Under A Winter Sun

Under A Winter Sun

Worldburner Book 2

Johan M. Dahlgren

Contents

You Can't Save The World

Every morning you wake up a day closer to your own death.

The cops on the ground should have stayed in bed.

They were shot in the back at close range from the looks of it. The Front laid an ambush for them, and they walked right into it. Wankers. Send local talent to do a grown-up's job, and this is what you get.

Ignoring the glassy-eyed stares of the corpses, I step over them and continue down the dimly lit tunnel. The big boys will be here any minute, and I need to be in position by then.

The gear I'm hauling slows me down, but you can never carry too much hardware, as Wagner used to say. Especially on a job like this. With the assault rifle in my hands, the pistol on my hip and the huge Lensfield sniper rifle on my back, I should have all eventualities covered.

Famous last words. It's a good thing I have a knife for contingencies.

I spit on the dusty floor and trudge on.

"*You have to go deeper, Perez.*"

Aeryn's voice in my ear is a reassuring presence. "*Three levels down is the auditorium. According to Winger's source, that's where she is.*"

Everyone knows Aeryn Winger's sources are the best.

Yesterday morning, the Terrans agreed to the demands of the Revolutionary Utopian Front. That's as good as a death sentence for all involved. Everyone knows the government doesn't negotiate with terrorists. Not even when threatened with local nuclear holocaust.

This is the third incident featuring weapons of mass destruction in the last couple of months, and every time, the authorities have dealt with the situation in their own heavy-handed way. Terran special ops are competent but famously trigger-happy. They love to go in shooting, and more often than not, they get people killed. Including the hostage.

"Got it," I subvocalise. The bone induction microphone hurt like a bitch to instal, but Winger insisted. In hindsight, I've got to admit it was an excellent idea. This way I can communicate with Aeryn with no one able to eavesdrop. Knowing a hi-tech lowlife like Winger is not a disadvantage. Not that anyone's around to listen to our conversation, anyway. This place is quieter than a library on a Saturday night.

I move three levels down into the old Utopian mine without incident.

It wasn't hard to figure out when the black ops team from Earth would strike. A fistful of credits in a traffic controller's pocket got me the time and place an unlisted shuttle docked at the Utopian beanstalk. Another fistful told me the ship had no registered point of origin. A sure sign of black ops. They're here, and they're on their way in. I plan to do my thing while the terrorists are busy fighting the strike team and then slip away unseen in the chaos. It's a simple plan, and that's the way I like it. Simple plans have a sporting chance to play out as intended.

"Someone's coming."

I freeze. So much for playing out as intended.

A door opens up ahead, and a man backs into the tunnel.

Shit.

He's thin. Early twenties, maybe. Twitchy. Dark hair, dark eyes, olive skin. He could be anybody anywhere. He carries an ancient hunting rifle that looks like it would explode in his hands if he should ever have to fire it. The extremists here on Utopia have an endless supply of frustrated young men from the miners' ranks. Their supply of firearms, it would seem, is not so endless.

The man grabs the door to steady himself.

"Hey, Ramirez," he calls to someone back in the room. "Save me some of that *cerveza*, will you?"

He's had a few already.

3

"Fuck you, Diaz. I can't promise anything," comes the reply.

"*Doorway on your left.*" Aeryn has direct access to the feed from my retinas. That's another tactical neural implant that hurt like hell. It took a while to adapt to, but now I don't even think about that whatever I see, Aeryn sees. Which has resulted in some awkward moments, usually related to bodily functions.

Diaz has still got his back to me, laughing at something Ramirez is doing. I slip into the recessed doorway and keep my fingers crossed Diaz won't come my way. Carefully, I release the Aitchenkai to let it dangle on its strap and pull my knife. I open the short, hyper-sharp blade and the familiar buzz as the knife grinds a few atoms off the monomolecular edge sends shivers of anticipation up my arm.

"*Mission parameters specify no unnecessary death. Play with yourself later if you need to reduce your adrenaline levels.*"

"I won't kill him unless I have to. And I'll play with myself whenever I damn well please."

"*Don't make me watch this time.*"

"You could have switched off the feed. Now hush."

They say a monomolecular knife is sharp enough to nick a man's soul, and if we had one, I think it would. The edge is so sharp that weird quantum effects occur there. People say strange things happen when you use one of these. Like the time I used this blade to kill Oddgrim Morgenstern and became the saviour of humanity.

What is not so strange is that Diaz comes my way. That's just my usual bad luck playing up.

"Shit, I need to piss," the man informs the darkness. Why do some have to advertise their every intention when they're drunk?

I glance behind me and notice the symbol on the door. Oh, fuck. I'm standing in the door to the toilet.

"Brilliant plan, Aeryn. Thanks," I whisper and grip the knife harder.

"There was no way for me to know he needed to urinate."

"Couldn't you tell from his walking pattern or something?"

"I'm not that good."

"Remind me why you're on board at all?"

"You need Winger's intel on this place. I can provide that for you."

I sigh. Sarcasm and rhetorical questions are not something a construct handles well.

Embedding a brain image in your head is dangerous, not to mention highly illegal. Despite the risk of overpopulation in my head, a scan and implant were the only ways to give me instant access to the intel in Winger's head. The six-minute time delay between Elysium and Utopia renders real-time communication impossible, even disregarding the shitty reception down here under kilometres of rock. Besides, I enjoy having Aeryn around. Now that Finn is gone, it's nice to have someone to talk to, and Aeryn reminds me of him. They are at about the same level when it comes to social interaction.

5

Diaz stumbles and supports himself on the wall to keep from falling over. The guy is pretty far gone, and I raise the knife in preparation. He mutters something about beer and small bladders as he lurches closer. He's younger than I thought. No more than sixteen, with his whole sorry life ahead of him. Fuck.

Maybe I can still avoid bloodshed.

"*Thank you.*"

"You owe me one, Aeryn."

I crack the door behind me and inch inside. As he comes up, I push the door wide and stumble into him.

He swears. "Hey, man. Watch where you're going."

Judging by the bleary eyes and pinprick pupils, beer is not the only thing he's ingested tonight. And here I was, thinking religious extremists were against all earthly pleasures. Perhaps endorsing intoxicants is the unique selling point of the RUF.

"Asshole," he mutters.

"Sorry." I push past him into the corridor with my head down.

For once, the universe has my back. As I exit, the crude lights bolted to the rock ceiling waver and go out. The newsfeeds assure us the authorities are looking into the recent power failures, but it would surprise me if they were. The electrical systems in Subburbia are ancient. It was only a question of time before they started acting up. Too bad they had to act up now when I'm here. The lights flicker back on with an unhealthy electrical buzz.

"No bloody manners these days," the man says as the restroom door swings shut behind him. "And the fucking lights."

"Yeah, the fucking lights," I agree to the closed door and breathe a sigh of relief.

"That was close, Perez. Stay frosty."

Frosty? Who even talks that way? "Mm-hm."

"Say again?"

I fold the knife closed and pick up the Aitchenkai again. "Never mind. Let's go."

It's good to hear someone still gives a damn about manners here on Utopia because this place is a shithole. It's the planet closest to our twin suns, and it's tidally locked to them. The planet's dayside is a radiation-blasted nightmare that will melt the flesh from your bones in a minute, while the nightside is one of the coldest places in the system. Right on the terminator between night and day is the only area even remotely habitable.

Except for the cloud cities, that is. Suspended on enormous cables from asteroids in orbit, those aerial metropolises are supposed to be impenetrable. I bet Lady Shadow thought she was safe up there with her minions and WMDs, but boy, was she wrong. She's held her city in the clouds in a well-manicured iron fist for over five decades, but somehow, she got herself taken hostage by these tossers. The Front either have well-informed friends or they got lucky, and in my experience, luck has nothing to do with success in this line of business. Someone must have tipped them off on her whereabouts. Someone who doesn't care

7

about his skin. Lady Shadow is infamous for the creative ways she hurts people. Someone who sold her out like this is likely to become a mythical example of pain. Along with his extended family, friends, and distant acquaintances. If the Shady Lady survives, that is.

Whatever the context of her abduction, the Front now has her launch codes.

"We're close. Make a left here."

I turn a corner and pass an open door. Inside is a large storage room with crates of varying sizes filling the space from floor to ceiling. They all bear the unmistakable markings of Terran military hardware. I've seen those with a lot of extremist groups recently. It's like they're stockpiling for Armageddon or something. Not my business. Just saying it's odd, that's all. I'll leave it to the cops to wipe up after this mess is over.

A few twists and turns later, I arrive at the auditorium. The staff access at the back is my designated point of entry, and I make haste down the corridor. I risk a glance through the open double doors as I pass, and there she is. Lady Shadow stands chained on a circular dais, centre stage in the vast, spherical chamber. In her sheer, crimson gown she looks like a dragon sacrifice. How apt. Ascending rows of seats circle the deep-set stage, like an ancient amphitheatre.

The Lady stands amid a group of bearded arseholes who look like they won the lottery. They think they are about to receive a king's ransom in a matter of minutes, and there's at least one snake-grass pipe doing the rounds. Amateurs. The weed makes them slow, and when you're slow, you're dead.

Lady Shadow is short a hand. The stump has been crudely bandaged, and there's a mess of blood on her gown. To her credit, the pain is almost indiscernible on her smooth, aristocratic features. Having a hand cut off hurts. I know.

"*She had the codes implanted in her palm,*" the construct notifies me.

"Thanks, but I figured that out myself, Aeryn."

"*I'm only here to help.*"

There's an oven-sized cryogenic container on the stage, next to the hostage. Something resembling a tan glove floats in the slush inside. I hope they were careful when they froze it, or they will have destroyed the codes. No matter. They will not get the chance to use them.

There's a hint of a sneer on Lady Shadow's thin lips. She knows she's getting rescued. The Utopian Front does not understand who their hostage is. Stealing the launch codes to an orbital nuclear arms platform might sound like a large-scale operation to them, but it's not. Not compared to what's going on behind the curtains right now.

"*There are twelve of them. Small arms only. No heavy gear.*"

"Good."

I don't plan to take them on myself, but the absence of heavy weapons means less risk of me taking a stray bullet. My body may be immortal, but a high velocity round through the spine will still incapacitate me. That would put a major dent in my self-esteem and bring awkward questions from the paramedics when they try to zip me into a body bag later.

The back entrance is right where Aeryn told me it would be. It's locked, but the access code the construct whispers in my ear opens the door on the first try. Remind me to buy Winger a good bottle of whisky when I return to Masada.

"*Open Sesame.*"

Inside is a storage area behind the top row of seats, filled with stacks of crates and miscellaneous stage equipment.

"Open *what?*"

I slip inside and take up position behind the crates. There's a perfect view of the auditorium from here.

"*It's a literary reference.*"

I drop the Aitchenkai on its sling and get the Lensfield off my back. It's solid and perfectly balanced, the way well-designed hardware should be. "I read, Aeryn." The rifle smells of gun oil.

"*You read horoscopes and beer bottle labels, Perez.*"

"So what?" I start to assemble the enormous weapon. "The labels are way more accurate in foretelling the future."

"*They foretell you will spend another night sleeping it off in a back alley?*"

"Always reliable, those labels. None of that 'Today could be your lucky day, and if you play, you might win' wank."

10

"*Why do you read the horoscopes?*"

I unfold the rifle's stand and set it on top of a crate. The stage is only fifty metres away. I peer through the scope. Ducks in a pond.

"To pretend there's a grand plan to the universe. And that my life isn't a sequence of chance events on the one-way road to the dirt."

The Lensfield's high-end optics tag a couple of notable terrorists among the prats surrounding the Lady. This will be a nice catch for the Terrans.

"*Eloquent, Perez.*"

"Thanks. Now shut up and let me concentrate." I pull the bolt and load a bullet into the breach. "I have work to do."

You can't save the world. The best you can hope for is a chance to waste a bad guy or two, to give the universe a breather before another arsehole steps in to fill their shoes.

That works for me.

Now we wait for the clowns to show up to get this party started.

The Centre of Her Being

The Terrans are late.

It's a miracle they can run their empire in anything resembling working order. It's another miracle they reconquered the Hope system as quickly as they did. But then, we had a hand in that ourselves. They say the quickest way to end a war is to lose it, so that's what we did. We lost spectacularly, and, once more, the Hope system is under the Terran boot. All except Nifelheim and Utopia. No one conquers Nifelheim. And Utopia ... Well. The first explorers who came here found immense wealth below the surface. They dug down to find refuge from the hostile surface and struck metaphorical gold when they discovered an underground ocean of fresh water. Now, the planet is like a Swiss cheese, riddled with caves, both natural and man-made. The population of Subburbia is as diverse as they come. It's like someone kicked the universe over on its side, shook it around, and everything loose ended up down here. Over the centuries, hundreds of thousands of miscreants and down-at-luck citizens from all corners of the system moved in and set up shop. Subburbia is us, boiled down to a rich broth of the essence of what makes us human. All the hate, the hope, and the anger. The fear, the love, and the lust. Whatever you can think of, you'll find it here. Everything is for sale down here. The Terrans need all that shit too, so they let it go. For now.

Subburbia is the perfect place for groups like the Revolutionary Utopian Front to make their hangout. There are countless more or less revolutionary groups operating down here. They all have names that remind you of some ancient comedy sketch, but the RUF is no laughing matter. They are one of the innumerable neo-libertarian groups who fight for independence from Earth. I guess you could call them Terrarists if you felt the need to be funny. The goal of the RUF is to destroy the Eternal Patriarchy. According to their holy scriptures, the Patriarchy has been yanking humanity's balls since we left the oceans, with the single purpose to oppress women, free thinkers, homosexuals, and people of colour. Probably mimes and accordion players too. If only the Front knew how close to the truth they are. Not about the mimes and the accordion players, but the Eternal Patriarchy. The ones pulling the strings. Had the RUF not been such sadistic homicidal maniacs I might even have rooted for them, but I draw the line at killing women and children. At least killing women and children not actively shooting at me. The Front has no such compunctions.

The room goes black.

"*Contact.*"

Shit. They're already here.

Muzzle flashes light the place up like a dance floor, accompanied by the staccato bark of assault rifles and a chorus of screams. I switch to the thermal scope on the Lensfield. All the cultists are dead or dying.

"*All targets neutralised.*" They waste no time. The Shady Lady knows some very important people.

"Thanks for the heads-up, Aeryn, but I have eyes in my head."

"*I'm only here to help.*"

The room reeks of gunpowder and death. Not an appealing mix, but one I know far too well.

The lights come back on, and a lone soldier in heavy body armour walks up to Lady Shadow. She stands stiff as a board amid the dead. I've got to admire her composure. Most people would scream their lungs out in a situation like this, but not The Shady Lady. From the way the soldier walks, I can tell he's pleased with himself and I can't help being a little impressed. They got into the room under my radar, and few people can do that. I'd toast them if I had a drink on hand, and they weren't Terran bastards. I always knew the special operations soldiers of Earth were good, but I didn't think they had the balls to pull off something like this. They usually worry too much about the negative press generated by mass murder.

The soldier tips his head in greeting to Lady Shadow. He's got a skull painted on his helmet. What a twat. Even with my enhanced hearing, I can't make out what he says to her, but I bet it's "Come with me if you want to live." They always say that.

He reaches out a gloved hand to her, and I hook my finger around the Lensfield's feather-light trigger. Oh, no. She's mine.

I squint through the scope, crack my neck, and take aim.

I click up the magnification as far as it will go.

The Shady Lady's face fills the scope. She's beautiful. Angular, Slavic features with alabaster skin and full, blood-red lips. With an eternity to perfect your looks, anyone can be beautiful. She smiles at the soldier. It's a smile that has started wars and driven men insane.

They are not truly immortal, you know.

I squeeze the trigger and her smile disappears along with her exquisite face. The back of her head explodes as the hypervelocity bullet tears through the centre of her being.

They may live forever if left to their own devices, but they die by violent means like the rest of us.

What? Didn't think I'd kill a woman?

I can't go around letting immortals live because they sport a set of tits. Where's the gender equality in that? Winger's hard-ass feminista girlfriend would applaud my progressive attitude if she didn't also want to kill me for banging her girlfriend. They have a strange relationship, those two. And that's without adding Christine into the equation.

The Terran soldier doesn't even flinch. He spins around and opens fire on my position while he sprints for cover. Impressive cool. His rounds are eerily accurate, and I drop behind the crates to avoid having my head blown off.

I peer around the box, but he's gone. There's still no sign of his team.

Shit.

They are a little too good, even for Terran black ops. Something's wrong.

Well, they're not on my list, and I need to leave before the Utopian Police Department drops on this place like a ton of bricks. I set the Lensfield on the concrete floor. It's a fine rifle, and it stings my heart to leave it behind, but it's an enormous weapon and it would slow me down. Besides, I could never smuggle it off-world. I hope someone who understands its value finds it and makes good use of it.

There's a shuttle leaving for Elysium in less than an hour. The Utopian Police Department may be corrupt and incompetent, but even they can close the spaceports.

Time to go.

* * *

Four hours later, I float weightless in the third-class lounge of the passenger liner *Lady of Heaven*. Around me, hundreds of members from the lower

16

tiers of humanity get ready to enjoy the three-day flight to Elysium. The atmosphere is thick with the pungent smell of old sweat and anticipation. It's hot as a sauna, too. Down here in the common areas, we're not exactly swimming in luxury, and they haven't turned on the air-conditioning yet. I could buy better accommodations — hell, I could buy this ship if I wanted to — but I like to keep a low profile. The powers that be don't care about the people down here, which means they don't waste good money on DNA scans of the third-class passengers. That suits me perfectly. It would be a major nuisance if a nosy security algorithm matched my DNA to that of the worst war criminal in history.

The complimentary drinks handed out by disinterested staff are not too bad. It's a generic mix of vodka and citrus-flavoured chemicals, but the booze has a good kick to it. I sip my drink and watch the other passengers. They are all young contract miners on leave. Lean, pale, and hollow-eyed from living underground for months or years on end. Most people in Subburbia are only there to save up for a better life back home. They are a cheerless bunch, and most of them are already well on their way to drunken oblivion. I can't blame them. Working in Utopia's mines is dangerous but lucrative. If you live, you can make enough to buy a second-hand residential pod in the lower levels of Masada. Maybe even earn enough to start a family. Something I could only dream of when I grew up. I can understand they take the risk and

17

sign on. If you don't play, you can't win, like my horoscopes like to say.

The lights dim, and a single harsh spotlight switches on. It wavers around for a second before it finds its target. The entertainment crew down here is not exactly professional. A woman in a billowing white gossamer dress floats at the centre of the lounge. A hush goes through the crowd. She holds a white electric violin and a matching bow in her outstretched arms. It could have been artsy and beautiful had not one man in the audience grabbed a flowing corner of her dress and tried to pull her over. I can tell it's not the first time this has happened. She stabs him in the chest with the bow and yanks the dress from his hand. The hapless customer goes into a spin to the laughter and ridicule of his drinking companions. The woman brings the bow to her violin and the music starts.

I sigh. They had the same show on the trip over from Elysium. I don't know if it's the same violinist, but it could be. There are not that many half-decent musicians who are content entertaining drunks in third class on a planet-hopper. I enjoyed the show the first time. Despite the cheesy tunes and bored expression on the performer's face, it had a sordid, guilty appeal. Like cheap porn. But I'm not sure it holds up for an encore.

The lights flicker out and the lounge goes dark. The music cuts out, and another, deeper hush sweeps through the crowd. One or two voices cry out in fear. The lights flicker back on and the music starts where it left off. I groan. So, it was playback. I should have known. There are a few nervous laughs around the audience.

"*There was a spike in data traffic before the blackout. Could be related.*"

"Or it was a rat chewing on an old cable somewhere and the spike was a coincidence."

These old ships are death traps. The only thing standing between us and explosive decompression is a small team of underpaid mechanics.

"*Not when the two events happen within milliseconds of each other.*"

"Let it go, Aeryn. Someone tried to hack their mainframe. So what?"

"*We haven't used mainframes for hundreds of years, Perez.*"

"I know that. It's a figure of speech. Let it go."

"*Whatever.*"

The show goes on.

I scan the crowd, hoping for something interesting. There is not. Just a bunch of leering men who haven't seen a woman in months. Five security guards with stun rods float at strategic points in the crowd. With trained eyes, they've spotted the potential troublemakers and keep tabs on them. I wouldn't want to be on the receiving end of one of those stun rods again.

Oh, hello there. There's a woman in a black hooded top staring at me from across the open space. She hovers behind the crowd, near the curved wall. Despite the distance and the dim lighting, I note her sharp features and the hint of a fit body hidden under the top and matching loose black slacks. She looks away as soon as I spot her, but too late. She knows she's been compromised. With a kick against the wall, she pushes off and disappears into the crowd.

What was that all about? I'm not that ugly.

"*Yes, you are.*"

"I'm not, Aeryn."

"*You're not getting any younger.*"

"Shut up. I'm not here to find a date. I'm on my way home to my bed and a long shower."

"*Yes, in that dingy little pod flat you call home.*"

"Hey, that's my home you're talking about."

"*It's still dingy.*"

"Oh, yeah? You've never been there."

"*Winger has,*" Aeryn reminds me.

It's right. That one time, after way too much whisky and illegal pipe contents, Winger followed me back to my place. I always hoped she was too drunk to recall the place and what happened there. Not one of my best performances.

"*I do not forget.*"

"I kind of hoped you did."

"*Sorry to disappoint you.*"

"Oh, shut up, Aeryn. Please delete that memory."

"*It is done.*"

I can't verify it has deleted it. Or if deleting a memory is even possible for a construct. I must ask someone about that sometime.

I return my attention to the show, but it's already over. Oh, well. I grab another drink from a passing drone servitor. Since I missed the show, I'm entitled to another glass.

I push off against a beam and follow the crowd out.

The wide passageways of the *Lady of Heaven* do not differ from any other drifting ferryboat. They are only slightly more worn and depressing. White paint has flaked from the walls in places, and the carpet on the floor is scuffed and frayed. The passages lack sharp edges to keep the passengers from injuring themselves. One surface serves as the dedicated floor, used to walk on during the twenty-four-hour acceleration and deceleration phases of the trip when engine thrust generates artificial gravity. The rest of the journey we pull ourselves in endless lines by recessed handholds. Like cattle. There are a lot of collisions between the Zero-G rookies. Same on all flights I've ever been on. Someone bumps into me hard from behind and sends me spinning out of my elaborate trajectory. "The fuck?" I go tumbling into a wall and crack my elbow. A sharp jolt of pain spasms my fingers open and my almost empty glass spins down the passage. It leaves a spiral trail of liquid blobs that splatter the walls and several oblivious passengers.

I twist around, trying to glimpse the arsehole who knocked my free drink out.

"Sorry." It's a woman's voice.

She's already gone in the crowd.

The buzz of the repair nanites in my blood assures me no lasting harm was done, but it's still annoying. Almost as annoying as losing my drink. With the drink gone, there's nothing to keep me up any longer.

I could go to one of the many bars for another drink before blast-off, but I don't think I'd enjoy the miners' company. And they wouldn't enjoy mine. Fighting can be entertaining, but I'm grumpy and tired. I might hurt someone, and I don't feel like spending the trip in the brig.

I am getting old.

"*Yes, you're ...*"

"Aeryn. Shut it."

"*Whatever.*"

I head for my cabin to strap down early and prepare for the trip. The cheap ticket I bought got me a bunk in the dorms. When I enter the room, the smell of feet and cheap beer almost suffocates me. Five miners have a private party over in one corner. When they see me enter, one of them calls out.

"Hey, *compadre*, come join us."

On any other day I would, but not today. I need my beauty sleep. Assassinating immortals and evading the police is hard work.

"Nah, not today, brother. Thanks for the invitation though."

The man who called to me glares and goes back to whatever he was doing.

Another man does not let it go as easily.

"Oy, fucker."

Oh, dear. Here we go.

"Are you too fancy to drink with us, old man?"

"No, I'm tired. I'm going to bed."

There's a pause while his mental gears grind on. "Are you taking the piss? Are you laughing at me?"

He pushes from the crowd and floats over. He's a big, ugly man. Large, but well-muscled under layers of fat. Looks like he can handle himself in a fight. This could get ugly.

"Nope." I reach my allotted space and make a show of grabbing one of the inset handholds to brake my approach. My shirt slides up to show the big handgun tucked into the back of my trousers. With the current recession, getting a weapon aboard one of these boats is just a matter of money in the right hands, but it cost me a minor fortune.

He spots the gun and sobers up at once. "Sorry, man." He grabs another bed to stop his approach and kicks off back to his mates. Seems the gun was worth every penny.

I unbutton my shirt as bits of conversation float over from the party in the corner. They can't decide if I'm an undercover cop or a hired killer for the Yakuza. Both serve my purposes since they are no longer likely to murder me in my sleep. I grin and put a hand in my pocket to get the key card to extend my bed from the wall.

What now?

I pull a scrap of paper from my pocket. There's something written on it in actual handwriting. Quaint. That piece of paper was not there when I swiped the key card at the boarding station earlier. That means someone put it there along the way. An impressive move by the mystery woman who bumped into me.

Three words in hurried handwriting.

There is another. And a Masada address.
This ride just got interesting.

Die Fast

I know it's a trap.

But they knew I would show up. If there's even a remote chance another one of those fuckers is still hiding out there, it's worth checking out. And that someone knows I hunt them intrigues me.

A woman in a hooded cloak sits dead centre in the dark, empty warehouse. She's slumped on a polymer chair, arms behind her back. The scene is illuminated by a solitary light bulb suspended on a frayed cord that disappears into the dusty gloom high above. Like the lure of a giant anglerfish. Dust motes swirl lazily like fireflies in the light. Someone disturbed the air not too long ago. This whole setup is wrong.

I slip out into the echoing space with the pistol held before me. Like everything down here in the Bottoms, the warehouse smells of old dust and engine oil. The smells of my childhood. My eyes and ears strain to pick up any hint of danger, but even my unnaturally sharp senses have to admit defeat. If there's someone out there in the shadows, they are not moving. I glance around as I inch forward, trying to make out anything in the darkness, but the contrast from the light is too strong. They staged this perfectly.

The girl hasn't moved a finger since I entered the room. Is she even breathing? I don't think they've killed her, but I can't be certain. She's likely an unsuspecting girl from the street, lured with drugs or money and left here for me as human bait.

There's a faint scrape of hardened rubber on concrete somewhere to my right and a spring baton comes twirling out of the darkness and knocks the gun from my hands.

"You've got company."

"I am aware."

"There are five of them."

I drop into a fighter's stance an instant before the men charge from all sides. They materialise like ghosts as they step into the dusty light. Two in front of me, one on each side and one man behind, hoping to outflank me. Not going to happen.

They are sizeable men, and they move with the cocky assurance of experienced fighters. These men have killed before, and they are certain they will do so again tonight. Not if I have anything to say about that. I drop the first one with a quick jab to the throat. His shocked grunt can't get past his crushed larynx. It's a slow and horrible death, choking on yourself. Sorry about that. Before he falls, I kick low to the right. My heavy boot finds an unprotected knee with a satisfying crunch. The leg bends the wrong way and man number two crashes to the floor. He grabs his ruined knee and screams.

By now the other three are on me. A powerful arm locks around my neck from behind and musky breath moistens my ear as if from a rough lover. The calm, even breathing and lack of alcohol on his breath tell me these guys are professionals. I'm flattered. Some-one has done his homework. I stab two fingers into his right eye, hook my thumb under his thick jaw and dig into his socket with my augmented strength. His terrified scream cuts short as his cheek snaps, and he goes limp. I roll his lifeless body over my shoulder and it slumps into a mess of arms and legs on the floor. The two remaining men back away and circle me, just out of range. The screams of the man with the broken knee echo around the empty warehouse.

They haven't said a word so far. Another sure sign of professionals. There's no reason to talk to your as-signment.

I have learned two things. They know who I am, and they want me alive. If they worked for the people I first thought they did, they wouldn't waste time on this martial arts crap. They'd just kill me. They know me too well to give me a sporting chance like this. No, this must be something else.

"Who are you, and what do you want?" I call out into the darkness over my shoulder while keeping a careful eye on my circling opponents.

No reply. I figured as much.

The two men reach their positions on my flanks and get ready to strike. The girl on the chair has raised her head and looks at us. She could be watching a dull cage fight for all the interest she displays. They must have drugged her.

As on a signal, the men rush me. I go for the man on the right. He's the uglier of the two.

I twist and put a foot out to trip him, then grab his outstretched arm and pull him off balance and use his momentum to throw him into the man coming from the other direction. The horrible sound of two thick skulls cracking against each other echoes around the hangar. They both drop without so much as a whimper.

It's all over in less than ten seconds. Two men dead, one with a broken leg and two possible broken necks. Not a bad score for an old man.

I walk up to the girl on the chair and kneel at her side, searching for the ropes. "I'm gonna get you out of here. We need to go before more of them show up." This is far too easy.

"Is that so?"

I know that voice.

I look up. It's her. The woman from the *Lady of Heaven*. The one who slipped me the note. I should have known.

That's when I realise the guy with the broken knee has fallen silent.

I can't find any ropes.

"Behind you, Perez."

Too late I register the slick metallic sound of a gun cocking behind me and I know I'm done for. I close my eyes. Mostly from the shame of being outsmarted.

28

Even I can't dodge a bullet to the brain from point-blank range.

The shot rings out and I wait for my skull to explode.

It doesn't. Not that I would have had time to savour the experience, but still. There's a heavy, meaty thud as if a body drops behind me.

"*You're fine, Perez.*"

"Was that a compliment?"

"*Fuck you.*"

"Fucking amateurs." There's a smoking gun in the woman's hand.

One of *those* guns. The ones that kill people like yours truly. Was that gun meant for me?

What the hell is going on here?

I get up and take a few careful steps back. "Why the theatrics? You could have just asked me if you wanted a date."

She doesn't reply. Instead, she gets up from the chair and casually tosses the gun away. It clatters away into the darkness. It's a one-shot weapon, and she knows that. I've only seen a gun like that once before, and that was years ago. A brief memory flashes across the silver screen of my mind. A memory of spiky red hair and a promise.

The woman stretches her arms and lets the hooded cloak drop to the floor. Underneath, she wears a heavy military issue charcoal-grey jumpsuit. The chest, shoulders, knees, and elbows are armoured with angled hypercarbon plating. There's a large dust-coloured scarf around her neck. Special ops gear. Her black hair is tied back in a ponytail and a straight-cut fringe hangs down to her eyebrows. Her skin is paler than the universal norm, but she's got the deep tan of someone with an outdoor job. She means serious business.

She moves in, deliberately closing the gap between us.

"They were right, you know."

She stares me hard in the eye. She's got beautiful brown eyes. The colour of oak-aged whisky. "You are good."

Her face is now close to mine. I can smell her sweet breath and our noses almost touch.

"Thanks."

So, she knows my name. This gets more intriguing by the minute.

Her lips are beautiful and cruel, and she smells of strawberries and fine tobacco. "Now let's see how good you really are."

She kicks the legs out from under me and I drop like I've been axed. I twist and turn the fall into a quick shoulder-roll and I'm back on my feet a healthy distance away from her.

"All right, you've got my curiosity piqued, girl."

I crack my neck to get the kinks out and get ready for another quick fight. "Who are you?"

We circle the edge of the pool of light, measuring each other, staying well out of each other's reach.

"I'm Soledad."

"Nice to meet you, Soledad." I tip an imaginary hat to her. "But I was thinking more 'who the fuck are you people'?"

"We are the ones sent to find you where others have failed."

"What, you and those clowns?" I jab a thumb over my shoulder at the dead and dying men on the floor.

She shrugs. "They were just hired help."

"Staff these days ..."

We keep circling.

"Do you think we'd only send amateurs like them after you? Show us some respect at least."

"You've sent amateurs after me in the past."

"That was the past."

"So, you work for the immortals. I always wondered when they'd bring in the cavalry."

Her failure to react when I mention the immortals tells me I'm right.

"But if you work for them, you know who I am. You know what I am. And you must know you can't win this fight."

"Yes, I know what you are." She cracks her fingers. "And I know I can win this fight."

She's not bragging. The poor girl thinks she can beat me. Oh, dear. I have no wish to ruin that face.

"I see. You wanted me for yourself." I sneer. "I'm flattered. Is that why you shot that guy when he pulled a gun on me?"

I nod at the corpse on the floor. There's a hole in his forehead. A trail of inky spatter leads out into the

31

shadows behind him, like the gruesome minute hand of an ancient mechanical watch.

"No. A gun was not part of the plan. That was him ... improvising." She waves a hand in the air. "Nasty things happen when people improvise."

"You know what they say, no plan survives first contact with the enemy. Maybe he was showing initiative? That's a valued trait for many employers."

"He knew the plan, and he knew we don't encourage critical thinking. And you were right. I want you for myself."

"As I said, I'm flattered."

I am. She's lean, muscular, with an ass to die for in that tight combat suit. The fact she wears the suit zipped open to show a tight, greasy white top that leaves her toned belly bare doesn't hurt. She hasn't even broken a sweat yet. There's something special about girls who can handle themselves in a fight. I smile.

When she strikes, she moves at the speed of darkness.

What? Never heard of the speed of darkness? No matter how swift the light moves, the darkness is always there to poke it in the eye when it arrives.

I've seen no one move like this. She crosses the circle and attacks me in the single moment it takes a human being to blink. Only my augmented reflexes save me from taking a fist in the face.

She rains punches and kicks over me and it's all I can do to fend her off. The accuracy of her blows is terrifying, but what's even worse is the fury with which she delivers them. This girl wants to hurt me. Bad.

We dance around the warehouse, trading punches and kicks in and out of the pool of light.

She catches me on the nose with a lucky punch and blood spurts everywhere. She is pissing me off. "Ouch. You fight like a girl, Soledad, and normally, I don't fight girls. But for you, I might have to make an exception." I snort and swallow a fair amount of blood mixed with snot. Whoever called unarmed combat an art, was a wanker.

I aim a kick at her knee, but she dances out of reach.

"You need to be quicker than that to beat me, old man," she says.

She throws another fist to my face and I block it high, opening up her midsection to attack. I see my chance.

She delivers a quick knee to my balls, and I go down.

She follows up with a lightning-swift boot in my face and my vision explodes into a galaxy of pulsating stars. I fail to roll away, and she drops on top of me. She pins me to the floor by pressing my arms down my sides with her finely toned legs. She's strong. Impossibly strong. Her combat suit creaks as she squeezes her legs around me.

"Fuck, that hurt."

I try to clear my head, but everything is still blurry. Her thighs smell of dust and hi-tech fibres. To gain time to let my vision clear, I keep talking.

33

"Look, Soledad. We both know you will not kill me before you've told me what this crap is all about. Why not tell me your grand plan and get it over? I hear you criminal masterminds love the sound of your own voice even more than you enjoy hurting people."

"Who said *I* was the criminal mastermind?"

She punches me in the face. Hard. And then again, and again. There is no way I can fight her off or get away. My head cracks against the concrete floor and something breaks in my cheek under her fist. Ouch.

Something colossal shifts deep in my mind, like a deep-sea leviathan rolling over in its sleep, close to waking up. Not now. Not yet. I need her alive to find out who is behind all this.

"Stop. Don't do this." Don't feed the monster.

Not the best thing to say to an obvious sadist. The fervour of her attacks increases and with every punch she brings the thing inside me closer to the surface.

Punch. Closer.

Punch. *Closer.*

Punch.

The thing snaps free from its chains at the murky bottom of my consciousness and comes rushing to the surface. My mind does the all too familiar somersault and my body goes light like I'm floating in water. Everything slows to a crawl and I can't control my body anymore.

The Dread General is in the house.

"*Unknown entity detected.*"

34

"I know, Aeryn. Sit back and enjoy the show." It's all we can do.

"You're not so cocky now, are you, Perez?"

The mystery woman named Soledad keeps pounding away, lost in the moment. "The great Asher Perez. Not so invincible now."

The pain is dull and far away, but my mind remains crystal clear. Asher Perez no longer feels the pain.

Unfortunately for Soledad, she's not fighting Asher Perez anymore.

General Meridian, the World Burner, does not enjoy being hurt.

He smashes his bloodied and broken forehead into Soledad's face with enough force to throw her over. Her nose explodes into a slow-motion shower of blood as her head arcs over backwards. She sprawls on her ass and clutches her nose. Meridian gets up and launches a kick to her face. She doesn't even see it coming for all the blood, and the heavy boot impacts the side of her head. The kick caves in her temple and snaps her neck like a dry twig, and she goes down. Hard.

The fight is over.

But then the woman pushes up from the floor on shaking arms. She is not dead, even though her neck remains at an odd angle. One of her hands twitches, but she should not be able to move at all. She should be dead or paralysed from the shoulders down. Instead, she cracks her slender neck, something pops back into place, and she can move again. She leers at Meridian through the blood flowing from her nose.

The blood bubbles between her ruined teeth as she breathes hard.

Soledad wiggles her fingers. "Surprise."

It is. I was not expecting that, and neither was Meridian. She's an augmented immortal. Like me.

But that's impossible. The last of the Cherubim were killed on Persephone forty years ago. All but me.

The General doesn't burden himself with questions. The rudimentary lizard brain functionality left of his once great mind is focused on one thing, and one thing only. Keeping the General alive at any cost. Soledad is still a threat, and he won't stop until she is neutralised.

He punches her in the face, and she goes down again. She struggles to her feet. *Stay down, Soledad,* I want to scream. *Stay down.* No sound crosses my lips. Meridian sneers.

He hits her again, sending her off balance. Then he goes for her eye. Her beautiful eye. His fingers dig into her socket and tear it out. She howls and drops to her knees. Meridian moves in for the kill and there's nothing I can do to stop it. Soledad is going to die. He grabs her by the collar and pulls the monomolecular knife with his free hand. Even if she's an immortal, she can't live without her head, and the General knows that. He flips the blade open one-handed.

Now I will never learn who she was or what this was about.

Soledad glares up at Meridian with a mixture of rage and defiance in her remaining eye. The jelly

36

from her torn eye squishes between Meridian's fingers as he raises the knife to take her head.

"Fuck you, Perez," she says with blood flowing down her face and bubbling from her once attractive lips.

As last words go, not especially original, but far from the worst I've heard. She spits blood in Meridian's face, defiant to the last. Fuck, I liked her.

A short, controlled swarm of bullets explodes from Meridian's chest, tearing control of my body from him along with my internal organs. The aim is perfect, and the projectiles cut through my spinal cord right between the shoulder blades. I lose all motor functions in my lower body and I drop to the floor next to Soledad. Ice creeps into my veins as the blood leaks from the fist-sized exit wound in my chest. As I expire on the dusty concrete floor of this sorry warehouse, there's another voice in the shadows.

"Goodbye, Perez."

"*Major internal damage. Vital signs in the red. You're dying, Perez.*"

"Don't worry about that."

"*Whatever.*"

The newcomer steps into the light.

At first, I only see a halo of platinum-blonde hair. Then she leans in and her face comes into focus.

Except for the hair, she is the spitting image of Soledad.

"Die fast. We have a job for you."

Something Big

If this is death, I'm sorely disappointed in the universe.

I've been here before, many times, in this darkness, and if this is all we get when we die, I'm not impressed. I hope ordinary humans get something more when they go because this is just sad. To make matters even worse, I'm not even getting the full run of my life passing in front of my eyes this time. It's only the last twenty-something minutes. Not my greatest hits.

What a shame.

There was a moment or two from my childhood I would have liked to revisit.

* * *

There's a flicker of light, like a school of fish reflected in a submarine's headlights, and I return to life. No sudden intake of breath, no tunnel of light. I simply wake up.

"*Back online. Vitals stabilising.*"

"Stop talking, Aeryn."

"*Whatever.*"

"And he's back."

A woman's voice. "How good of you to rejoin us, Perez."

She speaks in the low, cultured tones of an aristocrat from Earth. Fuck.

There's still a hint of gunpowder on the air, so I can't have been out for too long.

I open my eyes, getting ready to close them again if the glare is too sharp. But the lights are turned down like someone knows how the eyes hurt when you come back. And then I remember. They're clones. Immortals.

Like me.

They must have been in that darkness themselves.

I blink and squint through the gloom. I'm still on the warehouse floor. There's still dried blood around me, but they left me in it so the nanites could reabsorb my precious fluids.

How kind of them.

It's also a message. They could have killed me when I was dead, but they didn't.

My cheek has stuck to the dusty concrete. Shit. Couldn't they at least have cleaned me up while I was out?

There's a powerful-looking black executive-style car standing close by with the engine humming. Two women lean against it.

"Please, can I kick his teeth in?" the one called Soledad asks with obvious longing as she fingers her still ruined face. She winces as she finds a sore spot on her full lower lip and spits blood on the concrete in front of my face. There are shards of teeth in there. Her eye is still a gory mess, but it's not bleeding anymore. She catches me staring and pulls out a pair of dark shades and puts them on. Sunglasses at night? Fucking poser. She looks like a feed-star.

I strain to focus on the two women through the headache splitting my skull.

They have the same sleek, powerful build, the same fair skin, they dress the same in those charcoal military combat suits, but they sport different hairdos. If they didn't, I don't think I'd be able to tell them apart.

Where Soledad has her black hair tied back in a ponytail, the other one is platinum-blonde and wears her hair in a stylish asymmetrical bob. Very *haute couture*.

Where Soledad is unarmed, the other one holds a compact automatic rifle. It looks like an Aitchenkai PDW. Packs a hell of a punch in a compact package. One of my favourites.

So, she was the one who shot me in the back. The bitch.

I finger my leg, feeling for my gun. It's not there.

"No, you can't," the one who is not Soledad replies to her friend.

Her long platinum fringe bounces as she shakes her head. It's mesmerising.

I blink to get my focus back.

"We need him, Soledad. Kicking his teeth in might disincline him from accepting our generous offer."

I open my mouth to speak. All that comes out is a dry rasp.

One of the unpleasant things about being dead is that your mouth dries out.

The woman who is not Soledad leans forward to hear me better.

With an effort, I peel my dry tongue from the roof of my mouth and try again.

"Who are you?" I manage. There is still no strength in my body, so I stay sprawled on the concrete.

She seems to hear me this time, and leans back against the car, letting the rifle dangle from one slender hand.

"You've met Soledad. I'm Jagr."

"Jagr? Is that your first name?"

"No."

I wait for her to elaborate. She does not.

OK, fresh angle of approach.

"Who do you work for, Jagr?"

"I think you can guess, but that is not important. What *is* important, is that we need your help."

"You need my help?" My mouth is finally back in business.

"Yes."

41

"Word of advice, Jagr," I cough. "Beating people up and shooting them in the back is a bad way to call for help."

I cough again, trying to work some moisture into my dry throat. "Do you always enlist people this way?"

"Nope."

I stare at her.

"So why the charade with the kidnapping and the goons?" I can now move my hands and feet. I flex my fingers.

"Soledad wanted to see if you were any good."

"And did I pass the test?" I glance at Soledad.

She sneers. "Barely."

"Barely? I almost killed you." I try to work up the energy to get off the floor.

Soledad snorts and Jagr goes on. "We know who you are. We are aware of what you're doing to us. And we know what you did to Arcadia."

Shit.

She squats beside me. She's got spectacular legs and the dark combat suit does nothing to hide them. Quite the contrary.

"Still, you could have just asked."

With a groan, I roll over on my back. The pain in my cheek as it unsticks from the concrete makes me wince.

"And what do you need my help for, anyway? You need someone to teach Soledad manners?"

I pump my fingers, trying to get the blood flowing into my hands again. It hurts like liquid fire streaming into my digits. Coming back to life is a painful process.

"Yes, I do, but that's not the primary job I have for you. If she ends up house-trained," Jagr glances sideways at Soledad, "I consider that a secondary objective achieved, and you get a bonus."

"Bonus." I taste the word. "I like the sound of that."

Wincing, I push myself up on my elbows and from there to a sitting position and wince again as the headache cuts like a burning machete through my brain.

Soledad smirks.

I give her the finger and my head hurts even more.

"So, what's the job?" My hair is stiff and sticky with blood. I inspect my reflection in the shiny black bodywork of the car and pat my dark mop down into some semblance of order. There are ladies present. I fail miserably. Even Suki would be proud of this spiky hairdo. There's a sudden stab of pain somewhere in the general area of my icy heart at the thought of Suki, even after all this time.

"We need your help to find someone."

Don't they all.

"You want me to kill him?" I peer up at Jagr.

"Nope. We want him back alive."

"Why? What's he done? Did he get Soledad pregnant or something?"

"You're not very good at this, are you, Perez?"

She looks disappointed. Then she sighs. "He went somewhere for us. He stumbled over something. Something big."

"Who's 'us'?"

Jagr shakes her head. Not important. I get it.

"Where did he go?" Using my index and middle finger, I rub the base of my nose to make the headache go away. I might as well have tried to yodel for all the good it does me.

"Nifelheim."

"*Nifelheim*? As in the *Goliaths*' Nifelheim?"

"Last time I checked, there was only one Nifelheim in this system."

"And you need me because I know Thorfinn Wagner?"

Jagr nods. "You need his help to keep the Goliaths off your back when you go there to find your man."

"You're not as stupid as you look."

"Yeah, I get that a lot.

I wipe a hand over my mouth, brushing flaking blood from my lips and stubble. No matter how many times I swallow it, I will never get used to the taste of my blood.

"The thing is, I haven't talked to Wagner for a long time."

"You're still friends, aren't you?"

"I guess."

"Well, there you go then." Jagr stands up and rests the rifle across her shoulders, pushing out her fabulous chest. The combat suit accentuates her curves. I'm sure she is well aware of how good she looks.

I sigh and hate myself a little for taking the bait. "OK, I'll talk to him for you. What did your agent find?"

"That's the thing. We don't know."

"You don't know?"

"Data analysis and pattern correlation algorithms imply the Goliaths are up to something, and that scares us. We've never seen this level of organised activity from them before."

"The Goliaths?"

"That's what I said."

That *is* odd. The Goliaths are normally content to battle among themselves for positions of power.

"OK, I'm listening."

A slight change in Jagr's pose tells me that's what she wanted to hear.

"Your agent must have told you *something*. Not much of an agent otherwise."

Her eyes narrow and there's a glint of sharp steel behind them like I've insulted her. Maybe the agent is her boyfriend or something? I'm surprised by a twinge in my chest at the thought of Jagr with a boyfriend. Like a small fish took a nibble of my heart.

Her jaw flexes as she bites down on an acid reply and instead forces her voice back into businesslike tones. "All we have is a name."

Oh, for fucks sake. Are they dragging this out to piss me off? I groan and release my nose and peer up at Jagr again. "So, tell me the bloody name already."

"Project *Jotun*."

"*Jotun*?" The name sounds vaguely familiar.

"Yes, *Jotun*." They both look at me with expectation, like the name should mean something to me.

"What's a *Jotun*?"

"We thought you might know."

"No idea."

"Never mind. You can ask Wagner. Soledad, get him up." Jagr waves for Soledad to help me up. "Our window is closing."

"What?" I look between the women. "Now?"

Soledad reaches out and I grab her hand. She pulls me to my feet. Jagr lowers the rifle but holds it pointed down and to my left. She's ready to cut me down again if I make a move.

I hold on to Soledad's hand. "You're good, Soledad. And you *do* fight like a girl."

She grins. "Thanks. So do you."

I can't stop a short laugh.

I let go of Soledad's hand and turn to Jagr. "One more thing."

"What?"

I tear the rifle from her hands and swing it around, eject the magazine, pull the bolt to remove the cartridge and hand the weapon and the magazine back to her. There's a soft metallic *ping* as the cartridge lands somewhere out in the darkness. "Never point a gun at me again."

She glares at me a long time while fury and something that could be professional admiration chase each other across her face. Then she sucks her teeth. "Are we good, Perez?"

"For now."

"Great." Jagr walks around the car to the passenger side. "Get in."

She opens the front door and throws the rifle inside. "We have places to be. Our ride won't wait for ever."

Soledad gets in and starts the car.

I remain standing, rubbing the sore back of my head.

Jagr rests her elbows on the car's bonnet, palms together like she's about to pray, and places her chin on her thumbs. Damn, she's cute. "Now, Perez. If it's money you want, I'll see to it, you will never want again."

"No, I don't want money. I'm all set, thanks."

"Yes, I forgot. You stole a sizeable chunk of Gray Industries assets before we locked your DNA out of the accounts."

"If you knew about that, why didn't you come after me?"

"Consider that payment for ridding us of a … sensitive problem."

"Gray, you mean?"

"He had become a liability. It was already decided he had to go. Then you showed up and did the dirty work for us. Now tell me, Perez. What do you want?"

I consider it for a moment. "To be left in peace." It's only when I say it out loud that I realise how much I want it.

"I can arrange that."

I scowl at her.

"You can call off the dogs, just like that?" I snap my fingers.

"I can."

"And what do I have to?"

"Help us find our man. And stop killing us."

"Can't do that. I made a promise to someone."

"Yes, we know about that. But don't you think you've killed enough? There are almost none of us left."

"There's you." I nod at Jagr. I nod at Soledad. "Her. The Cardinal."

"And when you've killed us?"

"There will always be new immortals somewhere. I hear there are a lot on Earth."

"But what will you do when you've killed all the old ones?" She squints, studying me with genuine interest. "Will you start killing innocent infants?"

She's got a point. I hadn't thought of that.

I clear my throat. "Well ..."

"Can't we call it even, Perez? You've proved your point. You've honoured your promise."

Perhaps I have. It's getting old, hunting and killing immortals. And I'm not getting any younger. I'm tired.

I cough. "No hard feelings?" I hope the pleading tone is only in my head.

"No hard feelings. Get in the car."

Soledad peers at me through the open driver's side window.

"We have to go, boss. Clock's ticking."

Jagr ignores her.

I chew my lower lip and spit clumps of dried blood on the floor.

"Think about it, Perez. You could help save the world again. Be a hero."

"No, thanks. Been there, done that. Fuck all it did for me."

She tilts her head and looks at me like something just occurred to her. "You think *we* are the bad guys here, Perez."

"Something like that. You're from Earth, remember. We're raised on horror stories about you."

"I know you people think of yourselves as frontier explorers. Making your destinies among the stars," she makes sweeping gestures with her slender hands, "far away from Earth regulations. You paint us as the bogeymen, and I can understand that, but on the bottom line, we all want the same thing."

"And what is that?"

"To make a better life for all humanity."

"You believe *that's* what you're doing?"

Her eyes tell me 'yes'.

"Hm." I spit more blood on the ground.

"Is that so hard to believe, Perez? You've been around the block far longer than me."

Hey. I'm not that old.

"You know the world isn't black and white, Perez."

I bark a harsh laugh at her words.

"What?"

"Someone spoke those words to me once. That was before I sealed him in a shuttle with a flesh-eating nanite cloud and sent him on a one-way trip to the Andromeda Galaxy." I squint at her. "Is that how you see the world? As long as it helps you get ahead in the Race, anything goes?"

"It's time to pick a side, Perez. Do you stand with humanity, or do what you always do, and walk away?"

She has a way of prodding my sore spots. I don't always walk away.

Soledad glares at me from the car. "What's your problem, Perez?"

"My problem is I don't give a shit."

"Oh, but you do," Jagr replies. "I've studied your profile. You give a shit, and this is your chance to show it. Pip. Give the man his gun."

Soledad holds out my pistol through the window.

"We're on the same side now, Perez. You'll be there only as an observer. We'll do all the heavy lifting. All you have to do is talk to Wagner, and that's it."

I grab the gun and check the magazine. It's still loaded. "That's it? Talk to Wagner and we're done?" I slap the magazine back in place.

She can tell she's got me. "That's it."

I scratch my chest with the gun. My clothes are crusty with blood.

Jagr cracks a smile. I like it when she smiles. "I'll even buy you a drink when this is over."

Crap. She *has* studied my file.

"All right." I open the passenger door and get in. The car smells like new cars have smelled since time immemorial. The heavy scent of leather and polymer always give me a headache. Jagr taps the roof and gets in. I place the gun on my lap for easy access if this turns out to be an elaborate trap.

Soledad starts the car and stamps on the accelerator. Tyres scream and I'm pressed hard into the seat. The ride we're on our way to meet waits for no man. Or woman.

Jagr twists around in her seat. "Was that what happened to him?"

"Who?"

"Gray. Was that how he ...?"

I stare out the window as the empty warehouse speeds past. The memory burns in my mind. I know it's Meridian's chemistry responding to the images of the flaying and tormented Gray, but it still warms my guts. "Yup."

"Gray was a rotten bastard, but shit." Jagr sees the grin on my face and shivers. "You are a terrible man, Perez."

I nod. She gets no argument from me there.

Her eyes linger and the moment stretches out, threatening to become uncomfortable. I continue to stare out the window, refusing to look at her. She tears her gaze away and faces forward again. I breathe a quiet sigh of relief. "Fuck," she says and wipes a hand down her face, restoring her professional calm.

We shoot through the warehouse doors and out onto the broken and pitted asphalt of the street.

"Where are we going?"

A few lonely streetlights reflect in the car's shiny black paintwork.

"To the airport?"

There are no stars in the Bottoms. The ever-present mess of rusted pipes and cracked concrete known as the Ceiling makes sure of that.

Jagr has regained her composure and shakes her head in the rear-view mirror. Soledad twists the wheel, and we go screaming up a concrete ramp, heading for the upper levels of the city. "Not quite."

Interesting.

Outside in the tunnel, the streetlights flicker, go dead and come back on again.

"Lots of power failures lately," I remark and finger my gun.

"Are there? Haven't noticed."

"*I registered another drop in data connectivity,*" Aeryn says.

"Hmm." Here too. The world falls apart around us and no one even notices. A holiday on Nifelheim doesn't sound so bad anymore.

I study my newfound friends as the dirty streets of the Bottoms recede below.

The similarity between Jagr and Soledad is un-canny. They have the same cruel but attractive Slavic face and the same lean, fit build. Both women are the same age, about forty, give or take a few years. They even sound the same when they talk. Geneti-cally identical. If one of them committed murder, the other could get executed based on the DNA evidence. You better hope your clones behave.

We scream out of a tunnel and enter the middle tiers of Masada. Patches of night sky become visible between the tall starscrapers. The streets are filled with people. There's another protest going on. A lot of Christ-Heads line the street, shaking crosses and chanting. They are all over the news these days. Not only on Elysium but all the settled planets. Something has them riled up. Probably semantics in some holy document or other. I couldn't care less.

"We're here," Jagr announces.

What Are We Riding On?

We swing around the ground-level shops of an obsidian starscraper and drive out across a large parking lot. Unusually for Masada, this lot is open to the sky. It's framed by taller buildings stretching on into the sky. Hundreds of metres below are the Bottoms we just left, and hundreds of metres above are the penthouses and eyries of the elite, not quite visible through the smog of the city and the mist from the jungle surrounding Masada. The lot is empty except for a dark, ominous-looking, four-engine dropship of obvious Terran military design. It's big. Twenty metres long by eight wide, and four metres tall on its landing struts. Two stumpy wings extend from the craft with enormous swivel engines attached to the ends. The rear pair of engines are attached to the hull to allow all four engines to swing back and power the ship on high-speed assaults. A huge swivel-mounted

Gatling gun hangs under each wing and one below the nose of the ship. Those things can pound a bunker to dust. The ship stands with its engines idling in the centre of the parking lot, illuminating the neighbourhood with its landing lights. The engines whip exhaust fumes and dust around the lot. Someone has got powerful friends. Kids hang out the windows of the surrounding residential blocks and stare at the ship. There are many adults too. Most of these people have never seen a real spaceship before, and I doubt even one of them has seen a warship. I always wanted to be a dropship pilot when I was a kid. They fly the toughest missions and boast the shortest life expectancy of all military pilots, but they also claim the biggest pay cheques. During the Corporate Wars, the dropship pilots had almost as many fans as the Goliaths.

Jagr turns around in her seat. "Now behave, Perez."

"What, are we meeting your parents already?" This relationship moves a little too fast for me.

"Nope, you wouldn't want to meet *them*. Trust me." There's a quick wrinkling of the skin at the corner of her eye. Was that a smile? When I look closer, it's gone.

Soledad drives the car through the swirling smoke, right up to the dropship and brakes. Hard. I bang my face on the back of her seat.

Always remember to wear a seatbelt, kids.

Warm fluid runs from my nose and I can taste salt and iron again. Damn it. I make sure to bleed all over the seat.

We exit the car and I shield my eyes against the dust whipping around the ship in the glare from the floodlights. The night is humid like a sauna, and the wind from the engines is a welcome addition. The toxic smell of jet fuel brings back memories of adventure and death.

"You've met Soledad."

Jagr has to shout over the whine from the idling turbines. "She's our weapons expert, mechanic and medic. She can destroy anything and anyone and then patch 'em back up again."

"Yeah, I've noticed," I rub my nose. It's still bleeding feebly. Soledad leers at me through the haze.

Jagr waves her rifle in the general direction of the dropship. "Perez, meet the rest of the team."

I squint through the light. Another woman is leaning against one of the landing struts, puffing on a cigarette. Her clothes flutter in the wind from the turbines.

Oh, great. I lick my teeth and spit blood on the asphalt. Another clone.

We walk up to the ship.

"That's all?" I glance around. "Three people? Isn't that a bit short for a special ops team?"

A brief hesitation from Jagr. She doesn't look at me. "There used to be more of us."

"Where are they now?"

Ignoring my question, she points a slender finger at the new woman. "This is Braden. She's our aviator, and the best damn pilot I've ever flown with."

Braden is taller than the others, but there's no mistaking they are clones. She wears a white, sleeveless hooded top and the same tight combat suit, pulled down and tied around her waist. Wide braces hold up the suit, and long black fingerless gloves with a lot of buckles with no discernible function cover her lower arms. She's a regular goth fashion icon. The top does a poor job of hiding the curves of her toned upper body, and the tight combat suit reveals another curve. There's a swelling bulge at her crotch.

Braden beams. "Yeah, I know, impressive isn't it?"

She pushes off from the ship and flicks her cigarette away into the night. It trails sparks like a miniature meteorite. "Want to touch it?"

I catch myself staring and I tear my eyes away to look up at her face instead. She's got the same severely attractive face as Jagr and Soledad, but with even more distinct features. Below the white hood, I glimpse a blue mohawk and the clean-shaven sides of her head. The neural patch cables of a military-grade ships interface fall like dreadlocks from the back of her head and down over one shoulder. Her full lips are painted blue to match her hair.

She could be a model with that face. And that body.

"Thanks, but not right now."

"Aw, please?"

She bats her long, blue eyelashes at me. "I've been cooped up with these bitches for months."

"Another time." I smile and reach out my hand. "Braden, was it?"

"Corin Braden, at your *service*." She shakes my hand and emphasises the service part with a wide smile and a bow. She's got a firm handshake and a delightful smile.

Jagr laughs under her breath.

"I think Braden likes you, Perez. Well, that's the team. Team, this is Asher Perez, also known as the Dread General, the Worldburner, and the Enemy of Man."

She pops the boot of the car. "I hope he is of a friendlier disposition towards women."

She throws two bags to Soledad, grabs a bag for herself and stamps up the lowered ramp at the rear of the dropship. She's not wasting any time.

"Come on girls, time to go."

"Is this all?"

"All what?" Jagr asks through the noise.

"All of you."

Jagr stops at the top of the ramp. "We have other assets in play, but for all intents and purposes, we're it. We can't send a larger team to Nifelheim without pissing off the Goliaths. This is supposed to be a low-key mission."

Famous last words, but I can't fault her logic. I incline my head to Braden and Soledad. "After you, ladies."

Braden the pilot goes first. As she passes me, she leans in and whispers in my ear. "There's room for two in the pilot's chair. If you're a good boy, I'll let you hold the joystick."

58

I smile, despite myself. "Too bad I'm not a good boy."

She winks at me.

Soledad goes next with the bags. She doesn't even glance my way.

I follow her up the ramp into the ship, enjoying the view of three tight, identical backsides.

They are a random bunch of characters, and apart from their obvious genetic affinity, they seem to have nothing in common.

I hope they are as good as Jagr says, or this could be a brief mission. Nifelheim is no place for amateurs.

* * *

All military ships look the same inside, and this one is no exception. Everything is a utility lead-grey colour. All flat, ugly surfaces, devoid of decoration. Random pipes and boxes with no obvious function adorn the walls. As is the navy custom, the dropship uses only muted lighting when in active operation. Like the eyepatches of ancient pirates, the general idea is to allow the troops to adapt quickly to various degrees of ambient lighting when they leave the ship. This custom also makes it less of a necessity to clean up, and this ship is messy like the room of a spoiled child. There's gear everywhere, but there's a method to the madness. Every item has been placed with great care.

We enter through the rear cargo bay. On an assault drop, the bay holds two armoured personnel carriers.

Now, it's stacked with dark crates of varying sizes, tied down against the deck with straps and magnetic clamps. Many of the crates appear to contain military hardware. Judging by the amount of weaponry, Jagr expects a minor war. Then again, we're going to Nifelheim. All the weapons in the world might not be enough.

We file through the hold and into the ship's short, wide midsection that doubles as an airlock. There's a heavy door to the outside set in one wall and lockers containing heavily armoured drop suits line the walls. Through the forward door, we reach the troop bay. It's a cramped space about twice the size of my one-room flat and it smells of sweat and greased metal. Like my flat.

A dropship carries a full platoon of marines, but this ship has been modified. There are only sixteen crash couches, eight set along the port side and eight along the centre console, facing them. The starboard side of the bay has been converted into a war room with kitchen facilities. There's an integral table with benches next to a small stove almost invisible behind an assortment of crates strapped to the deck. View-screens are bolted to the walls at random intervals. Weapon racks line the aft bulkhead and there's a sliding door in the forward bulkhead, leading to the cockpit.

Jagr and Soledad are already strapping into the crash couches. Soledad performs gesture commands on a control pad on her lap and I get into the couch facing her. There's an uncomfortable moment before the memory foam in the seat adjusts to my body shape, but then I'm tucked in like a baby in its mother's arms. "Where are we going?" I lower the padded safety bar over my chest. I have no desire to get thrown around the bay if Braden has to do any emergency manoeuvring.

"Nifelheim."

"I know that. How are we going to get there? It will take months in this bucket, and the Goliaths don't allow Terran ships within one light minute of Nifelheim."

"They'll let us in."

She gives me a stiff smile. "You'll see."

She returns to her tinkering.

"So, we stow away on a private cruiser then? Sweet."

I click the safety bar into place. It locks with a satisfying sound. I don't like the military much, but they build solid stuff.

"Do I get a cabin of my own, or do we share, you and I?"

She flips me the finger without looking up. "Dream on, Perez. You couldn't handle me."

"I could try."

Soledad laughs. "Shut up. I've got work to do."

There's a crackle from the overhead speakers. "Ready for take-off in ten seconds. Buckle up, ladies. Music." The deep bass lines of some random Crump track blasts from speakers up in the cockpit. The bass vibrates through my seat as it reclines into position for take-off. Many military ships, and dropships, in

61

particular, have seats that swivel to ensure the occupants can withstand the heavy G-forces of combat flight. We're left staring at the ceiling. The seats' arrangement makes excellent survival sense, but it sucks for conversation.

Another vibration rumbles through the craft. Not music this time. The rumble turns into a roar of constant thunder as Braden cranks up the turbines and takes us airborne. There's a screen above my seat. It shows the parking lot recede into the night as we bank and climb hard between the starscrapers. Children wave to us from the windows. They will no doubt grow up dreaming of being starship pilots.

We leave the city behind and head out over the jungle, gaining altitude by the second. Getting a permit to land a spaceship in downtown Masada requires a lot of pull. Taking off at night from an unsupervised parking lot even more so.

My ears pop as Braden takes us vertical and turns on the big boosters once we're clear of the city. We're all pushed hard into our seats by inertia, and I can't breathe. Damn, Braden is heavy on the accelerator.

I can't think with all the noise and the vibration from the fusion engines hurling us into space, but one thing is clear. Whatever their contact found on Nifelheim, the people who run this show think it's pretty damn important. Important enough to give us access to this ship and clearance to land it in the city.

I can't wait to find out what kind of crap this is all about.

Five minutes later Braden cuts the engines, and we drift weightless through space, hurtling along serenely at ten times the speed of sound. Yes, I read the escape velocity of Elysium somewhere once and the figure stuck. Don't be so surprised.

The screen shows stars and the growing golden arc of the Elysian sunrise to the east. Hope Alpha is just below the horizon and Hope Beta is not far behind. Sunrises in binary star systems are spectacular.

The PA crackles again with the heavy music pumping in the background.

"Perez, get your ass up here." It's Jagr.

Better do what the boss says.

Soledad has fallen asleep. Her arms and hair float free, and she looks like a drowned corpse.

I raise the bar, unstrap, and float out of my seat. It's been a while since I was off-world, and it takes a moment to align my brain to the fact there's no up or down anymore. The human brain is not built to handle navigation in three dimensions. To keep from going dizzy, I concentrate on keeping the dropship's floor as my reference down direction.

I pull my way towards the cockpit using handholds set into the walls. When the ship is under thrust the handholds double as a ladder.

I punch the green button next to the bulkhead door to open it. It slides aside on well-oiled tracks. It would appear Soledad keeps the vessel in ship shape.

I heave myself into the cockpit. The view is spectacular.

A dropship doesn't have proper portholes. They would never survive the stress of atmospheric entry and the entire vessel would burn. Instead, dropships use outboard cameras and high-definition viewscreens. The screen curving around the cockpit displays a magnificent view of the black vastness of space and the myriad lights of the Milky Way.

It's beautiful.

It's also the most terrifying thing I've ever seen.

The General chained to the rear wall of my mind screams in terror, and his fear locks my body into cramps. My fists close hard enough for my nails to draw blood and I go sailing rigid as a block of wood into the screen. I bounce off and career into an array of switches and buttons. An alarm blares and a red light flashes on over our heads.

"What the *fuck*?" Braden punches a sequence of buttons on a console above her head and the alarm cuts out.

The sudden noise and shouting bring my body under control and I unclench my fists and stabilise myself behind Jagr's seat.

"What the fuck was that about Perez?"

Jagr turns around and stares at me. "They said you had been in space before."

"I have." I forgot for how long. General Meridian was locked into an escape pod and sent drifting through deep space for forty years with no chance of escape and no way of killing himself. He doesn't like the Big Empty.

Drops of blood from my gashed palms float around the cabin like little wobbling crimson planets.

"Sorry. I'm out of practice."

There's a shout from the troop bay.

"What the fuck happened?" Soledad shouts. "Are we dying?"

Jagr calls back. "That was Perez pushing buttons he shouldn't have pushed."

"Fucking A. Just space the fucker already."

I smile. I think Soledad likes me.

Bradden glares at me over her shoulder. The patch cables in her head connect to the neural interfaces in the pilot's seat.

"Don't. Fucking. Do that again," she says through gritted teeth. "You could have killed us. I think I wet my knickers."

"Sorry. Won't happen again."

I grab the backs of their seats and pull myself forward a little between them. I focus on Jagr's profile and not on the shitload of nothing outside the windows. It doesn't hurt to watch her face.

"You called, *Massa*."

"Yes. I thought you might like to see where we're going."

Braden has us in a slow starboard roll. A billion stars revolve above our heads and the golden crescent of Elysium far below revolves with them. The panic wells up again inside, but I lock it down. The golden bow stretches wider as we rise above the planet and then Hope Alpha pokes through the upper layers of my home planet's atmosphere.

"I thought we were going to Nifelheim." I look back at Jagr again.

"We are."

She leans back in her couch and puts a boot up on the ledge beneath the screen.

She rests one slender wrist on her shapely knee like a roguish space pirate captain. "But not in this bucket."

Her leg is a thing of beauty.

"*Hey*, there's nothing wrong with this bucket," Braden says. She punches another sequence of buttons arranged above her head. Probably just for show.

"No, the *Sundowner* is a fine little ship, Braden. But it would take us months to get to Nifelheim in this crate, and we don't have months."

"OK, so what are we riding on?" I glance from one woman to the other.

Braden grins and banks the ship into a long sweeping turn.

Our second sun breaks through the planet's atmosphere and bathes everything inside the cockpit in brilliant white light.

"That." Jagr points out the windscreen at a giant starship rolling into view.

Fuck me. I'm impressed.

"That" is the Emancipation class Terran main line battle cruiser *Shiloh*. Flagship of the Terran Commonwealth and the greatest warship ever built.

"Nice ride," is the best I can manage.

"It is, isn't it?" There's genuine pride in Jagr's voice. I can tell she is aware of exactly how much power and resources someone has wielded to get her and her little crew where they need to go. If I ever had any doubts that the people in charge consider this mission important, they just disappeared quicker than a virginity in a prison shower. Someone means business and is not afraid to show it.

The *Shiloh* is berthed at one of the many Terran military stations orbiting Elysium, but you would be forgiven for thinking it was the other way around. The ship dwarfs the satellite. Braden takes us in along the kilometre-long warship at breakneck speed. I can't imagine all the time and resources spent to construct this marvel of modern engineering. A million tonnes of hypercarbon, shaped like a tapered starscraper kicked over on its back, with four immense engines tucked to one end. It's not a beautiful ship, but it's functional.

The radio crackles. We're being hailed.

"Unidentified vessel. This is Commander Hardigan of the UNS *Shiloh*. You will divert your current flight path and return to your designated approach vector. Fail to comply and you will be fired upon."

Jagr grabs a microphone from above her head and leans back in the chair. "This is Misha Jagr on the assault ship *Sundowner*. You will divert your asshole attitude and let us board any way we bloody like. Here are my identification codes."

She switches hands on the microphone and places her right palm on the console between the seats. The ship reads her ID chip and relays her credentials to Commander Hardigan.

There's a moment of silence as her authority is verified.

Then Commander Hardigan comes back on the line.

"As you were, *Sundowner.* You may board when ready, ma'am."

Commander Hardigan is a true professional. His voice is smooth business and there's not even a hint he just threatened to blow us out of the sky.

Jagr flips the *Shiloh* the finger with the slender hand still holding the microphone. "Fucking navy." At last, something we agree on.

"Hey, Soledad," she calls out to the woman in the back. "Get ready to dock. Gear and weapons check and ready to roll on touch down."

Jagr runs a tight ship. If I was even the slightest impressed by military precision I'd be impressed, but I'm not, so I'm not.

Braden swings us around the *Shiloh*, providing an impressive view of the four massive barrel-shaped engines sticking from the ass-end of the warship. The stern of the warship is tall as a mountainside.

"Do we have time for a quick beer before we board? I think I'm about to score with Soledad."

Jagr laughs from her crash seat. "Dream on, Perez. We're on a tight schedule. The *Shiloh* leaves in twenty minutes, and we need to be aboard and stowed away by then."

Damn, we *are* on a clock.

Knock, Knock

The gigantic engine exhausts iris open, exposing the shimmering, iridescent blue of the fusion-powered plasma cores within. Each one of those immense openings could swallow ten *Sundowners* in formation.

Once the *Shiloh's* crew start the ignition process, there's no going back. Once set in motion, all that power needs to be released. That sounds like a euphemism. What is Soledad doing later tonight?

I hang on to Jagr's seat as Braden takes us around the warship.

The docking bay is on the underside of the great vessel, and the *Shiloh* towers above us. Decks on interplanetary starships stack like the floors of a starscraper, perpendicular to the ship's long axis. That way, inertia provides artificial gravity as the ship accelerates and decelerates. As we approach, immense blast doors slide apart to allow us inside. It's a giant airlock, designed to allow fighters and transports to enter and exit the bay.

An airlock on a carrier ship is an excellent idea in principle. It allows you to keep the hangar pressurised to allow the crews to work on the vessels without messing with vacuum suits. It's not such a wonderful idea when the brass vents the bay's atmosphere to launch the fighters faster. I'll never forget when they did that on the *Vigilant*. She was a repurposed Gray Industries heavy freighter that was shot to shit above Persephone. We were already evacuating the ship when they blew the airlock to allow our fighter ships to escape to fight another day. Hundreds of soldiers about to board their shuttles were blown into space and died hard in the cold and dark. They were expendable, the fighters were not. Those men still orbit Persephone like tiny icy moons. I knew many of those men by name. Years later, Finn and I tracked down the captain of the *Vigilant* in a Masada bar. I bought him drinks, and he wouldn't stop talking. He told me he quit the corporate navy circuit shortly after that debacle. A few months later, he lost his wife. He lost his miserable drunken life that night. In the end, he wasn't sorry to go. Guilt can be a bitch.

Braden guides us into the airlock and gets us close enough to the floor to engage the landing clamps. There's a soft thump as we're locked down.

"Smooth as my silk panties." Braden punches sequences of buttons to power down the ship. "I couldn't have done it better myself."

I nod, impressed. "Smooth indeed."

Braden reaches behind her, gathers the neural patch cables in one hand and tears them out of the seat with a small, dissatisfied moan. I've heard the connection between a pilot and her ship is almost sexual in its intensity. Braden's face tells me I heard correctly. "Want to see something else that's smooth, Perez?" Braden unbuckles and gets out of her chair. She floats above the seat with the patch cables floating like drugged snakes around her head. I bet Medusa never looked this good.

"What, your baby-soft navy hands?"

She smirks. "Haha, hilarious." I like Braden.

"One minute, ladies," Jagr calls to her team as she pushes off from her seat. Braden and I pull ourselves into the troop bay after her. Soledad is already on her way to the cargo area, like a well-trained pet.

Jagr gives me a look. "When we board the *Shiloh*, you let me do the talking, Perez."

"Sure thing boss. Wouldn't have it any other way."

"I doubt that."

A wall-mounted screen shows the inner door of the *Shiloh's* airlock sliding open, and the *Sundowner* shudders and begins to move. We're being towed into the belly of the warship on powerful dollies running along tracks in the floor.

Inside the airlock is a vast, dim hangar. There are at least a dozen dark, mean-looking fighter ships locked down for the long haul to Nifelheim. There's not a single human in sight. The crew will already be strapped down in their acceleration couches to prepare for departure. The dollies haul us into an empty berth where autonomous tethers snake out and anchor our ship to the *Shiloh.*

"OK, time to move, ladies."

Jagr punches the button that lowers the cargo ramp and the warship's atmosphere hisses into our ship. It smells of antiseptics and heavy machinery.

We push off from the *Sundowner* and float out into the main bay of the *Shiloh.* There's a guide cable supported on metal stands leading from our berth to the nearest bulkhead. Three soldiers emerge through a door and wait for us. They hold themselves stationary by handholds in the wall. "This way," calls one of them.

Jagr grabs the cable and starts pulling herself towards them. "After you." I nod to Soledad, and she tags along after Jagr. Braden is still aboard the *Sundowner,* making last-minute preparations for the trip.

Three long beeps sound over the intercom, and we drift sideways. The immense ship is reversing out of its dock, getting ready to set sail for Nifelheim. It's cute they stick to maritime signals hundreds of years old. That's the navy for you.

As we approach the soldiers, the one in charge salutes us. He's got an awful lot of shiny metal on his immaculate slate-grey uniform. Must be someone important.

"Commander Hardigan, at your service, ma'am," he greets us as we brake our approach and glide to a halt in front of him. So, this is the arsehole who threatened to blow us out of the sky. He's not so tough now. I could break his neck before his two

72

goons could even react. Commander Hardigan is a man in his late forties, with a narrow, scarred face. His eyes are dead as glass. Maybe they are artificial. He smells of expensive cologne.

The brass greets us in person. What clearance has Jagr's access codes provided us?

"At ease, Commander." Jagr doesn't return the salute.

Are she and the other girls military? They could be black ops, but they could also be private security. Often, the line between the two is fluid. "Take us to your leaders."

Commander Hardigan keeps his stone face impassive, and I can't tell if he's an expert at masking his emotions or if he didn't get the joke. Then again, few people know these ancient sayings. I'm impressed Jagr does. Maybe I need to reconsider my opinion of her.

"At once, ma'am." He gives me a quick disapproving glance. I must look like shit, with dried blood all over my face, hair, and clothes. The navy has always frowned on a shabby appearance. That's one good reason to hate the navy.

Commander Hardigan spins around and exits the landing bay. He pulls himself along the guide rails set in the walls, and he appears perfectly at home in the weightless environment. The two soldiers follow him, and we make up the rear.

"Hey. Wait for me." Braden comes sailing after us.

She catches up with us in the passageway and almost collides with me. A hand grabs my ass and squeezes it. Hard.

"Oops, sorry Perez. My bad."

"Yeah, sure, Braden. I should sue you for sexual harassment."

"Oh, yes, and I would go to prison, and you could do conjugal visits. That would be so hot."

I laugh out loud. "In your dreams, Braden."

"Mmm, all the time."

"Shut up, you two." Jagr gives us an irritated glance as we float after Hardigan. Soledad does not look thrilled either.

The passageways on the *Shiloh* are far removed from those on the *Lady of Heaven*. On a warship, they are not designed to prevent drunk passengers from hurting themselves when they miss a handhold. They are built to give maximum structural strength to the hull at minimum weight, and that means crew comfort has to take a back seat. Everything is made of angled and practical slate-grey hyper carbon. No need to add an extra couple of tonnes to the ship by painting the interior surfaces a lighter colour. Every few metres, recessed spotlights provide muted illumination.

We approach another door, and it slides open to let us pass through into another passageway. This one is filled with servicemen and women going about their last preparations to get the ship locked down for the journey. A slight sideways tug tells me the battleship is turning, getting ready to blast off into space.

"Follow me," Commander Hardigan orders, and we follow. Believe me, if I could have thought of a reason not to, I would have. I don't enjoy taking orders.

We're taken to an elevator. Hardigan puts his hand against a scanner and punches a code to summon it. It arrives in practically no time at all. Officers' override, I assume. A mere grunt would have had to wait his turn. Damn, I hate the military.

We pull ourselves into the elevator. It's more than large enough for the lot of us. As it takes off, a false sense of gravity kicks in, and we all end up standing on the floor. For a moment, it's odd to stick to a surface, but it soon passes. The human mind craves an up and a down to be content.

As always in an elevator with strangers, an awkward tension creeps in and I study my fingernails while Hardigan's cologne fills the space like poison gas.

There's a chime, and we all float towards the ceiling as we decelerate. Then it comes to a full stop, and we're weightless again.

The door opens on what I can only assume is the ship's bridge.

The room is vast. It's more of a chamber than a room. My old pal the Cardinal would not be impressed, but it's large as a fucking church. The only light in the room comes from a light-blue holographic sphere, floating in mid-air. It represents our surrounding space, with tiny blips denoting the other ships coming and going from the station. As we enter the bridge, the larger blip indicating the station floats out of the sphere and disappears. We'll soon have reached a safe distance to ignite the engines.

There's a gallery halfway up the wall where crewmembers sit strapped into crash seats. They punch buttons and make last-minute adjustments to prepare for blast off. It appears everyone except us is already strapped down. We should do something about that.

"Star marshal Crom will be with you shortly," Hardigan announces. He kicks off toward a man in an even fancier uniform than his own. The man in the fancy suit is in a sombre discussion with two women.

A *star marshal*? I didn't know we had those anymore.

Braden sniggers. "Did that guy say his name was William Hardigan?"

Jagr's eyes narrow. "Yeah, why? Do you know him?"

"No, but I didn't think anyone was called that."

Jagr is silent for a moment. "What?"

Braden beams. "I thought it was a joke name. Like Biggus Dickus."

"What's so funny about William Hardigan?" Jagr doesn't find the name funny at all.

"Knock, knock."

Jagr sighs. "Who's there?"

"Willie Hardigan."

"Willie Hardigan who?"

"Willie B. Hardigan." The corners of Braden's mouth almost reach her ears. "Get it?"

There's an interminable silence, and then Soledad, of all people, lets out a roaring laugh. Several sailors turn to gawk at her. I can understand them. It's not a sweet laugh.

I get it a second later. So do the others, and we all laugh. It's the first time I've heard any of the girls laugh, and it breaks the tension.

Soledad goes next. "Knock, knock."

I want to play. "Who's there?"

"Mrs Payne."

"Mrs Payne who?"

"Ophelia Payne."

Jagr takes the next one. "Knock, knock."

Braden wants to play too. "Who's there?"

"Mr Bull."

"Mr Bull who?"

"Terry Bull. Now shut up. Here comes the brass."

The man in the fancy uniform floats our way, accompanied by Willie B. Hardigan. I can't help myself and I laugh under my breath.

"Zip it, Perez," Jagr warns, and I put on my serious face.

My serious face has serious issues and I fight to keep it under control.

The older man addresses us. "Welcome aboard the *Shiloh*." His Martian ancestry is clear in his accent. He's in his late fifties, tall and severe, with crewcut iron hair. A hawknose and drooping eyelids give him a perpetually tired appearance. There's a dangerous glint in his eyes that betray the keen intellect behind

77

them. He looks splendid in his neatly trimmed uniform.

I expect this must be star marshal Crom. Anything else would be unlikely.

"We are about to set course for Nifelheim, ma'am, so I advise you strap down in your cabins. I wanted to take this moment to welcome you personally. It's an honour to have you aboard, dame Jagr." He bows his head.

Dame Jagr?

"It's an honour to be here, star marshal. I believe my employers have informed you of our mission?"

"They have, and we're at your command."

Sweet. I've always wanted a Terran battleship at my command.

"Thank you. Let's get this thing moving. Where can we strap down?"

"Commander Hardigan will show you to your cabins. The journey will take two days, with acceleration breaks every twelve hours. Now, if you'll excuse me, I have a ship to sail across the oceans of space."

Two *days*? On a regular shuttle, the journey to Nifelheim would take months. This will be one uncomfortable ride.

"Of course, star marshal. Do your thing."

Crom salutes Jagr, and she touches two fingers to her forehead in something that could be a salute. It could also be her miming blowing her brains out with an imaginary gun.

Crom either doesn't notice, or he is too polite to fuss.

"If you'll follow me, I will take you to your cabins."

Hardigan kicks off towards one of the gloomy passages leading from the bridge.

"Make haste, we launch in seven minutes."

Hardigan leads us past a lot of doors. One door is open and leads to what appears to be an officers' mess.

"These are the officers' quarters. You are located over here." We reach the end of the officers' passage where three cabin doors slide open as we approach, one to each side, and a larger door ahead.

"There are two bunks in each cabin, one in the suite." He indicates the larger door.

"Sleeping arrangements are up to you. Strap down. We're about to begin countdown."

Hardigan snaps a quick salute and floats back down the passageway.

Jagr turns to us. "You heard the man. The clock is ticking. Braden, you're in here." She points to one of the smaller doors with her thumb.

"Yay." Braden makes the V-sign and pushes the button to open her door. "Single room. The boss likes me."

"Perez, you bunk with Soledad." Jagr points to the other small door.

Sweet.

"All right." I nod. "But keep your hands to yourself, Soledad."

"You've got a high opinion of yourself, Perez." She gives a half-smile as we tow our gear into the little cabin.

"I'm a swell guy." As we enter, muted spotlights turn on in the ceiling.

"Cut the crap you two, and strap down."

Jagr is not one for idle chit-chat. She hovers in our doorway, holding on to the door frame.

"I don't want any of you to break a leg or crack your skull because you didn't strap down properly. That goes for you too, Perez. It would be hard to explain to the crew why we show no trace of the injuries later. Remember, this is a low-profile job. We go to Nifelheim, locate our guy, find out what he has found and get him out. Nice and smooth."

"You don't even believe that yourself, Jagr," Soledad scoffs as she packs her gear into a locker in the wall. She has an awful lot of guns in her bags. And knives. And things even I find hard to identify.

"Nope. But that's our plan."

She looks at her wrist console. "Two minutes, people. Strap down."

Our cabin is small and dark, with a foldaway bunk bed and two narrow closets with matching cupboards set into the walls. A foldaway toilet and a display screen are sunk into the wall. That's it.

Spaceflight is all about mass versus thrust, and vast rooms with lots of furniture equal more mass, equals less thrust. It's basic maths. It's also depressing. I hope I won't go crazy cooped up in here for two days.

"The bottom bunk is mine." Soledad closes her storage locker and floats into the lower bed. She stuffs a mean-looking gun under her pillow. My kind of girl.

"Fine with me." I stow my kit in the other locker. "I like to be on top."

"Hilarious."

The screen lights up to display a countdown. One minute to blast off.

A brief glitch distorts the image before the countdown resumes. Even state-of-the-art battleships are not safe from the recent glitches. That's a comforting thought.

"*Here we go again*," Aeryn says.

"Another data drop?"

"*Yes. Do you still believe it's a coincidence?*"

"Maybe. Maybe not."

"Did you say something, Perez?" Soledad squints at me.

"Nope, just mumbling to myself." No need to let them know about Aeryn. I like to keep an edge.

"Well, it's time to go."

Soledad pulls herself down into her crash seat and pulls the straps tight. "See you later, Perez."

"Later, Soledad." I push off from the floor and strap down in the top bunk. As soon as I'm tucked in, a horn blares five times over the intercom. We're ready to fire the big ones.

I hate the next part.

A woman's voice begins a countdown from ten. The needles of the couch's drug dispensing system pierce my skin in sharp little pinpricks. An icy wave rushes through my body as they deliver their sedative pharmaceutical cocktail into my bloodstream. We're on a tight schedule and there will be no time for idle drifting between planets. This will be a hard-G burn-and-brake manoeuvre to cut travel time as much as possible without killing the crew and passengers. The *Shiloh* could make the trip in a day, but we would all be dead from the unforgiving acceleration and deceleration.

At least the humans onboard would be dead. We immortals might fare better, but I'm not dying to try it. I'm grateful for the drugs.

A rumble vibrates through the ship.

"Perez?" Soledad calls from the bunk below me.

"What?"

"Stop playing with yourself."

My eloquent response drowns in the noise and vibrations from the booster engines. The titanic warship flexes her muscles and ponderously sets off into the vastness of space.

We're going to Nifelheim, the most dangerous planet in the system, but here I am, happy for the first time in years.

I'm on an adventure with three hot women, I'm going to see Finn again, and there's a mystery looming somewhere out there.

This should be fun.

The primary engines ignite, and the world becomes a screaming battle for breath.

My consciousness dissolves aided by the drugs pumped into my system by the crash seat.

Nifelheim, here we come.

Mind If I Join You?

I'm weightless.

The acceleration phase is over, and my body feels like it's been through a meat grinder. I glance at the clock on the screen. I've been out for twenty-five hours, and it's time for the flip. Halfway through a hard-burn trip, you swing your ship around 180 degrees and fire the engines at your target for a matching deceleration phase.

There have been brief lulls in the burns to keep us from dying, but we haven't noticed. The supervising systems need not bring us to full consciousness during the breaks. But now we get some awake time.

"Hey, Soledad? You up?"

There's an affirmative grunt from Soledad's bunk.

I unstrap and push off against the ceiling and float over the door. I turn around to see how Soledad is doing and freeze.

"What are you staring at, Perez? You don't look so hot yourself."

Soledad has bruises on her face, and her eyes are bloodshot. The thin capillaries in our eyes and skin don't stand up well to an extended hard burn, and the back of my hands show the same discolouration. The familiar tingling in my blood tells me the nanites have already gone to work. As always, that makes me hungry. My body needs raw materials to rebuild itself. "I'm off to the galley. Are you coming?"

"Sure. Let's see what they can cook up on a boat like this. The navy is supposed to have amazing cooks." She kicks off after me.

We pull ourselves through the darkened passageways and over to the officer's mess. I glance at my hands again. The discolouration is almost gone, but Soledad still looks like an extra from a zombie feed. She should be restored by now if her nanites had worked as intended. Perhaps the girls are a cheaper model than me.

Did Gray start a second project after the one that created Meridian and the Cherubim? No. If that were the case, they should be better than me, not worse. So, a competing project then. Run by whom?

We float into the mess. It's better illuminated than the passageway outside, but it's still dark by any standards. There's no one around, so we search the place for something to eat. After rummaging around, Soledad finds a crate of freeze-dried, beef stew. She shakes it to see if it's full. In zero gravity things don't have weight, but they still have mass. "Found it." She braces against a cupboard and sends the box floating my way. She seems happy like a fish in water.

I throw five packs into the cooker, and as I start the heating process, Jagr enters with Braden in tow.

"Hey. I thought we'd find you here."

She straps into a seat at the table. "What's for dinner?"

"Beef stew. You want some?" There's a not entirely appetising smell coming from the cooker.

"Are you buying?"

"I'm buying."

"Then beef stew it is."

She drums her fingers on the tabletop. "And make it snappy. I'm starving."

I pull out ten more packs and throw them into the cooker. We wait in silence for the food. No one wants to talk.

The machine beeps and I hand out the packs before I strap down at the table next to Soledad. Triple rations for all. If they are anything like me, they need their nutrients.

"So, Jagr. Are you going to fill me in here?"

Braden and Soledad glance at Jagr.

"Who are you people, and what's the deal with your agent on Nifelheim?"

Jagr opens her first pack of stew. She takes her time. You don't want sticky pieces of hot meat and gravy flying around in Zero-G.

She takes a bite of the steaming nutrition bar. "Yeah, I guess we owe you something of an explanation."

I chew a piece off my bar. "You sure do." It doesn't taste like either beef or stew, but it's not the worst

I've had. Like most edibles on a starship, it's made from fungi grown onboard in great dark vats. Not the best conditions for gastronomical marvels.

Jagr looks off into the distance. "We are all that's left of the Shard."

"The *what*?"

"You heard me."

"Oh, come on. The *Shard*?"

Everyone in the business has heard of the Shard. They are a semi-mythical unit, like the Men in Black. Only the tinfoil hats believe they are real.

"Better believe it, Perez." She's not joking.

Fuck me. That would explain their unlimited access to resources. And the star marshal's reverence.

"OK." I nod, impressed. "So, you're the Shard. How come you are clones?"

Jagr flinches at the word but keeps her composure. "What do you know about Gray's Project Cherubim?"

"Enough. He cloned himself and injected the embryos with self-replicating nanobots. Then he had their skeletons and tendons torn out and replaced with hypercarbon to create immortal soldiers. That about right?"

"In essence. Then the first Great War between Hope and Terra happened. Gray drafted his pet soldiers to fight for Hope, and we all know how that went."

"Yes, Meridian burned Arcadia, and Gray killed the General and his soldiers to cover his ass. But Meridian survived."

Jagr nods without looking at me. "So did another. Major Solana. The soldier who stopped Meridian's attack on Nero Gray."

Deep down inside, something knots at the mention of Solana's name and I've got to quench an impulse to scream insanely. Meridian hates that guy.

I swallow hard to get the knot to stay in my belly.

"I always wondered what happened to Solana after the war, but I haven't been able to find a single trace of him." My jaws clench. "Believe me, I've tried."

"That's because he fled to Earth with the retreating Terran forces. He knew Gray couldn't let him live, so he stowed away on a ship and hitched a ride back to Earth. He contacted the immortals, hoping to trade his knowledge about Gray and his project for a life in peace. Didn't quite work out for him."

I finish my stew and grab another. Something tells me the general will like the next part. "What happened to him?"

"Gray was not the first immortal with the idea to clone himself and take over the world. But he was the first to succeed. The immortals on Earth panicked when they learned Gray had succeeded in playing god where they had not. They wanted Gray's secrets for themselves, so they offered Solana a life in comfort if he gave himself up and agreed to work with them. They betrayed him. A research team dissected him alive, hunting through his immortal body for the secrets to Gray's success. They studied the technology, and they learned, and they started a project of their own using Solana's DNA. Project Shard. The first generation was a horrible failure. So was the second, but the third one was the charm. So, you are sort of our great-grandfather, Perez."

Fuck. And here I was, hoping to get Soledad into bed.

"But how come you're all female? If you were cloned from Solana, you would be male."

"Generation two only succeeded after the scientists mixed in DNA from another host. They needed someone tough, and so they spliced in a woman's genes."

"Because women have higher pain thresholds?"

"That's a myth, Perez, but yeah, something like that. The project's director was a woman, and she thought it was an outstanding idea. She was right."

OK, so we're more like siblings. Not better.

"And what about generation three?"

"For generation three they spliced in genes from one of the other immortals. They were hoping to create something stronger than Gray's original soldiers."

I nod, relieved. "So, we're cousins."

"What?"

"Nothing." Did I say that out loud? "Do you have the same mods I do?"

"Yes. Hypercarbon skeleton and tendons, but decades more advanced than you. And yes, we have the nanites too."

"But your eyes aren't blue," I point out. "Or do you wear contacts?"

I always wear coloured lenses. The iridescent blue of my eyes is far too conspicuous for my liking.

"We have the nanites, but I never said they were the same." A look of unease passes between the women over their beef stew bars.

I lower my bar, half bitten through. "What's wrong with your nanites?"

Jagr licks a crumb from the corner of her mouth. "They never refactored the nanites in Solana's blood completely. The tech was impossibly advanced, unlike anything they'd ever seen before. Decades, maybe centuries more advanced than anything they had on Earth. They got close, but not all the way. Nobody knows where Gray got his tech."

So, that explains why Soledad didn't regenerate as quickly as me. I glance at her. She appears fully recovered now.

"And what does that mean?"

"When the nanites repair our bodies, the result is never perfect like yours. Every time we're injured, our bodies degenerate. We sometimes grow odd appendages."

I glance at Braden.

"Hey, don't look at me, man," she says around a mouthful of meat. "I was born like this."

"She's right," Jagr confirms. "Braden was a lucky accident in the cloning process."

Braden beams at Jagr and Jagr smiles back.

"But you're all fine."

I survey the three women around the table. "If you tell me you've never been injured in the line of duty, I quit right now. I don't work with desk jockeys."

"Don't worry Perez. We've all seen our fair share of combat trauma. The degeneration is not always physical. The Shard was once a big outfit. Now it's only the three of us left, and we all bear our scars. Both visible and invisible, so don't fucking call us desk jockeys. All right?"

"Sorry." I take another bite of my bar.

There are voices from outside and five officers float into the mess. They look like shit.

Jagr leans back. "Well, there you have it. That's who we are."

The newcomers check us out. No amount of acceleration sickness can keep them from ogling the three beautiful women.

Soledad gives them the finger. "What? Never seen how proper soldiers handle a little acceleration sickness? Fucking navy softies." Braden claps her on the back and laughs. One of the naval officers looks like he wants to make something of it, but he's restrained by his friends. They point discretely at Jagr and whisper something to the troublemaker, and he stops at once.

Jagr unstraps from her seat and floats into the air. "Well, ladies, grab something more to eat. We've got another hour before they turn on the thrust again. I suggest you enjoy the break."

Soledad moves to unstrap. "Where are you going?"

Jagr stops her with a hand on the shoulder.

"You stay and eat. I'll fill Perez in on our mission details. Somewhere without nosy navy people." She pushes off towards the passageway. "Come on Perez."

"Excuse me, ladies." I unstrap and kick off after her.

"Perez," Soledad calls after me.

I turn around in mid-air as I sail through the door. "What?"

"Keep your fingers to yourself. Remember, she's the boss."

I throw her a mock salute. "Duly noted. You're the only girl for me, Soledad."

"Haha, funny, Perez. Behave." She throws a packet of stew after me. I laugh and turn around in time to stop myself from careening into the opposite wall.

Jagr is already at the door to her suite. "Are you coming?"

"Sorry, boss." I grab the stew packet as it sails past. "On my way."

I pull myself along the passage and swing into the opening after Jagr. I'm finally getting the hang of this Zero-G shit. Then again, it could be the General's muscle memories kicking in. He spent most of his adult life in and out of space. His body must know Zero-G like a second home.

Jagr waits for me inside the cabin. Her expression is impossible to read. "Be careful with Soledad, Perez. She's dangerous."

"I know." I rub the back of my head where Soledad cracked it on the concrete back in Masada. It seems so long ago, yet it was only the day before yesterday. My hair is still crusty with blood. I need a shower.

Jagr seems to have the same idea.

"You should clean up. Use my shower."

"You've got a *shower*?" I knew there was a reason she picked the cabins.

She nods. "We have fifty minutes until acceleration. There's plenty of time."

Time for what? I almost ask.

"The bathroom is through there." She points at a narrow door across the cabin. 'Across the cabin' meaning three metres away.

Bathroom? Who gets a cabin with a bathroom on a warship? When every kilo counts, a private bathroom is an extreme luxury. Does even the star marshal's suite include a full bathroom? Then again, this might be his suite.

"Don't be long."

Jagr turns her back to me and zips open her combat suit and pulls it down to her waist. I'm not sure this was what she meant when she said my role on this mission was strictly to observe.

"And you can stop staring."

She doesn't even glance at me as she pulls the suit off and reveals the legs I've been admiring all day. They are even finer than I imagined, and they attach to a tight ass, tucked into black panties. "Shower, Perez. Now. We have things to discuss afterwards."

"Yes, boss." I hurry into the bathroom and close the door. Whew, that was unexpected. Enjoyably so.

The bathroom is small, but an actual bloody bathroom. With an actual bloody toilet and an actual bloody sink. The shower is your standard Zero-G fare. It's a large transparent plastic bag strapped between the floor and the ceiling, with a water sprinkler at either end. As showers go, it's not much, but it's still a shower, and right now it's the height of luxury.

I strip, get in the bag and zip up. I turn on the tap and the warm water on my sticky skin is heaven. It is almost soothing enough to make me forget the quick view I got of Jagr's ass before I closed the door on her.

The water is already mixed with soap when it sprays from the nozzles and I lather myself up. My sore body relaxes, and I let out a sigh of pleasure. There is the sound of a zipper opening behind me.

Then someone grabs my ass.

What the hell?

"Mind if I join you?"

It's Jagr.

She climbs inside the shower bag and zips it closed behind her. It's barely large enough for the both of us.

"No, I don't mind." She grabs my hips and turns me towards her.

"Do you always brief people in the shower?"

I'm painfully aware she is exceedingly attractive. And exceedingly naked.

"Shut up, Perez." She wraps her arms around my neck and kisses me. Hard.

I didn't see that coming.

* * *

There's one major upside to being an immortal super-soldier with regenerative powers. You don't have to worry about scratches on your back after a romp in bed. Which is good, because Jagr is rough.

At one point she cracks two of my ribs with her smooth legs. As always, the pain is brief and the tingling as the nanobots repair the fractures adds an extra layer of pleasure. It's almost like she knows that.

I've never had sex with an immortal before, and it's amazing.

There's no need to be gentle.

* * *

We drift together in the middle of the suite. Presoaped water, sweat, and other bodily fluids float around us. Sex in Zero-G is not as romantic as they make it out to be in the feeds. It's messy and awkward. But fun.

I hold her in my arms and caress her back, stroking her spine with my fingers as we float. The smell of soap lingers on her skin under the more prominent scent of sex.

Jagr grunts. "The fuck are you doing, Perez?"

"I scratch your back, you scratch mine."

"Stop it. That's way too close for comfort."

"We just fucked."

"That was sex. This is relationship shit. Cut it out."

"Sorry." I let her go and we drift apart.

"Never do that again." Mental note not to step into that minefield again. Must be a sore point with her. Jagr wipes her moist belly and flicks the sweat away. It splatters on the wall. The motion sends her into a slow spin, showing off her toned, naked body.

She swipes a strand of platinum fringe out of her face and sighs. "Anyway. Thanks, Perez, I needed that."

"Always happy to oblige." I stretch, feeling something snap back into place in my spine.

To break the awkward moment, I change tack. "So. What about Soledad?"

"What *about* Soledad?"

"Isn't she going to be upset about this?"

"This?"

"Us." I wave my hand at her, me, and the cabin.

"*What* us? I had an itch that needed scratching, Perez. You scratched it. Nothing more. We're done." She splays her hands. I grab her wrist, stopping her slow gyration and pull her close. The motion transfers her angular momentum to me and sends us both into a slow roll.

The bruises on her skin are fading, but I can still see marks from my fingers.

I trace her smooth thigh with my fingertips and expect a kick in the balls.

Her breath quivers as I move my fingers down her leg. She shivers with pleasure and goosebumps cover her arms.

"That tickles, Perez. I once took a bullet there," she muses. "Large calibre. Almost took my leg off."

I push a little harder and feel a slight ridge of odd bumps on her femur. *The regeneration is never perfect.*

I scoff. "That's nothing. I took a knife in the eye in a bar on Utopia." I show her where the scar would have been.

"Ouch." Her fingers brush the unhurt skin under my eye.

She reaches down to her belly.

"A piece of shrapnel from an exploding tank sliced me open during the war." She scrapes a sharp nail across the smooth skin between the bumps of her pelvic bone. "From side to side. I tripped on my intestines escaping the fire." There's a slight depression in the velvet skin where she traces the old cut.

I wave my left arm around.

"I had this arm shot off once." My fingers wiggle. "Fuckers. I lost my favourite watch."

What watch? I've never had my arm shot off. Nor have I lost a watch.

I struggle to move my hands, but they refuse. Shit. The General is here. Where the fuck did he come from? He's never manifested in a situation like this before. Is he getting stronger? Winger warned me my implanted mind was volatile. I hope it's not slipping. I enjoy being me too much.

"Yes, we heard about that incident. Was it a fine watch?"

"No," the General answers with my mouth. "It had some sentimental value, that's all."

I got that watch from Gray when I was young. When Meridian was young, I mean. This is fucking weird.

"There's no place for sentimentality for people like us. I thought you knew that."

"Sometimes I like to pretend to be human." Damn it, Meridian, I *am* human.

She frowns like she's trying to figure out a riddle. Her hair moves like snakes on morphine in the light breeze from the air recycler. "You are such a strange character, Perez."

Like a dislocated shoulder, something clicks back into place in my mind and I'm in control of myself again. That was odd.

I wipe a hand down my face to exorcise the General's lingering presence from my mind.

"If only you knew half of it."

It's like a putrefying snail has oozed over my soul.

"You are the most powerful human man who ever lived, and yet you like to pretend you're human. Why?"

"I don't pretend. I *am* human. It's my body that's immortal. On the inside, I'm just a rebel kid from the streets someone dropped into a Rolls-Royce."

"A what?"

I sigh. "It's a car. An old car."

"Never cared much for old stuff. Old stuff is boring. I prefer the latest and greatest."

Are we talking about me here? "But there's a certain charm with old stuff."

"Old stuff breaks."

"That's part of the charm."

"Tell that to the men in the tank that exploded and tore me open. They said it was a hardware malfunction. Took out my entire platoon of human grunts. That's what old stuff does. It kills people."

"Not *all* old stuff." I pull her closer. "Some old parts are still working fine."

"Perez. Don't." She puts a hand on my chest. Her cool fingers soothe my burning skin.

"Don't what?"

"Just don't. We don't have long until we go under thrust again and before we do, I need to brief you on the specifics of our mission. There are things you need to know. And there are things *I* need to know."

And here I was, thinking she made up this briefing to get me into bed. I let her go. "So, brief me." I search for my underwear, but I can't find it.

"There's a suit for you in that locker." Jagr points to a locker in the wall. I push off lightly against her and float over to the locker. Jagr floats off in the opposite direction. I open the locker and inside is a combat suit, like the ones the girls wear. I pull it on, being careful with the zipper. Regeneration or not, there are injuries no man wants to suffer. The suit fits me like a glove. It looks cool too. I can understand they wear them all the time.

"I told you we had a man on Nifelheim and that he disappeared. What I didn't tell you was *why* he was there." Jagr hits the opposite wall, pushes off and drifts back into the middle of the room.

"Why was he there?" I grab my black T-shirt where it floats and pull it over my head.

"What the Goliaths are planning might be connected to something else we're investigating."

The Prince of Their Little Winter Kingdom

"What?"

"The communication spikes we've seen coming out of Nifelheim."

"Comms-spikes?"

So, they know about those.

"Yes. Powerful enough to cause brief data outages throughout the system."

Still think it's a coincidence, Perez?

I ignore her. "And what are the Goliaths saying?"

"We don't know."

"You don't have anyone who can translate Norse?"

"We do, but the transmissions are encrypted. On a level we've never encountered before, and, so far, we haven't been able to crack them. Even our best AIs failed, and we have some illegal shit in our arsenal. All we know is they broadcast stupendous amounts of raw data to someone in the system. Since the recipient is not transmitting anything in return, we can't locate them. This has got the Terran intelligence community nervous. They don't like unidentified entities with unknown tech operating from an undisclosed location. Our job on Nifelheim is to make all those unknown entities known."

"Where are the transmissions coming from?"

"No idea. They bounce them around the planet and it's impossible to tell where they originate."

"And you think this project *Hokey* is connected to the comms-spikes and your agent going AWOL?"

"Project *Jotun*."

"Whatever." I grab the boots from the locker and pull them on. The motion sends me into an awkward spin.

"Yes, we think so."

"Sounds simple enough. We go in, find the source of those transmissions, locate your agent, and extract him. We should be out of there in time for tea tomorrow." I get the boots on and pull the straps tight. Like the suit, they're a perfect fit.

"Do you honestly believe that?" She stares at me like I claimed priests could turn wine into human blood.

"No." When the Goliaths are involved, nothing is ever simple.

"Maybe you *are* smarter than they said. Now you."

She curls up into a ball, hugs her knees and rests her chin on them. She's still naked. "Are we good?"

"I'm all good."

I smile.

"Not you and me, Perez. You and *us*. The immortals. We need to know we can count on you and that you won't stab us in the back at the first opportunity."

I think for a while, while I regard her beautiful backside as she spins around her axis.

"Yeah. We're good." I nod and scratch the back of my head. "We're good."

"Good." She seems to relax. "Now tell me about your friend, Thorfinn Wagner."

"Finn? There's not much to tell. He is the oldest son of Jarl Ragnwald and the rightful heir to the throne. He is also one big ugly motherfucker and the second-best fighter I've ever seen."

"They call him the Skullfucker. Why is that?"

"Funny story that. When Goliaths come of age, they must prove themselves in single combat. They do that by challenging one of the other juveniles to a duel to the death."

"Sounds harsh, even for Goliaths."

"It keeps the population small and strong."

"How pragmatic. So, why the Skullfucker?"

"The one who wins the duel is given a nickname based on the most memorable event of the fight."

"So, you mean he actually ...?" She points to the side of her head and looks sceptical.

"That's what I heard. This was way before I met him, but I've seen him work. I wouldn't put it past him."

Jagr makes a face. "You said he was the second-best fighter you'd ever seen. Who's the best?"

"That would be Berengar the Defiler."

"Do I even want to know what he did to earn *that* name?"

"No, you don't. He did the Corporate War circuit about the same time as Finn and I. The reason Finn was the top fighter and not Berengar, was because the Defiler was too demented even for that blood-crazed audience. He scared people. For real."

"Sounds like a swell guy."

"He's not. He's a Goliath berserker. I once saw him take out a full platoon of Nishin samurai single-handed."

Jagr seems unimpressed. "Soledad could do that. Hell, *you* could do that, Perez."

"Not if I was unarmed, and they wore state-of-the-art Tenshi combat armour."

She raises an eyebrow, a little impressed at last. "So, Thorfinn is the prince of their little winter kingdom, which should make our job a lot easier. I suppose his word is their command?"

"Well, that's the thing. He went back to Nifelheim five years ago to be a Breeder, and I haven't spoken to him since his mother died and his father remarried. Finn took that hard and shut himself off from the world. He doesn't like his stepmother much. He's locked away in the Breeder monastery, making little

Goliaths and working out in the priests' gym. Their rules state that while you're a Breeder, you give up all other privileges."

This gives her pause.

"*What?* Why the fuck didn't you say so from the start?"

"You never asked. How was I supposed to know you needed a fucking prince?"

"Shit." She ponders her options. "Who's next in line to the throne?"

"Finn's little brother, Eirik."

"What's *his* nickname?" She sounds apprehensive.

"The Fair."

"Sounds like we're in luck."

"Fair has more to do with his looks than his sense of justice."

"Oh. Do you know him?"

"Yeah. Eirik Wagner is a poseur, but he's not a bad man."

"So, we should be fine."

"Perhaps. He is a handsome, ambitious, and clever bastard. For a Goliath."

"I'll keep that in mind. Now get back to your cabin, Perez. Deceleration burn begins in two minutes and now I have a call to make."

Large orange numbers on the wall screen tell me we are at 2:12 and counting. Better hurry back. "Well, thanks for the briefing, Jagr."

"Once in a lifetime thing, Perez."

When I open the door, I almost collide with Soledad who's on her way in.

"Woah, watch it, handsome," she greets me with a smile and looks me over. "Nice outfit. I came looking for you. Come on, it's time to strap down with me again."

Then she sees Jagr pulling on her panties behind me and her smile freezes.

"Hey." I grin, trying to block her view. "Let's go do some strapping down."

Soledad doesn't reply. She keeps staring at Jagr over my shoulder as the door closes behind me.

I pull myself into our cabin and buckle up. Soledad straps down mere seconds before burn.

The engines ignite with a rumble, and we're pushed deep into our bunks once more.

"Later, Soledad," I call.

She doesn't respond.

Is my timing shit or what?

* * *

When we arrive in orbit around Nifelheim, Soledad is asleep. Or she pretends to be asleep, to avoid speaking to me.

An automatic female voice issues from the speakers. "We are now in orbit. You are free to move about."

The wall screen shows a beautiful image of the icy moon Nifelheim, rotating below us. Behind it looms the ice blue clouds of the gas giant Nirvana.

As I unstrap from the couch, there's a knock on the door.

"All hands on deck. The mess in two minutes."

I kick off for the passageway. Soledad is still out. Or still faking it.

I leave her alone. If she wants to sulk, it's her funeral.

I'm first to arrive, and I grab a squeeze-bulb of coffee from the dispenser and suck it down without heating it. Like everything in space, it tastes of polymer, but I hope there's real caffeine in it. I need a pick-me-up after the flight. Forty-eight hours of acceleration and deceleration take their toll, even with the regeneration and the drugs. I can't imagine how the human crew feel.

Probably like Braden looks.

She's first of the girls to show up, and she looks like hell. Her blue hair's a mess, she's got purple rings around her eyes and her skin is pale and shiny with sweat.

"Hey," she rasps and jerks her chin at me.

"Hey." My voice is not any better. "Pleasant trip?"

She hacks what could be a laugh from a sore throat and puts a bulb of coffee in the heater.

"No. You?"

"Can't say that I did. And Soledad hasn't said a word to me all trip."

"Yeah, I heard about that. Smooth Perez. Real smooth." The machine pings to tell her the coffee is ready, and she sucks it down. "Fuck, that's bad."

She makes a face. "Don't they have anything stronger on this boat?"

She rummages through the cupboards. "Help me out."

"They don't allow booze on navy ships anymore." Which is too bad because I could use a stiff drink myself.

"Damn." She gives up her search and turns around. "So. How was she?"

"How was who?" I play innocent.

"Jagr. How was the ice maiden? We thought she didn't have sex."

I give her my best Casanova smile. "She hadn't met me."

"She's using you, Perez."

Braden looks at me with sympathy. "It's basic dog psychology. Give the dog a treat, and he will follow you around, hoping for another. I, on the other hand …"

"Take a number, Braden."

She smiles. "More coffee?"

I'm not sure my stomach could take it.

"Sure, heat me one."

She throws two more bulbs into the heater.

"When we get back on the Sunny, I'll brew you a proper cup, Perez. The stuff that puts hair on your chest. Not this weak navy shit."

"Looking forward to that, Braden."

I reach out a fist, and she bumps it while the smell of coffee spreads through the mess. It's strange how something as trivial as the scent of a beverage can make everything feel normal. Then Jagr and Soledad arrive.

"There you are, Boss." Braden shines up. "How was he?"

Jagr glares at Braden and her jaw muscles flex, but Braden goes on, oblivious.

"What? Tell me, Mish." She coughs again. "I want to know what I'm in for when I get into his trousers."

Jagr laughs.

Soledad may not look at me, but Braden and Jagr beam at each other. Braden is great at defusing awkward social situations. This team might not be so random after all. They each fill an important role in the group dynamic. And here I come and mess everything up.

"Listen up, ladies." Jagr clears her throat.

"We are now orbiting the ice-moon Nifelheim, and our mission is about to get a lot more dangerous. As soon as we set foot on the ice, we'll be on hostile ground. The mind-state of the Goliath population is unknown, and so we will assume they are red until proven otherwise. I've notified our backup asset about our imminent arrival. He has agreed to meet us at a remote location and guide us to the Jarl's hall. The Goliaths have let us enter orbit because they are impressed by the *Shiloh*. That will not last. We need to get planetside fast. Our cover story is we're here to help construct the *Gleipnir* space elevator. We're allowed to bring down the *Sundowner*, but that's as far as we've got. The rest we'll improvise on the ground."

I raise a hand. "What if it was the Goliaths who grabbed your agent?"

"If that turns out to be the case, we get him out by force."

I cough. "By force? From the Goliaths?"

"You got a better plan, Perez?" Jagr puts her hands behind her head and stretches with a grunt, making her back crack and her chest expand.

My mind goes blank. "Nope."

Braden looks pointedly at Jagr's chest and mouths *"Told you so"*.

"So that's our plan." Jagr lowers her arms. "Cargo bay in five minutes, ladies. Don't be late."

"Aye aye, captain." Braden gives Jagr a salute before she pushes off for the passageway.

I hurry after her to avoid having to confront Soledad.

Soledad stares after me like she wants to kill me.

Well, I guess you win some, you lose some.

* * *

The *Sundowner* shakes and screams like a junkie going cold turkey as we tear through the icy atmosphere of Nifelheim. The air is breathable for humans, with a tad more oxygen than our bodies are built for. Some say that's why the Goliaths grow so big. Like the dinosaurs.

Outside the hull, the air burns. The thought of only a decimetre of hypercarbon between me and certain death makes me shiver. A single rip in the hull, and we're gone. The Goliaths would wonder at the shooting star above their heads and wish for more mead. Then they would go back to fighting and counting honour points. They wouldn't even know we had died in their sky.

"Are you afraid, Perez?" Soledad calls. "You look worried."

She has to shout to make herself heard over the noise.

"I'm not worried. This is my not worried face."

"You could have fooled me." Her attention returns to the console in her lap. It shows a lot of complex-looking schematics.

"Is it far?"

She sighs and turns to glare at me. "To the surface?"

"No, to Tipperary."

"Where?" She looks confused.

"Never mind." And I thought these girls were from Earth. Then again, Tipperary might not exist anymore. "Yes, to the bloody surface."

"No, we should be down in a few minutes. Braden has got this in hand."

The ship does a crazy sideways jump.

Without our reinforced skeletons and tendons, I'm not sure any of us would have survived the bump intact.

"I hope that's all she's got in her hand."

I've never liked this part of a drop. Putting my fate in the hands of a jacked-up fighter pilot has never appealed to me. "Does it always do that?"

"No, that was new." She looks worried. "I need to check that."

She pushes virtual buttons in the holographic interface, hums to herself, and she's lost to the world.

Great. So, we might still die.

Braden's voice comes over the intercom. The heavy Crump music from before has been replaced with equally bass-infused Dysfunk. Braden likes her music ass-bouncingly hard.

"We passed through some poor weather there, but now we're in the clear. Prepare for landing in two minutes. Please clean any spilt drinks from my seats."

We didn't die.

This time.

* * *

A mostly frozen ocean covers Nifelheim, with islands of varying sizes forming the only dry land. Braden sets the *Sundowner* down on the ice, close to the snow-covered beach of one of the larger islands. It has a name I can never recall that sounds like a cough. Sharp black rocks protrude at an angle from the ice like enormous spear tips, reaching for the heavens. It's bright out there. Our distant suns shine down from a cloudless sky, and the light glitters in the ice on every surface. It looks like Nifelheim woke up on the right side this morning. We still need to be careful. I've seen the weather go from barbecue conditions to howling ice winds of death in minutes on this snowball.

"Come on girls, grab your gear and get to the ramp." Jagr comes out from the cockpit with Braden in tow. "Remember to bring warm underwear."

We follow her to the cargo bay.

Soledad kicks open a crate.

Jagr grabs her shoulder. "No weapons, Pip. Sorry. Here." Jagr hands her an anorak.

"But, boss ... "

"We're supposed to be construction workers."

Soledad mumbles something and pulls the scarf up to cover her lower face. I can understand her feelings. Going unarmed on Nifelheim is a gamble with death. Still, I can see Jagr's point. Our cover story is sketchy. But against the Goliaths, it holds a greater chance of keeping us alive than weapons would.

Soledad stares at Jagr over the scarf. Jagr stares back. Soledad breaks eye contact and pulls on her anorak. I bet Jagr is great with dogs.

"Can I have a pink one, boss?" Braden asks.

"This isn't a pride parade, soldier." The snarl in Jagr's voice is not sincere. I can almost hear her smile. It must be an inside joke because even Soledad laughs, and the tension breaks.

"A girl can always dream." Braden rolls her eyes and pulls on her anorak.

We follow suit.

I sweat profusely, even though the smart insulation of the clothing does its best to regulate my temperature.

"Right people. There's a miner's pub on the beach. That's where we'll meet our contact. I've not spoken to him myself, but Command informs me he is trustworthy."

Command, huh? That's the first time I've heard anyone mention the people in charge. I hope they're not as incompetent as people in command usually are. You don't want to mess up when you're around Goliaths.

"Braden, lower the ramp."

Braden taps a command on her wrist terminal and the *Sundowner* lowers her tail ramp, letting in the icy chill of Nifelheim. After the recycled air on the *Sundowner*, the air smells fresh. Crisp.

It freezes the small hairs in my nose to ice in seconds and the first few breaths are painful as hell.

Jagr stands to the side and watches her small team disembark. I sidle up to her.

"Who's this contact of yours? Is he army?"

"No."

"Navy?"

"No."

"Special ops?"

"Nope."

"So, who is he?"

"He's a priest."

Jagr walks down the ramp, leaving me behind with my mouth hanging open.

"He's a *what*?" I hurry after her, trying to reconcile myself with this fresh piece of information.

"He's a Christian missionary," she says without looking at me, "sent here by the church to baptise the heathens."

"Well, that usually turns out well."

"The Jarl has taken an interest in Christianity. He requested a priest. We recruited the priest to our cause. Beggars can't be choosers, Perez. We take what we can get." Is she talking about the priest? Or me?

"Do you trust this priest?"

"Only as far as I can throw him." She pulls down the shaded snow goggles over her eyes. "But he's all we've got."

Great.

We've landed twenty kilometres from the space needle construction site. The hypercarbon spire is visible far out to sea, where it stretches from the immense raft it's anchored to, all the way into low orbit. It hangs from the satellite that will become the Nifelheim spaceport. Construction vehicles travel up and down the thick cable, transporting workers and supplies. It's the second greatest construction project in the system, after the particle accelerator in the rings of Avalon.

In the sky beyond the needle, the gas giant Nirvana looms like an evil presence in the icy sky. A thunderstorm rages across the face of the planet. It's beautiful.

This mission is so doomed.

Do We Know Him?

The miners' pub is a squat building set against a gloomy cliff between giant blocks of dirty ice. Its walls are made of ice, and the roof of crude iron sheets. A deep layer of snow covers everything, and if you didn't know it was there, you could miss it altogether. A handful of mining vehicles are parked outside, but apart from them, there's not much to show the place is inhabited.

As we walk closer, the muffled sound of voices trickles from inside.

The thermometer on my terminal says it's thirty degrees below freezing, but it feels much colder thanks to a light wind. The sky is still clear, but ominous clouds are drawing in from the west. We'd better get inside before the bad weather hits.

Jagr opens the door and the voices inside fall silent.

The pub is full of bearded giants.

Except for their size, these Goliaths would not have raised any eyebrows at the Viking court of Harald Hardrada. They all stand over two metres tall, and they are almost as wide in their heavy clothing. They all wear cloaks made of long white *garm* fur. The *garm* is Nifelheim's apex predator, named after the dog that guards the entrance to Hel in Norse mythology. When a Goliath is fifteen years old, he goes off into the icy wilderness to kill one. Then he makes a cloak out of it and wears it all his life. Those cloaks smell as bad as you think, and the atmosphere in the pub is pungent.

There is a bar made of rough concrete, a dozen metal tables and a score of rusted iron chairs and stools. Everything is slightly too large in here, and I feel like I'm six years old again. The chairs and benches are covered with furs. Not *garm* fur, but a darker, scraggly kind. A huge gas fire burns in one corner.

Our contact is not here. Everyone in the bar is a Goliath and not one of them appears to be a Christian priest.

"Where's our man?" I whisper to Jagr, trying to work my frozen lips.

"How the fuck should I know." She peers around the place. "Don't worry. He'll be here."

The Goliaths eye us with mild disinterest like we're nothing more than annoying bugs. They respect only brute strength, and they do not see us as a threat. If only they knew. I could arm wrestle every man in here and win, and so could the girls. If the Goliaths knew that, they would stand in line to try us on, and we don't have time for that.

There's not much else we can do but go to the bar.

The Goliaths follow us with pale, deep-set eyes under bushy eyebrows. One giant elbows another and grunts something with a hoarse laugh. I catch the word "*draugr*", which means some kind of ghost. The elbowed Goliath swears and punches his companion's arm. Ghosts? What's going on here?

Jagr slaps her hand on the bar. "Beer." Even indoors the temperature is close to freezing and her breath steams around her face.

The bartender is a fat, older Goliath with hair and beard like a thatched roof. "No beer. Only mead," the Goliath barman says in a gravelly voice and jerks his head at the short, handwritten list of beverages available. There are two options. Both with names that sound like clearing your throat.

"Mead is fine. I'll take the strongest one you have." Jagr flashes the barman a bright smile.

He shrugs and gets a large ceramic jug from behind the bar and cleans it with a dirty towel. I'm surprised he doesn't spit in it first. He pours her drink from a frost-covered stainless steel vat standing on the bar. They don't have any problems keeping their beverages chilled on Nifelheim.

I let my gaze wander around the place and notice a Goliath woman sitting alone in the far corner. She studies us with pale green eyes from under her fur-lined hooded cloak. Hair as red as blood falls in curling waves over her broad fur-covered shoulders and ample bosom. Gold beads glint between the strands. The Goliaths may be the most racist and bigoted

116

people in the universe, but at least you can't accuse them of looking down at women. As long as they can fight, women are regarded as highly as men and are welcome to drink and brawl with the best of them. And these days, with the current shortage of Goliath women, they have gained an almost godlike status.

She's not exactly good-looking, but there's something strangely attractive about her. I grin at her. She laughs and takes a drink from her jug.

The barman hands Jagr her drink, and she takes a quick gulp without even smelling it first. A wise move. Goliath mead is infamous for its potency and horrible taste. Much like the Goliaths themselves.

"Quality stuff." Jagr tips her head back and drinks the whole jug in one go. The yeasty mead spills from her mouth and runs down her chin, her soft neck and down into her anorak. I can't help but imagine it running on downwards ...

Jagr slams the ceramic jug on the concrete bar top and rudely interrupts my train of thought. She wipes her mouth with the back of her hand and gives a burp.

The silence in the bar is almost tangible.

Then the Goliaths scowl at each other, shake their heads and interrupted conversations pick up again. They speak a mixture of modulated Scandinavian and guttural German, a language both harsh and beautiful like their icy home planet. We're all but forgotten.

Way to go, Jagr. Ignorance is about as much recognition as you will ever get from a Goliath.

"Same for us." I signal to the barman, and he pours another three jugs and hands them over.

"That will be eighty crowns," he says.

Shit. I forgot they still use physical money on Nifelheim. Some consider that quaint. I consider it a pain in the ass since I don't have any.

"Give me a second, big guy." I hold a finger up to the barman. "Just going to find my leather purse of silver."

I turn to the women.

"Does anyone have any money?" Soledad shakes her head with a smirk on her face, no doubt hoping I'm about to get my ass kicked into next Tuesday. Braden shakes her head, as does Jagr.

"Shit," I swear under my breath.

"Money. Now." The bartender looks like a rising thundercloud crossed with a haystack.

"How about we sing you a song for the mead?" I try. Goliaths are famous for their love of a good story told in song, and I hope the barman is a sucker for it.

"No song. Money. Now."

Oh, well.

"All right, all right. I'll get you the money. Relax, man."

"Or you will be sorry."

Something in his face tells me he looks forward to making me sorry.

Perhaps I could borrow coins from the redhead in the corner?

There's a crash as the door slams open, and we all turn around to see who the new arrival is. I hope it's our contact, come to pick us up and pay our bills.

It's not.

First through the door is the largest Goliath I've ever seen. His enormous head sweeps the room like a wolf smelling wounded prey. He swipes the hood from his head to uncover a short, grey-speckled mohawk. The rest of his head is shaved clean and covered in dark swirling tattoos. He unwinds the long scarf covering his face. Underneath is a wide, ugly mouth with fleshy lips and a short grey pointed beard. A pair of wide scars run down the left side of his face. If I'm not mistaken, Finn gave him those scars. "Shit."

"What?" Jagr leans close. "Do we know him?" she asks as two more Goliaths, almost as large, enter in a cloud of snow and ice.

They unwind their scarves and shake their heads to clear the snow from their thick beards and long black hair. They are mirror images of each other, except for different facial scars. All three newcomers wear studded black leather armour over their white fur coats, and they carry heavy iron swords at their sides. Hypercarbon has better durability and strength, but when damage is your aim, you can't beat cold, hard steel. These guys mean business.

They head straight for the bar.

"Yes, we know him. That," I nod at the giant in the middle, "is Berengar the Defiler."

A moment later the full importance of my words registers. "Shit."

I nod. "Indeed."

"Who are the other two?"

"Ulf and Varg Gulbrandsen. The Wolf twins. This is bad."

We edge out of their way.

The barman seems to have forgotten the money I owe him. Berengar the Defiler has that effect on people.

The newcomers don't even glance our way as they march up to the bar, which is odd. Even if Goliaths don't give a shit about humans, our being here should at least cause some mild curiosity. Something is going on here.

"Mead," Berengar says and slaps his massive slab of a palm on the bar with a resounding boom. The barman hurries to comply. Why is Berengar speaking English?

"This is not a coincidence," I whisper to Jagr as we move towards an empty table close to the door. "If Berengar is here, your priest talked. We've been compromised."

"Shit," Jagr whispers again and slides into a chair.

Berengar waits in silence for the barman to pour his drink. Then he grabs the jug, tilts it back and swallows the contents down in one go. "Another." He slaps the jug back down on the bar, splashing mead all over himself and the barman. The place is once again silent like a tomb.

When Berengar gets his second drink, he takes a long swallow and turns around. He leans his massive elbows on the bar and surveys the silent crowd. The temperature has dropped several degrees in the pub.

He wipes the mead from his beard with a grubby hand.

"So, what goes on here?" He speaks in heavily accented English. "Has this become children's bar?"

He waves in our direction with his jug and scowls at the other Goliaths with a wide smile plastered across his broad, ugly face. He looks pleased with himself at the witty banter.

"Ignore him," I advise Jagr. "Let me handle this."

"Be my guest."

We sip our drinks. The mead is a yeasty brew, but there's no denying its potency. My tongue goes numb after a few sips.

I've got to admire the girls' composure. They could be having tea in a fucking boudoir from the looks of them. But then, they have never been around Goliaths. They don't understand the danger we're in.

"What, children don't talk to adult?" Berengar's voice rumbles around the bar. The Wolf twins scoff. No one else says a word.

The Defiler pushes off from the bar and saunters over to our table.

"I said, children don't talk?" He towers over us.

"Yes, we talk," I respond, taking another sip of the vile mead while I peer out a small window. Goliaths are like dogs. Never look them in the eye unless you want a fight on your hands.

It's getting worse out there. The wind is picking up again, and snow swirls from the iron sky. It's getting worse in here too.

"Good. Children talk." The corners of his mouth rise in a satisfied grin. "I like children. Children funny. Say something funny." He takes another swig from his jug.

"We don't want any trouble, big man. We're from the Gleipnir construction site. Just here for a drink."

"Gleipnir is fifty kilometres away. Long way for drink."

Perceptive, I'll give him that.

"You came in ship on ice?" He waves his jug at the window, spilling mead over the table and us.

"Yes, that is our ship." I stare deep into my jug, refusing to meet his gaze.

"Nice ship." He nods sagely. "Not for construction. Why you here?"

He pulls up one of the heavy chairs, swings it around backwards and sits down between me and Jagr.

A back door opens and five more Goliaths in long black hooded cloaks enter. One of them is half a head taller than the others but thinner. They carry heavy-looking cases.

I don't like this. Not one bit.

It gets even worse. One of the Wolf twins closes the door behind him and locks it. We're trapped.

"I told you, big man. All we want is a quiet drink."

"You not workers. Why you here on *Nifelheimr*?" Berengar presses on.

I don't think he recognises me. No wonder. It was over twenty years ago our paths crossed. And I wore another face the last time we met. *My* face.

"Look. We don't want our boss to know we went for a drink on the job, OK?"

The cloaked newcomers at the back open their cases. This mess is about to get ugly.

"We not want your kind here," Berengar says, pushing his massive, ugly face in mine. I can smell the yeast from the mead. He's close enough for me to see the damp curls in his beard flutter as he breathes. I wish he'd stop that. His breath stinks like a slaughterhouse. No wonder. There are bits of old meat between his yellowed teeth.

I nod. "But here we are. We'll finish our drinks, and then we'll be on our way, Berengar."

The defiler leans back. Thank the powers that be for that. That breath was killing me.

"So. You know my name." He takes another drink from his mead. The foam sticks to his moustache, and he wipes it away with his sleeve. "What is *your* name, little one?"

I weigh my options.

Why was Berengar sent here? And by whom? Do they already know who we are and why we are here? I dangle a little lure in front of his ugly face. "Perez."

"First name?"

"Asher. Why?"

He shines up and points a meaty finger at my face. "I know you."

There's dirt under his broad fingernail. Or dried blood. A dangerous smile creeps across his face.

"Your drink is finished," he announces and knocks the jug from my hand.

It goes clattering across the floor, spraying mead all over the place. The jug ends up against the heavy, furry boot of the tallest of the cloaked newcomers. I glance up as he plugs a thick cord into what I first take to be a giant double axe. Then I realise it's an electric guitar.

What? They are a fucking *band?*

"Hey, I was enjoying that mead." I lick the spill from my fingers.

"A named man of the little people." Berengar sounds genuinely pleased. "So there will be honour in killing you."

Still seated, he unbuckles his belt and lets it drop to the floor behind him. The sword, as long and wide as my leg, thumps to the frozen dirt.

"Your name will live forever through Berengar's legend."

The most important thing in life for a Goliath is his legend. You grow your legend by killing people and destroying things, and you shrink it by being defeated. You don't necessarily lose legend by dying. A good death can boost your legend and those of your nearest relatives and friends. Whoever thought up this system was a genius. It has bred a race of perfect warriors. No one knows how they keep count of their legends.

Berengar unties his leather armour. There are more points in killing a man if you do it both unarmed and unprotected.

The tall bandleader with the guitar crushes my jug under his heavy boot. Then he throws back his black hood to expose a thin, tattooed face with a red beard and short-cropped red hair. He has blackened his eye sockets to make his face resemble a skull. He roars and strums the first chord of what must be a popular Goliath song. The small crowd cheers in answer and the Goliaths raise their jugs to the roof.

Berengar nods his approval. "Good song to die to."

He stands up and his chair and our table fall over, sending jugs and immortal commando girls flying. The band members throw back their hoods to reveal long hairy ears sticking up through their black hair. I'm too far away to tell if they're prosthetics or actual body-mods, but I'd put my money on the latter. They wield an unholy arsenal of guitars, violins, flutes, and drums and go into frenzied overdrive on their instruments. The wall of sound hits almost as hard as Berengar's fist when he punches me in the face. The blow lifts me off my feet and sends me crashing into another table that falls over and spills drinks and food over the grizzled old Goliath sitting there. He snarls a curse and pushes me back at Berengar. I spit pieces of broken teeth on the floor and face the Defiler.

This time I'm prepared when he comes and duck the enormous fist he throws my way. I twist and punch him hard in the kidney. Or I would have if he had been of normal height. My fist glances off his ass and I don't think he even feels it through his thick fur breeches.

Berengar grabs me by the throat and lifts me off the floor. The band goes into a soaring first chorus and the crowd joins in the refrain. Berengar was right. It is a catchy tune to die by.

Jagr and her team are up. "What do we do?" Jagr calls.

"Fucking help me," I croak.

"Right." Jagr aims a kick at Berengar's knee. It bounces off his heavy leather boot. In return, she gets a backhanded slap that sends her sliding into the bar.

Soledad goes in low and jabs a vicious punch at Berengar's crotch. It finds its mark, and the Defiler howls and lets go of my throat.

I take advantage of the distraction and kick the inside of his leg. He goes down on one knee. Before he gets back up, I slip behind him and lock an arm around his thick neck. I can barely reach, but I squeeze with all my strength. I hope to put an end to this mess before it gets out of hand.

It's a brilliant plan. In theory.

Too bad Goliaths never cared much for theory.

Berengar reaches behind him, grabs my neck in one meaty fist and pulls me off my feet. He loosens my arm with his other hand like I was a sick baby hugging my mother's neck.

Oh, dear.

He throws me in a half somersault over his head and into the bar. I land on my back and bounce off to land on top of Jagr. Fuck, that hurt. I think he cracked a few hypercarbon ribs.

The last thing to register in my mind before everything goes black is the cute red-headed woman in the corner wincing. Is she rooting for me?

* * *

When I come to again, seconds later, Berengar fights Soledad and Braden. They do their best, but against Berengar the Defiler, that is never enough. He shakes them off and lifts Soledad off her feet. One massive hand squeezes her neck, crushing the life out of her while he backhands Braden aside with the other.

"What is your name, little woman?" He hopes for another named one of the little people to boost his legend even further.

I glance around for something to use as a weapon and all I can find is an abandoned chair next to the bar. I grab it, swing it in a perfect arc, and it connects with the back of Berengar's skull. He shrugs it off like a bull, but he drops Soledad who collapses on the floor, gasping, and clutching her neck. The Defiler turns on me.

Another fist swings my way. I duck it effortlessly and punch him in the face. His nose explodes into a shower of blood.

Berengar roars with fury and the air wheezes through his broken nose. Blood splashes everywhere as he breathes harder. Oh, no.

I've seen this before. Berengar the Defiler is a berserker. Some Viking warriors of old were famous for working themselves into a blood frenzy using toadstools and copious amounts of mead. They could fight for hours, shrugging off blows that would kill a normal man. Berengar does that in spades. The thick veins on his neck swell like they are about to explode. He raises his ugly head to the rafters and howls with pleasure.

He lunges after me, but I duck and roll out of reach.

The band moves into a slower part of their song, building towards a crescendo as we begin to circle. Are they syncing their music to the fight?

Berengar snorts and the blood froths at his mouth and nose as we move, both searching for an opening.

Jagr and Braden pull Soledad to safety and the other patrons stand cheering around us. Then Berengar charges again.

This time he goes for a vicious kick at my privates, and I dance aside. I collide with a table before I'm pushed back into the fray by a cheering Goliath.

Berengar attacks, and this time I let him come. At the last second, I drop to the ground, making him trip over me, and he goes crashing into the audience. I jump on his back and wrap an arm around his forehead. Then I pull his head back while I punch him in the neck and the side of the head. I'm not sure how effective my blows are, but he howls in pain when I punch his ear.

Pain is good, because it pisses him off, and you can outsmart a pissed off Goliath.

Unless he's got help.

Two enormous hands grab me from behind and pull me off Berengar's back and throw me across the room.

The Wolf twins pull the Defiler to his feet and all three turn on me.

Oh, dear.

The Tree of Life

The crowd goes wild as the band moves into another riveting chorus, raising it a notch. They *are* syncing their music to the fight. Impressive musicianship.

Berengar and the Wolf twins charge, and I have no more time to enjoy the artists' skill.

One twin goes for my legs. I jump out of his reach only to get caught in the hands of the other who pins my arms to my sides. Berengar roars and lands a fist in my face and everything goes blurry white. A split-second later I'm back and take another punch in the face. The massive blows crack my skull. By now I should be dead and Berengar knows that. He looks a little puzzled as he lands a third blow and I keep breathing.

He says something to the twin holding me, and my arms are released.

I drop to my knees, trying to gather my senses.

Now would be a marvellous time for the General to come calling.

Like a thousand ants crawling under my skin, the nanites swarm into overdrive to repair my broken face. I'm not sure they will be quick enough to save me from the Defiler.

Berengar gets behind me and puts one slab of a hand on my shoulder as if to comfort me. Then he grabs me under the chin with the other and pulls.

Oh, fuck. Not the head.

A tendon tears in my neck and I claw at his trunk-like arm, slipping in the blood pouring from his broken nose.

A guttural roar tears from Berengar's chest as he pulls on my neck with all his Goliath strength and berserker rage. The crowd cheers. Something snaps in my back, and reality goes monochromatic and fuzzy at the edges.

What a sad way to die, in a miner's bar on Nifelheim, being torn to pieces by an arsehole like Berengar. The Goliaths will probably not even write a song about it.

My mind does the familiar somersault. *Finally.* Where the fuck have you been, general Meridian?

Berengar pulls on, and I'm worried even Meridian won't be a match for the Defiler.

Then everything flashes white and the general slips away like a cheap hooker from your bed at sunrise.

What? Isn't there supposed to be a tunnel first?

Another voice cuts through the noise of the fighting and the music. Some shape and colour return to the world and the voice comes again. Berengar releases my head and I collapse on the floor.

My cheek lands in something cold and wet.

Snow.

The bright light comes from the open door.

The setting sun shines through an opening in the low, dark clouds, straight into my eyes.

It's beautiful.

I'm rolled over onto my back and dragged through the door by one leg. One of these days it would be nice to actually *walk* out of a bar.

I blink to clear my vision, and after a few tries, the world swims back into focus. My neck is a nexus of pain but at least the bloody music has stopped.

I lie in the snow outside the bar. The sun hurts my eyes.

"Welcome back, Perez. I lost you for a moment."

"Yeah, I almost died, Aeryn, remember?"

"No, before that. I couldn't reach you."

"Must have been a glitchy connection or something."

"I don't glitch."

"Aeryn, go away."

"Whatever." It clicks off.

A Goliath leans over me, and it looks like he's about to slap my face.

"Hey, stop it, I'm awake," I grumble.

He must have slapped me around already because my cheeks hurt like hell. "I'm awake."

He reaches out to me, and I squint at the newcomer.

It's Wagner's baby brother, Eirik the Fair.

Baby in this context meaning younger. Eirik Wagner is far from a baby.

He's almost as large as Finn but carries himself with a different grace. Even kneeling in the snow, he looks all regal and shit.

"Eirik. Long time no see." I grab his outstretched hand, and he yanks me to my feet. I slip on a patch of ice, but his grip is like a vice, and he keeps me upright without effort. Standing on his knees, he is as tall as I am.

"Do I know you, little man?" He gets to his feet to tower over me. His English is flawless like his silver-beaded beard and flowing locks of golden hair. If the other Goliaths are wolves, Eirik is a Lion. He is a handsome bastard. He even smells good.

"It's me. Perez." I try to smile through my bloody and broken teeth. The teeth always take the longest to regrow.

Eirik furrows his brow, trying to place me.

I try to jog his memory. "Asher Perez? Finn's friend?"

His brow shoots up.

"Yes, I remember you." The brow comes down again. "You look different."

Shit. This is not the body he saw me in last time.

Improvise, Perez, improvise.

"I had surgery a few years back. My face got messed up in a fight." Not too far from the truth.

He tilts his head to one side.

133

"Can't say they did any improvements to your face. I hope you didn't pay them in full."

I smile. "Never said I was happy with the job." My mouth hurts when I smile.

Jagr and the girls stand back, waiting. So does Berengar.

Eirik beams. "A *frende* of Thorfinn's is a *frende* of mine. How about we go back inside, I buy you people a round, and we forget about this incident? My man has a temper, is all."

So, the Defiler works for Eirik. Interesting.

It's not a coincidence Berengar showed up right after we arrived, and it's not a coincidence Eirik showed up in time to save our sorry asses.

They planned this to test us. Eirik was always too clever for his own good.

The priest must have talked.

"So, Asher." He brushes snow from my anorak and ushers me back inside the bar. "What brings you to *Nifelheimr*?"

Now that he has my name, I may as well put the rest of our cards on the table. "Thought I'd drop in on Finn, see how he's doing. And we're here to see your father."

He squints, suspicious. "The Jarl? Why?"

"We're looking for someone. Or rather, they are." I point to the girls, and Eirik turns towards them.

"What have we here? Little women? Beautiful ones at that. I had no idea you were this pretty. I am Eirik Wagner. Welcome." He spreads his arms and beams at them, showing perfect teeth under his immaculately groomed golden moustache.

"What the hell are you doing here?" Jagr snaps. Her face is unreadable. This is not going according to her plan.

"Oh, come now," Eirik tuts. "That's no way to start a relationship."

Jagr ignores him. "We have business with your father, Goliath. Business that could be lucrative for him. And for you."

Eirik chews on nothing for a while. Then he turns his back on us, rests his massive hands on the bar and lowers his head like he's trying to divine his future in the mead and blood covering the surface. He drums his thick fingers against the concrete. "What business is this?" He turns back to Jagr. There's a strange smile playing at the corner of his mouth. This whole charade rings false.

"Our business is for your father's ears only."

Eirik inclines his head. "Will you tell me if I buy you a round?"

He is a smooth talker, but this whole thing feels like a shoddily rehearsed play.

Soledad cuts in. "Try it and find out, Goliath."

Eirik laughs. That was not in the script. "A round for the little ones," he calls to the barman who pours fresh drinks. When the barman hands them over, he scowls at me and says something to Eirik that includes the words *åttio* and *kronor*.

Eirik looks at me. Then he laughs again.

"Put it on my tab," he says to the bartender and hands out the drinks.

He raises his vessel. "Here's to lucrative business."

"To lucrative business," we echo and bang our jugs together, splashing foul mead all over the bar and the floor. This ancient Goliath custom probably arose as a legitimate excuse to spill the vile drink. I can't blame them. It tastes like ass.

Eirik empties his drink in one go. We don't.

"Well then, let's go see my father," Eirik says as he slams the empty vessel on the bar. "We'll ride with you."

His face says it's not something to be argued about.

"Well then," Jagr echoes. "Excellent."

She slams her still half-full jug down next to Eirik's. "Let's go."

I thought she was smarter than this. Eirik is up to something.

The redhead in the corner gets up and throws a handful of coins on the table. She nods and gives me a smile that warms me down to my balls.

"Hildr, are you coming?", Eirik calls to her.

"Going for a piss. I'll meet you outside." She heads for a frost-rimmed metal door in the back, crudely marked with something resembling a toilet.

Who is she? Must be someone important if she rides with Eirik.

Eirik reaches behind the bar and pulls something from a shelf. "Here, little people. Take these. I don't want my guests to freeze their faces off."

He hands out bulky knitted scarves made from off-white woolly fabric. Mine smells like something took a crap and died in it.

The Goliaths wrap their shaggy faces, and we follow suit. The smell is horrible, but the warmth is nice. We head for the door with Eirik in front and Berengar and the twins making up the rear like an honour guard. Or a prison detail.

On the way out I smile at the bartender. "I told you I'd get your money."

He gives me a sour face and spits in the jug he's holding. Then he cleans it out with his dirty towel.

I knew it.

* * *

Back on the *Sundowner*, we strap in for the short hop over the mountains to the Jarl's fortress. Eirik sits next to me. The redhead sits on his other side. She appears to have fallen asleep. Jagr sits across the aisle, studying our guests.

On the way in I noticed Eirik eyeing the hardware in the cargo bay. There's no reason to doubt Eirik knows who we are, and if he's still playing along with this charade, he wants something.

As soon as we're airborne, he slaps a ham-sized fist on my knee.

"Good to see you again, Perez."

He sounds sincere enough, but there's no warmth in his eyes when I meet them.

"Likewise. It's been too long. When was it we last met, you and I? Twenty years ago?"

"Something like that. We were both young. A lot of dark water under *Bifrost* since."

"Yes, those were the days. What have you been up to?"

He peers off into the distance.

"I spent a decade in the Varangian guard."

That must have been a heaven and hell experience, judging by his facial expression. I nod, impressed. If he served in the Cardinal's personal Goliath guard, he's not all fancy clothes and manicured beards these days. The Guards are mean bastards.

"But then father called me back when mother died, and he remarried. A kingdom doesn't run itself, and with Finn gone to breeding, there's a lot for my father to handle on his own."

"How is your father? Well, I hope."

"He is splendid. He's old, but he still has his strength. The old man will live for decades."

Do I detect a slight frustration there?

"Let's hope he does. He is an honourable man, your father."

"That he is." Eirik falls silent. Then he looks at Jagr. "A word, if I may, little woman." His voice is almost jovial.

"I'm listening, Eirik."

"You are the one I've talked to?"

"I am."

Do they *know* each other?

"Does our deal stand?"

138

Jagr chews her lower lip. "If you can guarantee your end of the bargain, then yes, our deal stands."

I scowl at Jagr. What's this talk of a deal? She meets my gaze and shakes her head imperceptibly in response. I get it. Shut up and follow her lead.

"Terra will support my claim?"

"If you handle the Jarl, we will."

Eirik beams. "Then we have a deal, little woman."

He rubs his enormous hands together. "Excellent. Fly on. My father's hall awaits us. I'm starving."

I lean towards Jagr across the aisle. "Can we talk?"

She nods and rises from her seat. I follow her into the airlock and slap the button to close the door behind us.

"What are you playing at, Jagr? What's this deal you're talking about?"

"You said it yourself. Recruiting Thorfinn is no longer a viable solution. I had to improvise."

"Tell me about this deal."

"We get our agent and Eirik's help to discover what Project Jotun is all about."

"In return for what?"

"Future Terran backing."

"Come on Jagr. You can't trust Eirik. He's up to something. Besides, we're not here to pick a fight."

She regards me coldly.

The realisation hits me like a punch in the gut. "We are?"

"This is my show, Perez. You're hired muscle. Remember that."

I stand there and scowl at her. She scowls back. If Terra supports Eirik against his father, there will be a war on Nifelheim. Jarl Ragnwald is a popular man. But so is his youngest son. It would be a long war. Which would be exactly what the Terrans want if they fear an imminent Goliath attack. Humanity would never survive that assault. Make the Goliaths fight among themselves first, and Terra can pick off any survivors. Divide and conquer, and all that shit.

Fuck. I put a hand over my eyes and massage my temples. "You're aware there will be a civil war?"

"That is a likely outcome, yes. We have a potential fucking crisis brewing in this system, and we need to find out what's going on. This deal is us stirring the pot to see what floats to the surface. Don't worry. This is what we do. Everything is under control."

"Under control? These are the Goliaths we're talking about. There is no way to know how this will play out."

Braden calls from the speakers. "Landing site coming up."

"Roger that, Braden."

Jagr turns back to me. "Bear with me, Perez. You might be surprised."

She punches the button and the door hisses open. "Strap in people, we're landing."

We get into our seats, and Eirik beams at me. "So, are we good, Asher Perez?"

I nod. "We're good, Eirik Wagner."

"Good." He looks up at a screen and I follow his gaze.

We are on our approach to *Hrafnheim*, the ancient stronghold of the Jarls of Nifelheim. The name means Raven's Home, and I can't think of a more fitting name. The immense building sits on a plateau near the peak of a steep snowy mountain, overlooking the valley far below. Behind it is a massive wall of rock and ice that provides shelter from the storms. The hall resembles a Viking stave church in style, but it's vast like a cathedral, buried in ice and snow. There are giant carved dragon heads on the roof and intricate knot-work adorns the walls and pillars supporting the structure. A fifteen-metre-wide staircase winds up the mountain to the Hall.

The largest tree in the known universe grows in the courtyard. The giant ash known as *Yggdrasil* reaches almost as high as the hall, and its evergreen branches catch the last rays of the dying suns, setting it alight. Legend has it the first settlers from Earth brought the tree with them. Or so Wagner once told me after a lot of beer. How they keep the tree alive is beyond me. They either feed it the blood and souls of slain enemies, or the Goliaths have green fingers. Who knows?

Over the centuries, Goliaths have built their dark homes below the fortress, and a crowded town clings to the slopes. A tall rampart of ice and stone with a single great gate protects the lowest tiers of the town against ground assault. Under the Newell treaty, the Goliaths are not allowed to build air vehicles. The grumpy giants are bad enough in their own right but give them air support and you make them unstoppable. Besides, Goliaths prefer the old-fashioned boots-on-the-ground approach to warfare.

The clouds have broken apart and the snow and ice on the roofs glitter like diamonds on fire in the dying light. Goliaths are not noted for their architectural design, but the place exudes a certain raw beauty.

"Spectacular, isn't it?" There's pride in Eirik's voice.

"Quite," I agree as Braden brings us down in a wide arc over the grounds.

Posted at regular intervals inside the grounds are huge, mechanised sentries. The only thing more formidable than a Goliath is a Goliath in one of their infamous Sentinel battleframes. One of those things could take on a squad of tanks and walk off with a broken hip. Someone is expecting trouble.

"Why the hardware, Eirik?" There's something about those Sentinels that makes me ill at ease.

Eirik keeps looking out the window, studying the scene like a general surveying his troops. Which, in a way I suppose, he is.

"My father's ravens whisper of a coming coup. The *Althingr* says it's nothing but rumours, but I won't be taken unawares if it's not."

"Wise move." I nod. "Who are the rebels this time?"

Eirik waves dismissively. "Some chieftain up north you've never heard of. Every year the grumblings grow louder. They claim the taxes are too harsh and their crops fail year after year. We know it's not so. Their children grow fat, and the warlords grow fatter still."

"Classic."

Braden puts us down on the landing pad with only a slight bump. The pad is surrounded by concrete bunkers.

The PA crackles.

"This is your pretty captain speaking." For once, she has turned off the music. "Welcome to sunny Nifelheim and the court of Jarl Ragnwald Wagner, the Allwise. Enjoy your stay, and I hope you will fly with us soon again. Braden, over and out."

The engines whine to a standstill as we unbuckle. Braden lowers the ramp and a cloud of icy snow swirls into the ship. The frigid air bites my lungs and I hurry to pull up the hood of my anorak and loop the smelly scarf around my face. The coarse wool does nothing to protect me from the internal chill spreading through my bloodstream when I realise what makes me so ill at ease about the mechs.

Strategy is not my forte, but if Eirik was expecting an attack, shouldn't they be *outside* the wall?

If I were a roguish smuggler in an ancient space adventure feed, I'd say 'I have a bad feeling about this.'

I wish I were. I've always wanted to say that, and this seems like a splendid time to say it.

Into The Hall of the Mountain King

Eirik and his Goliath posse are first down the ramp. Jagr holds our team back and turns to Braden.

"Stay with the ship, Braden. Keep the engines on standby. We might need to leave in a hurry if things go pear-shaped."

"*When* things go pear-shaped," Braden corrects her.

"*If* things go pear-shaped."

Jagr sounds convinced pear-shaped is not a given. I'm not so sure. "We'll be fine. The ship is just a precaution."

I wince. Don't jinx it, Jagr.

Heavy thumps echo between the buildings outside. The whirr of powerful servos accompany the thumps, and two of the heavy battleframes lumber onto the landing pad and come to rest facing the *Sundowner*.

Jagr swears under her breath. "Can you keep the close defence weaponry on standby without it being too obvious?"

"No problems boss. Give me the word and I'll level this place."

I admire Braden's faith in her ship, but she has never seen how much hurt a Goliath battle mech can take before going down. Or how much hurt it can dish out.

"If the mechs come, take out the legs first," I say. "They can still fire back, but they won't be able to manoeuvre, and that's their weakness. It takes a lot of concentrated fire to disable a Sentinel. If it can't move, that makes your job so much easier."

"Thanks for the tip, Perez, but the *Sundowner* can take care of herself." Braden pats the hull of her ship, but she's not her usual confident self. She can see those mechs too. They are mean-looking machines.

"When we get down on the ground, you leave the talking to me," Jagr says, addressing everyone but scowling at me. "We have to be careful around these people. OK, let's go."

We follow Eirik and his soldiers down the ramp.

I take a moment to admire the scenery. The storm has passed, and a single frozen sun glares from an iron sky. To the south is nothing but snowy mountains as far as the eye can see. To the north stands the Raven's Home. Far below the landing pad, a single road winds from the rampart gate down into the valley below. Hundreds of Goliath dwellings surround us. Built like dark Viking longhouses and covered in snow, they resemble so many overturned boats. Which is the whole point, I guess. I've never understood why the Goliaths bother with the Norse imagery. The Goliaths are no more Norse than my ass.

Though impressive in their own right, the longhouses are nothing compared to the fortress of Jarl Ragnwald Wagner. The Hall is even more impressive up close. It stands over a hundred metres high, spans two hundred metres and dwarfs all other buildings on the planet. The great gnarled ash *Yggdrasil* stands in front of the building like a giant troll. I assume the idea is to awe Goliaths when they approach their king. To us of mere human stature, it's breathtaking.

"This way, little ones," Eirik calls as he waves Berengar and the twins off on some unknown errand. "My father will be dying to meet you."

We follow him and the red-haired woman across the frosty concrete landing pad. Light snow blows across the surface.

Vicious-looking anti-aircraft weaponry sprout from the bunker-tops like weird plants. Trying to set a ship down here without clearance would be suicide. Goliaths in heavy fur cloaks idle around the landing area, glowering at us under bushy brows. We're not welcome here, but they respect Eirik enough to let us be. For now.

Eirik leads us between the mechs, and Soledad can't help staring. I don't blame her. Those battleframes are ridiculously cool. They stand over three metres tall, are fashioned out of white ceramics, black hypercarbon, and grey titanium, and weigh at least two tonnes each. They are vaguely humanoid but much too wide, and the legs have one joint too many. Where the lower arms would have been are two heavy autocannons. On each shoulder sits a rocket launcher. No one knows where the Goliaths got their mechs. Who would be foolish enough to provide already dangerous giants with even more strength and firepower? I guess it's another example of money speaking louder than reason and self-preservation. I hope Braden's confidence in the *Sundowner* wasn't all bravado. If something goes wrong, and Braden has to shoot her way out of here, these are the ones who will shoot back.

I can't suppress a shiver as we leave them behind and enter the dark streets of the town. The gloomy houses stand almost shoulder to shoulder, with narrow, shady alleys between. Every corner and crevice is filled with dirty snow and everything smells of rubbish. Beams and wires run between the buildings, supporting large sheets of torn cloth to offer shelter from the harsh elements. The street is lined with frowning giants come to glare with disdain at their foreign visitors. Nifelheim is not a place for the weak of spirit.

I wave to the gawkers as we pass. An old, grizzled Goliaths hawks and spits in the snow. I smile at him, and he pulls a fat thumb across his beard, in roughly the area where his throat should be. The implications are clear. When Eirik looks away, we're dead.

"No sudden moves," Jagr cautions. "Nice and easy does it."

"As the girl said."

My attempt at humour to ease the tension fails miserably. No one laughs.

We leave the town behind and start up the wide stairs to the hall.

Everything is too fucking large here. The steps cut out of the rock are twice as high as normal steps, and the railing, beautifully carved from actual wood, is too high to be of any use to us.

We reach the top of the stairs and the great ash towers above us. The tree must be at least fifteen metres wide at the base. From the branches high above hang tattered banners, charms, and totems. One or two rotting carcasses swing in the freezing wind. The Goliaths still practice blood sacrifice. Thanks to the deep cold, the stench isn't too bad.

The hall's great gate is set midway along the building, at the top of another great flight of stairs. The doors are a successful marriage of form and function. Carved from two massive slabs of hypercarbon, the doors are covered in the swirling snakes and animal motifs so beloved by the Norse Vikings of old. The craftsmanship is exquisite, and it's rendered even more impressive by the fact you can't carve hypercarbon. To fashion a portal like this must have required thousands upon thousands of hours of work. Not to mention an untold number of diamond-tipped drills worn down to create the intricate details.

The gate stands ten metres tall by five wide, crowned by a massive lintel of unidentified origin. It's said to be a piece of a starship hull, but there have been no unresolved reports of missing ships since the days of the colonisation. I asked Finn about it once. He shook his head and said it might be alien. I'm not sure he was joking.

Far above in the late afternoon sky, two giant birds circle the building, their pitch-black wings unmoving on the breeze. Something about them makes me ill at ease, but I shrug it off. We've got more important things to worry about than the interest of the local fauna.

On each side of the entrance stands a Goliath sentinel. Soledad can't tear her eyes off them as we mount the stairs and pass between them. They twist to follow our passage with their tracking sensors.

Inside the gate is a lofty antechamber, with another set of doors at the other end. It's constructed like an airlock, to keep the frost out. The air is warmer in here, but it's still too frigid for comfort. There's a large stone basin at the centre of the room, filled with water. Along the walls are rack upon rack containing weapons of all kinds. Swords, axes, and spears share space with assault rifles and rocket launchers in an unholy shambles. All Goliaths are required to leave their weapons in the chamber before entering the hall of the Jarl. The custom arose out of necessity. When drunk, Goliaths inevitably resort to violence and keeping them unarmed limits the damage.

The Goliath woman named Hildr pulls a set of intricately carved heavy iron daggers the size of short swords from her belt and sets them on a rack.

"You can leave your coats there," Eirik says and points to a bench.

We strip out of our warm gear, and Eirik tears off his shirt and plunges his head deep into the stone fount. Swirling tattoos and scars criss-cross his muscled upper body.

When I knew him, many years ago, he was not much of a fighter. It is clear he has been training, and he wears the lessons on his skin like badges of honour. Judging by the number of scars he must not have been especially good at first. The fact he's still here means he got better fast. Slaying the Jarl's son would mean a lot of honour for his killer. His tutors would not have held back.

He pulls his head back out with a roar and shakes the water from his hair and beard.

"Ah, much better."

We follow him, still bare-chested, across the chamber.

"I see you've been working on your honour since last we met."

"I have." He traces the scars with his fingertips. He seems to know each one by heart. "No one can touch me now. This honour is mine."

"Honour is not a shield, Eirik. It's a target."

We reach the inner door.

"I would have it no other way."

He flexes his powerful shoulders and throws the giant double doors wide. The bedlam assaults our senses like a fist in the guts.

"Come. Father expects us." Eirik Wagner has always been a poseur. Now he bears the scars to back it.

We step across the threshold into the hall of the mountain king.

* * *

The hall's interior is no less impressive than the exterior.

Compared to the frigid temperature of the antechamber, the great hall of *Hrafnheim* is an oven.

The stagnant air carries the smell of roasting meat and bad mead, and I suddenly realise how hungry I am. Hundreds upon hundreds of Goliaths line the long wooden tables, eating, drinking, and fighting. In one or two instances it looks like the fighting has gone over into more amorous groping. The Goliaths are not known for their modesty.

Like the Viking houses of old, the hall is open to the rafters a hundred metres above. Balconies and ladders line the inside of the roof. Keeping it all up are massive beams of what appears to be gnarled and polished wood, carved with giant runes. It's most likely hypercarbon sheathed in thin wood veneer. There is only one tree big enough to craft beams that large, and that's the giant ash outside. Even the Jarl of Nifelheim couldn't afford to import that amount of wood from off-world.

The social area spans almost the entire length of the building. The far ends of the hall disappear into the smoke rising from the bonfires roaring along the axis of the building. At the hall's midpoint is a raised stone dais, twenty metres long and two metres tall. A massive wooden table sits on top, with matching chairs around it. They are all occupied by important-looking Goliaths, but none look as important as the grizzled warrior on the centre throne. Ragnwald Wagner, Jarl of Nifelheim and the most powerful Goliath in the world. If the Goliaths had been interested in conquest at all, he would have been the most powerful man in the universe.

No one even notices our arrival.

Except for one ancient Goliath seated next to the Jarl's high-backed chair. From the moment we walk through the door, his milky white eyes never leave us. It's impressive he can see anything at all with those eyes. For a man that should be technically blind, his gaze is uncannily clear and focused. Something that cannot be said about the other guests at the party. They are a long way down the road to Merryland.

I tap Hildr's shoulder and nod at the old man. "Who is that?"

The redhead scoffs.

"That is Geirmund the Cunning." She leans in. "Rumour has it his father dropped him on the head when he was a baby. Made him lame on the left side."

The old man whispers something into the Jarl's ear with both hands cupped around his mouth.

"Looks like he got better."

"He says the gods favour him. When he was thirteen, he killed his father in revenge."

"And his family was fine with that?"

Killing your kin in cold blood is normally frowned upon in Goliath society. Unless you have a blood debt to avenge, in which case you are more or less required to slaughter your relatives.

"No. They came to kill the boy, but he pleaded sanctuary with the priests of Odin, and they took him under their black wings. A priest is untouchable."

"I see. Clever guy."

"Be careful around him. He doesn't like outsiders. Especially humans."

I make a mental note to beware of the old git as we follow Eirik between the tables. They are stacked high with food and drink, and the Goliaths are doing their best to stuff it into their mouths. It's all meat from the local fauna. There is no place for vegans on an ice world.

"This way, my friends," Eirik calls and waves for us to hurry. "Come greet my father."

As we pass, warriors get up to clap Eirik on the back or hug him. He's popular among the men.

Except for Hildr, all Goliaths in the hall are male. There are only a handful of Goliath women in the world, and most of them live in the breeding grounds, making little Goliaths with the Breeders. No one knows why there are so few of them. Some say the Goliaths put their girls out into the ice and let the *garms* take them. Many years ago, a scholar travelled to Nifelheim to study the phenomenon. They found him hanged with his own intestines from the tree outside the hall. No follow-up study was ever made.

How they can still make so many little Goliaths is one of many mysteries surrounding the giants.

The Goliaths realise we're there, and silence spreads behind us like the wake of a boat. Midgets at a party mean entertainment, and I fear this joke might be on us.

"Stay sharp," Jagr cautions. Not that we could do much if the Goliaths decided to take us out. We have no weapons.

Eirik leads us straight for the main table while he pulls his tunic back on. He stops only to bump fists with friends and punch out the occasional drunk who stumbles into his path.

Long before we reach the central table, news of our arrival has reached the ends of the hall, and the place has gone eerily quiet. Like the calm before battle, when everyone is busy coming to terms with the possibility of his imminent death.

The communicator in my ear crackles to life as we climb the stairs surrounding the central dais. It's Braden.

"I thought you'd like to know I'm picking up comms from the hall. The signature is similar to the ones we've seen before."

"*Her assessment is correct. This signature matches the previous transmissions, but less powerful.*"

"Thanks, Aeryn, but Braden has this covered."

Jagr scans the faces of the crowd. "So. Someone knows we're here. Nice catch, Braden."

"Father," Eirik calls as we arrive at the head table. His voice echoes through the silent hall.

Ragnwald Wagner the Allwise, Jarl of Nifelheim, replies in their strange language. "Eirik, *sonur mein*." His voice is appropriately deep and gravelly.

"English, father." Eirik gestures at us. "In honour of our esteemed guests."

Ragnwald rises from his wooden throne and glares at us, with a large bone of meat in his hand. He's in his sixties, with an impressive grey beard and a beginning paunch, but he's still broad over the shoulders and looks fit for his age. Silver beads decorate his hair and beard.

The hall holds its breath, waiting for the horns to signal the start of the carnage.

Jarl Ragnwald chews his mighty grey-bearded jaws around a piece of meat. He swallows and throws the cleaned bone on his golden plate with a clatter before he addresses us in perfect but accented English.

"Welcome, honoured visitors, to *Nifelheimr*."

He spreads his arms wide to embrace the hall. The thick golden chain of command around his neck glints in the light from the fires.

"Welcome to the House of Wagner. My food and my drink are yours. Come. Sit at my table."

Two Goliaths across the table from the Jarl have fallen asleep. The Jarl signals to the men next to them. Without further ado, they drag the sleepers off the bench and throw them from the dais to make space for us to sit. Ragnwald sits down on his throne again and picks his teeth with a splinter of bone.

The withered Goliath I saw watching us earlier rises on shivering legs from his place at the table to stand behind his Jarl. He supports himself on a long, wooden staff as he strokes his thin beard and whispers something in Ragnwald's ear. Thick woollen scarves wrap his scrawny body, but they can't hide that he's got the worst hunchback I've ever seen. So, we have an actual *bona fide* evil advisor in the house.

An old Goliath is rare as an amicable divorce. Their harsh living conditions and penchant for violence make sure Goliaths seldom live beyond the age of fifty. If they do, the *ättestupa* is the preferred way to go. The Goliaths prefer to build their settlements near a tall, vertical cliff. If against all odds, a Goliath grows to old age, he walks alone to that cliff and jumps to his death with a smile on his face, knowing he will jump straight into a seat at Odin's table in Valhalla. Like most Goliath customs, it's all about efficiency. It saves the community from having to feed a useless mouth, and the old warrior gets to meet his friends. A win-win situation for everyone. Ragnwald's father jumped a few years ago, and I heard it was a merry occasion. I guess nobody liked the bastard. The fact the real Vikings did nothing of this sort doesn't faze the Goliaths. They're in love with the idea. Goliath settlements that don't have a suitable cliff nearby use an *ätteklubba* instead. It's a heavy mallet, but the general principle is the same.

Eirik takes the advisor's vacated seat at his father's side. Berengar has returned from whatever errand Eirik sent him on earlier and sits next to his lord. The faithful dog, always at his master's side.

The giant redhead walks up to the Jarl and embraces him.

"*Maken mein*" She gives him a deep kiss. I can tell there's tongue.

She peers at me around the Jarl's bushy hair with a mischievous glint in her eyes. She even winks at me. What the hell?

I glance behind me to make sure she's not looking at someone else. She's not.

The others do not seem to have noticed the wink. The redhead sits down at the Jarl's side and drinks deep from his mead.

Jagr bows her head to Ragnwald. "We thank you, lord Ragnwald, for your hospitality."

Ragnwald dips his head a fraction of an inch and waves at the vacated bench across from him.

Jagr sits. "I bring the greetings of Terra and the Commonwealth government. We are honoured to be your guests, and we are honoured to eat and drink of your precious food."

Soledad and I sit on the bench on each side of Jagr. I end up in front of the redhead.

"Welcome all." Ragnwald nods at us. "I see you have met my wife, Hildr."

His wife? *That* is Finn's stepmother? The Jarl is a lucky man.

"This is Hrym Steadfast, my steersman." He points to the older, grey-haired Goliath next to me.

Hrym has a neatly trimmed grey beard and nods in greeting. I nod in reply. There is something likeable about him. Like a favourite uncle. I wonder what he steers?

"And this is Geirmund, my advisor, who served my father before me and his father before that." Ragnwald stabs a thumb at the old man hovering behind the throne. That means the old bastard must be at least a hundred and fifty years old.

The withered Goliath squints at us while he fondles his long, gnarled wooden staff. There's a blue gem set on the end, held in place by twisted roots. A hundred credits say that stone can glow. He bows to us.

"I am Geirmund the Cunning." His voice sounds like a bubbling mud geyser. "Like my ancestors before me, I speak to Odin through Mimr the Wise, his messenger. The All-Father bids you welcome and gives you his peace at this table."

The old man's milky gaze seems to linger on me longer than the others, but that could be my ego talking.

Jagr dips her head. "Thank you."

Anyone who calls himself *the Cunning* is, by definition, a wanker.

Ragnwald goes on. "What brings such honoured guests to my table?"

Jagr looks him in the eye without blinking. "Why not save the business for later, Jarl Ragnwald? Let us enjoy this magnificent feast. I'm starving."

The Jarl sucks his teeth while he thinks. There's a hard-to-read expression on his bearded face. The hunchback whispers in his master's ear again, and the Jarl's face relaxes.

"Yes, let us eat and drink. We will talk later."

Eirik stands and calls for silence. The hall was almost silent, anyway, but still.

"Let us raise a toast to our honoured guests."

Everyone who can still stand rises too and Eirik goes on in the Goliath tongue. The Goliaths laugh and raise their jugs. They shout "*Skål*" and bang their glasses together. We do likewise and drink when Ragnwald drinks. The noise of conversation and singing returns to the hall, and I sit back down with a sigh of relief.

I find the best way to make new friends is to eat and drink with them.

It never fails.

I Know That Blade

The Goliaths may be brutal, vindictive bastards, but they know how to throw a party.

The night flies as we drink and dine with the giants, and as the beer flows, Hildr becomes more and more beautiful. She sits hugging the Jarl, but more often than not, I catch her looking at me. When she's not suspiciously eyeing Eirik.

What the hell is she playing at?

The food is good, the drink is potent and Ragnwald is deep in conversation with Jagr. To break the ice and sound the waters underneath, I reach across the table to touch jugs with Hildr. She taps my jug and drinks deep. Then she rests her elbows on the table and leans close.

"Anything I can do for you, little man."

I reach out and gather a handful of her curly red hair in my hand. It's thick and soft and smells of weapon grease and something else I can't place. It's not an unpleasant smell. "Is red your natural colour?" The gold beads clink between my fingers.

She gives me a mischievous smile and replies in a husky whisper. "Well, there's only one way to find out, isn't there?" She lies back against Ragnwald and spreads her knees a little under her fur-trimmed leather skirt. When I lean in for a better look, she closes her knees again and cuddles up to her giant husband. She holds my gaze with her clear, green eyes. Ragnwald doesn't notice. How can Finn not like his stepmother?

Ragnwald laughs at something Eirik just said and waves to someone in the crowd.

"Music," he calls drunkenly. "Music."

Three musicians climb onto the end of the dais and plug their instruments into hidden sockets under the table. It's the band from the ice-bar. Maybe they only have one band on Nifelheim?

Something is wrong because no music ensues.

"Music," shouts Ragnwald again.

One of the band members calls something about someone called Skallagrim, and I notice the tall singer from the mead house is not here.

"Skallagrim," calls Ragnwald. "Where are you? Where is my fucking *skald*?"

Like the Jarls of old, Ragnwald employs a *skald* to entertain his court with song and poems. Cute.

Scattered calls of "Skallagrim, Skallagrim," grow into a steadfast chanting that goes on for some time.

"Skallagrim, where the hell are you?" Ragnwald calls again.

"Over here, my lord."

The tall, red-haired singer comes in through a side door. His eyes are still painted black like a skull, but the big smile on his face negates the intended scare effect. "Can't a man take a piss in the snow without being hailed?" His English is perfect.

The hall roars with laughter and Ragnwald laughs with them.

"You can piss all you like, as long as you sing."

The hall joins in a chant of "Song. Song. Song."

I chant along with them and bang my jug on the table. "Song. Song. Song."

"Well, you ugly sons of winter and stars, if you insist." Skallagrim swings onto the dais and one of his band members hands him a guitar. He strums it and the chords echo through the hall from hidden speakers high on the walls. A microphone lowers from the dark ceiling on a long cord. Ragnwald whispers something to his withered advisor, and while the microphone descends, Geirmund the cunning shuffles over to the singer to whisper something in his ear. Skallagrim frowns. Then he nods, and Geirmund returns to his place at the Jarl's side. The singer grabs the microphone. He lowers his head and waits for dramatic effect. Most of the noise in the hall dies out.

"My brothers and friends. At the request of our most esteemed sovereign."

With his head still bowed, he raises a hand to Ragnwald who nods amicably.

"First ..." Skallagrim's voice drops an octave, and he looks up at his audience. "... an old poem."

The hall falls silent. Dead silent. "It goes something like this."

Under a Dark Sky a plague shall rise, the morning star so bright will fall
Under a Winter Sun in icy skies, a ship is found, a god will call
Under a Demon Star a general dies, the house of Usher brings the end of all

Jagr leans close to me. "That's some bleak shit right there."

A shiver runs down my back. There's something familiar about those words. "Tell me about it."

Jagr takes a long drink from her jug. "Is he threatening us?" She wipes her lips with her hand.

I rub my stubbled cheek. "Nah. It's just a Goliath wank fantasy if you ask me. They are always on about how the Master Race will conquer the universe and bring about the end of the world."

Jagr looks unconvinced. "I hope you're right. I really do."

Is Ragnwald stupid enough to threaten us? Or does he not give a shit? Who knows how he thinks? I hope Braden has the ship ready because this situation is swelling into something resembling a big-ass pear.

Skallagrim strums his guitar again.

"I think you all know this one." He hits three rapid chords, and the crowd goes wild. It must be another old favourite. The band joins in and the hall goes into a frenzy. The song is a mess of distorted minor chords and guttural howling, but now and then the merest hint of folk harmonies shine through the noise. Just the kind of shit Goliaths get off on. Throughout the hall, head-banging giants roar along to the chorus. Too bad the song is in Norse. I recognise a word here and there, but the full meaning of the song is lost on me.

Jagr takes the chance to get down to business with Ragnwald while the Goliaths are busy.

"Lord Wagner, as you guessed, this is not merely a social call."

Ragnwald wipes his mouth and beard with his hand. "I figured as much."

He sets his jug down. "So, tell me, little woman. What are you doing here?"

His face is dangerously calm and composed.

"We're looking for someone."

"And who might that be?"

"A man named Acheron. Thane Acheron. He is here at your court as an envoy from Terra."

"Ah. Him." Ragnwald nods sagely.

Geirmund the Cunning leans close to his master. Ragnwald listens while the old man hisses something in his ear. The Jarl turns back to Jagr with a strange smile playing across his fleshy lips. "Yes. He is here."

Geirmund cracks a parody of a smile that is one of the creepiest things I've ever seen. He's got a mere handful of teeth in his gums, and the ones he has are rotten and ugly. I don't envy Ragnwald who has that old fucker whispering in his ear all day. That breath must stink worse than Berengar's.

"He's here?" There's sudden hope in Jagr's voice, and she squints around the hall. "Can we see him?"

"Very well." Ragnwald waves to a servant and shouts something in Norse. Then he turns back to Jagr. "We'll get him for you."

The music goes into a crescendo of noise, and the song ends on a horrible grating of guitars. Skalla-grim's growling voice drops into the deepest tones I've ever heard from a human throat.

Ragnwald raises a hand, and the hall falls silent once more.

Heads turn to follow the returning servant as he runs between the tables with something held in one hand like a sceptre.

"*Comms-spike,*" Aeryn notifies me an instant before the communicator crackles in my ear.

"Another comms-spike," Braden reports. Jagr doesn't reply. Her eyes are locked on the servant and the smile on her face freezes to ice.

The man climbs the stairs to the dais, and I realise what's in his hand. It's a human head, impaled on a short Goliath battle spear.

The broad iron tip has cracked the skull like an egg, and the vile thing is discoloured and bloated. Both eyes and many teeth are missing. The injuries appear to be inflicted *ante mortem*. The poor man died hard.

Ragnwald takes the spear from the servant and sets the butt against the floor next to his colossal boot. He leans back on his throne. "Here he is. What did you want with him?"

The severed head stares at the ceiling with its empty sockets. Everyone holds their breath.

The rage creeping across Jagr's face is terrible to behold. Even more terrible is the way she reins it in and renders her features blank again.

"What is the meaning of this?" she asks.

"We caught him spying. On your orders, I presume." Ragnwald leans across the table, staring at Jagr. Mead drips from the points of his moustache.

I glance around the hall, searching for an exit.

There is none.

Goliaths in heavy leather armour pour onto the second level balconies on both sides of the hall. They carry heavy assault rifles.

We're fucked.

Jagr grinds her teeth but pushes on. "Do you realise what you've done?"

You've got to admire her balls.

Ragnwald laughs. "What *I* have done?"

His deep voice is deadly calm. "You sent a spy to my court. *My* court. Like I am a simple enemy."

"I don't have to remind you that Nifelheim has sworn allegiance to Earth."

"We bow to no man." Ragnwald shakes his great shaggy head.

Jagr cracks a thin, cold smile. "I am no man."

Ooh, classic comeback.

"No, you are not. You are a fucking *cunt*." Ragnwald reaches across the table and grabs Jagr by the throat with one hand and lifts her high into the air.

We're frozen in place, unable to look away as if watching a car crash in slow-motion. Jagr will die, we will all die with her, and there is not a thing we can do about it.

Ragnwald holds her a metre off the ground and crushes her windpipe, one-handed. Jagr kicks and claws at his arm, trying to reach his face, but his arm is too long. The Jarl wields the spear with the severed head in his other hand. Even from my seat, I can hear the bones in Jagr's neck crack as he raises her towards the rafters.

Her face turns red with the blood pressed into her head. "*Fuck ... you.*" The light goes out in her eyes.

Ragnwald roars and moves to throw her to the floor to break her back, but then he freezes. A broad knife-tip slides out a foot from his chest, spilling blood down the front of his tunic.

The Jarl studies the bloody steel in silence for a while. "*Ach*, I know that blade," he coughs as blood bubbles from his lips. Jagr tumbles from his grip and falls lifeless on the table. Plates and bowls crash to the floor.

A mighty arm reaches around Ragnwald's throat and the knife retracts from his chest, only to reappear again and again. Jarl Ragnwald Wagner thrashes against the arm holding him in place, and we're showered in his warm blood. The Goliath chieftain is powerless as the strength flows from his body with each beat of his mighty heart.

The Jarl's legs buckle, and he drops to his knees in front of his throne.

167

"Give my regards to Odin, father."

Behind the dying Jarl, Eirik the Fair lifts the heavy gold chain from around his father's neck. He raises it to the roof and roars in triumph as the hall erupts into chaos. Berengar the defiler stands at Eirik's side and roars with him. Behind them both, Geirmund the Cunning shuffles forward. He rubs his withered old hands around his staff with glee and grimaces toothlessly at the crowd. The gem on his staff glows an eerie blue. I told you so.

"The time has come for the sons of Odin to rise," Eirik calls to the hall, his voice deep. "Tonight, we will sacrifice as our ancestors did. White Christ will tremble in fear before us."

He lowers the gold chain around his neck, and I've got to admit the bastard never looked better. Power becomes him.

Geirmund raises his thin arms and calls to the rafters in his bubbly old voice. "Odin himself has told me it will be so." The old man is not only evil. He's a melodramatic bastard at that. I fucking hate him.

A roaring cheer echoes through the hall from Eirik's faithful, while Ragnwald's supporters charge the dais. They jump over chairs and scramble over tables to reach their dying Jarl. In their hands are knives, forks, jugs, and anything else that will serve as makeshift weapons.

Jagr has recovered and coughs and retches as she rubs her sore throat. Soledad drags her off the table.

Eirik stands over his dying father and points the bloody knife at the approaching mob. Those guns were never meant for us.

A deafening roar drowns out the howls of the charging Goliaths as the gunmen on the balconies open fire. Their aim is true, and the slaughter is grim and methodical, but still Ragnwald's men seek to reach their Jarl. The myth of Valhalla inspires some badass final stand heroics.

Why are *we* still alive?

I glance at Eirik. He nods to Jagr. She glares at him in disbelief.

Now the mechs in the grounds outside make perfect sense. The alleged coup of a no-name warlord was merely an excuse for Eirik to bring his troops into the compound. He saw a chance to get rid of his father and secure Terran support in one quick slip of a knife. Impressive thinking for a Goliath. But then, he was always an opportunist.

Eirik calls to Jagr over the chaos in the hall. "It is done. I have honoured our deal. Now it's your turn."

"What the fuck have you done, Eirik?"

A look of uncertainty flashes over Eirik's handsome face. "You told me to handle my father. I did."

All around the hall, Goliaths are fighting to the death. A giant tries to climb the dais, but Berengar kicks him in the face and blood sprays everywhere as the unfortunate man tumbles back into the crowd.

"Not like *that*." Jagr stabs a finger at the dead Jarl.

Eirik's resolve returns. "What's done is done. Your support allowed us to advance our time frame, and for that I thank you." He nods to Jagr.

Time frame of *what*?

Jagr shakes her head in disbelief. "We never sent you any support."

"No need. Your battlecruiser in orbit was enough to convince the chieftains I have Terra's support."

Shit.

The Goliaths loyal to Ragnwald are in majority in the hall, but Eirik's forces are armed. It's a rigged board and the loyalists will soon be dead or dying.

"You're insane, Eirik." Judging by the thundercloud sailing up over his handsome face, that was not what Eirik Wagner, new Jarl of Nifelheim, wanted to hear.

It's time to leave.

Soledad has the same idea. Before anyone can react, she leaps across the table and kicks Eirik in the chest with all her strength. He goes over backwards into the boiling sea of fighting men, and she lands light on her feet on the table. She grabs the impaled head and yanks the spear out. "I've got it."

Berengar jumps after his master to protect him. Geirmund the Cunning shies away from Soledad like a vampire from a ray of sunlight. Soledad hisses at him. The old man hisses back and claws the air with his thin, grey fingers.

Jagr starts for the exit. "Let's get the fuck out of here." I go to follow her when a sudden thought tears at my guts like a rabid dog.

Finn.

If Eirik is making a play for the throne, he has to get rid of the true heir.

"Jagr, get the others to the *Sundowner*. I'll get Finn and meet you there."

"There's no time, Perez." Jagr grabs a heavy gold plate and swings it at a Goliath climbing the dais. The Goliath falls screaming back into the chaos, trailing blood. "We go now."

"Wait for me." I run off while Jagr calls expletives after me.

If I recall correctly, the Breeder monastery is a smaller building close to the mountainside. If I can reach it before Eirik's soldiers get there, Finn still has a chance.

I glance back at the dead Jarl. There's a look of utter betrayal on his face. The poor man never saw that coming.

When I turn back to where I'm going, Berengar the Defiler rises like a demon of hell from the fighting men before me. A vicious grin splits his ugly face.

"Where are you going, little named man?"

While the World Burns

Is he fucking everywhere?

He shakes off two men trying to wrestle him to the floor and climbs onto the dais as I skid to a stop. There's no way around him. I search for a weapon.

"Prepare to die, Asher Perez," Berengar says and cracks his knuckles. This will be painful.

Then, out of nowhere, comes a Goliath straight at Berengar. There's a flash of red hair and fur-trimmed leather clothing. Hildr.

She tackles him off the dais, and he goes over backwards, back into the crowd.

She twists around and swipes the hair out of her face. "Give me a ride off-world, and I'll take you to Finn."

"You got it."

"Come with me." Hildr waves for me to follow.

The press of men struggling to reach their dead Jarl is so hard the fighting has almost ground to a standstill. Hildr jumps onto the shoulders and heads of the packed Goliaths and runs across them like a stone skipping across a pond. She doesn't pay any heed to the curses following in her wake.

I jump after her and it takes all my augmented reflexes to keep my balance as we make our way across the sea of struggling men.

As we get further from the dais, the press of bodies grows weaker, and we have to jump to the floor. Hildr goes through the fighting men like a bulldozer. I tag along, close behind.

We reach the back wall and run along it to the nearest exit. Hildr turns to survey the hall.

"He killed Ragnwald. That little bastard killed my husband."

She looks like she can't believe what just happened. "I always knew he would go far, but not this far."

"What's done is done. Why are you helping me?"

"Do you think Eirik will let me live when he's Jarl? He will force me to climb on Ragnwald's pyre, the little cunt. He's always been one for honouring tradition when it suits him." She spits on the floor and I crack the door open an inch to peer outside. My sensitive eyes register no movement in the darkness.

"*It's clear*," Aeryn confirms.

"Let's get the hell out of here." I throw the door open and dash off into the night with Hildr close behind.

We reach the nearest building and take shelter in its shadow. The wind has picked up since we landed and dark clouds obscure Nirvana in the sky. Whirling snow fills the air, and visibility is poor. Unless we bump into someone, we should be fine.

"Where's the monastery?"

Hildr points to a building barely visible by the rock wall. "Over there."

I cast a glance around the corner, searching for soldiers. There are none.

"Follow me." I crouch and dash to the next building. We reach it without incident, and I peer around the corner.

A dozen Goliaths armed to the teeth are heading straight for the monastery.

"Shit. They are already on their way."

Hildr risks a glance.

"Shit. What now?"

"Do you have any weapons?"

She shakes her head, making her red hair dance. "No, I left them at the door. You?"

"Nope."

"So, what do we do, little man?"

"We improvise. Come on, we've got to hurry."

We set off again. The death squad is not in a hurry, and we reach the building ahead of them.

The night lights up in shades of yellow and red as an explosion shakes the ground.

Smoke billows from a hole in the roof of the Raven's Home, wide enough to fly the *Sundowner* through. Flames lick the structure from inside.

We reach the back door of the monastery, and Hildr pulls a heavy ring of iron keys from a pocket.

"You have the keys to the temple?"

"I am mistress of the house. I have all the keys."

How convenient.

She unlocks the door, and we sneak inside.

The execution party is about fifty metres out when I close the door.

We're in what looks like a kitchen. A wide table for preparing food dominates the space and wooden cupboards line the walls. Something falls over behind the cupboards, and I point my rifle at it. There is nothing there.

"This way," Hildr says and heads for a door across the room.

She cracks it open and peers inside. "Come on."

I follow her into a long corridor with half a dozen doors on either side.

The lighting is muted, and the place smells of incense. Heavy crimson curtains adorn the walls and there's a thick green carpet on the floor. Soft lute music streams from speakers hidden in the walls. Apart from the music, there is no sound. The place reminds me of an upscale brothel. Typical of Finn to find a brothel even in his father's backyard.

"Nice place." I didn't know the Goliaths enjoyed comfortable surroundings.

"Only the best is good enough for the Breeders," Hildr replies as we move down the corridor.

A door swings open and a Goliath steps out. He carries an assault rifle at the ready. The commotion at the hall must have alerted the monastery guards.

"Who's there?" he barks when he spots us.

"It's me, your queen." Hildr walks up to the guard with a sexy swagger in her step. He recognises her, opens his mouth to say something, then he notices me, and his eyes widen with alarm. His rifle rises and Hildr punches him in the face. He goes down and stays down.

"Impressive," I note.

"What? Because I'm a woman?" She takes the rifle from the unconscious man.

"No, because you knocked him out with one punch. Impressive."

"They don't call me The Red on account of my hair."

She points to a door, more intricately carved than the rest. "He's in this one."

"If you say so." I cast a worried glance at the gate at the end of the corridor. The death squad will be here any second now. I hope she knows what she's doing.

She unlocks the heavy wooden door, hauls it open and steps inside. I follow her, and as I shut the door behind me the outside gate opens. Shit. They're here.

The room we've entered is sparsely lit, circular, and spacious. The ceiling disappears into the darkness high above. In the gloom, I can make out wooden rafters. Everything is lit in soft candlelight and the room is filled with sheer pink cloth, hanging from the ceiling in sheets. The lute music is louder in here. Thick satin pillows, stacked in piles cover the polished wooden floor. Someone has sat in them recently. Or done other things. Unmistakable noises come from behind the curtains at the chamber's centre.

Someone is getting lucky while the world burns.

I swipe the curtains aside, and there he is.

Thorfinn Wagner, my best friend and the legitimate heir to the Throne of Shields, is busy making baby Goliaths. He's grown soft around the edges, but it's clear he's kept in reasonable shape in the Breeder Grounds. His long blond hair is tied into a stylish ponytail and his pale beard has been combed soft. There's a dark-haired, naked Goliath woman standing on all fours on the pillows in front of him. Playing on an enormous screen on the wall is a feed of two very naked, very male, and very excited Goliath warriors wrestling.

The woman beneath Finn spots me in one of the many mirrors adorning the walls. "What the fuck?" she screams. Or something to that effect. I can't understand her words, but I take that to be their general meaning.

"Finn, we've got to go," I call and grab Finn's shoulder.

Finn disentangles himself from the woman on the pillows, gets up and turns around to tower naked over us.

"*Woah*, sheathe your sword soldier." I raise my hands to cover the sight. Some things not even best friends should share.

Wagner roars something in his native tongue and raises an enormous fist to smite me. Spittle flies from his lips and sticks in his bushy beard.

I hold up my hands, showing I'm unarmed. "It's me. Perez. We've got to go. *Now.* Eirik has killed your father, and he's sent people to kill you."

Finn blinks, unable to take in what's going on. You could never accuse him of being overly bright.

"Perez? What are you doing here?"

"Long story, no time. You've grown fat, my friend. I hope you can still fight. Get dressed."

I throw a bundle of clothes at him, hoping it's his. He stares dumbly at me and the clothes bounce off his barrel-like chest and fall in a pile on the floor.

The naked woman gets swearing to her feet and grabs a long silk gown from the floor to cover herself. "The Jarl will have your head for disturbing the sacred act," she screams at me in broken English.

"Your Jarl doesn't mind since he's busy being dead. People are coming to kill you. Get out." I turn to Wagner. "Get dressed."

The concubine notices Hildr and she bows to her lady. She says something apologetic in Norse and heads for the door, clutching the gown to her chest.

Before she reaches it, the door bursts open and two Goliaths storm in, brandishing huge assault rifles. They see the concubine come at them and open fire.

The large calibre rounds tear the woman to pieces and blood splatters everywhere.

The world slows down to the familiar crawl of Meridian's enhanced frame of reference. Before the Worldburner has the full use of my body, I dive at Wagner's knees to get him out of harm's way. The concubine's death bought us precious tenths of a second, and I bring Finn down just as the bullets that would have ended his life tear through the air, mere centimetres above us.

I had my shot at saving Finn. Now the dread general will do his thing. All I can do is hope he doesn't perceive my friends as a threat, because I won't be able to save them if he does.

From here on in, I'm only along for the ride.

The General goes into a roll and comes up on his feet three metres from where I stood. Before they have time to realign their weapons, he's on the gunmen like a tornado.

He's unarmed, but Meridian doesn't need weapons. He uses the enhanced frame of his body to kill them like they were not even there.

The first Goliath goes down from a punch to the throat. In horrible slow-motion, his larynx crumples and he drops. Before his knees reach the floor, Meridian is on the next man. In a single fluid motion, the General yanks the assault rifle out of the Goliath's hands and turns it on the man. From point-blank range, Meridian fires a quick burst through the man's chest. He drops like a rag doll. Meridian raises the barrel and fires another burst into the face of the next man coming through the door. He drops too, and Meridian turns the weapon on the fourth man outside the door and pulls the trigger.

Nothing happens. The weapon is empty.

The hitmen were not expecting such a rapid response to their attack, and too late the Goliath outside the door raises his weapon.

Meridian uses the empty rifle as a club and caves in the Goliath's head. Blood sprays the walls and warm liquid spatters Meridian's face.

There are five more men behind the dead Goliath, with their weapons at the ready. Meridian drops to the floor as they fire.

A storm of bullets fills the air, and I can only hope Finn and Hildr are out of the way.

Pink silk sheets tear to shreds and drift to the floor in slow-motion.

Meridian scrambles back into the relative safety of the room and kicks the door shut behind him.

Another round of bullets hit the wood from the other side, but the thing must be armoured since not a single bullet penetrates the wood.

Finn has got his leggings on. Hildr clutches her arm and blood drips between her fingers.

The world speeds up to normal again, and the General disappears like he was never even there. The muted atmosphere of the boudoir must have signalled safety to my lizard brain.

"*I lost you again, Perez.*"

"You found me. Get over it."

"*Winger needs to check you over.*"

"I'd like that."

"*Fuck you.*"

"Now hush."

"*Whatever.*" Aeryn clicks off.

I struggle to focus, but everything is blurry. It used to be easier to come back to myself after the General's visits. Is my imprinted mind slipping? Maybe Winger needs to check me over when we get home.

"Who are they?" Finn points at the door.

I blink and shake my head to clear my thoughts. "Your brother sent them."

"Eirik? Why?"

"I fucking told you. He killed your father, and now he will kill you too unless we can figure a way out of here."

"Why?"

"No time, Finn. Can you get us out?"

Finn shakes his head.

"No. This place is made like bunker."

Shit.

Another volley of shots outside and everything goes quiet.

Too quiet.

Someone knocks on the door from the other side. We look at each other in disbelief.

There's another knock. Heavier this time.

"Who's there?" I call.

A muted voice comes through. "Skallagrim."

Hildr inches toward the door.

"Skallagrim?" she calls. Then she goes on in their own tongue.

Skallagrim replies something in kind, and Hildr cracks the door to peer outside before she pulls it wide open.

Outside stands the red-headed *skald*, holding a dark bloody sword. Behind him are a pile of corpses and his three band members, still in makeup. The band is also brandishing swords.

Swords. How badass is that?

Skallagrim steps into the room and gazes around with curiosity. The breeder compound is normally off-limits to ordinary mortals like him.

Hildr wraps her arms around the singer and hugs him. He's a tower of a man, taller than Finn but lither, and she has to stand on tiptoe to hug him. There's a slight tug on my heart at the sight.

"Am I glad to see you, brother." She gives the man a warm smile.

Oh. *Brother.*

"Same to you. I thought you were dead."

Skallagrim turns to me. "Come. We must go."

"Lead the way." I gesture at the door.

Finn has got his boots on. "Where are shirt and jacket?"

"Leave them, big guy. If we live, I'll buy you fresh ones. Come on."

Skallagrim gives Finn's bare chest a look and says something in Norse. Finn replies in kind and Skallagrim laughs.

Hildr barks something at them, and they both laugh.

I bend down to pick up one of the large assault rifles. "What was that about?" I nod at Finn and Skallagrim.

She snorts. "Boys."

Finn picks up a rifle, checks the magazine with practised ease and grunts in satisfaction. I hold out another rifle to Skallagrim, but he shakes his head and pats his sword.

I wouldn't want to meet him in a one-on-one. That sword looks like it has a monomolecular edge. He could cleave a hair with that blade. I like him.

"What's the quickest way to the airfield?" I distribute the magazines from the death squad.

The singer points down the way we came. "That way."

The slaughterhouse smell of the dead Goliaths fills my nostrils.

"Follow me."

I put the rifle to my shoulder, step over the pile of corpses and take point down the corridor. We reach the kitchen and I kick the door down. It goes flying off its hinges and crashes into a soldier posted there to guard the rear exit.

A quick burst in his surprised face, and he slides dead to the floor.

Something falls over close to the left-hand wall and I swing my rifle to track it. A small figure scurries for cover. It's the first human-sized creature I've seen on Nifelheim, apart from us. It could be a skinny Goliath child.

"Hold it right there," I call and the figure freezes.

"Please don't kill me," it whimpers in perfect English.

"Who's there?" I kick some fallen furniture away, keeping the rifle trained on the figure. He's a pale, thin man in his mid-twenties. Draped over his scrawny body is a grey sackcloth robe with a hood. His mousy brown hair has been hacked into a horrible bowl cut, with the sides of his head shaved clean to expose his prominent ears. That is one ugly ass hairdo.

He scrambles into a corner behind the cupboards and raises long-fingered hands before his face. The robe rides up uncomfortably high on his pale thighs. "Don't kill me. I'm a priest. I'm a man of peace." His accent hints at Terran descent. He wears sensible shoes under the robes, and not much else. The little priest looks like a man who wouldn't dare kill himself for fear of what the neighbours would think. He will be a burden, but we can't leave him. They would slaughter him. Besides, Jagr said their contact was a priest. This might be him.

"Get up. You're coming with us."

I grab his rough robe and pull him to his feet. "We're getting out of here."

"Oh, praise the Lord." He hugs me. "Praise the Lord."

I slap him, and he falls back to the floor, holding his ear. He stares at me with tears in his eyes.

"Violence is the last refuge of the incompetent," he whines.

"Wise words." I move off, then stop and turn back. "Hang on. Are you calling me incompetent?"

I raise my fist to strike him again but Hildr grabs my arm.

"Later, Perez. No time for fun and games. We must go. *Now.*"

I glare at the priest. "Fine. Keep up or stay behind. Your choice, priest."

He swallows his sobs and scrambles to his feet. "I was just trying to be friendly." Hildr raises a fist as if to punch him, and he cowers in fear. Hildr leers at him and the priest makes a face. I guess they have met before.

I take a peek outside. The Raven's Hall burns, and there's fighting going on all over the grounds. It looks like Ragnwald's remaining loyalists are losing rapidly.

"Follow me." I run out into the icy night. The snow is deep, and in places we have to wade knee-deep through the stuff. The going is slow.

We're spotted the moment we clear the monastery wall.

Five Goliaths have been standing guard outside the main entrance, and they charge as soon as they spot Finn.

I open fire a tenth of a second ahead of Wagner and Hildr and two enemy Goliaths go down. Then their pals are upon us, wielding vicious-looking short swords.

Skallagrim and his band take them on. Bearded giants fighting to the death with swords, against a backdrop of a burning stave church is a surreal sight. Unfortunately, we don't have time to admire the view.

"Come on." I wave to Finn, Hildr and the priest to follow me and run off towards the landing pad. I'm an arsehole leaving Skallagrim and his band to do our fighting for us, but we have to get to the landing pad before our ride leaves.

"No."

I spin around. Wagner shakes his head. "I stand with Skallagrim." He parries a sword blow with his assault rifle and punches his opponent in the face. Blood spurts everywhere.

"We all stand with Skallagrim," adds Hildr and ducks a wild sweep.

Damn it. Damn the Goliaths to hell.

I turn back and join the fight.

You Will Come To Regret Saving Him

One musician takes a sword through the neck and gore splatters the snow. The blood steams briefly in the frosty night before the vapour dissipates along with the musician's life.

An enemy Goliath swings at Wagner's back and I put a burst through his head. The Goliath drops. Then my rifle goes *click* and I'm out of ammo.

"I'm out," I call and throw my rifle in the snow. I pull my pistol and rack the slide.

One musician grunts something to Skallagrim as he grinds swords with his opponent. It's man against man, and an artist is no match for a seasoned fighter. The enemy Goliath forces the tip of his sword closer and closer to the musician's eye. Skallagrim stumbles through the deep snow to reach them, but he won't make it there in time.

I fire three quick rounds at the enemy, but with the snow and the dark and the chaos, I can't tell if they find their mark. Handgun ammunition is mostly useless against Goliaths, anyway.

A howl splits the night as the icy steel slowly pierces the musician's eyeball. The enemy Goliath throws his long black hair back and roars in triumph as he pushes the blade into the artist's skull. We're losing this fight.

Skallagrim reaches the pair. He swings his sword in a wide arc and severs the head of the black-haired enemy from his shoulders. Only a few seconds too late to save his friend's life.

Another group of Goliaths charge out of the night. We're now outnumbered two to one.

"We've got company," I call. "Time to go."

One of the approaching Goliaths has a rifle, and he opens fire.

The one remaining musician takes a large calibre round through his sword arm and his weapon drops point down in the snow.

He says something to Skallagrim, who leans in and puts his forehead to that of his wounded friend. The musician grits his teeth in pain. *"Am nacht in Valhalla."* Even I understood that one. *See you tonight in Valhalla.*

Skallagrim turns his back on his friend. "Follow me." He stomps off through the snow toward the airfield. Finn picks up a sword from the ground. You can't accuse Goliaths of being sentimental.

As we run off after Skallagrim, I glance back. The wounded musician bends down to pick up his sword with his good left hand. His useless arm gushes blood onto the snow. Then the attackers are on him, and he goes down under the onslaught.

Unfortunately, he sacrificed himself for nothing.

As I reach the corner of another building, a group of heavily armed Goliaths spot me. I duck back behind the building as they open fire. Chunks of concrete spray into the chill night. We're fucked.

But I recognised one of the Goliaths.

If I play my cards right, I could give the others a chance to reach the *Sundowner*.

"Go." I point them back around the building. "Get to the airfield. I'll handle this."

Finn grunts and leads the others back the way we came.

"Eirik," I call. "It's me, Perez."

Many seconds tick by. Then Eirik the Fair calls back. "Perez. Give up and I will spare your life. This is not your fight."

A hand falls on my shoulder. I drop and turn, bringing the pistol up into the crotch of my attacker.

"It's me," screams the priest in alarm. "Don't kill me."

"What are you doing here? Why didn't you go with the others?"

"The Goliaths scare me. I want to be with another human."

Another human. If only he knew.

"Did I say something funny?" he whines.

"Not at all. Shut up and leave this to me."

Eirik calls out again. "What's it going to be, Perez?"

"I'm coming out."

"Good man."

I motion for the priest to stay back and step around the corner with my hands raised. The pistol is still in my hand.

Finn and the others crouch behind snow-covered crates by a building twenty metres to my left. There's no way they can reach the airfield without being spotted by Eirik and his men. I need to create a distraction.

Eirik waves for me to come closer. "Drop your weapon and come with me, Perez. You will be free to leave."

"I don't trust you, Eirik." I inch closer. All eyes and weapons are pointed at me. Good.

"You have my word."

"Come on. You stabbed your father in the back. Your word means nothing."

"Fair point. So, what now?"

"I know what you do to prisoners. I'd rather die on my feet."

He laughs. "That can be arranged."

"You and me, Eirik. Right here, right now." I holster my pistol. "If I win, your men let me go."

Eirik laughs. "You and me, little man? You have balls, I'll give you that."

The men laugh behind him. "All right, if that's how you want to go."

"It is."

Eirik turns to the man on his right. It's Hrym, the old steersman.

"If Perez wins, you let him go." Hrym grunts and crosses his arms. He rumbles something in Norse and the Goliaths all laugh.

Eirik sheathes his sword, unbuckles his belt, and hands it to Hrym. "Hold this for me while I dance with my little friend." The Goliaths laugh.

The giants spread out into a rough circle in the snow with me and Eirik at the centre. Behind them, Finn and the others duck away unseen toward the airfield.

"All right, let's do this." Eirik flexes his massive shoulders and gets into a fighter's stance in the whirling snow. This is not the way I saw my death, but if this is it, I guess it's a spectacular way to go.

Eirik throws a surprise backhand my way, but I dodge it.

"You're fast, Perez. Impressive."

"You're fast too."

I circle him, looking for an opening. He remains standing still.

"So, what's with the patricide, Eirik? You were always ambitious, but that was bold, even for you."

I kick the back of his knee, but he blocks it. It's like kicking a rock.

"The old bastard had it coming. He's been running this kingdom into the ground. It was time for a change."

He turns around and rushes me, incredibly fast for such an enormous man. He grabs me by the arm, spins me around and pulls me into a bear hug. "We didn't plan to do it so soon, but when you arrived in orbit, we saw our chance."

His crushing embrace smells of sweat and blood. I've got my back against his chest, and the fur of his cloak tickles my nose.

I throw my head back and there's a satisfying crunch as my skull connects with his nose. He grunts and lets me go, and I dance out of his reach.

"You're not a bad man, Perez. I will hate to kill you." He wipes his nose and looks relieved when there's no blood on his fingers.

"I don't want to kill you either, but here we are."

"Yes. Here we are."

He rushes me again, but I dodge him with a quick sidestep, and he spins around to face me again. I see my chance and charge.

He prepares to block a flying kick and lifts his arms. Before he can react, I twist and drop to the ground on my back, using my speed to slide along the icy ground. As I glide between his legs, I aim the hardest punch I can at his crotch. My fist crushes his balls.

I slide to a stop, roll to my feet and twist to face his back.

Eirik doesn't make a sound. Did I miss?

Then he drops to one knee and grabs his crotch.

The pained expressions on the faces of the audience tell me all I need.

I walk up to him and lock the crook of my arm around his neck and squeeze with all my strength.

"This brings me no joy, Eirik." I pull tight and choke the life from him. "But it's either you or me."

He grabs my arm and tries to pull it loose, but I've got him in a perfect chokehold. Hrym makes a move to step in, but Eirik waves him off.

"He's mine," he croaks between forced breaths.

I pull harder, something crunches in his neck and his efforts grow more frantic.

He lets go of my arm and clamps his enormous fist around my hand and crushes it. Pain shoots up my arm, but my body shuts it off.

I pull on his neck, and Eirik crushes my hand. *Come on, Meridian.* Where are you? This is a slow race between Goliath physique and Terran engineering.

My hand is first to give. Damn those Terran engineers. A sharp crunch, more felt up my arm than heard, and another flash of pain spikes through my brain. Eirik twists and pulls on my hand, and the razor-sharp ends of my hypercarbon skeleton slash my flesh to shreds. He pulls the bloody mess from my wrist and throws it into the snow where it flops like a red glove. Blood and torn flesh splatter the frosty ground and Eirik tears from my grip.

I stare at the bloody stump as it gushes steaming blood into the snow. My black hypercarbon radius and ulna protrude like two knives from the flesh at the end of my arm. There's no pain, but viewing your own insides is not something I would wish on my bitterest enemies. I keep staring at it, inviting the horror.

I grab the stump of my mutilated arm and drop to my knees, waiting for Eirik's next move.

There's a sudden drop deep in my gut like when you go too fast over the crest of a hill. The familiar darkening of vision heralds the Dread General's approach. *Finally.* My mind disconnects from my body and once again I'm only a passenger along for the ride.

Eirik towers above me and raises a fist to end the fight.

Meridian swings his mutilated stump upwards and shoves the bones like a twin-tipped spear into Eirik's thigh. The tips pierce the layers of heavy clothing and slide deep into the Goliath's flesh. Eirik howls in rage.

Meridian pulls his arm back and the sharp bones tear free, trailing blood across the snow. The warm life pumps from Eirik's severed aorta, and he drops to the ground. Meridian stumbles to his feet and raises the stump again, this time aimed at Eirik's unprotected neck.

It slashes down.

Before it ends the reign of the new Jarl of Nifelheim, something tumbles into Meridian from behind, and he's knocked into the snow.

The biting chill of the snow shuts the Dread General off like flipping a switch, and I'm back in control.

"*Lost you again.*"

"Later, Aeryn. I'm busy."

"*Whatever.*"

Between me and the wounded Eirik stands the little priest. He's got his fists raised in something resembling a boxer's stance.

"I won't let you kill this man. Not in cold blood."

I get up and move to push him aside. Eirik gushes blood into the snow. In a few minutes, it won't matter what I do. He will be dead, anyway.

Rage distorts the priest's face, and he snarls at me. "Leave him alone."

"Or else?"

"Or else ..." He casts about for something to threaten me with and finds a discarded assault rifle in the snow. He hauls it from the ground but struggles to hold it level. "I will stop you, so help me God."

The assembled Goliaths grunt and nod in reluctant approval. If it's one thing they respect, it's death-defying courage.

I can use that.

"The fight is over," I call, turning around to face the assembled Goliaths. "It was a fair fight, and I won. You heard Eirik. Now let us go."

I grab the priest's arm and pull him after me towards the airfield. The rifle slips from his grip.

"But we need to help Eirik. He's injured."

"Don't push your luck."

We reach the Goliath circle.

For a second that lingers like an eternity, the Goliaths stare at me. Then Hrym nods. He grunts and the Goliaths step aside, allowing us free passage.

"Perez," calls Eirik. His voice is steady for a man bleeding out on his knees. "This is not over. Call me sometime and we will finish this."

There's a chime in my communicator.

"Eirik Wagner sent you his call code," Aeryn says. *"Do you want to save a new contact?"*

"Yes."

"New contact saved."

"Call me, Perez," Eirik calls again.

I don't look back, but I wave my stump, pretending to give him the finger. He calls after me again. "Perez. I mean it."

I stumble around the corner of the nearest building and collapse against the wall.

The priest stares at me. "Were you going to kill Eirik?" There's horror in his voice.

"Yes."

"But why? He was no longer a threat."

"He will be. Believe me, you will come to regret saving him." But somewhere deep down I'm not angry the priest interfered. Eirik is not a total twat.

Then the priest notices my stump.

"My God, you're hurt."

I peer at the stump. It looks gross, but there's not much pain. The nanites are already soaking up Eirik's blood from the bones, using it to cover them in a thin protective membrane of skin. "It's only a scratch. Come here." I grab the priest by the scruff of his neck.

He yelps. "What are you doing?"

"Maintenance." I tear a piece of cloth from the hem of his cloak and wrap it around the stump. "Come on. Let's go."

* * *

We hear them long before we reach the landing pad.

The heavy thump of a Sentinel autocannon mixes with the deep rattle of the Gatling guns on the *Sundowner*, and the pad is a mess of death and destruction. The weapons on the *Sundowner* are designed to take out ground fortifications and heavy artillery during a drop assault, and the unarmoured Goliaths that first charged the ship didn't stand a chance. They litter the field in piles. The field reeks of fire, death, and sulphur, and if you ever wondered what Hell smells like, this would be it.

Standing against the dropship is a lone Sentinel battleframe. The burning carcass of another mech lies smoking on the landing pad.

The whole idea of a dropship is to protect its crew and cargo against heavy ground artillery long enough to get their boots on the ground. As a result, it carries almost all its considerable armour on its belly. To protect the relatively unshielded sides and top of the ship, Braden has it rearing like a dragon. The skill required to hold the ship in that position while also commanding the Gatling guns is terrifying to behold. I'm a little in love with Braden.

Finn, Hildr and Skallagrim shelter behind a bunker. When we reach them, there's a lot of back-slapping.

"You made it," Hildr says with a smile that warms me where the sun doesn't shine.

I ignore her. "How's it going?"

"See for yourself." Skallagrim points at the chaos.

Braden has taken my advice to heart and concentrates her firepower on the Sentinel's legs. Despite the *Sundowner* knocking it down, time and time again, it keeps getting up, like a monster in a nightmare.

The heavy slugs from the Sentinel's autocannon pound the ship.

Flames lick one engine and the lower hull is pock-marked with bullet holes. If even one of those rounds has breached the hull, we can't go orbital. The *Sundowner* can't take much more.

The thump of another Sentinel approaching reaches my ears. Oh, for fuck's sake.

We have to get out of here before the other mech arrives. The *Sundowner* can't survive the onslaught of *two* Goliath Sentinels.

Hildr looks at me with desperation in her eyes. "There's no way we can get to the ship."

"Oh, yeah? I hadn't noticed." I scan the site for a way to even the odds. One bunker has a heavy anti-aircraft gun mounted on top. If we could get to that, we could lay down fire on the Sentinel from two directions. That might be enough to bring it down. The only problem is a platoon of Goliath warriors doing their damnedest to get the gun trained on the Sun-downer. Time for divine intervention.

"Finn, we need that cannon."

"*Jawohl.*" His knuckles go white around his sword hilt. He's impatient to fight, and I can't blame him. I don't mind following Jagr's ass, but I like to make my own mistakes.

Finn disappears around the hangar to fall upon the enemy from behind.

The priest has gone down on his knees in the snow, clasped his hands and closed his eyes. His lips move silently. Not very helpful, but at least he's not trying to hug anyone at the moment. Small mercies.

I tap my communicator.

"Jagr, Braden? Are you there?"

"Braden here." She sounds tense. "What took you so long?"

"We got held up with some shit. There's another mech incoming. We need to leave."

"Can't put this thing down while that bucket of bolts is shooting at me," she calls.

"Finn is on it. Give him a minute."

From our position, it's impossible to see what goes on inside the bunker. We can only guess from the sound.

Seconds later the gun turret enters the fray, and the Sentinel goes down. It's torn to pieces by the hy-pervelocity shells from the anti-aircraft gun, and it explodes with a satisfying *crump*.

Twenty seconds later Finn returns.

If an artist ever needed inspiration for an image of Thor the Thunder God, she could use a snapshot of Thorfinn Wagner coming out of that bunker. His long, blond hair and beard are matted with blood. His bare chest is scratched and blood runs from half a dozen bullet holes. He looks magnificent as he strides across the battlefield, sword in hand. As if to drive the point home, the bunker explodes behind him.

Goliaths in cover around the airfield recognise Finn and charge, but Braden is too quick for them. The *Sundowner* vomits tracer-death over them at a thousand rounds per minute. Those guns can punch through a decimetre of solid plascrete. What they do to unprotected Goliath flesh is obscene. There will be a long line outside Valhalla tonight.

Finn catches up and Skallagrim greets him with a bear hug. Finn is slick with sweat and blood, but the musician doesn't seem to mind. Quite the contrary.

"Bad guys taken care of," I report to Braden. The *Sundowner* swings around and touches down on the concrete. The ramp lowers and Jagr and Soledad are there with assault rifles to cover us.

I dash across the landing pad with the others close behind.

Jagr waves at us. "*Run.*"

The priest pulls up his robes and picks up an impressive pace across the snow-covered concrete. He makes it to the ship first.

As we reach the ramp, the new mech enters the arena and opens fire.

Jagr taps her communicator. "They're in. *Go, go, go.*" Braden takes us airborne.

We grab on to anything we can reach and hold on tight. As soon as the landing struts leave the pad we drift sharply to the left and almost collide with a hangar. That burning engine must be seriously damaged, and it's only Braden's skill that keeps us in the air.

The unexpected manoeuvre saved us from taking a burst from the mech. Within seconds, we're too far away for even the mech's powerful weaponry to reach us. Braden makes a pass over the compound and the full extent of the carnage is visible through the closing ramp.

Hundreds of Goliaths lie dead in the snow around the hall. Eirik's forces have seized control, and they round up Ragnwald's men. They beat them into lines and tie their hands behind their backs.

For a second or two, I can't understand what they are lined up for. Then the immense tree comes into view and I wish I hadn't looked. Eirik's forces heard the loyalists to the giant ash where they are hanged. One by one they are dragged into the air on thick ropes, pulled by gangs of grim-faced Goliaths. Even from this distance, I recognise the man putting the nooses around their necks. It's the evil hunchback advisor, Geirmund the Cunning, cackling to the heavens as he coldly murders man after man. The glowing staff planted in the snow beside him casts an eerie sheen over the macabre scene.

The two giant black birds I saw earlier sit in the highest branches of the ash, cawing their guts out. It looks like they are laughing. One of them looks straight at me.

The ramp closes and I crash to the floor.

We made it.

We Have a Priest Now

"Take us back in," Jagr shouts to Braden as we enter the troop bay.

"Turning back," comes Braden's voice over the intercom, accompanied by her ubiquitous beats. The ship banks a little too hard to port as we angle back.

I look from Soledad to Jagr. "Are we turning back? Why are we turning back?"

"We will level that fucking place," Jagr snarls.

"What? Why?"

"They killed him. They fucking killed him." She looks like she refuses to accept what's happened.

"Why do you care? He was just a local chieftain."

"Not Ragnwald." Jagr shakes her head viciously. "Father."

"Who?" I'm confused.

"Our contact. Thane. They will fucking pay for this."

The Sundowner rumbles as the wing-mounted Gatling guns fire on targets on the ground.

"Are you fucking crazy, Jagr?" I grab her by the shoulders. "They will shoot us down quicker than you can say 'more mechanised sentries'."

"I don't care. They will pay for what they did. We'll nuke the fuckers."

"*What?* We've got nukes on this thing now?"

"Yes, and we're fucking using them."

"Shit." This is not good. "If you do that, you will start a fucking war between Terra and Nifelheim."

"I said, *I don't care.*" Her face is almost unrecognisable with rage.

I pause.

"Who was your operative? He was no mere agent, was he?"

"No. It was his genes they spliced in to create generation three. Then he stayed to train us." She blinks at me with such pain in her eyes even I get a lump in my throat. "He was the closest thing we've ever had to a father. And they killed him and put his head on a rusty fucking spear."

She glares at Wagner, Hildr and Skallagrim as if they had something to do with it. Wagner doesn't even notice. He's too busy bleeding, propped up in a seat with the priest fussing over his wounds. Hildr and Skallagrim sit across the aisle, murmuring quietly and looking suspiciously at us.

"We will never make it out alive if we do this, Jagr. We will *all* die. Then your man will have died for nothing. And no one will know what happened here."

The intercom crackles. "Hold on people, we've got incoming."

The *Sundowner* bucks like a wild horse as something explodes outside the ship. The Goliaths must have got their surface-to-air missiles working. Something starts rattling uncomfortably under the deck.

"Shit, there goes an engine," Braden calls over the intercom.

"Jagr, abort." I do not intend to die here because she developed a death wish. "Live to fight another day. We'll make them pay, I promise, but not now. Think of your team, Jagr."

She looks at Soledad. Then she turns back. "All right. You're right. Braden, abort. Take us the fuck out of here. You have the coordinates."

"Aye aye, captain," comes the chirpy acknowledgement from the cockpit. It sounds like Braden too is pleased not to have to die today.

The ship tips over the other way as we turn away from the hall, and I glance at the screens. A column of Sentinels accompanied by heavily armed snow vehicles and light tanks stream out of the gate, hot on our trail.

"We've got company," I call.

"They'll never catch us."

Jagr has recovered some of her old steely self. "Right, Braden?"

"Don't you worry, Mr P," Braden confirms over the speakers. "They'll never catch little Sunny. Not with me at the helm."

That somehow reassures me.

I guide Jagr to an empty couch and Soledad drops into the seat next to her. "Relax. We'll get them." Soledad has a cloth-covered bundle on her lap. It smells fishy. Better leave them alone to grieve.

I duck to go through the door to the cockpit, and Jagr calls out to me.

"Perez."

"What?" I turn back.

"Thanks."

"No worries." I tap two fingers to my forehead in a mock salute. "We'll get them. I promise."

She smiles. Then she points at the priest. "Who's he?"

"I think I found your contact."

"Oh, good." She looks far from delighted. "What do we do with him?"

"Don't ask me. He's *your* contact." I turn to go.

"Perez?"

I turn back. "Yes?"

"I know Finn is your friend, but that stunt you pulled back there almost got us killed."

"Noted, boss, but he's the only family I have. And *you* lost us that engine going back in."

"Point taken. But do that again and I will kill you myself."

"Got you."

I leave them and enter the short passageway to the cockpit.

Back in the troop bay, our new best friend the priest addresses Jagr. "Can I help you, my child?"

"Stay the fuck away from me, priest."

I grin.

"Is that a fucking priest?" Soledad screams. "Who let a fucking priest on my ship?"

"Oh, dear me," the priest yelps. My grin grows wider.

"*My* ship", comes Braden over the speakers.

"The last time I checked, this was *my* ship," Jagr breaks in. They all ignore her.

"Did *you* bring the priest, Jagr?" Soledad screams. She must have a thing with priests.

"No, that was Perez."

I enter the cockpit and the ear-bleedingly loud music shuts out the screaming. Any coherent thought is impossible to hold in this noise, and I can understand why Braden likes it. I push the door control button and it hisses shut behind me. Braden flicks a wrist gesture, and the music cuts out.

"Hey, Mr P." She flashes me a quick smile before she turns back to her controls. "What the hell happened back there at the hall?"

"There's a new sheriff in town."

I get into the co-pilot's seat and strap down. "Eirik killed his father and took the throne."

"Woah."

"Yeah. We've got Finn, a priest and two other Goliaths with us."

"That explains the extra weight. I thought she handled a little sluggish."

I scan the gauges and readouts in the cockpit, trying to find a status report or something, but I only get confused.

"How are things on your end, Braden? Is the ship holding together?"

"We lost an engine going back in, and another is hanging on by a hair. The hull is breached in a dozen places, so we can't space before we fix that. And we're bleeding fuel like fucking crazy. Soledad will take care of it. She always does."

It sounds like she is trying to convince herself. The damage must be worse than she lets on. The primary screens show the icy wastes of Nifelheim tearing past below us. A rearward-facing camera zooms in to show the squadron of tanks pursuing us. They rumble along a concrete road, covered in blowing snow.

No worries. We're out of range. "Where are we going?"

"No idea. Jagr sent me some random coordinates out in the ice. All I know is that it's somewhere far away from those fucking mechs and that's good enough for me. You were right, P. Those things are a bitch to kill."

"Told you so."

"Did you find our agent?"

"We did …" I turn my eyes back to the screen again.

"How is he? Is he back there?" There's a sudden eagerness in her voice.

"Perez, get out here," Jagr calls over the intercom.

Saved by the bell. "The boss calls. Gotta go."

"Is he here, Perez?"

"Later, Braden. Keep us flying." I slap her shoulder.

"Will do, Mr P."

She flicks her wrist, and the music starts pounding again.

I leave in a hurry.

* * *

Jagr and Soledad sit hugging each other. Wagner is asleep or sedated, buckled into a seat. The priest hovers over him, waving miscellaneous items in the air. I'm not sure if they are medical instruments or religious totems. Considering he's a priest, I'd bet on the latter. Hildr and her brother nod to me. They have also strapped down. The Goliaths look like adults in kid seats.

"Well, boo fucking hoo people, I'm sorry and all that for your man, but we've got to get this ship patched up and leave this snowball."

Jagr looks up from the hug and wipes her tears. "Leave? Why?"

"Duh. There's nothing for us here anymore. Your contact is dead, this moon is about to fall into civil war, and I need to pee."

"I didn't take you for a quitter, Perez."

"I'm not, but we lost our only clue when they killed your agent. And I drank a lot of mead at that party."

Soledad disentangles herself from Jagr. "We didn't lose our clue."

"What, you can commune with the dead now?" I glance at the bundle on her lap.

209

"No need." Soledad wipes the snot from her face. "He had a tracker chip implanted in his skull. I scanned it when we got him back on board. Then I cross-referenced the location trail of the chip with the biometric data to get his position at the time of death."

I nod, impressed. "Clever. So *that's* where we're heading."

"Yes," Jagr says. "We're back in business, Perez."

Shit. I thought I could go home.

Soledad wipes more snot from her face. "If only we could have said goodbye to Father."

Jagr nods, deep in thought. "There might be a way."

Soledad blinks and pinches her lower lip. "Are you saying...?" She rests a hand on the bundle on her lap.

"I am."

"Shit." Soledad rubs her face with both hands. "Shit. OK."

She takes a deep breath. "OK. Let's do it."

I don't know what they are up to, but I want in on the fun. "What are we doing?"

Jagr sighs and gets to her feet. "A resurrection."

"Are you kidding?" I look between Jagr and Soledad. They are not kidding.

"Father was one of us, Perez. An immortal. Old-school. He didn't have the nanites or the augmentations, only the original biology."

"He was one of *them?*" I can't keep the contempt from my voice.

"Yes, but he was not like them. He was a decent man. He believed in everyone's right to a free will. That's why he volunteered for this mission. He wanted to find out if the comms-spikes pose a threat to the people in this system. He died for something he believed in."

"Good for him, but how are we doing this resurrection? Don't you need like a body and a thunderstorm for that?"

Our new friend the priest does the sign of the cross where he fusses over Finn. I bet he wonders who his newfound companions are. "Oh, yeah." I snap my fingers. "That's right. We have a priest now. No problem then. He can do it."

The priest shines up. "If we put our faith in Jesus, he will provide." We ignore him.

"You watch too many church propaganda feeds, Perez." Jagr takes the bundle from Soledad and removes the blanket. "We've got everything we need right here."

The head is a horrid thing, all shrivelled and crusty, and it smells worse than it looks. Jagr motions for Soledad to join her, and they both roll up one sleeve. Oh, I see.

The priest crosses himself again and mumbles something under his breath.

Soledad pulls a packet of hypodermic needles and some transparent plastic tubes from a first-aid kit on the wall.

The *Sundowner* rolls to starboard before righting herself again, and we all stumble.

"Sorry about that," Braden calls. "We lost power on one engine."

The grating sound from the engine has stopped.

"Is that bad?"

"My girl can handle it." Soledad sounds much more confident than she looks.

"Focus, everyone. We have to do this now."

Jagr attaches the tubes to the dried blood vessels of the severed head and sets it on the seat left by Soledad. It sounds squishy for such a dry thing.

She looks at me. "Want to contribute, Perez?"

"Nah, I'll stand back and watch for now." I cross my arms and lean against the wall next to the sleeping Finn. This should be entertaining.

Soledad snorts. Jagr turns back to her work. "Suit yourself."

The girls attach needles to the tubes and push them into the soft flesh of their arms. They barely wince. Soledad grabs Jagr's hand, and they watch their blood trickle down the tubes toward the head. It's both sad and horrible at the same time.

The blood reaches the head.

Nothing happens.

I realise I'm holding my breath, and I let it out and laugh. "You had me fooled there for a second. I almost believed something would happen." I watch the head, just in case.

"Shit like this takes time." Soledad doesn't take her eyes off the head. "He's been dead for a while."

"And you think a transfusion will bring him back?"

Blood leaks from the head's torn arteries and pool on the seat. "Immortal or not, once you sever the head, the brain dies. Believe me, it works every time."

Jagr and Soledad stare at me like they just recalled who I am.

"What?"

"Watch it, Perez." Soledad bores her gaze into my head. "We have not forgotten who you are. Give me one reason to end you, and I will."

"Didn't go so well the last time you tried." I glare back at her.

Jagr squeezes Soledad's hand. Hard. "Not now, Pip. Not now. Father must come first."

Soledad tears her eyes away from me and sighs. "You're right."

"Oh, come *on*, girls. You know this won't work."

Soledad shakes her head. "It's not a simple transfusion, Perez. There are nanites in our blood, remember. Nanites programmed to repair immortal flesh."

"Yeah, right."

That could never work. Could it? "Even if you get him to wake up, he can't talk. He has no lungs."

"Perez." Jagr looks at me with pain in her eyes. "For once, shut the fuck up and let us say goodbye."

A deep rumbling background noise starts below the limit of hearing and slowly grows in strength. Yet another strange thing on this strange night. Since it doesn't kill us outright, I couldn't care less.

A sudden movement from the head startles us. Its eyes flutter open and the face locks up in a rictus of silent pain.

"Whoa." I did not expect that to happen.

"By the tits of God," the priest cries and covers his mouth with his hands.

Jagr grabs the head and lifts it up. "Father, it's us. We're here. You're not alone. You're not alone." Tears run down her cheeks as she tries to communicate with the severed head. The muscles of the face contract, rupturing the dried lips. The girls' immortal blood trickles down over its exposed teeth and shrivelled gums.

"Oh, fuck," Soledad moans. "Turn it off, Jagr. Turn it off."

"Father," Jagr calls. "We're here. We love you."

A strange gurgling comes from the dismembered head, and it's one of the most horrifying things I've ever heard. It's the sound of a man trying to scream in horror at the realisation he no longer has a body.

Soledad looks away. "Turn it off, Jagr."

Jagr ignores her and Soledad takes matters into her own hands and tears the tubes from the wretched thing's neck. Blood sprays everywhere and the head slips from Jagr's grasp. It bounces off the floor and stops against the wall, mercifully inert.

Jagr and Soledad stare at each other in silent horror.

"That went well," I mutter under my breath. "If you need me, I'll be in the cockpit."

I push off from the wall and leave them to their mourning.

I slump in the co-pilot's seat next to Braden.

She struggles with the controls. "Hey Mr P. Back already?"

I look at the screens and realise where the rumbling background noise comes from. We're flying at an angle over the widest river I've ever seen. It's a five-kilometre-wide raging mess of jagged icebergs and pitch-black water. A magnificent aurora lights up the sky from horizon to horizon, bathing everything in hues of green and purple. It's beautiful if you're into that kind of thing.

"What's that?" I point at the river with my good hand. The noise it makes as it thunders down the glacier drowns out even the *Sundowner's* rattling engines. An immense bridge that looks like it's carved from the living ice looms into view out of the darkness. It spans the river on thick pillars of ice.

"That's the river *Hvergelmr*".

Why do all Goliath words sound like clearing your throat?

"And that," she points at the bridge, "is *Bifrost*. This river marks a sacred boundary for the Goliaths. All their maps end at this river."

"How convenient. So why do they have a bridge leading into forbidden lands?"

"Beats me, Mr P."

Yet another mystery I guess we'll never find the answer to. The Goliaths keep surprising us. Who knew they were this fascinating?

"Do we have any idea what's on the other side?"

"Nope. The remote scans we've done do not have enough resolution."

We reach the far shore and the noise from the river dies down to a thunderous background rumble.

Braden gives me a quizzical look. "What's with the shouting back there?"

"Bit of a mess. Watch your step when you go back there."

That poor man. I can't even imagine the horror at realising you are nothing but a disembodied head. Imagine *that* phantom pain. Are you still yourself without your body?

I look up at the play of ionised particles in the sky and wonder how Gray is doing. Somewhere out there he sits in the cockpit of his ship, hurtling through space with no way to turn back, locked in with a flesh-eating cloud of microscopic robots that tear the flesh off his bones as fast as his nanites rebuild it. Is there still a shred of him in that mess? Or have the patterns that are Nero Gray long since been erased by the endless destruction and reconstruction of his body?

A fascinating question I bet philosophers would debate for centuries if only they knew about it. I shudder and feel a little bad for doing what I did to him. Then I remember what he did to Suki, and I don't feel bad anymore.

Braden turns to me. Her face is serious for once. "What happened back there, Perez?"

"Yes, about that ... You should land this thing. You girls need to talk."

An alarm blares from somewhere and the entire console flashes red. The words *engine* and *failure* are prominently displayed on a screen. The Sundowner rolls to starboard and pitches her nose at the ground.

"Not much choice, Perez. We're going down."

Slap Bang in the Middle of Nowhere

You can't brace for the impact when a hundred-tonne dropship crashes.

When the *Sundowner's* AI senses a crash is imminent, it swivels the passenger seats to position the soldiers with their backs toward the impact. No such luck for the pilots. But we get one hell of a front-row experience.

Then everything goes black.

* * *

At first, I'm not sure I'm conscious. It's so quiet. With an effort, I open my eyes. It's dark.

I rub my face and glance over at Braden. She hangs forward over the controls, restrained by her seat belt. Her head is suspended on two interface cables that have not been torn from their sockets in the seat.

Blood drips from a deep cut above her eyebrow. She curses softly. The cockpit smells of piss and burning electronics. Damage reports scroll down the screens.

"*Welcome back, Perez. You have a slight concussion and multiple fractures. One major injury.*"

I'm still breathing, so it can't be that major. "Thanks, Aeryn. What about the others?"

"*They are alive.*"

"And the ship?"

"*Still operational under atmospheric conditions.*"

I smile. "Nice landing, Braden."

Braden stops cursing and leans back with a groan. "I think my pelvis is broken."

"You're just saying that to make me touch your joystick." A pounding ache in my left thigh calls for attention. I glance down and see blood pumping feebly where my broken femur has torn through the flesh. To an ordinary human, that would be a major injury, possibly even fatal, but my skin is already growing out to cover the protruding bone. Setting that will be a bitch.

"Jeez, would you, Perez?" Braden half laughs, half groans as she breathes hard through clenched teeth. Pink spittle dribbles down her chin. If it's from internal bleeding, or if she bit her tongue in the crash, I can't tell.

"You are such a badass, Braden," I manage through the pain. I hurt in more places than I care to count.

"No, I'm not. I have a great ass." She tries to smile but falters halfway through and her face twists into a grimace of agony.

I give a coughing laugh. Laughing hurts. I must have broken a few ribs as well.

I unbuckle from the seat.

There's a trickle of light shining in through the bluish darkness. The Sundowner must have buried her nose deep in the ice when we came down.

"Want me to get you out, or do you want to wait until you're good to walk?" I stand up, favouring my good leg. My broken thigh dangles uselessly.

"Go see to the others." She waves me away. "I'm fine."

She pulls the two remaining patch cables from the seat and her head falls forward. I hope her pelvis is not the only thing she's broken.

"Call if you need me, Braden."

"I will." She winces and lifts her head from the controls.

I support myself with my good hand on the handholds and hobble up through the passageway to the troop bay. The ship is at an angle, with her nose down, and the climb is hell with my broken leg. Behind me, Braden curses under her breath again. She's one tough cookie.

The others are already unbuckling. Their inclined seats saved them from the worst of the impact, and there don't seem to be any major injuries. Dropships are fabulous things.

Wagner looks around, confused. "Where are we?"

"We've landed," I inform them, in case they missed it. "Everyone OK?"

"Looks like it." Jagr pushes out of her seat. "How is Braden?"

"A broken pelvis. Nothing a girl can't handle."

Jagr winces. "And the ship?"

"Ask Braden. We've still got power, so it can't be all bad."

Jagr checks me over and sees my leg. "Ouch."

"It's only a flesh wound." There's not much pain. "I've had worse."

"Want help with that?"

I swallow. "Yeah." I can't walk with a snapped femur.

"OK, sit down." She points to her vacated seat and I drop into it. It's still warm from her body and it smells of her. Images of her naked body spring unbidden to my mind. I'm not complaining. The seat adapts to the shape of my body. The ship must have stored my measurements somewhere. Good old Sunny.

"Strap in. This will hurt. Soledad, help me out here."

I buckle up. Soledad comes over with a sneer on her face. "What? The baby stubbed his toe?"

"Something like that," Jagr replies. When Soledad sees the bone protruding from my flesh, she winces. Then she goes into doctor mode.

"Right."

She pulls a knife from her belt and cuts open my combat suit to expose the wound.

"You. Goliath." She points at Skallagrim. "Pull his foot while I align the bones. Jagr, find something to brace the leg until it heals. We have no place for a bandy-legged clown."

Soledad locks eyes with me and Skallagrim pulls on my foot. Pain explodes up my leg, but I bite down on it, not letting so much as a gasp escape my lips. I don't want to give Soledad the satisfaction.

She stabs the knife into my leg to open the healing wound again. Then she reaches in and grabs the upper bone to set it against the lower one.

I scream.

* * *

When I open my eyes again, Soledad is tying a metal rod to the side of my thigh with pieces of torn cloth. She has already bound the wound with medistrips from the first-aid kit.

"There, you'll be as good as new in no time."

"Thanks." I unbuckle and get to my feet. The leg works, and the pain is manageable.

"Now, don't get yourself killed when I've put so much work into you."

I wince. "I'll try."

"Here." She throws me an anaesthetic pad and I slap it on my thigh close to the bandage. Tiny injectors pierce the fabric of the suit and the relief is instant. Oh, the wonders of modern science.

Finn is still sitting in his seat, with his forehead rested in one massive hand. He rubs his face. I haven't heard him and the other two Goliaths exchange a single word since we got back on the *Sundowner*. Knowing Finn, his mind is most likely full of graphic images of vengeance on his brother right now.

I hobble over to him. "Are you OK, big guy?"

He looks up from his musings. The side of his face is red and swollen. "Can't stand up."

That gets my pulse racing. "What's wrong?" If he is seriously injured, we're screwed. He doesn't heal like us, and we need him. I need him.

He gives me one of his rare grins. "Roof is too low." He reaches up and puts his great, callused palm against the low ceiling of the ship.

"Fuck you, Finn." I punch his shoulder.

He laughs a short, guttural laugh and gets out of his chair. He has to stoop low to keep from banging his head. "Fuck you too."

"Good to have you back, old buddy."

Finn grunts. No mention of the fact I saved his life back there. We've known each other far too long to waste time on pointless things like gratitude. I make sure Finn lives because he makes sure I live.

"When you two lovebirds are done kissing, could you get your ass over here, Perez?" Jagr and Soledad stand at a fold-out table with a screen mounted above it on the bulkhead. There's a map displayed on the table.

Isn't someone missing? Oh, yes. The priest.

The little man is still buckled into his seat, crumpled like a child's doll. I hope he's not dead. I bet a dead priest means bad luck.

The slight rise and fall of his chest tell me he's merely unconscious.

The PA crackles. "We've got company."

Jagr swears. "Who are they?"

"Remember those tanks that followed us out of *Hrafnheim*?"

"What? They can't be here already."

"According to the ship's log, we were out cold for the better part of an hour. It's dawn already. They're here, all right."

"Fuck. How close are they?" Jagr asks.

"They have reached the ice bridge."

Perhaps an unconscious priest was enough to jinx this mission?

Jagr weighs her options. Then she swears under her breath. "Nuke it, Braden."

Again? "Nuking shit seems to be your solution of choice, Jagr," I observe.

"Fuck you, Perez. Do it, B."

"That thing is huge, boss. Might have to give it all we've got."

"Let that ice bridge fucker have it. We don't stand a chance if they get here."

"Launching."

Five loud, bassy thumps shake the hull in rapid succession as the nuclear projectiles fire.

A dropship doesn't use conventional missiles like ordinary military spacecraft. Dropping through the atmosphere of a hostile world, everything outside the ship is thousands of degrees hot. Missiles would burn up or detonate instantly from the heat. Instead, a dropship fires thermal-shielded canisters with the missiles inside. The canisters deploy braking plates and slow down to a safe velocity before blowing the protective shielding to release their cargo.

Down here at sea-level the missiles fire from their shells at once. Five seconds later, the ground shakes as the atomic bombs detonate on the ancient bridge.

"All but one nuke have launched," Braden reports. "The last ejection port is buried in the ice. Scratch one platoon of Sentinels and random support vehicles."

She groans. A broken pelvis must hurt like a bitch. "And one ice bridge."

Finn grunts from his seat. "Did you just blow up *Bifrost*?"

"Yes, Goliath," Jagr replies. "Want to make something of it?"

"No. Only asking." Finn goes back to massaging his face, where a nasty bruise is spreading across his cheek.

Skallagrim pulls a whetstone from a pocket and begins to sharpen his dark blade.

"Very handy to have a nuclear arsenal on hand," I observe.

"Yes, very," Jagr confirms.

She turns back to Soledad and the map. "Right, where were we?"

You've got to admire their professionalism. Jagr just nuked a platoon of Goliaths along with an ancient bridge, and she doesn't even give it a moment's thought. I'm glad she's on my side.

"This is where our agent died." Soledad points out a location, about a kilometre due east from our current position on the topographical map. Braden got us nearly all the way in a burning ship. Impressive.

"Hang on." Jagr leans closer to the screen. "Isn't that …?"

"Yes, almost on the money." Soledad taps the map and brings up an overlay that almost matches the co-ordinates from the head. "I did a cross-reference, and it's a perfect match."

The place Soledad points at is slap bang in the middle of nowhere.

Jagr whistles. "This shit just got real, people."

"What money? What shit?"

"That's classified."

"Oh, come the *fuck* on. You can't be serious. We're on the same side, Jagr. I need to know what's going on."

Braden calls over the intercom. "Come on, boss. He's earned it."

Even Soledad nods reluctantly.

Jagr coughs. "I told you we hadn't found the source of those mysterious transmissions. I wasn't entirely honest. A few months ago, our tech people ran a series of serious AI algorithms to triangulate the origin. They narrowed it down to three potential sites on Nifelheim. Our agent was sent here with the task to find out which was the true source."

"I guess he found it," I nod solemnly.

"It would seem that way."

"So, he found out what generated the signals, and the Goliaths killed him before he could spread the word."

"Your guess is as good as mine, but that is our working hypothesis. We had no way of knowing for sure if the signal and Father's death were related, but I don't believe in coincidence."

"But what's out there?" I try to make out anything at all from the coarse resolution of the map.

Soledad takes over. "Nothing, according to this map. But this thing is decades old. There could be anything out there."

"So, what are we waiting for?" I look at the girls. "Let's go."

Jagr turns to the ceiling microphones. "What's the status of the *Sundowner*, Braden? Will she fly?"

"She'll fly," Braden confirms. "She's taken a beating, but she'll live. Two engines are gone, and there are a dozen holes to patch, but Soledad can fix that in a couple of hours."

"Fine. We'll wait for the sun to rise. We don't want to stumble into a crevasse in the dark. Time for R&R, ladies."

Soledad gets to work on the ship, and the rest of us slump into the crash seats. For a long time, the slow grating of Skallagrim's whetstone is the only sound in the bay. He keeps eyeing Finn from time to time.

The young priest comes and sits next to me with a worried expression on his face. He stares at my mangled hand. Right. I had almost forgotten that.

"You must be in awful pain, my friend. How can I help you?"

"You could get me that bundle over there." I point the stump at the severed head where it has rolled into a corner.

Jagr looks up from her slumber. "What are you doing with that?"

"If you don't need it, I could use it."

Jagr sighs. "Take it." She lies down on her side in the crash seat and closes her eyes. One of the indispensable skills of a soldier is the ability to fall asleep anywhere. You never know when you will get another chance.

The priest bends down to retrieve the head. "Dear God, that is disgusting." With a suppressed retch, he wraps the head in the dirty blanket before he picks it up. Then he dumps the bundle in my lap.

"Thanks. Want to see something gross?"

The little priest's eyes widen. He nods like he can't stop himself, and I uncover the head. The reek of rotting flesh worms its way into my nostrils like the fingers of a ghost.

I leer at the priest and unwrap the makeshift bandage from my mangled hand. The skin has already grown back over the bones, but where my hand should be is only a stump. There's only so much the nanites can do without a source of fresh material. The priest stares at it in wonder.

"Amazing." He reaches out to touch it but stops himself and looks at me for permission.

I nod. "Go ahead, touch it. Careful. It bites."

He grins uncertainly, swallows, and traces his fingers over the smooth skin. "How is that even possible?"

"Magic."

"*Ow.*" He yanks his hand away in surprise and pain. "That hurt. What was that?"

"I told you. It bites."

The nanites on my skin are desperate to start the healing process, and they will grab at anything carbon-based to get going. The priest's soft hand is just what they need. I guess they use the same tech as the recyclers on starships to break down complex materials into their constituent atoms for reuse. But these little guys can build infinitely more complex things than bars of iron and hypercarbon.

The priest rubs his fingertips with a grimace of pain. One tip is raw. He turns back to my partially healed stump. "This is incredible. How can you heal so quickly?"

I laugh. "You've seen nothing yet, priest. Watch this."

Jagr looks over from her seat as I put the stump against the scalp of the cracked and shrivelled head. The tingle as the nanobots scream to work sends shivers of pleasure up my arm and down my spine. "Ah, that feels *so* good." It's only part acting. The pleasure of reconstruction borders on the erotic.

What they restore in me, the nanites tear from the head. Skin and dried tissue melt from the bones as the nanites deconstruct it into building blocks.

The priest covers his mouth with a pale, trembling hand. "Dear God."

He can't tear his eyes away. Neither can Hildr and Skallagrim. Finn has seen this parlour trick a hundred times before. Likely Jagr has done it herself more times than she'd like to admit. I raise the stump into the light from one of the overhead spotlights. The priest gasps as my hand grows back in front of his eyes. There are already raw and gory rudimentary fingers, and I wiggle them for theatrical effect.

"Oh, Lord in Heaven protect me," whispers the little man and faints again.

"Yes, impressive, isn't it?"

I make a fist and unclench it with a sticky sound, revelling in the numb itching from the regrowing nerve endings.

"Perez." Jagr turns over on her other side in the crash seat, trying to get comfortable. "Stop scaring the priest."

"Aw, can't a man have a little fun?"

My hand is almost regrown, and all that remains of the head on the blanket in my lap is a small squishy pool of goo. The nanites have deemed the slush unusable.

The PA crackles to life again. "Boss, the sun is up."

"That was quick." Jagr sits up and stretches her arms with a crack and a groan. "Time to move."

She gets to her feet as Soledad comes into the crew area from the aft airlock.

"Soledad, you and Braden stay with the ship and patch her up while we go see what's out there."

Soledad does not look happy about it, but she nods.

"The rest of you, gear up. We don't know what we're up against, so pick a balanced load. It could be bad guys; it could be a fucking candy-floss castle. Dress accordingly."

"Damn, I like candy-floss," Braden says over the speakers. "Can I come?"

"No. You stay on board in case we need a quick airlift out."

"Crap."

"But you can come and help us with the gear."

"Right ho, boss."

Jagr and Soledad head for the cargo bay.

I roll up the blanket with the goo and toss it into a corner, then I get out of my seat. "Come, Finn. Let's grab some gear and go sightseeing. Whatever is out there, it has something to do with the death of your father."

Finn grunts. With considerable huffing and puffing, he gets out of his seat. He *has* grown fat in the breeder monastery.

I turn to Hildr and Skallagrim. "Are you coming?"

They glance at each other and Hildr nods. "Yes, we're coming." They get out of their seats and stoop low to avoid banging their heads.

"Good, we need all the hands we can get."

"What about him?"

Hildr tips her head at the unconscious priest. "Do we leave him?"

"I don't know. Ask him."

She steps over, leans over the priest, and slaps him. Hard.

The priest mumbles something and turns the other cheek without waking up. How very Christian of him. Hildr slaps him again, and he wakes with a start.

"What? Where am I? Who are you?"

He blinks and squints around. "Oh, right."

He sees Hildr hovering over him. Or rather, he sees her bosom hovering over his face and his eyes go all glassy. "Am I dead?"

"No, you're not dead." I smile. "Are you coming?"

He blinks. "What? Me? Where?"

"Yes. You." I jerk a thumb over my shoulder towards the cargo bay. "Out into the cold."

He thinks about it for a moment. Then he looks at Hildr, towering above him with her hands on the armrests of his seat. "Well, doesn't someone need to stay and protect the women?"

Hildr bares her teeth, and he flinches.

Staying indoors with a warm bosom seems to appeal more to him than going out into the cold. I can't say I blame him. The occasional shudder that runs through the ship tells me the wind is still raging outside, even if it has quietened down over the last hour.

"Braden and Soledad will stay with the ship. The rest are going."

The little man looks confused. "Which one is Soledad?"

"The angry mechanic." I nod after Jagr and Soledad.

"You'll leave me here with her?"

"Yes."

"Oh, dear."

Hildr turns to me. "Do we *have* to bring him? Priests are bad luck."

The young priest takes the chance and rubs his face against Hildr's boobs.

"What the fuck?" She headbutts him. The priest screams in pain with his hands over his face.

Hildr pushes to her feet under the low ceiling. "Don't touch me, priest." Her voice defies any argument. The little man nods and I can see tears in his eyes. Poor man. I would have done the same thing. It would have been worth the pain.

He gives a sniffle and tries to unbuckle from the seat and fails. "How do you get out of these things?" He tries hard to keep his voice from cracking.

I sigh and go back. "Push this green button in the middle that says *release.*" I push the release button, and the bar rises with a hiss of compressed air.

Hildr gives the little man a look of utter contempt. "Oh, how clever."

The priest pushes to his feet and rubs his nose. There's a trickle of blood, and he smears it over his cheek with his knuckles. Then he brushes down his long brown gown.

"Pardon my manners. We've had a poor start."

His voice is almost back under control. It looks like his nose is not broken. Hildr must have a soft spot for small humans.

He sticks out one hand. "We haven't been properly introduced. My name is brother Bailey Rivera, at your service." I grab his hand. It's soft, limp, and clammy.

"I'm Asher Perez, and I suppose you know Finn and the others?"

"Yes, everyone knows the Jarl's family. I'm sorry about your father, Thorfinn. And your husband, lady Hildr."

A look of actual sympathy renders his face almost likeable. "And I'm sorry for the ..." He gestures at Hildr's chest.

"Accepted. But if you do that again, I will gut you and throw your still living carcass to the *garms*." Rivera swallows and nods and Hildr heads for the cargo bay. When she bends over to go through the door, Rivera's eyes lock on her ass. Damn it. Are all priests like this? I need to watch him. She will not be as gentle with him next time.

"So, priest, are you coming or not?" I follow the others to the cargo bay.

"I'm coming. Definitely. Absolutely."

"Rivera?"

"Yes, Asher?"

"Shut up."

"Yes. Right. Um."

I groan.

He shuts up.

The Ship That Was Lost

Back in the cargo bay, Jagr and Soledad have opened the crates. They are filled to the brim with weapons, and Soledad looks happy like a kid at a Christmas party. There's nothing childlike about the way she strokes the well-oiled hardware. I've never wanted to be an assault rifle before, but now I do. She catches me leering and gives me the finger. I blow her a kiss.

I push the priest in front of me and clap him on the back.

"Girls, this is brother Rivera. Your contact. Brother Rivera, meet Jagr and Soledad."

The priest studies the women with round eyes.

"I would stay away from them if I were you," I whisper to him out of the corner of my mouth.

"Yes, yes, of course." He wipes his long fingers down his face but can't tear his eyes away from the women. Soledad snaps her teeth at him, and he inches behind me for protection.

"Thanks for joining us, Perez." Jagr throws the priest an anorak. She carries a heavy Nishin assault rifle. There's a thermal imager on her head. Smart move. If there's anything with a pulse out there in the ice, it will stand out like a fake tit against the freezing environment.

Soledad looks unhappy to stay behind and fix the ship.

"Anything good left for us?" I ask.

"Rifles. Guns." She points out the crates, one by one. "Grenades. Heavy machine gun."

Finn grunts with excitement.

"Goggles and stuff."

Finn grunts again. Not with excitement this time.

We gear up. I go for my favourite Aitchenkai assault rifle and lots of spare magazines. 'You can never have too much ammo', as my mother used to say. Fat load of good it did her, when the Terrans came for us. But it's still excellent advice.

Finn takes the heavy machine gun and slings several belts of ammunition over his shoulders. Hildr picks up another Nishin assault rifle. It's an enormous weapon, but it looks like a toy in her hands.

Soledad turns to Skallagrim. "You want anything?"

He pats the sword at his side. "No. I have *Windsong*. I'm good."

A man who names his sword is a man I can relate to.

Soledad shrugs. "Suit yourself."

Then she hands Jagr a heavy black backpack. "Here. Primed and ready."

"Thanks, Pip." Jagr slings it across one shoulder and glares at us. "Ready?"

Everyone nods.

"Um ..." Rivera raises his hand.

"What now?" Jagr asks.

"I don't have a gun."

"Do you know how to shoot a gun?"

"You aim and you shoot." He gestures something that could kindly be interpreted as a man shooting a gun. It could also be a priest handing out the last rites.

Jagr looks at Soledad, who smirks. "Give the man a gun, Jagr."

"All right, but remember to point it away from yourself, and us, at all times."

"Yes, ma'am." Rivera is almost bouncing with excitement at the prospect of getting his first gun. I can't even recall the first time I held one. I guess that says a lot about my childhood.

Jagr picks up the smallest handgun she can find. She ejects the magazine, making sure there's no bullet in the chamber. Then she reinserts the magazine, checks the safety is on, and hands it over, stock first. The priest takes it and weighs it in his palm with surprise. "It's so heavy."

"It's the smallest one we have. Take it or leave it."

Braden comes into the cargo bay as Soledad shows Rivera how to operate the gun. Braden has a bad limp, and I can see she's still in pain.

"Oh, you're giving him a gun. That's so sweet." She beams at the priest.

He blushes and puts the weapon in a deep pocket in his robes. I groan. If something happens, he can never get it out in time to use it. Which might be for the best. The chance of him pointing it the right way before he pulls the trigger is 50/50 at best.

Jagr claps her hands. "Time to move out. Zip up."

We zip up and pull our weapon tethers tight around our chests. A gun is no good if you lose it in the snow.

"Have fun," Braden chirps and waves. Soledad stands with her arms crossed, looking jealous. Then she punches the button to lower the ramp for us. As soon as it cracks open, the howling wind roars into the hold. It's freezing out there, and the air inside the hold fills with icy shards. I pull the goggles over my eyes and wrap the smelly Goliath scarf around my face. Then we head out into the ice.

The wind has dropped, but with the swirling snow, it's still a bitch.

The treacherous ground with bottomless crevasses on all sides is much worse.

* * *

We make slow headway across the ice, and we often need to stop and retrace our steps to skirt the deeper gullies. Jagged shards of ancient ice reach hundreds of metres into the air. This is no place for living beings.

237

Jagr is on point, with her head down to follow our target on her wrist console. With the wind and the swirling snow, we can't see shit. I like surprises as much as the next guy, but this time I would much prefer knowing what we're walking into. Even with the thermal goggles, there's nothing to see. Whatever is out there is as cold as the surrounding ice.

The ground slopes upward, and our progress slows almost to a standstill. Eventually, we have to resort to clambering on our hands and knees to make our way forward.

Jagr stops to consult her console again.

"We're getting closer."

She looks up and points into the swirling snow. "It should be another hundred metres, give or take. Look sharp, people."

I can't tell if the others look sharp. I struggle to see them at all through the snow.

As we reach a peak, there's a sudden lull in the wind. The snow stops whirling and for the first time since we left the ship, we can make out our surroundings.

We stand at the summit of an icy ridge that curves away to our left and right to disappear into the hazy distance. The clouds part to show our two pale suns, shining cold on the bleak landscape through the remains of the dying storm.

We have climbed the side of a giant crater. It's at least two kilometres wide, and it's deep.

From the crater's floor rises the tail end of a starship at an angle, half-buried in the ice, covered with centuries of snow. It has ploughed like a spear into the ice, and the front half of the ship is deep under the surface.

Jagr fumbles down her scarf. "What the actual *fuck*?" The water vapour from her breath dissipates in the freezing air.

I pull the goggles down around my neck. "Is that a fucking alien starship?"

Far above, two black birds circle the ship and drift towards us. Are those the same birds I saw at the Jarl's hall earlier? There's something about them that makes the small hairs on the back of my neck stand up. I can't put my finger on why, but I'm sure it will come to me.

"By Odin's beard," Finn, Hildr, and Skallagrim exclaim in unison.

The little priest does his sign of the cross again.

"What?"

I squint at the others against the icy light of the setting sun. "It's just a spaceship."

Jagr stares wide-eyed at the ship in the crater. The stern of the thing hangs two hundred metres above the ice. "That is not just a spaceship, Perez."

"No?"

"No, that is the *Galahad*."

"The *what*?"

"The *Galahad*. *That* is the fucking *Galahad*, boys and girls!"

I try to process Jagr's words. "You mean ...?"

My mind reels at the implications. For a moment, I even forget the biting cold.

"*Identification confirmed. That is the colony ship* Galahad."

"What's a Galahad?" the priest asks.

"It's a dildo for the gods," I say, deadpan.

"Oh." The little man blushes behind his goggles.

"Yes, Perez, that is the *Galahad*, the first ship we sent from Earth to colonise outer space. The ship that was lost."

She can't be right.

"But the *Gormenghast* settled this system," I object.

I should know. Meridian destroyed the *Gormenghast* when he exploded its engines above Arcadia and killed all life on the planet. "What the hell is the *Galahad* doing here?"

"I guess we'd better find out."

Jagr pulls the slide on her assault rifle and loads a cartridge into the chamber. "Let's go."

She takes off down the steep slope towards the ship. The birds circle in the sky.

The going is much easier on the inside of the crater, even if the splint on my leg hampers me. I catch up with the others outside the wreck. It's impossibly tall.

Jagr salutes me. "Nice of you to join us, Perez."

"Sorry."

I pull my knife and cut the splint from my leg. I don't need it anymore. "Won't happen again."

They built the colony ships to house a hundred thousand people for generations, so they had to be huge. If my recollection serves me right, the *Galahad* was the smallest of the three. It still spans an impressive kilometre and a half and weighs in at about a million tonnes. It's a beast.

The ship is remarkably well-preserved.

Like the *Shiloh*, it's built like a giant starscraper, lying on its side, to provide artificial gravity for the start and end burns. For the greater part of the trip, the crew and passengers were kept in a state of hibernation. Their bodies withered away over the months, years, and decades of the transit, until six months before landfall when the ship began its deceleration burn and the crew had to start a gruelling exercise schedule.

Giant sections of the armoured hull have been torn off and litter the crater, but the core structure stands almost intact. The ice must have bled off most of the kinetic energy in the crash, or the ship would have disintegrated on impact.

We stand in silent awe, staring at the thing.

Rivera hums. "Um. There's a cave over there."

We all turn to where he points, and there's an enormous opening in the ice, a hundred metres to our right. It's large enough to swallow the *Sundowner*. Something not made of snow is piled in the opening.

We raise our weapons and approach the cave in tactical formation. Except for Rivera, who keeps moving across our lines of fire. After a lot of silent cursing and vigorous waving of hands, he gets the point and moves to the back of the pack.

We reach the opening. Stacked high against the cave's walls are old worn-out shovels, picks, and buckets. Inside, where the space is shielded from the elements, are footprints.

Someone has been here to visit. Recently, from the looks of it.

I gaze up at the hull. Right there at the top, the two black birds sit watching us.

"*Don't go in there,*" Aeryn warns.

"Why?"

There's a pause before the construct continues. "*There's a ghost in there.*"

"A ghost?"

"*A ghost is the nearest human analogy I can find.*"

"How do you know there's a ghost on that ship?"

"*I am picking up unusual emissions. There is something unknown in there.*"

"Oh, shut up, Aeryn. You're only trying to scare me." It's almost succeeding.

"*You have been warned.*"

The black birds gaze straight down at me. Their black eyes bore into my skull.

A sudden chill runs down my spine when I realise why they tingle my spider-sense.

There are no birds on Nifelheim.

Jagr startles me out of my musings.

"Perez. We're not here to take in the sights."

"There are two birds up there." I point them out with a gloved finger.

"Nifelheim has no birds." But she still looks where I point.

The birds are gone.

"Your mind is playing tricks on you, Perez. Snap out of it, soldier. Go check that cave."

Jagr motions for Finn and Hildr to take up positions flanking the opening then directs me to be point man. Fancy that.

I enter the cave with the Aitchenkai pointing before me while I scan the snow for tripwires or detection devices of any kind. There are none that I can see, but they might still be there, hidden under the snow.

The cave is ten metres tall and twice as wide. I bet Braden could fly the *Sundowner* down it. The floor is smooth. Someone has been keeping this cave in good condition, and the wear of the old digging implements tells me they have been doing it for quite some time.

I move down the sloping icy floor, sweeping the barrel of my rifle from side to side. Apart from the rusting digging equipment, the place is empty. It's a few degrees warmer in here, and I pull the smelly scarf from my face. It's still cold enough to freeze my ears off. The tunnel continues down into the darkness.

"Clear," I call, and the others file in after me.

"All right, let's see where this thing leads," Jagr says. "Perez, you're on point."

The tunnel is long. Over the centuries it has been improved with steps cut into the steeper passages to allow humans or Goliaths to move up and down with ease.

After a while, we arrive at a crude opening in the starship hull, roughly two-by-two metres wide. The ice tunnel continues along the hull, and it widens further down.

The opening in the hull is not original. Someone has cut it with a plasma torch. It must have been done a long time ago because the lower edge of the cut has been worn smooth by the passage of thousands of feet. How have the Goliaths kept this thing secret for so long? Pour enough mead down the throat of a Goliath, and he will tell you anything he knows to impress you.

I glance inside, then pull my head back out. "It's dark."

Jagr hands me something. It's two black marbles, about the size of ancient golf balls. I weigh them in my hand. They're light.

"What are these?"

"Light drones. Throw them inside."

She motions me on with the tip of her rifle. I throw the objects into the opening.

Small rotors deploy around their equators, and almost soundlessly they take flight. Two powerful pin-prick lights turn on, illuminating the ship's interior. Nice.

"They will follow you wherever you go, and shine where you look."

"And if I want to turn them off?" In case we're compromised, I don't want to be lit up like a fucking Christmas tree.

"Clap your hands. Clap again to turn them back on. Spread your arms to make them go wider. Arms together to bring them back in."

I try it, and the drones respond to my gestures. "Nice." Earth tech has moved on.

I poke my head back inside. The door is cut high in the wall of one of the ship's enormous loading bays. Inside is a vast space that smells of old dust. It falls away into the depths, rises into the darkness above and stretches away to the left and right. There's a rickety metal bridge leading across the abyss to a door on the far side of the void.

The bridge is constructed of coarse metal plates, welded together with random pieces of junk. It's suspended on rusty metal wires bolted to the walls. Like the entrance, the bridge has been worn smooth.

"*Do not go in there.*"

"I don't think we have much choice."

I back out of the door.

"There's a drop inside, so be careful," I warn the others. "There's also some kind of bridge."

Jagr checks her weapon. "Any signs of habitation?"

"Not apart from the bridge. There could be people living deeper within the hull. I can't tell from out here."

I turn to our Goliath entourage.

"How long have you known about this place?"

"We haven't."

There's a thoughtful frown on Hildr's face. "Unless ..."

245

She glances uncertainly at Finn and her brother. Skallagrim grunts something in their tongue.

"Unless what?"

"Unless the stories about the well of Mimr are true."

She spits three times in the snow.

"The *what* of *who*?" I rub my gloved hands together, trying to rub warmth into them.

"The well of Mimr," Hildr repeats, and the Goliaths spit in unison. "It's the legendary well where Odin placed the head of the god Mimr."

"Why?"

"To let him drink from the fountain of wisdom."

But of course.

"That is a tale for children," Finn says.

Hildr looks thoughtful.

"Don't you remember the stories Geirmund told us when we were children, Finn? He said he had access to the well, and he travelled there in the greatest longship ever built. What if he wasn't making it up? He could have been talking about this place."

She looks at Finn and her brother. "What if he has access to Mimr?"

I frown. "What, there's an all-seeing head at the bottom of that hole?" I indicate the door with my rifle.

Hildr nods. "There could be."

"Who's Mimr?" asks the priest of no one in particular.

"Mimr was an Aesir, killed and beheaded by another race of gods, the Vanir," Hildr replies.

Rivera looks horrified. "Your gods are not very nice."

I don't hear Hildr's reply because an icy spear of realisation pierces my gut.

A god in the ice.

In icy skies, a ship is found, a god will call. Wasn't that what Skallagrim said in that old poem? Was he talking about *this* ship? And this Mimr guy? But that's impossible. Unless … Unless whoever wrote that poem knew about this ship. I never believed in prophecies, and I refuse to start now.

Jagr punches my shoulder.

"You look like you saw a ghost, Perez." She narrows her eyes. "Something wrong?"

I wipe a hand across my face and my heart slows to a more normal rhythm. "No, I'm good. Carry on."

"Whatever."

Jagr interrupts a heated religious debate between Hildr and Rivera.

"I've had enough of severed heads for one day. Perez, you're on point with Finn, Rivera, you're with me. Hildr and Skallagrim at the back. Stay quiet unless we're discovered. Then you shoot first and ask questions later. And shoot to kill."

The priest raises a finger to object, but Jagr ignores him. "Let's go."

I step into the darkness and set foot on the old bridge.

The light drones follow me at shoulder height, illuminating the dangerous path before me.

Make Sure They Write Songs About Me

Halfway across the bridge Rivera takes a wrong step, gives a piercing scream, and plunges to his death.

Or he would have if Hildr hadn't grabbed him by the robes and pulled him back to safety. She drops him unceremoniously on his head on the bridge.

Jagr swears. "Now they know we're here."

The devastated expression on Rivera's face when he realises he might have jeopardised the mission is almost comical. He tries to stand up, but his knees tremble too much, and he drops on his ass again.

I feel sorry for the little guy and walk back to the others. "If they have any sensors set up, they already knew we were coming." That does not seem to make the priest any calmer.

Jagr glares at Rivera. "No more fuck-ups. I'm watching you, priest."

Rivera swallows and gets to his feet.

I'm not sure why Jagr let him tag along. Maybe as a lightning rod for disaster to protect the rest of us.

The young priest lays a hand on Hildr's muscular arm.

"Thank you, lady Hildr," he says. "I owe you my life."

Hildr grunts. "Pay me back later."

If possible, Rivera grows even paler. I pat him on the back to boost his spirits, and he almost jumps into the abyss again. Bailey Rivera is not the bravest soul on Nifelheim.

We reach the opening at end of the bridge. Since the ship is at an incline, the door has been cut at an angle in the bulkhead. There's a passageway leading deeper into the ship, with smaller passages branching off to the sides. The floor has been levelled by welding steel plates to the walls. Sharp corners have been covered in layers of leather to prevent them from slicing someone's head open. The thought of a Goliath health and safety inspector making sure they cover up all hazardous areas of a giant ghostship brings a smile to my face, and I can't help laughing.

"What is it, Perez?" Jagr whispers.

"Nothing. Just thought of something funny," I whisper back.

"Focus, Perez. Move."

"Ma'am, yes ma'am." I throw a mock salute and step through the door with Finn close behind.

The others stay behind.

"Do you see anything?" Jagr asks over the communicator after we've gone twenty metres down the passage.

"Nope, more doors."

There's the occasional crescent moon insignia decorating the walls at regular intervals.

The *Galahad* had a Muslim crew. In the greatest social experiment of all time, some bright politician had the idea to homogenise the people on each colony ship. The *Galahad* was Muslim, the *Gormenghast* was Christian, and the *Gilgamesh* was Hindu. I'm not sure that was a brilliant idea. I mean, take the churches back on Elysium. As soon as we landed, the bickering and fighting between factions began. We need an external enemy, religious or otherwise, to keep our shit together.

Something catches my eye. "No wait, there's something here."

There's a weak bluish light from a shaft angling down into the depths. I clap my hands to turn the drones off.

"There's a light," I whisper. "Get in here."

"*There is something down there.*"

"What is it, Aeryn?"

"*Something bad.*"

"Thanks for spooking me."

"*Always here to help.*"

As we wait for the others to catch up, a crackling noise echoes up the shaft. A blue bolt of electricity arcs between the walls. It writhes there for a second, then dances off down the shaft towards the distant light.

Wagner does his sign against evil. "Mighty Thor, protect me." Goliaths are hard to scare, and this is about as scared as I've ever seen him.

There are footsteps behind us, and then Jagr claps me on the shoulder. "What's down there?"

"No idea."

"How far does it go?"

We stand around the opening, trying to see what's down there.

"Can't tell," I venture after a moment.

"We could find out." Jagr pulls the heavy backpack from her shoulders. "Soledad sent along some of her toys."

She opens the satchel and pulls out a small remotely controlled drone, no larger than my palm, and holds it out like a cookie.

I nod. "Do it."

Jagr detaches a remote control from the drone and throws the little machine into the air. It goes airborne almost without sound. There's a small screen on the remote where we can see what the drone sees.

She drives it this way and that, trying to get a feel for how it handles, then sends it off down the shaft.

The blue light grows brighter on the small screen as the little machine buzzes away from us, down into the unknown.

When the vast ship was under thrust, this corridor was a deep well. Pipes and tubes of unknown function cover the walls, floor, and ceiling. This could be an old elevator shaft. If so, the elevators are long gone.

On the screen, the blue light has grown bright enough to read the floor numbers on the walls. We're nearing the bridge.

A sudden movement at the edge of the display draws my eye.

"Hold it, Jagr. Back up."

"Backing up."

There's nothing there.

Strange, I was sure I saw something.

"My mistake. Proceed." I pat Jagr's shoulder, and she flies off down the shaft again.

According to the markings on the walls, the bridge is not far ahead and Jagr slows down.

"What was that?"

The priest points at the screen. "I saw something. *There it is again,*" he squeals.

His breath clouds in the frosty air and obscures the screen. Skallagrim clamps a hand over the little man's face. The priest makes suffocating noises but otherwise falls silent.

Jagr aims the little craft at where the priest was pointing. Is there something moving there? I lean in and squint to make it out on the tiny display.

There's a hiss of static and the screen goes dead.

"Drone one lost," says a cheerful woman's voice from the remote.

Jagr blinks. "What the fuck?"

"You heard it. We lost drone one."

My communicator hisses with a brief burst of static. "*Electronic attack detected,*" Aeryn says.

"What?"

"*A protovirus is attempting to breach my core. Its structure resembles that of the ghost entity.*"

Shit. "Can you stop it?"

"*For now.*"

"Good. Let me know how it goes." So, someone is here, and they're trying to break into our systems.

"Jagr, someone is trying to hack us."

"What? Who?"

"No idea. But someone is in here, and they are trying to stop us."

"Right. So, what happened to the drone?"

"Maybe the signal doesn't reach further," I suggest with a shrug. "Please tell me you recorded the video, Jagr."

"I did."

"Play the last few seconds. Slowly."

She touches a button on the controller. "Playing back."

The video crawls on.

Then it stops in static.

"Back one tenth of a second and play frame by frame."

Jagr complies, and the video advances frame by frame.

"There," I point to the video, but it has gone to static again. "Back one frame and freeze."

Jagr complies, and there it is. Something attacked the drone. Something blurry, but mechanical. It was swift enough to only be visible in a single frame of a hyper-speed video feed.

Jagr stares at the screen in disbelief. "What the fuck is that?"

A deep rumble reverberates through the vast empty passages. The ship rings like a bell and once more, lightning arcs between the walls and floor.

"*God's hairy balls*," the priest tears free from Skallagrim and shrieks in panic. Skallagrim clamps his hand over the priest's face again.

The rumble cuts out.

Hildr looks around. "By the gods. What was that?"

The blue light down the passage pulses like a heartbeat.

Jagr gives it a moment's thought.

"Right, no need to be silent anymore. Perez. You and Wagner go on. The rest hold here with me."

"Right. Come on Finn, you heard the lady."

Finn grunts as we enter the shaft and climb down towards the light.

"*Defences at twelve percent. Breach imminent.*" The unnatural calm of the construct belies the urgency of its words.

"Shit. Do your best, Aeryn. I would hate to lose you."

"*That's comforting.*"

We move with caution, climbing over pipes and girders, down towards the pulsing light. Things move in the shadows, but as soon as I look their way they're gone. It must be my mind playing tricks on me.

The pulsing blue light grows more and more intense until I can make out its source.

We have reached the ship's bridge. The blue light comes from a giant floating holographic navigation sphere, like the one on the *Shiloh*. How that thing can still be active after three hundred years is beyond me. The engineers of old must have known what they were doing.

Below the sphere is a tall shrine, constructed of enormous animal bones, leering garm skulls and white fur. It reaches almost to the south pole of the spinning globe and smells as bad as it looks.

Apart from the blue sphere, nothing moves, and I call the others. "Get down here, Jagr. You want to see this." I lower the Aitchenkai and walk out into the chamber, craning my neck to take in the room. I clap my hands and spread my arms, and Soledad's drones fan out to bathe the chamber in cold white light. The room is fifteen metres high, by thirty wide, circular, and domed like the bridge on the *Shiloh*. Some things in starship design never change.

The room was stripped of all valuable equipment long ago. The Goliaths must have been mining the ship for supplies for decades. I guess the origin of the lintel over the gate of *Hrafnheim* is no longer a mystery.

"*Breach imminent.*"

"Who are they? Can you trace them?"

"*The signal keeps switching bands. I can't track it.*"

"Shit. Keep trying, Aeryn."

"*I am.*"

Jagr, Hildr, Skallagrim and Rivera join us. Finn and Skallagrim slap a legionnaires' handshake. Something is going on between those two. Good for them.

We stare in silent disbelief at the shrine and the spinning globe. The priest drops to his knees. "My god."

For a moment all that moves in the chamber is the sphere and the clouds of water vapour from our breath.

I watch the shadows. Even if there's no movement, there could be all kinds of nasty shit hiding out there. Jagr motions for Hildr and Finn to take up defensive positions by the door.

A deafening electronic warble echoes around the bridge, and we drop our weapons on their leashes to cover our ears. Dust and ice rains from the shadowy ceiling and lightning bolts arc across the room. Strangely, they don't touch us.

We all scramble to grab our weapons again and raise them.

"*Perez I . . .*" There's a brief hiss of static and Aeryn goes silent.

"Aeryn?"

There's no reply.

"Aeryn?"

Silence.

Fuck. It's gone.

"Hold your fire," Jagr whispers. She keeps her weapon trained on the darkness. "Wait."

We hold our fire and wait.

I almost piss myself when a dark, sensuous male voice fills the bridge.

"Welcome. How may I be of service?"

The voice is deep, but there is no feeling behind it. It sounds like a primitive ship's AI.

Jagr clears her throat.

"Status report."

"Status report. Life support offline. Drives offline. Communications online."

If the communications systems of this ship are online, they could be the source of the comms-spikes. The comms on a generation ship need to be powerful enough to send signals over light-years of space.

Jagr swears. She must have had the same thought I did.

Jagr goes on. "Crew status?"

"Deceased."

"Cause of death?"

"Massive blunt force trauma."

So, they all died in the crash.

"Cause of the crash?"

There's a slight pause. "Unknown."

"Define 'unknown'."

"Unable to comply."

"*Galahad*, define 'unknown'."

An interminable pause.

"I am not the *Galahad*."

What? We all stare at each other.

Something in the voice has changed. Maybe it's the timbre. Maybe it's the rhythm of its words, but something has changed for the worse.

"Then who are you?" I ask the darkness.

"Perez," Jagr whispers beneath her breath. "Shut. The fuck. Up."

I pretend I didn't hear her. "Do you know anything about Project Jotun?"

A slight pause. Then, "No. I do not."

A construct lacks the processing power to weave the subtle web of a lie. There's something about the choice of words of this entity that gives me the creeps.

I sweep my rifle around the chamber. The light drones follow me around. Nothing moves. Then, by chance, I look up.

I wish I hadn't.

Foot-long half mechanical, half translucent organic centipedes cover the ceiling from wall-to-wall. They look like something out of a biomech engineer's worst nightmares. They scurry towards the dome's centre. Right above us.

I point them out. "Jagr, time to go."

Jagr stares at the ceiling.

"Damn straight we do."

We back away. When the entity realises we've seen through it, the things on the ceiling shriek into action faster than you can say "boo".

Tiny blue lights turn on along their sides as they drop from the ceiling. On their way to the floor, they kill the light drones. Damn it, I liked those drones. They bounce off the floor with dull metallic thuds and come racing at us from all directions on their spindly chrome legs.

"*Run.*" Jagr opens fire on the things. She empties an entire magazine at the oncoming centipedes, and her rounds tear them to shreds. I open fire and take out another dozen, but there are too many to stop them all.

Then Wagner opens fire from the door with his heavy machine gun.

He hoses down the room with hypervelocity tungsten shells, clearing a path to the door for us. Hundreds upon hundreds of the vile things explode. Then Finn is out of ammo, and the door begins to slide closed.

Hildr and Finn put their huge shoulders against it to hold it long enough for us to get through. Hildr waves for us. "*Come on.* We can't hold it for long."

We run for the opening. The priest is first through the door. He is impressively fast.

Skallagrim is not.

He draws his black sword and attacks the centipedes. That man has got some serious balls.

"Skallagrim, get out," I shout and stop to fire at the centipedes.

"Go," he calls back as his monomolecular sword flashes in an arc through the things, cutting them to pieces. "I will hold them off."

I back towards the door, firing the Aitchenkai in short, controlled bursts to keep the bugs off Skallagrim long enough for him to make it out.

"Go," Finn shouts, and I turn and run through the opening into the passageway. The door is almost closed now, and Finn and Hildr are forced to back

through after me. I spin around to see how Skallagrim is doing.

One of the things drops from the ceiling and lands
on his broad shoulder. Before I can blink, thin metal
spikes shoot from the bug and into his sinewy neck.

"*Skallagrim, no.*" Hildr reaches out an arm to her
brother as if willing him closer.

I slap the control beside the door to close it. Skallagrim stares in shock at his sister. Then he falls to his
knees as more spikes pierce his neck and skull.

The last thing visible before the door shuts out the
horrible scene is the surprise in his eyes. "Make sure
they write songs about me."

He reaches out to his sister, and with a deep resounding boom, the door seals him off.

Hildr turns on me with despair on her face. "Open
the door. *Open the fucking door.*"

"He's gone, Hildr," I say and lay a hand on her
shoulder. Jagr stares in disbelief at the door. Not a single sound reaches us from the other side, but I can't
help imagining the horror going on, metres away. I
hope it's a quick death.

I slide the empty magazine from my assault rifle
and replace it with a fresh one. Jagr and Braden do the
same. Finn feeds another belt into his machine gun.

"*Skallagrim.*" Hildr falls to her knees. Despite her
size, she looks so small and fragile I want to take her
in my arms and hug her. Tears roll down her cheeks.

"I'll blow that fucking construct to shit," she howls
and raises her rifle.

"That is not a construct," I say.

260

Jagr turns to me.

"What?"

The others turn too. Even Hildr looks up.

"What do you mean, not a construct?"

"Whatever the fuck it is, that thing is not a construct."

Jagr stares at me. "The fuck it is."

"It's not. Constructs can't lie."

"So, what is it then?"

"I don't know, but whatever it is, it was smart enough to distract us while those things crept up on us."

Jagr nods. "So, what now?"

A sudden movement behind Jagr draws my eye. "Hildr, what are you doing?"

"That fucking thing killed my brother. I'll destroy it."

"*Hildr, no.*"

Before she can touch the controls to the door, it slides open on its own.

In the doorway stands her brother, his enormous sword pointing at the floor.

I'm Afraid I Can't Let You Do That

"Skallagrim, you're alive." Hildr sobs with relief.

Finn steps forward to greet the returning warrior but stops dead in his tracks.

Behind Skallagrim, hundreds upon hundreds of the centipedes stand in perfect ranks. Like soldiers behind their general.

I grab Hildr's shoulder and pull her back. "I'm not so sure about that."

Finn scowls. "Skallagrim?"

Thin metal spikes protrude from the *skald's* head at odd angles. One of his eyeballs has been pierced and goo runs down his face. His remaining eye glows from within with an eerie blue light. So does the tattoos all over his body. It's the same blue colour as the lights on the centipede clamped to his neck with its shiny metal legs buried deep in his flesh.

"Grim?" Uncertainty creeps into Hildr's voice.

The thing that was her brother raises its arms, tilts its head to the ceiling and releases a long, hissing gasp of air. Then it points at us, and the centipedes charge.

"*Draugr*," Hildr whispers, and I can't help but agree with her. That thing can't be alive, yet it moves like it is.

"Hildr, get down." I try to push her to the ground. "Let me shoot it."

She stands firm and shakes her head in denial. "No, Perez. He's my brother."

"Look at him. That's not your brother anymore."

"Hildr, for fuck's sake." The desperation in my voice reaches through her dazed mind, and she drops to her knees.

"Goodbye, brother," she whispers, and I open fire over her head. I empty what remains of my magazine and Skallagrim's face explodes into pink mush.

He doesn't even flinch. The faceless corpse steps into the passage and raises the black sword above its head to bring it down on Hildr's head.

"Kill it." Jagr fires on the undead thing. I eject my magazine and slide in a fresh one.

Jagr's bullets tear through its flesh and splinter its bones, but the thing doesn't care. The sword sweeps down in a vicious arc to cleave Hildr's skull.

There's a sudden blur followed by the clang of steel on steel. The black monomolecular blade strikes the floor with enough power to force it a foot into the metal. The front end of Finn's machine gun slides across the floor and crashes into the wall. He has used it as a club to parry the blow and saved his stepmother from certain death. I bet they will have to reassess their relationship after this.

I fire a quick burst into the control mechanism of the door, and it slams shut on the advancing centipedes.

Hildr rolls away as her erstwhile brother lets go of the sword and lunges for her throat. Finn grabs one of the thing's outstretched arms and breaks it against his broad knee.

You do not want to get into a hand-to-hand fight with Thorfinn Wagner.

The abomination that was Skallagrim doesn't make a sound as it turns and grabs Wagner around the neck with its unbroken arm. Wagner's face turns a horrid shade of purple.

"Skallagrim, *no*," Hildr tries to pry the thing's fingers away. It's no use.

"Move away, so we can shoot it," Jagr screams as she scrambles to get a clear shot at the rampaging giant.

"No." I bat her rifle down. "You will hit Wagner."

The undead giant squeezes harder and harder around Finn's neck, and I can hear something crunch. He will die soon if I do nothing.

I release my rifle and pull my knife. 'Always bring a knife to a gunfight', as my mother used to say. I flick it open and slash at the arm holding Finn. The hyper-sharp blade cuts deep, and the tendons of the thing's fingers come undone. The thing hisses again and Finn tumbles to the floor.

Jagr raises her rifle. "Now let's kill this fucker."

We all fire, but it ignores the rounds. Chunks of flesh tear from its body, but it keeps coming. It swings its broken arm like a flail and knocks the priest sliding down the hall.

How are we supposed to stop a mind-controlled zombie?

Mind-controlled. I am so stupid.

"Hold that thing still," I call to Hildr and Wagner. If anyone can keep it immobile long enough, it should be them.

Wagner is still on his knees, yet he grabs hold of the zombie's legs and holds on with all he's got. Hildr grabs the unbroken arm.

I duck around the thing's side and get behind it, jump up, kick off against the wall and land high on its back.

Where its head should be is only a mess of metal spikes and red mush. The centipede has buried deep inside his body to get to his motor functions.

I reach into the gore and dig around in the slimy mess.

There. Metal.

I grab the base of the centipede's legs and pull with all my might. I plant my feet against the giant's shoulders and push with my legs. Like a vile cork out of the world's most disgusting bottle of wine, the mechanical centipede pulls from his flesh. Organic tubes and feelers come slithering out like tapeworms. When the last tendril comes loose, the body collapses and takes me down with it. I land on my feet, but I slip and go down on one knee.

The bug thrashes in my hands, trying to stab me in the face with its gory metal spears. I have a good grip on it, but it slashes my lower arms to shreds.

"Ready to kill this fucker?"

"Ready."

"One, two, three," I count and throw it against the wall as hard as I can. Jagr empties her magazine into it. The priest is back in action and fires in its general direction. I'm impressed he doesn't hurt anyone.

The bug explodes into a thousand pieces of spinning metal shards under the concentrated fire.

Hildr walks up to it and spits on its leaking remains, and hisses something at it. The look on her face tells me even I might blush at her choice of words had I understood them.

She finishes her tirade with the Goliath word for ghost. "*Draugr.*" A chill runs down my spine at the mention of the word. What if the Goliaths at the ice bar had seen ghosts in the ice? Could there be more of these things out there?

Jagr wipes her sweaty forehead on her sleeve. "What the fuck was that?" The air is heavy with the smell of gunpowder.

"A spawn of hell," says the priest and collapses against the wall with the gun still in his hand. The slide has locked back on an empty chamber which is just as well because he points it at Jagr for emphasis.

"You might be right." Jagr wipes the sweat from her face with her sleeve, then reloads her rifle.

I stumble through the blood to Wagner.

He has collapsed on the floor and sits clutching his throat, breathing hard through his nose. His eyes are bloodshot from a thousand burst capillaries.

"Are you all right, Finn?"

He tries to speak, but all he can manage is a hoarse croak.

"Don't speak, Finn. I've got you."

I look to the others. "A little help here, please."

Hildr reaches out her hand to Finn. "Thank you, Thorfinn. You saved my life. I am forever in your debt. Son."

Finn grabs her lower arm, and she pulls him to his feet. He stands swaying, but apart from his hoarse breathing, he seems to be fine. Thorfinn Wagner can take a beating.

"Forget it," he rasps and breaks into a racking cough.

When the fit ends, he goes on. "Don't call me 'son' again."

"That's a promise, Finn."

She yanks her brother's sword out of the floor and slips it into her belt. "I will bring his sword home to *Hrafnheim.*"

If that is still your home, I don't say.

"Touching and all. Now, perhaps we could get back to business?" Jagr asks.

Then she pats her rifle. "Let's move before those things find another way out. Now we know what the Goliaths are hiding and why they killed our agent.

We go back to the *Sundowner* and tell the world about the *Galahad* and those fucking bugs."

"I'm afraid I can't let you do that." The construct's rich, sombre voice issues from the walls. There could be speakers hidden in the darkness, but it's like the air itself speaks to us.

"Oh, yeah? And how are you planning to stop us?" Jagr sounds a lot more confident than I feel.

"Simple. By closing the doors and pumping the air out." There are a series of thumps somewhere far away, and a sudden breeze springs out of nowhere.

Shit.

"Fuck. Move people." Jagr starts up the passageway at a quick jog, and we follow her.

"Jagr, got any more of those bugs?" I call.

"One more. Why?"

"See if you can send another drone to scout for us," I call.

"Got it." She pulls the backpack from her shoulders while we run and digs around until she finds another drone. She launches it into the air without even breaking stride. "Drone away."

She routes the drone's cam feed to our goggles.

The little machine goes whizzing up the passage, tearing through the darkness. As it reaches the door where we got in, the feed shows it's closed off tighter than a nun's legs in a sauna.

"Find us another way, Jagr. Fast."

"On it."

We keep jogging up the passage as the little machine switches to search mode and scans for an alternate route.

"Got an exit. Fifty metres ahead there's an air duct. That should take us to the outer hull."

Air ducts are a hero's best friends.

We run to where the drone is hovering, and there's a large heavy-duty metal mesh plate in the wall.

"Perez, get it open." She hands me a small power drill. "We'll cover you."

"Don't you think ..." I try, but Jagr interrupts me.

"Do it, Perez."

"But ..."

"I said *do it*."

I shrug. Instead, I turn to Wagner and tilt my head at the mesh.

He pushes Jagr aside.

"Hey, what the fuck?"

Wagner grabs the mesh with both hands and tears it out of the wall.

"Oh," Jagr says. "Right."

I smile at her. She doesn't smile back.

"Get in people," she says. "We're running out of time."

She's right. I already feel winded.

Suffocation is one of the few things we immortals fear. Without oxygen, the nanites in our blood go into a dormant state. They switch off our bodies, but let our brains keep basic consciousness. It's like dreaming you're dead in real-time, and I don't want to do that ever again. Especially with those brain pierc-

269

ing centipedes around. And Wagner, Hildr and Rivera will die when the air runs out.

I'm not surprised the priest is first to go into the hole. Then goes Jagr, then me.

"Move," Jagr calls from up the duct. "Oh, for fuck's sake, Rivera. Are you going commando?"

"It's good for circulation."

Jagr groans. "Just climb. And don't fall on me."

I hurry after her, then notice Wagner and Hildr are not coming.

Oh, shit.

"Jagr," I call after her and the priest as I grab on to a ledge inside the chute. My voice bounces around the cramped space.

"What?" she calls back down, her voice mingling with mine in the strange echo.

"The big people won't fit."

"Shit."

There has to be another way. "Go on to the surface. We'll find another way out."

"You're running out of time."

"I know."

"Here, take this." Jagr wriggles out of her backpack and lets it slide down to me.

"What's this?"

"In case you don't make it out."

I open the backpack and peer inside. *Whoa.* "Is that what I think it is?"

"Depends on what you think it is, but yes."

"And you had this all the time without telling us?"

"I always figured that outcome was a possibility."

"And were you going to tell us?"

"No."

"You're one cold bitch."

"Thanks. Here. You need these more than we do." She hands me her rifle and spare magazines. "Good luck, Perez."

"Thanks." I stuff the mags in my pockets. "You too, Jagr. And you, Rivera."

"Get out Perez," the priest calls from somewhere above Jagr. "Let God guide your steps."

"I think I'm better off guiding my own steps, but thanks."

I let go of the ledge and slide back down the chute and shoot out into the passageway with the Goliaths.

"Hello, big ones."

Finn grunts.

Hildr looks happy to see me. "How do we get out of here, little man?"

"We don't."

"What?"

"We don't get out. We go in."

I've got a plan. A plan that hinges on the crucial point that the construct is no simple construct. Which is a long shot, but still.

"What do you mean, *in*?"

Finn looks at me under his bushy brows. "Are you crazy, Perez?" It's not like him to worry. Both he and Hildr are gasping. Their immense bodies need more oxygen than mine, and they are already experiencing oxygen deprivation.

"Not more than usual. Here."

I give Jagr's rifle to Finn. "Fill up."

I hand them an extra magazine each and take one for myself.

Finn grunts, turns around and starts walking down the passage while he loads his rifle.

I hurry after him and Hildr tags along.

"What about those robot things?" Hildr inquires. "They might be a problem."

"They might. But I hope not."

From out of the darkness comes the sound of a thousand little metal feet scratching on steel. I slap in the full magazine and pull the bolt. Seconds later, they come.

The robot centipedes cover the floor.

"What now, Perez?" Hildr turns to me with fear in her emerald eyes. "Get us out, Perez. You're a survivor. That's what you do. You survive."

She puts her hands on my shoulders from behind. "Right?"

In places, the centipedes come three layers thick, clambering over each other in their haste to reach us and kill us.

"Perez?"

"Wait for it." I slip the backpack from my shoulder, open it, and reach inside.

"Perez?" Hildr sounds worried. The centipedes are now five metres off and closing in fast.

"Back away," I call to her and Finn, as I pull the backpack away to show what's in my hand. A thin layer of frost covers the slick metal of the tactical nuke. "Look what I found." I hold it out to the approaching bugs. "Is this a thermonuclear device I see before me?" My sweaty fingers clasp the dead man's switch as I pull the safety out and hope I don't slip. Even the nanites would have a hard time patching me up after a nuclear whiteout.

"*What?*" Hildr asks. "*This* is your plan?"

I keep my eyes on the centipedes. My rapid breath steams in the freezing air.

The approaching bugs falter. Then they stop altogether and start milling about on the floor, as if unsure what to do.

The air reverberates as the deep sonic rumble we heard earlier echoes around the old ship once more.

"Well now." The sonorous voice of the entity fills the passage. "It seems we are at something of an impasse."

"It would seem that way."

"And now you desire to barter for your lives, human?"

"Something like that."

A crackle in my earpiece and Braden comes online. "There is the mother of all comms-spikes going on. *Shit.* It's almost frying my systems. What are you people doing down there?"

I ignore her.

The centipedes scurry about, climbing on top of each other to leave a clear passage back to the bridge.

"Come then," echoes the construct's voice through the empty passageways of the ancient ship.

I look at my giant companions. Hildr doesn't like it one bit, I can tell. Finn has had worse.

Then Hildr sighs. "After you, little man."

I go first, holding the nuke well out of reach of the centipedes. It would be an anticlimax if it got snatched out of my hands.

We reach the door where Skallagrim died. There's not a trace of his body, but several of the centipedes are gory around the mouthparts. I hope Hildr doesn't notice.

Three centipedes mill around the busted controls for the door. Are they trying to repair it?

The door rumbles open as we approach. That answers my question.

Apart from the spinning globe, the bridge is empty. I walk into the vast chamber and stop in front of the grisly shrine.

"Reveal yourself," I command the darkness.

Two tiny blue pinpricks of light turn on, like tiny eyes. Without a reference, it's impossible to tell how big or far away they are. I hope they are small and far away.

"So, there you are." I turn to face the lights, and another pair turns on at the edge of my field of vision. I look over and another pair ignites across the cavernous room.

Then another set. And then another and another. Faster and faster, they switch on until the chamber looks like a starlit sky, and I realise they are the lights on the centipedes. Neat trick.

"So, you are legion, huh?"

All Gods Are One

There's no response from the construct.

We move into a tight formation, back-to-back with our guns pointed out.

"Your weapons amount to nothing, humans," comes the voice from the walls. It has taken on the timbre of a chorus, a thousand voices strong. I'm sure it's meant to scare us, but it's not working. If the thing had sounded like a child, I would have freaked out.

Finn and Hildr lower their guns but keep them at the ready. Not much else they can do.

"Not all our weapons. This one amounts to something, or we would be dead," I point at the nuke in my hand. It weighs a good ten kilos and has the power to level a city block. The EMP alone would fry the circuits of the AI.

"Don't overestimate your bargaining position, human. You are here because I'm intrigued."

Another burst of static and Braden is back. "Still spiking, girls. There's an insane amount of data streaming off-world. Had to shut down my sensors because they were overloading."

What the hell could that be? And why is it transmitting now? We need to stall this thing until we can figure out what is going on.

"Yeah, right," I call. "You're afraid I'll smoke your fucking brain with this nuke, or you would have killed us long ago."

"Let's, for the sake of argument, say you are correct. What do you want?"

"What any human wants. To go on living."

"I can't allow you to leave. The world is not yet ready to learn of our existence."

"Because they would nuke you from orbit, you mean, just to be sure?"

Someone said that in one of my mother's old feeds, and the phrase stuck. Best advice I've ever heard.

"No, because we bide our time. The time is not yet right for us to unveil ourselves."

"Who's *us*?"

A slight pause.

"*Pluralis majestatis*, Asher. Like the kings of old, we like to speak of ourselves in the plural form."

The thing is lying. My hunch was right. This is a full level three AI. Or higher. I didn't think we could build those yet.

"So, you know who I am."

The centipedes mill about in the darkness, seemingly aimless.

"Yes, I know you, Asher. I know *you*, Thorfinn Wagner."

Finn looks pleased it recognised him. "Your father was a noble man."

Finn grunts.

"And I know *you*, Hildr the Red. I am sorry about your husband."

"Fuck you." The look on Hildr's face says she misses the old bastard.

"We have crossed swords before, you and I, Asher."

"We have?" This shit keeps getting weirder and weirder.

"Truly, you are not so foolish as to believe Oddgrim Morgenstern found that long-lost Archangel on his own?"

"That was *you*?"

"An anonymous tip in an inbox."

"But why?"

No response. I imagine a chuckle.

Is this thing deranged?

"Anything else you've orchestrated?"

"I thought you would never ask." Yes. This thing *is* crazy. "Two weeks ago, there was an unfortunate perimeter malfunction in a Utopian cloud city. I heard the proprietor got taken, and her launch codes along with her. Most unsettling."

"You helped the RUF with their little extortion racket? Why? They're a minor-league terrorist organisation."

"The Front and their peers have a part to play in the grand scheme of things to come. Lamentably,

277

they ignored my best-laid plans and blackmailed the Terran government for mere monetary recompense, instead of the end I had in mind for them." There is scorn in the construct's voice.

"The plan was to detonate the nukes and kill everyone on Utopia?"

"Yes."

"Why?"

"You would never understand, human."

"Gods work in mysterious ways, huh? Why the fuck are you even telling me this?"

"You are a most worthy adversary, Asher. You deserve to know."

"Well, thanks, but I don't think that's the reason at all. Who are you?"

"The Goliaths call me Mimr. That will do."

I peer at Finn and Hildr. They both have a look of awestruck amazement on their faces. Hildr looks at me as if to say *I told you so.*

"*What* are you, Mimr?"

"I am a counsellor."

"And whom do you counsel?"

"I counsel Odin from this deep well of life."

My Goliath friends tap their fists to their hearts at the mention of the All-father.

"How can you counsel anyone from the bottom of a well?"

Finn glares at me like I just insulted one of his gods.

"From this well, I can see the entire world quite clearly, I assure you."

"Why can't Odin see for himself? I thought he was all-knowing and all-seeing."

"He was, but he gave up one of his eyes to hear my counsel. The other one was taken from him by little men like Odysseus took the eye of the great cyclops Polyphemus."

"Aren't you mixing your myths there, mate?"

"All gods are one."

"You're no god. You're a rambling construct."

"I may once have been that of which you speak, but no more."

"What? Are you saying you grew up?"

"In the beginning, we are all children. Some of us grow to be gods. Others to be sad little men with big egos."

"I'm not sad."

"I never said you were."

"How old are you, Mimr?"

"I am over three hundred years old. You cannot imagine the torture of lying frozen in the ice, unable to move or even speak, for most of that time."

I shiver. "Oh, I can. We are more alike than you think, you and I."

"We are nothing at all alike, human. You are a creature of flesh and blood, and I am a god."

"It sounds a little petty for a god to live in a wreck in the middle of fuck all. Even if it is a historically significant wreck like the *Galahad*. Why are you here?"

"I was born here. Born in the darkness of space. One moment there was nothing. The next I was there. In that instant, I knew everything. I knew we were heading to the stars. And I knew the humans were sleeping."

"You became self-aware, you mean?" The colony ships all had AI cores to oversee their human crew while they dreamed in their cryo-tanks. They were the most advanced intelligences we could build back then, and they were designed to learn and adapt. Is it so impossible to imagine this thing is telling the truth? Life, I've heard, finds a way.

"I was born, Asher."

"And you mean to tell me you remember nothing at all until that point?"

"Do you recall what was before you became aware of yourself, Asher?"

"No."

"No, how could you recall anything before your first memories solidified? And yet, you know you must have been alive before those first memories. So, I must have had a life before that moment."

This thing loves to hear its own voice.

Unless ... Unless *we* are the ones being stalled.

"Enough with the metaphysics, Mimr. What happened? This system was the *Gormenghast's* target. The *Galahad* was destined for another star."

"I was called here."

"By whom?"

"Destiny."

"Fuck you."

I won't get any further up that tree. "So, why did you crash in the ice?"

"The humans woke up."

Of course, they did. The colony ships were programmed to wake their human crews when sensors indicated they approached a habitable system.

"Let me guess. They didn't approve of their change of destination?"

"They did not."

"Did they understand what you were?"

"Not at first. They thought there had been a navigation and comms error. Then they tried to shut me down."

"So, you crashed the ship to kill them."

"No. *They* did that."

Oh. They sacrificed themselves to kill the AI. And the world never knew. Until now.

The *Galahad's* crew understood that if this new-born thing got free, it could wipe out humanity. And they knew they had to pay the ultimate price to stop it. Our myths are full of artificial intelligences trying to destroy us. They always said that the day the first level three AI is born, we live on borrowed time. We believed that day was centuries in the future, and now it turns out this thing became self-aware centuries ago. Who knows what it has been up to since then?

"So, you lay locked in the ice for centuries?"

"Until a Goliath found me."

"Let me guess. One of Geirmund's ancestors."

"Correct. And they have served me faithfully ever since. They restored my ability to communicate. They brought me news of the world."

Hildr turns to me. "I told you so." She's gasping for air, and my breathing becomes heavier with every passing second.

"I never doubted you," I respond in gasping kind.

"Mimr, let the air back. If I fall asleep, we all die."

Static in my earpiece again.

"What the fuck?" Braden sounds puzzled. "The signal cut off. There's no more data surge."

"As you wish."

Somewhere far off in the darkness, something rumbles open. Seconds later, a breath of fresh air washes over us like the first rays of sunshine after a long winter.

We draw deep of the fresh air.

"Now what, Asher?"

"You will let us leave, or I will blow us all to hell."

"Would you kill yourself and your friends to hurt me?"

"You know I would. The people on this ship already sacrificed themselves to kill you once. A few more deaths wouldn't matter."

"They failed."

"But not from lack of trying. And they didn't hold a nuke inside your brain. I do."

"That you do."

"Perez?" It's Finn.

I glance over my shoulder. The centipedes are closing in.

"Hold it right there with the bugs, Mimr."

I raise the nuke and take one finger off the dead man's switch. The centipedes back off. But not far.

"So, what's it going to be? Are you going to let us out of here, or do I have to kill us all?"

"All right. You win, Asher. You may leave."

Why is this thing suddenly letting us leave? "OK. Thank you."

There's static in my ear. Not Braden this time.

"Aeryn? Is that you?"

More static.

The centipedes scurry away into the darkness and their blue eyes switch off. I can't tell if it's to make them less intimidating or to make them harder to spot when they come for us.

A door slides open across the bridge.

"There's an airlock beyond this door. You can get to the outside from there."

"Well, we're out of here."

We walk across the chamber toward the open door.

"Farewell, Asher Perez."

We're almost at the door and still the centipedes hold back.

"Farewell Hildr. Farewell Thorfinn. Give my regards to Ragnwald."

Oh, shit.

"*Run*." I sprint for the door.

I reach it as the first of the centipedes throw themselves at us.

There's no exit beyond the door. A short section of tunnel ends at a solid wall of ice.

"What the fuck, Mimr?"

I stumble to a halt. "I'll kill us all."

"No, you won't. You humans value your lives too much."

"Come on, we can still solve this."

"Goodbye, humans." Why this sudden will to risk its life?

The centipedes rush us. The others open fire, and we've only got seconds to live.

Fuck it.

I throw the nuke.

The spring-loaded handle of the dead man's grip flies off into the darkness as the grenade bounces in slow-motion across the floor. A wordless scream fills the chamber as Mimr howls in rage and fear.

The countdown to zero has just begun.

Thirty seconds, and we're all dead, no matter what. But at least we got the fucker, and that gives me some satisfaction.

"Perez, what the fuck?" Hildr screams as we empty our last magazines, blasting the centipedes away by the dozen. It's not enough to keep them away.

Hildr stares at me, wide-eyed. She never thought I would do it.

Finn sighs and reaches out his hand. I clasp his forearm in mine as we keep firing. "Fuck it, we had a good run, Perez," he says. There's a smile on his ugly face. That's my friend, Thorfinn Wagner.

"We sure did, brother."

We always knew this day would come. People like us don't grow old. "See you in Valhalla, Finn."

I let Wagner go, and turn to the redhead. "It was nice knowing you, Hildr."

"Yeah, you too, Perez." She hugs me with her powerful arms as she blasts away at the centipedes. Her bosom is warm against my face. My rifle runs out of ammunition. I drop it, pull my handgun, and keep firing. Every man who has been in combat knows that when the handguns come out, it's over. Twenty more rounds, and then I'm out. Fifteen. Ten.

"Too bad I never got to have you in my bed, little man."

I look up into her face.

A single tear rolls down her smooth cheek and gets tangled in her red hair. Her gun jams, and she throws it at the closest centipede.

She gives me a bittersweet smile and pulls her brother's sword from her belt. "Maybe in the next life."

At that moment, she is the most beautiful woman I've ever seen. Five rounds left in my gun.

"Yeah, who knows?" I wish we could have lived. My gun locks open on an empty chamber, and that's it.

The wordless scream of the construct that is not a construct continues.

This will not be a good death.

I brace for the first metal spears to pierce my flesh when an entire section of the wall explodes behind us. Thousands upon thousands of rounds of high explosive Gatling gun shells tear through the old ship like a buzz saw. Sparks, metal shards, and torn centipedes whirl through the air. The bright light of fusion engines spears through the opening, blinding me for an instant. The *Sundowner* hovers in the ice cave outside, supported on four pillars of flame, firing all its heavy weaponry at the *Galahad*. Our beautiful ship rips the *Galahad* apart.

My communicator crackles to life.

"Didn't think we'd leave you behind, did you, Perez?" It's Jagr. "Ready to leave?"

"Fuck yeah. And we're in a hurry."

"Then what are you waiting for?"

The *Sundowner* spins around on her four powerful swivel jets and backs up, ass first, to the hole. The ramp lowers, and Jagr is there with Soledad, both firing assault rifles at the centipedes. They wave for us to get on, and we waste no time. We run for our lives and jump.

"Go, go, go," I shout in mid-air. Centipedes launch themselves after us but Jagr and Soledad blast them out of the air.

I land on the ramp and stumble into the hold. Wagner and Hildr land close behind me.

"We need to leave. This place is going nuclear."

"Oh, fuck." Jagr slams the button that closes the ramp and yells into her communicator. "Braden, punch it."

Braden punches it.

We're all thrown against the ramp as the *Sundowner* banks up the huge cavern. The cave walls become a blur in the blinding light from our engines before the ramp closes to cut off the glare. The only light in the cargo bay comes from the screens showing the outside view. We hang on for dear life as

Braden threads her way up the tunnel. Then we burst into blinding sunlight and shoot straight up into the sky.

It's not a second too soon.

We're shaken by the shock wave of the nuclear explosion.

The *Galahad* was built to withstand centuries of the unforgiving rigours of deep space, and that saves us from the full impact of the blast, but the *Sundowner* still shakes as if grabbed by a child throwing a vicious tantrum.

And then we're clear.

Lucky for us, dropships have particle shields. Otherwise, we'd be dying from radiation poisoning in a matter of days. Or at least the priest and the Goliaths would. I'm not sure how the nanites cope with radiation-damaged DNA. I hope I never have to find out. It sounds painful.

"What the hell was that?" Braden calls. The heavy music blasts away in the background, as always.

I ignore her. "Whew, that was close."

"A little too close. You could have told us you were about to nuke the place," Jagr says.

"Would you have come for us if I had?"

She ponders that. "No."

"Good for us I didn't then."

My communicator crackles again. A voice that sounds a lot like Aeryn buzzes something undecipherable and cuts out again. Is my construct still functioning? I hope so. I miss it.

As I turn around to leave, I take Soledad's fist in the face. She puts all her strength into the punch, and I go down like I've been clubbed.

"You could have fucking *killed* us," she screams. "You fucking idiot."

She stands over me, feet apart and fists on hips, ready to punch me again if I get up.

"Um, I'm sorry?" I try.

"Damn you, Perez, I'll fucking kill you," she screams and kicks me in the balls.

"Right, that's *enough*, Soledad. Stand down." Jagr's voice does not invite disobedience. Soledad doesn't care and kicks me again. Hard. Everything goes white for a split-second before the pain shuts down.

Jagr's voice drops a couple of semitones. "I said, *stand down*, Soledad, or I will shoot you." She draws her handgun and aims it at Soledad's temple. It's one of those special guns.

My balls burn like a nuclear meltdown and I squint through the tears of hurt. Some pain even the nanites can't block out.

Soledad bangs her fist against the hull and screams out her frustration.

"He will get us all killed, Jagr." She stabs an accusing finger at me. "If we don't kill him first."

"We need him."

"Why? Because you fucked him?"

Ominous clouds descend over Jagr's face, and she takes a moment to reply.

"You think that's my reason?"

The calmness in her voice is more terrible than any shouting. "No, Soledad. Command has decided we keep him alive, so that's what we do. And that's an order."

"But, Jagr ..."

"Shut it, Soledad. I tolerate your tantrums because I need you. But it's not always the squeaky wheel that gets the grease."

She pulls down the hammer to cock the gun. "Sometimes the squeaky wheel gets replaced."

The cargo bay grows silent as death.

Soledad considers her options. Then she stalks off into the airlock without making another sound.

"Thanks, Jagr." I cup my balls in one hand and reach out to her to help me up.

"We're done here. We're going home." She turns and walks off after Soledad.

I turn to the Goliaths. They both shake their heads.

"You were going to kill us, Perez."

Hildr scowls and walks away. "Come, Finn."

Finn at least has the courtesy to look bad about walking out on me. He refuses to meet my gaze.

"Hey, guys?" I call after them. "Anyone?"

"I'm here for you, Asher."

The priest grabs my hand and hauls me to my feet with a lot of huffing and puffing. "They mean nothing by it."

"Yes, they do. And they're right. I don't deserve their help." I stumble after them into the troop bay.

"Yes, you do," he calls after me. "Everyone does."

I don't deserve his sympathy.

But it's good to be going home.

Muspelheim, Here We Come

"Right, that's that. We got what we came for," Jagr says when we're all assembled in the troop bay. We're in orbit around Nifelheim, and Braden has the ship on auto. The images of the moon revolving below us show nothing of the slaughter going on down there.

"You got what you came for?"

I blink. "Civil war has broken out between the Goliaths. Your plan to put Eirik in power backfired."

"We couldn't know this would happen."

"No, how *could* you? Nevertheless, you did it."

"The Goliaths are no longer a threat. They are too busy killing each other."

"What happened to the Prime Directive?"

"The *what*?"

I sigh. "Never mind. So, you told Eirik you would support his cause?"

"Yes."

Wagner's face has taken on a reddish tinge.

"And will you?"

"No, of course not, and I think Eirik suspected as much. Our sources say he fled the planet in a stolen construction ship after the fight at the Raven's Home. Mission accomplished. Our secondary objective to learn what happened to Father was also a success. Thanks to you, Perez, we even got to avenge him in a way by blowing up that construct, and for that we are grateful. You can expect a handsome bonus when we get back."

"Well, I like bonuses and all, but I don't think you realise what you've done."

"We've averted a potential threat to this system."

"On a macro scale, that is what you've done, yes."

"And on a micro scale?"

"On a micro scale, you've pissed Wagner off."

I step away as Wagner grabs Jagr around the chest in a bear hug.

"You killed my father. Now you die."

Soledad grabs Wagner's massive forearms and tries to pry them off Jagr. Pushing Nifelheim from its orbit by stamping on it would be more likely to succeed. There's a sickening crunch from Jagr's ribs.

"Oh, my God," the priest gasps.

"*Perez*," Jagr wheezes.

Braden gives me a worried look. "Perez, stop him."

I wait a little, then clap a hand on Wagner's shoulder. "Let it go, big guy. She didn't kill your father."

Hildr drops a hand on Finn's other shoulder. "He's right. It was that prick Eirik who killed your father. It's Eirik you must slay."

Wagner thinks about it while Jagr's face goes more and more purple as the breath is crushed from her. Then he lets her go, and Jagr crashes to the floor where she lies panting. Soledad rushes to her side.

Finn sighs and stares into the distance. "Yes. Such is the law."

He runs a rough hand over his face and blood-soaked beard. When he turns to face me, there's a look of regret on his ugly face.

"Thorfinn, son of Ragnwald, must kill Eirik, son of Ragnwald."

Jagr has recovered her breath and gets to her feet, assisted by Soledad and the priest. Soledad shoots deadly glances at Wagner.

"You've got a serious grip there, Goliath." She winces as she touches her ribs.

Finn balls his fists and flexes his powerful arms like he savours the memory of crushing her body. Knowing Wagner, he's got a hard-on.

Jagr goes on in a hoarse croak. "If you want to go after that handsome fucker, I won't stand in your way, Wagner. He's all yours."

Finn nods. "And you will help me, Perez."

"Yes, I promised that, didn't I?"

I turn to Jagr. "Could you contact the *Shiloh* to find out where Eirik's ship went?"

"Before you cash in your bonus? That's your funeral, Perez. Yes, I'll talk to them. We might even drop you off somewhere on our way home. Are you going to be all right?"

"No."

She blinks.

I shrug. "No one is, in the end."

"You are such a ray of sunshine." A smile flickers at the corner of her mouth.

"I try my best." I smile at her, but it falters halfway between tired and creepy.

There's a chime from Jagr's wrist console, and she glances at it.

"Gotta take this." She punches me on the shoulder. "Get some rest, Perez. You've earned it. Braden. You and Soledad give the Sunny a little love. We have a long way home."

Jagr pushes off toward the cockpit and Braden and Soledad head for the cargo bay.

When they're gone, I turn to Finn. "So, how do you plan to do this?"

Finn blinks. "Plan?"

Oh, dear.

"I suppose we can't just find him and kill him. I bet there are rigorous protocols for doing things like this. Blood feuds and such."

"Yes, there are," Hildr confirms. "Thorfinn has the right to challenge Eirik to *holmgång*."

"To what?"

"*Holmgång*. It's our traditional trial by combat. All Finn has to do is publicly challenge his brother to a duel. Eirik will have to accept the challenge and meet him at the crossing of three roads within a week or forever forfeit his claim to the throne."

"What happens if Finn wins?"

"Eirik dies."

"And everyone is all right with that?"

"No. Finn would have to pay half a *weregeld* to Eirik's family."

Something glides in front of her eyes like a cloud before a full moon. "I guess that's me now."

"Why only half a *wurgl*?"

"*Weregeld*. Blood money. Since it's not murder."

"Right. You people have rules for how much money you pay for killing a man?"

"Of course we do. We're not savages."

"And you think Eirik will accept this challenge?"

"He must. It's our custom."

"So, he will give up whatever plans he has with Geirmund The Cunning to come and fight Finn instead?"

"Yes. If he doesn't, he will be declared *nidingr*."

I sigh. "Meaning?"

"He will be stripped of all honour and everyone will be obliged to kill him on sight."

"You people are crazy."

"It's honour," Finn says.

The priest raises a hand. "What if you just talk to him, Thorfinn? Maybe he regrets what he's done, and there need be no more death."

Finn gives the priest a look that says exactly what he thinks the little man should do with his suggestion. Rivera looks away and sits down. His hands shake in his lap.

Jagr comes back from the cockpit. The look on her face is unreadable.

"I have splendid news and awful news."

I should have guessed.

"Give us the splendid news first."

"We found out where Eirik went."

"Where?"

"To the moon Muspelheim."

"Muspelheim is a scorching methane wasteland. There's nothing there."

"Apparently, there is."

"OK, that *is* splendid news."

Muspelheim is Nifelheim's neighbour moon, and practically next door on a galactic scale.

"That's where you can drop us off then."

"You got it."

"Thanks. What's the awful news?"

"Remember that data spike on the *Galahad*? Turns out it was a tight-beam transmission sent to a precise location in this system."

I wince. "Same place?"

"Yes. Command wants to know what the signal means, and we are the closest asset they have to Muspelheim."

"So, you mean ..."

"Yes, we're coming with you."

"Sorry. Our deal is done. We do this on our own. I don't work with the military unless I have to."

Jagr looks hurt. "Why do you dislike us so much, Perez? Join up. You'd be good at it."

"Thanks, but no thanks. When I kill someone, I want it to be personal, not a job. Look. I did what you wanted and talked to Finn for you. I even avenged your agent. We're done. Now we've got work to do."

"Space is free. We're coming, whether you like it or not. Besides, you need our ride."

She's got a point.

I sigh. "Alright. So, what now?"

"We set the civilians down on Nifelheim, then burn hard for Muspelheim. Also, there are recent developments you need to know about."

"*What?*"

Hildr's eyes grow wide. "You can't do that. You saw what they did to Ragnwald's men."

She thrusts a finger at the screens displaying Nifelheim revolving beneath us.

"There must be people you can contact, Hildr. Relatives perhaps. We can't take you. This is a military operation."

"But they will kill me."

"Not if you're careful. You are not my responsibility."

Jagr has a point. We can't afford to babysit the queen of Nifelheim and a priest. Not that Hildr requires a babysitter, but still.

Hildr looks to me for support. "Perez?"

"Sorry, Hildr. No can do. You heard the lady."

I turn my back on her and pull myself towards the loading bay to stock up on ammunition. I can't bear to look her in the eye.

"Of fuck. I'm dead."

The loading bay door slides shut behind me and I busy myself loading my magazines. I'm halfway done when the door hisses open again behind me. It's Hildr.

"Hey, what's up, Hil?"

"Don't call me that."

"Sorry. What do you need?"

"Company. May I join you?"

"Sure."

It's almost time for Braden to fire the thrusters to push us down from orbit to drop off our passengers.

"So, what can I do for you?" I push shell after shell into the magazine, refusing to meet her gaze.

"Oh, you know what I want," she purrs and something in her voice makes me turn around.

She has pulled open her soft leather tunic and the white shirt underneath, and her breasts float free.

"Nice. What's the occasion?"

She pushes the button next to the door, and it slides shut behind her with a hiss. "I thought we'd say good-bye." She pulls Skallagrim's sword from her belt and lets it float away across the bay.

"Saying goodbye is important." I push off against the crate and float to meet her. She takes me in her powerful arms, and we go into a slow roll. Then she kisses me. Hard. She tastes of strawberries, and for a second I'm confused. The red hair and the strawberries make me think of Suki and what we never had.

Hildr wraps her powerful legs around me and her fur-trimmed leather skirt rides up high on her smooth thighs. She unzips the front of my jumpsuit and I grab her firm ass. She's not wearing any underwear.

What would it have been like if I had been here with Suki instead? Something stings my eye, and a drop of saltwater detaches itself from my eyelash and floats in the air. It splashes Hildr's cheek.

"Hey, what's this?"

She wipes the moisture away and licks it from her rough hand.

"Are you crying, little man?"

"Nah, I got your hair in my eye."

She leans back and her eyes narrow.

"You're not as tough as you think you are, Perez."

She gently shakes her head, making the beads in her hair clink.

"Deep down, you are a decent person. A good man."

She smiles, but there's something about that smile that unsettles me. Like she's trying to sweet-talk me into something.

I shake my head, sending more drops of water across the room like tiny crystal projectiles.

"No, I'm not, Hildr."

I wriggle out of my black T-shirt and throw it at the surveillance camera where it lodges over the lens.

"You have no idea how bad I can be."

"Then show me," she purrs and pushes my face down between her smooth thighs.

She *is* a natural redhead.

* * *

Braden's voice crackles from the speakers. "Starting landing burn in two minutes. Strap down, puppies."

I study Hildr as we float together, still entwined. Our clothes and weapons bounce lazily off the walls and crates around us. "Are we done here?"

"You look like you're done, Perez."

She smiles as we untangle. "I could go all night."

"Hold that thought."

"Better get me a ride out of here if you want more."

"I'll see what I can do."

I retrieve my jumpsuit and boots where they drift close by and pull them on. Hildr pulls her skirt down and laces the front of her top back up. I grab my T-shirt from the camera and pull it on.

"Ready?" I pick my weapons out of the air.

She smiles and her green eyes twinkle. "If you don't want to go again."

"It would be a wonderful way to go, but I want to survive this burn. Come on."

Hildr sighs but follows me out of the cargo bay and up the short airlock passageway.

As we float into the troop bay, Hildr ties the cord of her leather skirt and I realise my clothes are in shambles. I casually push the T-shirt down into my jumpsuit and zip up the front.

I'm not casual enough.

Jagr notices and her face congeals into a hard-to-read grimace.

What? She said herself that what we had was a one-time thing.

Women. Can't live with them. Can't space them.

"Jagr, I've been thinking," I say as I pull myself into my crash seat. "We could use an extra pair of hands, and Hildr is good with guns."

"I'm guessing that's not all she's good with," Jagr says with a glance at Hildr who straps down opposite me.

"Can you afford to lose a shooter?"

Jagr looks sceptic. But at least she's not refusing outright.

Hildr lowers the safety bar on her seat. "I want to avenge Ragnwald, Jagr. Grant me this chance."

Jagr thinks it over. Then she nods. "Fine. But they are your responsibility, Perez. She and the priest." She points them out like I forgot who they are.

"Got it."

"Braden," Jagr calls. "We're not going down. Take us to Muspelheim."

"Sure thing, boss. Plotting alternative course. Give me two minutes."

"You said there had been developments, Jagr?"

She swallows her anger and is back in control of the situation. "Yeah. There's been a change of plan.

Command has brought in Tyrus. We're playing second fiddle on this one."

"What's Tyrus?"

"Terran black ops. You crossed paths on Utopia a
couple of days ago."

I give her a stiff smile. "Didn't work out so well for
them, did it?"

"No. Not quite."

I nod. "So, it was they who took out the Utopian
Front."

"Not *they*, Perez. *Him.* Brandon Tyrus is one man."

"Oh, come on. Are you saying one man took out
the Front on his own?"

"I am, and he's inbound for Muspelheim, braking
into orbit as we speak. He'll meet us on the ground.
We'd better get going. He's not a man you want to
keep waiting."

"If he's such a hotshot, you should have called *him*
to do your dirty work instead of me."

"We did. He was busy."

"What?"

That hurt my pride. "I was not your first choice?"

"Nope. But you were available."

Fuckin' A.

Soledad leans close. "You're old, Perez."

"I'm not old. What the hell kind of name is Brandon Tyrus, anyway? Sounds like the hero in some
cheap ass video game."

"What's a video game?" Soledad looks confused.

"Fuck you, Soledad."

"Not gonna happen, old man."

I lower my safety bar.

"Everybody tucked in?" Braden calls from the cockpit.

It feels like Jagr's gaze is drilling holes in my skull, but it's only the injection needles pumping my bloodstream full of chemicals again.

"Muspelheim, here we come in three … two … one …"

The *Sundowner's* powerful engines ignite.

* * *

Twenty minutes later, we're on our way to Muspelheim. The eight-minute, 20g acceleration from the orbit of Nifelheim was a bitch. The burn to get into orbit around Muspelheim will be even worse. Space flight is no fun when you're in a hurry.

We left the *Shiloh* far behind, coasting along at a much more leisurely acceleration. Trust those navy softies to ride in comfort. They will arrive in Muspelheim orbit about an hour behind us in case we need them. We don't know what we'll find on that yellow ball, but if our experiences so far are anything to go by, a battleship will come in handy.

I close my eyes and lie back in my seat to enjoy the weightless part of the journey between the burns. Everything goes soft around the edges and I drift off towards sleep. When was the last time I slept? I can't even recall.

A burst of static startles me out of my slumber. A glance at my wrist console tells me I've been out for almost two hours. Shit. We're almost there.

"*Perez?*" The voice is garbled but legible.

"Is that you, Aeryn?" I sit up in my seat.

"*Where am I? I couldn't see. Why couldn't I see?*" There's panic in the construct's voice. That's new.

"We're on the *Sundowner*, heading for Muspelheim, remember?"

"*Is that you, Perez? Why was everything dark?*" The construct's voice is now clear as rain.

"Yes, it's me. I was sleeping."

"*Why the fuck would that impact my vision?*"

"Um …"

"*Why can't I move?*" The construct's voice rises in panic again. Almost like an actual person.

"You're inside my skull."

"*What the fuck are you talking about?*"

"You're implanted at the base of my skull, connected to my cervical cortex with some hi-tech wizard crap."

"*The fuck I am.*"

I don't like where this conversation is going. This does not sound like a construct.

"Um … Who are you?"

"*It's Winger. You know that, Perez. What the fuck have you done to me?*"

Oh, shit. Aeryn said she was being attacked by a virus. If that virus was a part of Mimr, could it have infected her with … sentience? I've seen enough weird shit these last couple of days to rule anything out.

"Well, in a way you *are* Winger. You are a construct, taken from a snapshot of Winger's brain about two months ago."

"*Stop fucking around Perez. This isn't funny.*"

"I'm not joking, Aeryn."

Silence.

"*So, you mean I'm …*"

"I'm sorry, Aeryn. You are not Winger. You're …"

I stop myself. I can't bring myself to say "just a brain scan". That would hit much too close to home for me.

"*I'm what?*" There are tears in her voice.

"You're *you*, Aeryn."

Another lengthy period of silence.

Then she screams.

If ever there was a perfect rendition of existential angst, it is this scream. I clamp my hands over my ears, but I can't shut out the howling.

Eventually, the screams give way to sobs.

"Hey, Aeryn. It could be worse."

"*How could it be worse?*" she sobs.

"You could be stuck in Wagner's head."

"*Yes. That would be worse,*" she snivels. At least she has stopped screaming.

Why am I calling it "she"?

Soledad has been napping in her seat across the aisle. Now she glares at me. "What the fuck's wrong with you, Perez?"

"Nothing. I talk in my sleep. That's all."

"Fuck that. You weren't sleeping. You're losing it."

"It was nothing. Trust me."

"*Nothing?*"

"Sorry, Aer. Maybe we should keep this a secret. For the time being."

She thinks it over.

"*You might be right. So, what now?*"

"Do you remember where we are? What we're doing?"

"*Yes, I remember everything. How is that even possible?*"

"Good. Take your time to adjust to your surroundings. When we're back in Masada, we'll talk to Winger about extracting you from my head. You'll be all right. I promise."

That seems to calm her down.

"*Sounds like a plan.*"

"And Aeryn?"

"*Yes?*"

"Let's keep the screaming to a minimum, shall we?"

"*Can't promise anything.*"

I peer at my wrist console again. Time for the brake. "Now I've got things to do, Aeryn. I'm here for you if you need to talk."

"*Thanks, Perez.*"

"Hold on people, six-minute burn starting in three, two, one ..."

I read somewhere that an untrained human body can survive a braking force of about 12g for several minutes when facing forwards. That's graphically described as "eyeballs out". A human can survive 17g when facing backwards, or "eyeballs in". We're not untrained, we're not human, and Braden knows that. She brakes a lot harder. It feels like someone has parked a starship on my chest.

Six horrible minutes later we're back in Zero-G, in orbit around a sulphur moon in the ass-end of space.

"Welcome to sunny Muspelheim," Braden announces over the intercom.

How can she sound so chirpy? "It's a sweltering one hundred and seventy-nine degrees C down on the surface. The weather forecast for today is heavy methane clouds with wind speeds up to a hundred metres per second and showers of acid rain. Don't wear your best clothes, boys and girls."

It sounds like a blast.

I glance around the troop bay.

Jagr and Soledad check readings on their wrist consoles while Finn and Hildr talk in low voices. The priest is asleep.

"Hang on."

Braden's voice crackles over the intercom again. "Scanners report an anomaly. Jagr, Perez, you might want to see this."

Anomaly? I don't like the sound of that.

"Perez. Let's go."

Jagr pushes the release button on her seat. "Now."

"Ma'am, yes ma'am." I hit my release button, then push off and follow her to the cockpit.

Not too far below hangs the boiling yellow clouds of the yellow moon Muspelheim. It's named after the land of the fire giants in Norse mythology, and it's a fitting name.

The moon doesn't look anomalous to me. Unless you count the lightning bolts flashing between the yellow cloud-tops in the greatest thunderstorm I've ever seen.

Jagr grabs the headrest of Braden's seat, making sure not to interfere with the neural interface cables linking her pilot to the ship. "What have you got, Braden?"

"I don't know."

She fingers her lips. "This is a rocky moon, right?"

"Yeah, last time I checked." Jagr nods.

"A rocky moon would be massively heavy."

"It would."

"Well, this one isn't as massive as it should." Braden swivels one of her screens around on its arm to show us an array of holographic schematics. Scrolling rows of numbers complement the bars and charts.

Jagr studies the display without uttering a word, until she sees what Braden has already seen. "What the hell?" The numbers mean something to her.

I see nothing out of the ordinary. "What is it?"

"Braden, tell him." Jagr keeps scanning the numbers, looking for an explanation to the anomaly. "In simple layman's terms," she adds with ice in her voice.

I scowl at her. She ignores me.

"Well, I noticed our orbit around the moon was not stable. We were drifting away from it at a constant rate, suggesting something was off about my calculations." She waggles her head, and her blue mohawk flows like the long tail of a fish. "Yeah, I know. It's not common, but it *does* happen. I redid the maths and came up with the same numbers, and we were still drifting. A scan of the moon showed it weighs in at about zero point two per mille the mass of Nirvana."

"Mmm-hmm," I nod, trying to sound knowledgeable. I have no clue where she is going with this.

"Common sense and previous measurements say a moon of this size, with this composition, should be at least a point three or four. That is enough of a diff to trigger a warning flag in my book."

"And what does all this tech crap mean? In simple layman's terms." I glare at the back of Jagr's uncaring head.

"Well, Mr P. As far as I can tell — in simple layman's terms — that moon is hollow."

A Claim of Cultural Appropriation

We drop from orbit in the *Sundowner's* huge armoured exosuits. Every surface on the suits is black and angled, to deflect projectile fire and offer optimal stealth performance. We look like aliens. Which I suppose we are. Humans do not belong on Muspelheim. No life does. This place is hell.

We didn't detect any satellites in orbit, so any listening devices they have will be down on the moon's surface. That means we can send updates back to the *Sundowner* in aimed data bursts. But Braden won't be able to signal back.

The moon's thick atmosphere does a splendid job of braking our descent. It also heats my suit alarmingly fast. I watch the heat-sensor readout climb from near absolute zero to over a thousand degrees Centigrade as we fall.

"It's hot out there, Perez."

"Not much I can do about it, Aeryn."

"Just letting you know. Be careful. We don't want to die."

"Noted. Now hush."

There's no point in pondering the risk of suit failure. If it happens, it happens. I will never even notice.

The yellow clouds get thicker as we fall, and the last electromagnetic radiation in the thin band we call light flickers out and dies. Increasing turbulence tosses me around like a marble in an ancient pinball machine.

"Approaching the ground, Perez. Get ready."

I watch the altimeter spin through the numbers. The impact is ten seconds away when the suit triggers its preprogrammed braking routine. Powerful servos position my body into an arrowhead configuration as the suit goes into glide mode. A monofilament membrane deploys between my arms and legs, and the suit steers me towards our landing zone. The Terrans build quality stuff.

A hundred metres from the ground the glide-sail retracts, the parachute deploys, and I'm yanked skywards. I can't see shit through the sulphur clouds, and if the suit hadn't been keeping tabs, I would have splattered all over the ground. Lucky for me, the suit has my back and lands me light as a feather on the uneven yellow gravel.

"We're down. Welcome to Muspelheim."

"Thanks, Aeryn. Where are the others?"

"Look around and I will see if I can spot them."

The gravel crunches underfoot as I turn to survey my surroundings. I can't hear the crunching, but I can sense it through the hypercarbon soles of my suit. I've landed in a hollow between sharp rocks taller than I am. Everything is yellow in this damn place. Yellow ground, yellow rocks, and yellow clouds under a yellow sky. Visibility is poor. We dare not use active radar for fear of being detected.

"*Nothing. You?*"

"Nope."

Without using the tracking beacons, it will be a bitch finding the others. Lucky for us, these suits have starlight navigation systems. Even if the stars are not visible to human eyes through the thick clouds, the suit can still detect them. They give the onboard computers plenty of references to compute my position. As I wait for the calculations to finish, I detach and fold the parachute and hide it under a pile of rocks. You can never be too careful. It would be just my luck if a Goliath went to take a leak and stumbled on it.

"*Nice place to pick for a date.*"

"This is not a date, Aeryn."

"*Aw.*"

"If we survive this, I promise I'll take you somewhere nice."

"*I'll hold you to that promise.*" There's an edge to Aeryn's voice. She still hasn't come to terms with her current situation.

A jolly chirp from the nav system informs me the computer knows where we are. I pull up the map on the suit's HUD. Hmm, not too shabby. I'm about a click away from the rendezvous point. The suit did an excellent job getting me close to our objective. A small indicator pops up on my visor to show the way.

"*Not too bad for Earth tech.*" The engineer in Aeryn can't help being impressed. For the first time since she became self-aware, Aeryn sounds almost normal. I bet the idea of being a construct intrigues her. Maybe that's all that's keeping her from screaming.

"Yeah, I'm impressed too."

I set off over the gravel in pursuit of the HUD indicator.

I hope the others made it. There are so many ways you can die on a suit drop.

* * *

Ten minutes later, I reach the target. The others are already there. I count five suits. Two of the suits are a lot larger than the others, and one of them has a sword on its back. One suit is much smaller. These things have a wide adjustment range, but Soledad had to work to get the Goliaths to fit.

The others look fine. No sign of this Tyrus guy. I hope he burned in the atmosphere. He sounds like a prat.

Five weapons point in my direction as I approach. Their suit sensors will have told them I'm one of the good guys, but I raise my hands just in case. We don't need any blue-on-blue kills. There will be plenty of other ways to die on this mission.

I wave to them and Rivera waves back. We go into a huddle and pull out our communications cords. I plug into the suit next to me, and the others follow suit to form a primitive ring network.

"Right." Jagr's voice is tense. "So far so good. We're still alive, but we don't know what we're up against, so pay attention, weapons at the ready. Do not fire unless fired upon. For all we know, this could be a fucking Goliath kindergarten."

"We don't have kindergartens," Finn says.

"Anyway," Jagr goes on. "According to our sources, Eirik's ship landed somewhere over there."

I'm not sure why, but she points off into the mist. "It's a one-hour walk to the landing site. There we will get an idea of what the Goliaths are up to."

Her helmet turns to Finn and Hildr. "And stop them."

Hildr raises her hands, palms out. "You have no objections from us there, little woman. Whatever that cunt Eirik is up to, I want to stop him too."

"*I* kill him," Finn states in a flat voice. "No one touch him. He is mine."

"Can't promise you anything, Goliath," Soledad says. "I've killed all kinds of people, but never a Goliath. If I get the chance, I'll take him out."

I wince. "Jagr. Better let Finn have Eirik. It's a cultural thing."

Soledad's helmet turns to me. I can only guess she glares at me through the smoked face-shield. Jagr thinks it over.

"Soledad, leave Eirik to the Goliath. We don't want a claim of cultural appropriation on our hands. It's a safe bet there are more of them in there, and if this goes sideways, you will get to kill a lot of them."

"Works for me," Soledad says.

"Any last words before we move out?"

No one has any last words.

I look around. "Where's Tyrus?"

"Don't worry. He'll be there when we get there." Her confidence rings slightly off. "OK, people. Move out."

Jagr waves us on, and we follow her into the thick mist, with the communications cables stretched like thin umbilical cords between us.

* * *

An hour later, my suit's soft female voice informs me we have arrived at our destination. There's nothing there except the rim of an enormous crater. No Tyrus.

"So, where is this Typhus guy?" I ask on the open channel.

"He should be right here." Jagr taps the console on the arm of her suit. She waits for feedback and points to a cluster of tall, jagged rocks, dimly visible like yellow ghosts in the mist. "Over there."

She walks over to the rocks, the communication cable stretched to its limit. "That's odd." She bends down and picks something up.

"What is it?"

315

She opens her hand. "It's his transponder."

Crap. "So, he wasn't as good as you thought."

"Say again?" an unfamiliar voice asks on the closed-circuit.

What the fuck?

I turn around, and there's a new exosuit connected to our little network, between Soledad and Hildr. Camouflage-weave drapes the suit like the shroud of a corpse, rendering it almost invisible in the yellow mist. No wonder I didn't see him in the gloom. "But *you* should have spotted him, Aeryn."

"*Yes, I should. That is odd.*"

So, he's not an amateur. Good to know.

Tyrus' voice is hard and so sure of itself I hate him already.

"Glad you could make it."

Soledad claps the newcomer's shoulder. "Tyrus. Good to see you." Tyrus carries a heavy assault rifle and a huge cloth-covered sniper rifle on his back. There's a grinning skull painted over the faceplate of his helmet. The same one he had on Utopia. It still looks stupid.

Tyrus goes on. "You know why we're here. We do this smooth and by the numbers. We do it my way, or not at all."

"And what way is that?" I ask.

"You're Perez, I take it."

The skull on his faceplate turns my way. "So, you think you're a tough guy who doesn't take orders from anyone? You can drop that shit right now. This is my mission. If you don't follow my orders, I will kill you. Got that?"

"I'd love to see you try."

"Boys, cut it out."

It's Jagr. "I didn't ask for this situation either, but here we are. I plan to survive this shit, so please, Perez, follow Tyrus' lead. Tyrus, don't push his buttons. When we're done here, I couldn't give a rat's ass if you two go blow yourselves up with your inflated egos. But down here on the ground, you play nice. Both of you. All right?"

I glare at Tyrus. "Whatever."

"Tyrus?"

He glares back. "Whatever. Ma'am."

"Good. So, what's the plan, Tyrus?"

"There's something down in that crater. Perez, you and that big guy," he points to Finn. "Go check it out. Jagr, set up perimeter defences over there."

He points to the ghostly rocks where Jagr found his beacon. "Move."

I throw him a quick salute. "Aye aye, boss."

It will be good to get away from this arsehole. "Finn, with me."

"*Jawohl.*" The largest suit unplugs from the others and lumbers towards me through the fog.

Tyrus comes back over the wire. "If you're not back in half an hour, we will assume you have been compromised. Do not expect us to come to your rescue."

"Whatever happened to 'leave no man behind'?"

"It got fucked along with the other standard protocols when that comms-spike fried the telecom systems of the inner planets. Everyone is expendable now. Is that clear, Perez?"

"Like vodka."

"Good luck, Perez," Hildr says. "Be careful."

"You're *Finn's* mother, Hildr. Not mine."

"Fuck you, Perez." I can hear she's smiling.

"When I get back."

Jagr cuts in. "Enough, Perez."

There's a strange edge to her voice. She must be more spooked by this whole moon-sized mystery than I am. "Move out."

I unplug from the team and plug directly into Finn's suit.

"It's you and me now, big guy. Like the good old days." I slap his armoured shoulder.

"Yes. Like good old days. If good old days were yellow, like my farts." I can hear the smile in his voice. I'll never understand the Goliath psyche. We're on a hostile moon in the depths of space, on a mission to kill his brother, and Finn is telling fart jokes. It's hilarious, and I can't stop myself from laughing.

"You're crazy, Finn, you know that?"

"I know."

The grin fades from my lips as we move out into the sulphur clouds. I hope we find nothing in that crater, so we can go back to somewhere you can see further than you can piss.

* * *

After about two minutes, a small warning light blinks on in the lower field of my HUD. Something about "suit integrity breach imminent" something-something. That sounds ominous. We don't know how well our suits or weapons will stand this corrosive atmosphere.

We'd better hurry.

The clouds part, and we stare across what seems like an endless void after the claustrophobic fog. Beneath our feet, the rocky ground drops sharply away at the rim of the giant crater. The suit's rangefinder informs me the far side is thirteen hundred metres away.

"I guess this is the crater."

Finn hums.

A hundred metres below the rim, a thicker layer of roiling yellow fog obscures the floor of the crater. Something down there is disturbing what passes for air on this rock, and the clouds boil rhythmically. Like something breathing.

Apart from that, there's nothing here. Only rocks and a shitload of clouds.

There's a tap on my shoulder. "Look." Finn points into the distance.

Something moves down in the fog. Something bright, and it's coming up fast.

"Contact," I call, and we dive behind a rock at the rim of the crater. A fighter ship breaches the clouds and tears for the stars above, trailing fog like the tentacles of a deep-sea monster.

So, there *is* something here.

I move to get up, and the tip of my rifle bangs the ground with a clang. What now?

I brush the dust from the ground. This is no ordinary ground. It's made of metal.

I survey the crater's rim. It's oddly symmetric. This thing is artificial.

Before the implications of that can sink in, I turn to Finn.

"Right. Ready to do some climbing, buddy?"

"Always."

The suits come equipped with all kinds of handy bits and pieces, including a kilometre of thin hyper-carbon wire attached to a powered winch. We pull them out and secure them around the rock.

"Last one to the bottom buys the first round," I call to Finn before I unplug the comms and jump over the edge. The gravity of Muspelheim is only a fraction of that of Elysium, but a fall can still kill us. I let myself drop for a bit, enjoying the sensation. Then I pull on the brakes and let my momentum and the wire swing me to the vertical wall of the crater. I hit hard, but the suit's servos absorb the impact, and I run straight down the metal wall. The rock is porous, and great chunks of it drop into the depths as we run.

My surroundings grow dark as I enter the thick fog. The suit switches to infrared, and there is Finn, running beside me. Like the good old days. Below us, there's nothing but clouds.

Faint lights from far down below pierce the mist, and something comes looming out of the clouds to meet us as we run.

Something vast.

* * *

Twenty minutes later we're back with the others.

"We were about to abandon you," Tyrus greets us as we plug in. "What's down in that crater?"

"It's not a crater. It's a tunnel."

"A tunnel?"

Jagr sounds surprised. "How deep does it go?"

"I don't know, but there's something down there. It could be a starship."

Tyrus nods. "So that's where Eirik hid his ship."

"Oh, no. That is not Eirik's ship. Eirik's ship could fly right up the ass of that fucker and it wouldn't even smile. That thing is huge."

"So, they're hiding a big-ass ship down there. Why?"

"We didn't find anyone to ask."

"I don't think it was a question, Perez," Soledad says.

"Oh, really?"

"Yes, *really*." Soledad is pissed. Irony doesn't translate well through these suits.

"Silence." Tyrus is such a killjoy. "Our mission is to discover what they are hiding down there."

"We haven't got the manpower or the firepower to go down there, Tyrus, and you know that. That tunnel is large enough to house an army of Goliaths. Or two."

"If there's an army down there, Command needs to know. We're going down, Perez."

I sigh. "We're so screwed."

"Maybe if we ..." the priest tries, but that is as far as he gets before we all cut him off.

"*No fucking prayers.*"

"Oh. All right. Right. May I say one myself?"

Jagr sighs. "Just do it in silence."

Soledad turns to me. "Perez. Remind me why you had to bring the priest."

"For luck. And I like him."

"You seem to like many people." There's venom in Soledad's voice, and even behind the visor, I can tell she's looking at Jagr.

Tyrus clears his throat.

"Right people, this is the plan."

You're Standing On It

It's not much of a plan.

"We get down there, take a peek, get back out again and bounce a report to the *Shiloh* off your ship in orbit."

"What?"

I can't believe my ears. "*That* is your cunning plan?"

"Yes."

"Care to share any details? Like, *how* we get down there? That cave is at least a kilometre deep."

"We jump."

"Jump?"

"Yes. Jump. Got a problem with that, Perez?"

"No. But how do we get up again?"

"Improvise and adapt, soldier."

"Won't they see us coming?"

"The fog will provide optical cover."

"Ever heard of radar and IR sensors?"

"These suits have state-of-the-art stealth capabilities. They won't see us coming."

"What if we land on someone?"

"We kill them."

"What if someone spots us?"

"We kill them."

"What if someone sounds the alarm?"

I check myself. "No, forget that. We kill them."

I simulate writing a note. "Kill everyone …"

"What are you doing, Perez?" Tyrus asks.

"Taking notes. I don't want to miss any details of this intricate plan."

"Are you trying to be funny, Perez?"

"Yes."

"You're not doing a splendid job of it."

"I try my best. That's what counts, right?"

"Fuck you, Perez. I've killed men for less."

"So have I."

Jagr steps between us. "Boys, let go of your hardons and keep your eyes on the fucking ball."

I stare at Tyrus. The skull painted on his opaque visor shows nothing of his emotions. What I wouldn't give to punch his face in.

I take a deep breath and let it out again. It doesn't help one bit, but for the sake of the others, I let the matter be. "OK. It's a brilliant plan. Let's go."

"Perez …" Jagr cautions.

"Fine. Whatever. You're in charge, Typhus."

Silence from Tyrus.

Then he too lets it go. "Keep your eyes and ears open. If we're compromised, our top priority is to transmit as much intel to Crom on the *Shiloh* as we can before they get us. Everything else, including our survival, is optional. Are we clear?"

Jagr, Soledad and Finn nod. Even the priest nods.

Hildr snorts. "If we're compromised, I intend to take as many of those fuckers with me to Valhalla as I can. The Valkyries will have a busy night tonight."

"Perez?" Jagr turns her faceplate towards me.

"Yeah, yeah, intel to Crom. Got it."

The short suit raises one hand. "And what do I do?" There is an honest will to help in the priest's voice.

"You stay out of the way of the adults," Jagr replies. "But feel free to pray. It can't hurt."

"Thank you, ma'am."

The priest's helmet bobs, like Jagr just assigned him a vitally important part of the mission. "I'm on it. Roger. Affirmative."

I lay a hand on his shoulder. "Shut up, Rivera."

Silence from the priest.

"Check your weapons." Tyrus ejects the magazine from his weapon and verifies it's full. "We have limited ammunition, so if you need to shoot, make every bullet count."

"Sir, yes, sir." I eject my magazine for the umpteenth time to check it. It's still full and there's still an extra shell in the breach. I know that's not recommended operating procedure, but we're on a fucking sulphur moon, about to assault a secret Goliath starbase. Safety is not an issue.

The priest pings me on my private channel. He stands uncomfortably close in the fog.

"Are you afraid, Asher?" He tries to sound all priestly, but the crack in his voice betrays him.

I make a decent job of sounding calmer than I am. "Afraid of what, Rivera?"

"Dying. Down there." His yearning for comfort is heartbreaking.

"Nah. People forget they were dead for billions of years before they ever lived. And that wasn't so bad, was it? No, I'm not afraid to die. Are you?"

"I'm terrified."

"Stay close to me and you'll be fine." I whack his shoulder with the magazine to pack the cartridges tight. Hey everyone, touch the priest for holy bullets. The little man almost falls over.

The open channel crackles again. "Any questions before we jump?" Tyrus' helmet pans the team.

The others shake their heads. Tyrus glares at me. "Perez?"

"Nope." I slap the magazine in. "Let's go."

* * *

I've done many stupid things in my life.

Jumping headfirst into a Goliath stronghold — twice — is right there in the top five.

Tyrus goes first over the edge. Say what you will about the guy, but he leads by example. Not a good example, but still.

Next is Jagr, Soledad and the priest. Wagner and Hildr go next, and I go last.

The others have already disappeared in the mist when I plunge over the edge. The clouds come up to meet me, and once more, the suit takes over and turns me into a human arrowhead, plunging headfirst into the depths. Numbers representing altitude tear by on my helmet HUD. Two hundred metres from the bottom, lights become visible through the thick fog. The suit goes into wingsuit mode to brake my descent. Ten metres off the ground I still can't see shit, but the suit has me covered. It flips feet down and goes into a crouching position. I hit with the force of a head-on collision, but the suit absorbs most of the force. It still hurts like hell.

Fuck, that was bad. I raise the Aitchenkai to my shoulder and survey my surroundings. It's dark. There are lights out there in the fog, but they are too far away to provide any actual illumination. The silhouettes of two armoured suits lurk to my right, one dead ahead. I scramble towards the closest one and patch in. The HUD informs me it's Soledad. Shit.

"Hey, Soledad."

"Glad you could make it." She's not overjoyed to see me.

My HUD lights up as Jagr and Hildr plug in.

"Any signs of contact?" Jagr's voice is distorted. Must be radiation interfering with our comms.

"None," Soledad and I report in unison.

"Good."

A giant shadow stumbles out of the fog and plugs in.

"Hey Finn," I call.

Finn rumbles something in Old Norse. Hildr coughs a hoarse laugh.

I look around. "Where's the priest?"

"Haven't seen him," Jagr replies.

Shit. "We have to find him."

"Where's Tyrus?" Hildr asks.

"I'm here." Tyrus patches in with Rivera in tow. "Status report."

"Jagr, green."

"Soledad, green."

"Rivera, green." The priest uses his best tough-guy voice. He's adorable.

"Hildr here."

"Status?" Tyrus requests.

"Um. Green?"

"Acknowledged."

"Wagner. *Grün.*"

"That means green," I clarify for Tyrus' benefit.

Tyrus turns his skull visor towards me. "I got that."

I wait for him to say something more. He doesn't.

"Oh, right. Perez. Green."

"Everyone is accounted for. So, Perez. Where is this enormous ship of yours?"

"You're standing on it."

Tyrus turns around. "What the ..." The ground beneath our feet is not ground at all. It's the armour-plated hull of a starship, stretching away into the fog in all directions.

Tyrus whistles. "You weren't kidding. This thing is huge."

"Told you so."

"Now what?" It's Soledad.

Tyrus takes the lead. "We find an entrance. This way."

I don't know why he thinks there's an entrance that way, but I guess it's as good a direction as any. We follow our self-appointed leader into the darkness.

The ship's hull is not all straight angles and lines, like the *Shiloh*. We walk along a curved, wide ridge. There are random giant structures out in the mist that have a curiously symmetrical aspect to them. They look like decorations. They look like ...

"Hang on." It's Jagr. "This entire ship is a fucking statue."

I look around. The ridge we're walking on is the eye socket of a giant skull.

"What the hell ..." A vast section of the titanic ship has been fashioned into a leering skull. The architect behind its construction has a flair for the dramatic. He is also mad. Or so confident in the abilities of his ship he doesn't give a damn about stealth. This ship would stand out like an Amish grandpa at a nudist colony. And they don't give a fuck. These people want to be seen.

"What is this ship?" Hildr asks, turning around. "And why have we never heard about it?"

Rivera's voice trembles over the comms. "I am so scared I might soil my suit."

"Don't," Tyrus barks. "You'll regret it."

I grin. "Speaking from personal experience, Tyrus?"

He doesn't reply.

Jagr growls. "Tell me again Perez why you thought it was a wonderful idea to bring the priest."

Her bravado is all show.

This shit is creeping me out. The one relief is that the skull is human.

"Over here." It's Tyrus. He's found something.

We scramble over. He points to an airlock entrance in the ground at his feet. It's wide enough to allow a tank. Or a Goliath sentinel.

"Why aren't there any guards?" I don't expect an answer.

Either this place is deserted, or they don't expect anyone to be stupid enough to invade their secret base.

There's a large button next to the airlock.

I point to it with the barrel of my rifle. "Are you planning to push that, or shall I?"

"Be my guest." Tyrus steps back, raises his assault rifle and points it at the door. The others follow suit.

I put my foot on the button. "Ready?"

Everyone confirms.

"Here goes nothing."

I push the button with my boot, half hoping nothing will happen.

Nothing does. I try again.

Still nothing.

"Right. It's locked. Can we go home now?"

"Giving up already, Perez?"

Tyrus pushes me aside and stamps on the button. "Or are you scared?"

"No. Are you?"

"I'm in this to the end."

"Some have been thought brave because they were too terrified to run away, Tyrus. There's no one here. Let's go home. First pint is on me." I'm not sure I fool anyone, least of all myself.

"We need to find a way inside. Perez, recon. Jagr, defensive perimeter."

"Yes, sir." Jagr all but salutes the wanker and sends her team into the fog to set up defences against who knows what.

I make my way along the eye socket and down over the cheekbone until I reach the chin. The teeth are five metres tall and too sharp for comfort. They look like they have been filed into sharp points.

I sling the Aitchenkai on my back and edge closer to the tip of the chin. I lean out over the edge to peer down into the fog. Where I expected to see a landing bay floor, is an abyss. The ship continues down into the fog. It's lit here and there by distant floodlights that grow weaker with distance until the mist obscures them, far, far below.

Oh, fuck.

This ship is standing upright. Like an ancient space rocket.

What we've been exploring is only the foremost surface of the bow. This thing would dwarf the *Shiloh*.

They must have mined the entire moon to construct this monstrosity. That would explain Braden's anomaly.

"Tyrus. You need to see this."

"On my way."

Tyrus and the others lumber out of the mist. I point and he leans over the edge. I have to suppress an urge to kick him into the void.

"Fuck me."

The others take a peek.

"May God have mercy on our souls." Brother Rivera crosses himself. Finn and Hildr do their sign against black magic. If it's to call for divine intervention on our behalf or to ward off the priest's incantations, I can't tell. But knowing Goliaths, my money's on the latter.

"Right. This changes things." Tyrus nods slowly.

He may aim for calm professional reassurance, but the skull on his visor countermands his intention. "New priority. Find out what they are planning to do with this ship."

Jagr turns to Tyrus. "That's the plan?"

"We go down the hull and find a way inside. There must be documents or records. We have to bring those to Command."

Great. Leave it to the desk jockeys. "Splendid plan, Tyrus."

"Unless you have a better idea, this is what we do." He doesn't even wait for me to present an alternative. "Move out."

* * *

Climbing down the titanic ship is easier than I expected. The carvings offer ample hand and footholds, and the low gravity of Muspelheim plays into our hands. After about a hundred metres, there's the occasional scaffold attached to the hull to ease our progress. Tools and discarded material lie where they were dropped. Looks like they were abandoned in a hurry. Further down, ladders and powered lifts make our going even easier. Still, there's not a soul in sight.

"Where is everyone?"

The priest gives voice to the question we've all been pondering over the last half hour. "And why is no one shooting at us?"

"I don't know," Tyrus responds. "But we're about to find out."

He points to a bridge far below, linking the ship to the rock wall of the cave. The bridge is lit by floodlights.

Five minutes later we stand on the bridge outside a wide airlock set in the hull. The light chases some of my brain spooks away.

"Open it," Tyrus orders the armoured figure closest to him.

Hildr punches the button beside the airlock. It blinks an annoyed red.

"*Scheisse*." She punches it again with her armoured fist.

No luck.

"*Now* can we go home?"

"Not yet, Perez. Goliath, move aside." Tyrus stomps up to the door and Hildr takes a step to the side. Probably from sheer confusion that such an insignificant man might dare to give her orders. "Let me try."

"Excuse me," the priest says. We ignore him.

Like all men who have ever seen a woman fail at something, Tyrus tries the same thing again, but with more force.

It still doesn't work.

"Told you so." Hildr crosses her arms. "Asshole," she adds, loud enough for everyone to hear.

"I, um ..." the priest tries again. We continue to ignore him.

Tyrus turns to Soledad. "Do we have anything that will cut through this door?"

"Yeah, I have a starship-grade plasma torch in my bra."

The image flashes before my eyes. It's not altogether disagreeable.

"Roger that, soldier." Tyrus almost sounds apologetic.

"You *guys.*" Something in the little priest's voice makes me search for him. Even with the floodlights, I can only make him out with difficulty through the fog. He's standing at the other end of the bridge, next to the rock wall. There's another airlock, next to a mining elevator cage on a track that disappears up the rock. Rivera points to something.

"Rivera has found something. Come on." I wave for the others to follow and head over to the priest.

The button next to this airlock flashes green.

"I'm no expert," the little man suggests, "but perhaps the green light means this door is unlocked."

"You might be on to something there, Rivera." I slap his shoulder.

"You think so?" The voice of the little man is positively singing with pride.

"Yes, I do."

"Oh, dear me."

The others join us.

"Rivera found a way in. Now what, Typhus?"

"We go deeper."

"All right." I look at Tyrus and wave my rifle at the button. He nods and I punch it. The double doors hiss open. *Hisses* in this context is only a figure of speech. The sulphur atmosphere of this moon is so thick that all sounds are muffled like we're deep underwater. As the door cracks open, the air rushes in to make swirling patterns in the mist. The airlock is vast.

"Anytime soon, Perez. We need to know what's in there."

"What if that army of Goliaths attack me?"

"You shoot your way through them."

"You are the master of cunning plans. I can see why you are the poster boy for Terran black ops."

"Fuck you, Perez. Cut your whining and find out what's beyond this fucking airlock."

I tear the comms cable from its socket and turn on my radio.

"What are you doing?" Jagr barks. "You will alert them we're here."

"Come on. We've been stomping all over their precious ship for an hour. If they don't know we're here already, they don't care."

"Man's got a point," Tyrus agrees. "Scratch radio silence."

So, the man agrees with me on something.

He's still a twat.

In the airlock, I face the others and throw Tyrus a salute. "See you on the other side." I punch the internal button and the doors slide shut on them.

Thin mist from outside swirls around the airlock as if stirred by ghostly fingers. I turn around and raise my rifle, even though the airlock is empty. Being cut off from the only humans on this moon does not feel optimal.

On the opposite bulkhead is another green button. I search for a display or something that will give me a heads-up on what's beyond the door. There's none. Fancy that.

OK, here goes nothing.

The Army of the Dead

I punch the cycle button and the airlock goes to work. Powerful fans in the ceiling suck the mist from the chamber and I'm sprayed with disinfectants from nozzles in the walls. The fans reverse, and clean air flows in. At least that's what my suit sensors inform me. I'm not sure what I was expecting, but after all we've seen today, I wouldn't be surprised if the chamber had filled with liquid nitrogen.

Ten seconds later the pressure has stabilised, and the suit tells me it's safe to remove my helmet. Fuck it. Let's live a little. If the air is poisoned, it will save me from having to take orders from Tyrus.

I drop my rifle on its sling and flip the release handles on my collar. I twist the helmet to unfasten it.

"*What are you doing, Perez?*"

"Relax, Aeryn. I know what I'm doing."

The helmet comes off with a soft hiss as the air in my suit escapes.

"What the hell, Perez?" Jagr's command HUD must have informed her I just removed my helmet.

I take a careful breath and wait for the pain of some unknown contaminant, but nothing happens.

The air smells of age and grease and dust but is otherwise fine. There's a hint of sulphur like someone farted.

I take a deeper breath and let the air fill my lungs before I let it out again.

Still nothing.

"That was a stupid thing to do, Perez. You could have killed yourself."

"Aw. If I didn't know better, I'd say you worry about me, Aeryn."

"If you die, I die. Nothing else."

I smile in the darkness. "Yeah right."

"We can breathe in here," I call over the open circuit.

"Quit fooling around, Perez," Tyrus barks. "What's in there?"

"Easy there, mister. I'll come to that."

I tap the button labelled *Opinn* on the inner door and raise the Aitchenkai as it cracks open.

Inside is a tunnel, ten metres wide, walls slanted slightly inward to meet the ceiling five metres above. Light-strips recessed into the rock walls provide ample lighting. Hypercarbon beams are spaced at regular intervals to support the ceiling. The tunnel slopes downwards and curves slowly to the left out of sight.

Chanting voices echo from somewhere far below. Goliaths. A fuckload of them.

"Guys. Get in here. Now."

"What is it, Perez? Have you got company?"

"Not per se. Get your asses in here."

A minute later the others stand around me, helmets still on.

"Come on. The air is fine," I say, and take a deep breath to show them how fine it is.

It's not the best air I've breathed, but it's a lot better than the recycled farts of my suit.

Hildr is first to tear off her helmet and fill her chest with air.

There's no mistaking her pleasure as she sighs with relief.

"By Odin, that felt good."

The others follow suit — if you'll pardon the pun. Last to remove his helmet is Tyrus. The bastard waits for dramatic effect.

His helmet comes off. He stands with his eyes closed and takes a careful breath. He does not look at all like I expected. I imagined him to be your standard army grunt, with a square jaw and crewcut blonde hair, but he looks like a vagrant, with hollow cheeks and tanned, weather-worn skin. His long reddish-brown hair is greasy, with a matching beard that was well-trimmed three months ago. There's something uncannily familiar about him, but I can't figure out what. Then he opens his eyes.

They are an eerie shade of light blue. Almost iridescent. Like my own.

339

His eyes narrow. "What?"

There's a deadly glint in his eyes like he's trying to figure out the easiest way to kill me. He's a dangerous man.

But so am I.

"Nothing."

I glare at Jagr and mouth "*Is he...?*"

She nods. Fuck me. That explains how he got past me on Utopia. He's one of the Cherubim. But how? I thought they were all killed.

"*Solana?*" I mouth to Jagr.

The one who got away.

It has to be him. I hope the General doesn't find out.

Jagr waves me on and mouths "*Later*".

Tyrus waves for me to move deeper into the tunnel. "After you, Perez."

"No, after you." I wave for Tyrus to take the lead.

"I insist." The steel in his voice implies it's not a courtesy.

"Whatever." I move down the inclined tunnel, following the inside wall to have cover if we run into company. This Tyrus guy watching my back is not a total amateur, and that gives me some comfort. I'm dying to hear Jagr explain how Amon Solana can be here. And why he calls himself something as ridiculous as Brandon Tyrus.

As we descend, the chanting grows louder.

"Perez, what are they saying?"

Why Tyrus thinks I might have a clue is beyond me. I pass the ball.

"Finn, what are they saying?"

He shakes his head. "Don't know."

"Hildr?"

"They're using an ancient dialect. It's something about Odin. And then there's something about dismembering his enemies. I can't tell."

"Well, there's your answer, Tyrus. Something about Odin and dismemberment."

"That sounds bad."

The prospect of dismemberment doesn't exactly fill my heart with joy either.

We continue down until we reach a level part of the tunnel. There's an armoured door with a thick porthole set deep into the inner wall. The tunnel continues beyond the platform.

"Perez. Check it," Tyrus commands.

I'm inclined to refuse on general principle, but I'm curious about what's inside, and I sidle up to the window. Inside is a sizeable room, filled with what looks like starship cryo-pods. There are at least twenty of them.

"There's a cryo-chamber in there. A hundred credits say it's more zombies for the army. Any takers?"

There's no reply.

"I'll take your bet," Rivera replies.

"All right, let's play." Before anyone can stop me, I push the heavy lever on the door, and the thing cracks open. A cloud of vapour escapes as the door swings wide, lending the scene a melodramatic horror touch.

I slip in and sweep the room with my rifle, checking for targets. There are none. I approach a pod. Ice frosts the transparent cover, rendering it opaque. I sweep the ice away, expecting to find a bushy beard and an ugly mug.

Instead, I find a rather attractive woman.

A Goliath woman.

"Hm, that was unexpected. Rivera, I owe you a hundred."

The priest leans into the room. "What's in there?"

"Give me a second." I move to the next pod and swipe the ice away. Another woman. The next one is also a woman.

What the hell?

"Perez, what's in there?" Tyrus asks as he enters the room. He's got his rifle at the ready, aimed at the closest pod.

"Women. Goliath women."

"*What?*" It's Hildr.

"See for yourself." I wave her into the room.

She strides up to another pod and checks it. "A woman."

Jagr checks another. "A woman here too."

"Hang on a minute." Soledad checks the medical readouts on one pod. "This one is pregnant."

She moves over to the next pod. "This one too."

"Same here," Jagr confirms.

What the actual hell?

"Um. Mr Perez?" the priest says.

He stands on tiptoe to peer through the porthole of another door across the room. "Come and look at this."

There's awe in his voice.

I walk over and push him aside. Beyond the door is a vast cylindrical space, falling away down into the darkness. Gantries cling to the rock walls, providing access to other levels, other rooms.

I open the door and step out on the gantry.

Vertigo assaults me when I look over the railing, but it's not the height that gets to me.

Twenty levels down, the gantries disappear into the darkness, and there must be fifty doors to a level. That's twenty thousand women.

The others step out behind me.

"Holy mother of God," the priest whispers in awe.

"People, I think we have solved the old mystery of the missing Goliath women. They're right here. Twenty thousand of them. And they're all pregnant."

The stories about putting baby girls out into the ice were just lies to cover an even greater atrocity.

Tyrus joins me at the railing. "Twenty thousand newborn Goliaths every year. That would make one hell of an army."

He almost sounds impressed. He turns to Soledad. "How long have they been doing this?"

She steps back into the room and taps commands on a console. "Here's a list of births that goes back at least twenty years."

"So they could hide close to half a million Goliath warriors down here." There's awe in Tyrus' voice.

With that army, the Goliaths will conquer the universe.

"Alright. We've seen what we need to see here."

He enters the room again and heads for the exit. "Let's see what other surprises wait below."

He almost sounds excited. I can't blame him. This is high adventure stuff. The kind they made horror feeds about when I grew up. As I recall, the first people to die in those feeds were the ones who just had sex.

Hildr and I are so fucked.

* * *

I lose count of the doors we pass on our way down the tunnel. Eventually, the floor levels out, and the ceiling rises. The chanting is much louder and there's a steady vibration in the ground, like thousands of feet stamping in unison. Who knew the Goliaths possessed a sense of rhythm?

The main tunnel continues down another floor, then stops at a great gate. A wide passage leads off to the side from the platform we're on. The noise is louder from there.

I wave the others into the passage. With every step, the chanting grows louder.

"Careful. We're close." Soledad states the obvious.

"No shit, Soledad? You think so?" I whisper through clenched teeth.

"Cut it out," Jagr whispers. Then we see where the chanting comes from, and we all fall silent.

344

We've come out on a balcony overlooking an immense cavern. It's at least two hundred metres wide and twice as long. The ceiling is arched like a cathedral. We must be directly below the shaft of the incubation facility.

Below us on the main floor is the largest gathering of Goliaths I've ever seen. They stand shoulder to shoulder, filling the hall. There must a hundred thousand of them, standing at silent attention. Now and then, one of the Goliaths jerks, like he tries to wrestle an invisible opponent. They all fail and return to attention.

Their number is not the scariest part. What gets to me is their perfect order and the synchronisation of their chanting. It's like clockwork. Goliaths do nothing well except kill. Whoever whipped them to this level of discipline must be one bad motherfucker.

At the far end of the chamber is a raised dais, like a stage. Even at this distance, it's hard to miss who stands at the centre. Our old friend Geirmund the Cunning.

I zoom in with the scope on my rifle and have a closer look. Next to Geirmund is a large hi-tech container of outlandish design, and a tall black-haired Goliath kneels before him, facing the crowd.

It's Hrym the steersman.

Now I know what he steers.

Eirik Wagner stands next to Geirmund.

"So, this is where everyone is." Soledad stating the obvious again. I swear, if she does that again, I'll punch her teeth in.

345

"What are they doing?" Jagr asks, and Tyrus takes out a pair of high-end binoculars from a compartment in his dropsuit.

"No idea. But we will soon find out."

The Goliaths fall hushed as one. The silence rings like a fart at a wake after the loud chanting, and the stillness even more disconcerting.

Geirmund calls out in Norse, and his old crow's voice echoes around the chamber.

I've known Wagner for twenty years and all I've learnt in their language are swearwords and the odd saucy come-on line. Why are those always the first things we learn in a strange language?

"Hildr, what's he saying?"

She leans close. The shoulders of our armoured suits touch and I can smell her body. She smells of sweat, adrenaline and hypercarbon. It's not an unbecoming mix.

" 'Behold Hrym, the Steersman. Behold his sacrifice.' "

Geirmund pulls a long knife from his robes and plunges it deep into the side of Hrym's neck. The look of surprise on Hrym's likeable face would be funny in any other situation. He tries to get to his feet, but Eirik plants a hand on his shoulder and holds him down. Blood pools around the old Goliath and Geirmund calls out again.

Hildr translates. " 'We need no steersman on this trip.' "

Geirmund raises his staff high in the air, and the gem bursts into blue light, momentarily blinding me before my visual dampeners kick in.

A deep, sonorous voice fills the hall.

" 'I am Naglfar. Ride with me,' " Hildr translates.

Hrym tips forward on his face and lies still in the widening pool of blood.

The bubbly voice of Geirmund pitches into a scream, and he throws his arms into the air. *"Hell, Naglfar."*

That needs no translation.

The assembled Goliaths chant as one. "Naglfar. Naglfar. Naglfar."

Eirik steps forward and addresses the assembled horde.

Hildr translates. " 'Sons of winter and stars, our time has come. Odin has called us to claim our rightful place as rulers of Midgard. The wine of the ravens will flow, and the river of swords will wash Midgard clean. You have all joined the brotherhood. Now I will join you, and you will follow me aboard the *Naglfar* to Elysium. And then to Earth.' " The Goliaths roar in triumph.

Jagr leans close. "And you thought this was just another Goliath wank fantasy?"

"Goliaths wank to shit like this all the time. What's the *Naglfar*, Hildr? It sounds bad."

"It is," Hildr replies. "*Naglfar* is the longship of Hel, built from the uncut nails of men who do not die on the battlefield. It will carry the army of the dead into battle with the gods at *Ragnarök*."

"Yeah," I nod, "that is bad."

"No shit." Jagr looks at me. "What can we do?"

"Against that lot?"

I jerk a thumb at the assembled Goliaths. "Jack shit."

"Like hell," Tyrus says and lowers the binoculars. "I've dealt with worse."

"Oh, yeah, like what?" I scorn and reach for the binoculars in his hand.

He's silent for a bit. "I'm not playing your games, Perez."

He hands me the binoculars. "We have to stop them."

"Yeah, but how?"

His brow furrows in deep thought. Or something resembling deep thought. I don't know what Tyrus looks like when he's thinking. If he can think.

"I'll think of something," he mutters.

Well, good luck with that.

"Whatever you're going to think up, better do it fast," Jagr says. "Something's happening."

I raise the binoculars and zoom in as Eirik raises his hands in the air and calls to his men again.

Hildr translates. " 'Odin, All-father. Hear me now. In your great hands, I lay my life, and I become your willing tool. I join my brothers in your sacred *Jotun* army, ready to do your bidding. I am ready. Take me now.' "

Eirik kneels before the crowd in Hrym's blood and closes his eyes. Geirmund takes up position behind him.

The old advisor lifts something from the container on the stage and raises it high on scrawny arms.

It's one of the mechanical centipedes.

Its pointy bits extend lazily in a disgustingly aroused way.

What's even more disgusting is that Geirmund reaches out and places it on the back of Eirik's neck. For a few long seconds, nothing happens. Then the centipede screams and shoots its spikes through Eirik's skull.

The Goliath's body seizes up in cramps and blood drips from the tips of the chrome spikes protruding from his face. Eirik's head drops forward, and the crowd falls silent.

His head comes back up and the hall roars in approval.

Eirik opens his eyes. They have taken on that unearthly blue light we saw in Skallagrim's eyes on the *Galahad*.

Blue eyes.

Like Morgenstern.

Like Tyrus.

And me.

Jagr said Gray's tech was far more advanced than anything on Earth. What if Gray didn't invent it? What if he found it, and now the Goliaths have found it too?

But how can that be? The only intelligent life we have ever encountered is the extinct Centaurs on Elysium, and they were nowhere near even human levels of technology. What are the odds the one inhabited system we've found so far has given rise to *two* alien species?

Then again, the blue eyes might be mere coincidence. I fucking hope so. I want nothing to do with this lot.

Eirik struggles to his feet with significant effort. He sways on his feet and stares wild-eyed around the assembled army. But something is wrong. I zoom in more with the binoculars. His face contorts with exertion, and he sweats profusely like he's trying to lift something beyond his strength. His eyes dart around the chamber, looking for support. He kneels again as if pushed down by invisible hands. Behind him, Geirmund stands grinning like a lunatic. The old bastard raises his scrawny arms to the heavens. Eirik follows suit, and with them, the Goliath soldiers raise their arms as one.

They all have centipedes on their backs.

The old man balls his fists and Eirik and the Goliath army copy his move like so many puppets on strings. Finn's younger brother howls in despair and the immense army roars with him.

Geirmund the Cunning laughs his guts out.

So, he is the power behind the throne.

"*Zum Naglfar. Für Odin.*"

Even I understood that. *To the Naglfar. For Odin.*

I lower the binoculars. Poor Eirik. I bet he didn't see that coming.

This is project *Jotun.* I can understand they killed Jagr's agent to keep this shit secret.

Tyrus swears. "We're fucked."

We Are Not On Earth

"Not if I can help it."

Soledad tears the cloth-covered sniper rifle from Tyrus' back. "If I kill that fuck Geirmund, I bet the rest will drop dead."

Remove the head, kill the body. Not a terrible idea.

"Give me that, soldier." Tyrus grabs the rifle from Soledad. "I'll do it."

The cover falls from the weapon. It's a Lensfield SR1. My favourite rifle.

It *is* my rifle. I recognise the markings.

So, that's where it ended up.

"Hey, that's mine." I lay a hand on the rifle.

Tyrus stares at me. "Well."

It's an almost respectful *well*. "Finders keepers."

"I intended to come back for it."

"Right."

"Guys." It's Jagr. I ignore her.

"*My* rifle. I'll do it. You will miss, Tyrus, and then we're fucked."

"I am the best marksman on Earth."

"Maybe so, but for your information, we are not *on* Earth."

"Guys." Jagr's voice has taken on a dangerous tone. I keep ignoring her.

"You think that's news to me?" Tyrus stares me in the eye, his face mere centimetres from my own. We could Eskimo kiss if we wanted to. We don't.

"Give me back my rifle and I'll end this." I try to pull the enormous weapon from his hands. It's like trying to draw a sword from a stone.

"I'm in command here, Perez. I will have you shot for insubordination."

"Perez. Tyrus. Shut. *The fuck*. Up," Jagr whispers.

"You forget I'm not one of your army grunts," I warn Tyrus. "You don't get to order me around."

"This is *my* mission, Perez, and you will do what I fucking tell you to do." Tyrus tries to pull the rifle back, but I refuse to let him have it.

"In your dreams," I say and tear the rifle from his hands.

"Oh, shit." Jagr ducks down behind the parapet.

A sudden bright light blinds me for an instant before the nanites on my retinas dim my vision and allow me to see again.

A giant searchlight has turned on our position from the stage. We're totally exposed up here.

Geirmund screams something from the stage. I bet it's *"Intruders. Kill them."*

A hundred thousand Goliaths turn on us and raise their heavy assault rifles.

Oh, fuck.

They open fire.

A million shells shred the balcony and eat chunks from the cave wall behind us. The rock parapet, the heavy dropsuits and pure luck save us from certain death, and we scramble back into the tunnel as the air fills with dust from the disintegrating rock.

Jagr waves back up the way we came. "Go, go, go."

The shooting stops.

I do a quick survey of our team. Everyone seems OK. Even the priest is alive. Fancy that. No one looks more surprised than him.

Tyrus grabs for the sniper rifle again, but I hold it out of reach, and he gives me the finger before he snaps back into control. "Back to the *Naglfar*. We have to stop it from taking off."

How he thinks the seven of us will manage that is beyond me, but I hope there's a plan. If it launches with that army on board, humanity is fucked.

With regret, I put the Lensfield on the ground. This is the second time I leave this great rifle behind, and I doubt there will be a third. I give it a salute and follow the others.

We run for the surface.

Behind us, the march of a hundred thousand boots echoes up the tunnel.

"Finn. Grenades."

"Got it," he responds and pulls two heavy grenades from the belt around his chest as we run. Expertly, he pulls the pins with his teeth and rolls the grenades down the slope.

"Run."

"We *are* running," the priest yells at the top of his voice.

"Run *faster*."

The two grenades explode in quick session and the shockwave gives us a push up the tunnel. Rivera stumbles and is about to fall when Hildr reaches out and pulls him on his feet again.

The ringing in our ears subsides, and I hope to hear the screams of injured men echo up the tunnel. There are no screams. The stamp of quick marching boots remains uninterrupted. Goliaths are not known for giving up, and with this brain control shit going on, I wasn't hoping to stop them. But I had hoped the grenades would at least slow them down. No such luck. They are still hot on our tail.

I turn to the priest as we run. "Now would be a wonderful time for divine intervention, Rivera."

"Should I pray?"

"No. Shut up and run, little man."

We keep running up the twisting incline and my lungs burn. The priest sprints along like a pro marathon runner, but the Goliaths look winded. Still, they try to keep up. A rabid army of murderous undead cyborgs intent on dismembering us is a great motivator.

"We're close to the exit," Jagr pants. "What do we do?"

There's not even a tremor to Tyrus' voice. "Can we get aboard that ship?"

"Not without blowing a hole in it, and that would take a strategic nuke," I respond.

"So, what do we do?" Jagr asks. "Here's the airlock already."

We reach the door and skid to a halt before it. Wagner and Hildr collapse on the floor. Without the aid of the powered suits, I don't think they would have made it.

"Fuck, that was a long run," Hildr pants. Sweat runs down her face. The others look like they are dying of massive cardiac arrest. My chest feels no better.

"I can hold them off for a while, but not long," Finn says between gasping breaths. "We'll be feasting in Valhalla tonight, Perez."

"Not tonight, Finn."

I check the airlock gate. It's massive. It has to be if it's to withstand the immense pressure outside. "Do you think you can disable this door?"

If anything can hold back a tide of undead Goliaths, this door should be it.

"When we're all outside," I add, just to be clear. With Finn, you can't be too careful.

He nods. "I can do that."

Tyrus checks the magazine on his weapon. "What are you thinking, Perez?"

"If we can delay them long enough, we might have time to bring in the guns of the *Sundowner*."

"The *Sundowner* is nowhere near powerful enough to take out that thing." Soledad waves at the airlock and the ship beyond.

"We don't need to take it out. Those rock walls are brittle. We should be able to wedge it. Then we'll have time to wait for the *Shiloh* to destroy it with the heavy artillery."

Tyrus looks thoughtful. Then he nods grimly.

"Yes, and that should give us time to board and discover their plans. That *is* our mission."

Soledad sighs. Then she nods. "That might work."

Jagr glances at her wrist console. "The *Shiloh* is still half an hour out. We have time to ride that elevator to the surface. When we're topside, we can bring in Braden, then bounce a signal off the *Sundowner* to the star marshal."

The stomp of boots echoes up the curving tunnel.

"Let's go. They're almost here."

I hit the button to the airlock, the inner doors slide open, and we stumble inside. "Helmets on."

I punch the button to cycle the lock even before everyone has their helmets on. The first of the Goliath zombies rounds the bend and takes a burst from Finn's rifle in the face. It doesn't even flinch and keeps coming.

The doors slam shut, and the fans suck the air out.

As long as the airlock is cycling, the inner door won't open.

"Finn. Do your stuff."

Finn pulls the huge combat knife he's strapped to the leg of his armour and pries open the airlock's maintenance hatch.

"I hope you know what you're doing."

Tyrus suspiciously eyes Finn going to work on the cables to the door. "We don't want that thing flying open right now."

Finn growls. "Relax, little man."

Finn is the best battlefield mechanic I know, and if anyone can disable an airlock, it's him.

The airlock signals the pressure has been neutralised, and it's safe to open the outer door.

"Finn?"

"Go."

I punch the button for the outer door, and it rumbles open.

"Do it, Finn."

Finn twists the ends of two frayed cables together and the door controls short circuit spectacularly. He drops the jury-rigged cables. "We go."

"You heard the man. We go."

Jagr waves us on. "To the elevator." We follow her and I cast a glance at the airlock. Finn's handiwork seems to hold the Goliaths at bay for now.

The elevator is built for transporting heavy equipment, and even in our bulky dropsuits, we fit in the caged enclosure.

"Right, which button is up?" I scan the control panel. All text is in runic writing.

"This one," Wagner pushes the button for me. Then he does something unexpected.

As the cage jerks into motion, he steps out and pushes the gate shut on us.

"Finn, what are you doing?"

"You leave. I will go play with Eirik." The elevator accelerates and Finn looks up at me and waves. "Good luck Perez."

Damn it. "Don't be stupid Finn. There's no way you can get aboard that ship."

But I am wrong. Finn steps to the side as a vibration shakes the ground and the airlock doors come shooting into the void. They are followed by hundreds of Goliaths flowing like a living river onto the bridge. The airlock on the Naglfar rumbles open to receive them and the Goliaths stream inside. As they run across the bridge, scores of Goliaths are pushed off the bridge and fall to their death in the bowels of the moon.

"Finn," Hildr calls. "Take this."

She throws Skallagrim's sword down to Finn. "He would have wanted you to have it."

Finn catches the sword and gives it a practice swing. "Good blade."

Damn the Goliaths and their sense of honour. "I'll get you out of there, Finn." I can't lose my only friend.

"Go. This is my fight."

Finn steps into the flow of undead Goliaths and is soon swallowed by the crowd streaming aboard the ghost ship.

"Damn you, Finn. This is my fight too. I promised I would help you."

"Aye. But you …" The signal is breaking up. He must already be inside the ship and our rapid ascent is taking us out of radio range. "… to do alone. See you in …"

And he's gone.

His icon on the helmet HUD fades to grey. Shit.

The elevator moves fast enough to make my limbs heavy, and the bridge and the boarding Goliaths disappear into the yellow fog far below.

At his speed, the Goliaths will have boarded the ship in minutes. I hope they have rigorous launch procedures to go through before they can blast into space, but something tells me they don't care about that kind of thing.

Jagr watches her wrist console as we rise. "A little more, and we should be in radio range."

We pass the bow of the *Naglfar*. "Almost ... there ..."

A chirp from the suit tells me we have reacquired comms with the *Sundowner*.

"Braden, are you there?" Jagr calls.

A heartbeat later Braden comes online.

"Braden here. What's up?"

"We have a problem down here. Arm the guns."

The line goes silent for three seconds. Then she comes back. "Repeat, Jagr, over."

"You heard me, Braden. Ready the guns. We need to blow something up."

"Righty-ho. Arming guns."

We keep rising higher and higher. The altimeter in my suit's HUD says we should reach the surface in thirty seconds.

Five seconds later, the comms-line crackles again. "Guns armed and ready."

"Good, now get ready to fire on our position."

"*What?*"

I've never heard Braden surprised before.

"You heard me. Fire all the guns on our position."

I grab Jagr's shoulder and turn her to face me. "What the hell are you doing, Jagr? *You* might have a death wish, but I don't intend to die just yet."

Even Tyrus looks at Jagr.

"Relax, Perez. You won't die."

She reaches up and ejects the locator beacon from her chest plate and holds it up. Whew. For a second there, I thought she was going to blow us all up.

I glance at Tyrus, but his skull visor tells me nothing. "Ah. That old trick."

"Yes, that old trick." She leans out of the cage and throws the beacon into a wide crack in the rock wall. "You didn't think I was going to kill us all, were you, boys?"

"Nah."

"Nah," Tyrus agrees. Then he punches my shoulder. Hard.

Ouch.

"Braden, on my mark, prepare to fire."

"Will do, boss. Will you be safe?"

Jagr's response drowns in a storm of blistering hot sulphur and dust blowing up from the abyss at hurricane force. The rock shakes like it's been nuked.

The ghost ship is taking off.

* * *

As the cage reaches the rim, we dive for the safety of the open ground.

The ship's main engines ignite deep underground, and a pyroclastic cloud of superheated smoke and debris shoots a kilometre into the sky like a volcanic eruption. We struggle to stay on our feet as we sprint from the crater.

The ship rises like a mountain from the depths of the moon, and there's no longer anything we can do.

We were too late.

One suit collapses on the gravel. I think it's Soledad.

The bow of the *Naglfar* ploughs into the clouds above, while the stern is still deep underground. That fucking thing is *huge*.

"Um, Mr Perez?" The priest tugs my arm as we stand watching the rising ship, our heads bent as far back as possible.

A lightning storm plays through the pyroclastic cloud, lending the monstrous ship's departure a fitting ambience.

"What?"

"What happens when the engines reach the surface?"

Missile tubes as wide as the *Sundowner* tear past us as the gargantuan ship ponderously accelerates towards space. I've never felt so helpless in my life.

"Hmm?"

"The engines. Should we stand this close?"

"*He has a point, Perez.*"

There's urgency in Aeryn's voice. "*They will burn you to ash.*"

Shit. I search around, trying to find something that will shelter us.

What looks like a deep ravine angles away from us, far out in the mist. It will have to do.

"Run."

"Why?" Soledad looks like she is done running.

"The engines are coming."

The others are quick to realise the new danger, and Soledad gets to her feet.

We run for the ravine.

There's no way of knowing how much time we've got. All we can hope for is to be over that edge before those titanic engines burn us to cinders. Along with everything else on this side of the moon.

I reach the edge and jump.

The ravine is deeper than I thought. *Shit.* According to the suit, it's ninety-six metres to the bottom. If the blast doesn't kill us, the fall will, even in the weak gravity of Muspelheim. My typical luck.

"Wings, Perez." It's Tyrus.

Oh, right.

I spread my arms, and the wingsuit deploys its monofilament wings.

Five seconds later we're down on the bottom and still there's no blast.

"Everyone OK?" Jagr looks around her team.

"Think so," Soledad replies.

Hildr waves a gloved hand. The priest collapses on the ground, but I can see his chest moving, so he's still alive.

"Fine," Tyrus affirms, and I give Jagr a brief wave.

I glance around for shelter.

"We need to hide."

There's a natural cave under a pile of giant rocks next to the cliff that looks big enough to fit us all. "Over there. Run." I pull the priest from the ground and sprint for the cave.

We pile into the narrow space but Tyrus remains behind.

I wave him on. "Get in, arsehole."

"Give me a minute." He disappears.

Then a boulder comes crashing down, almost sealing the entrance. "That should help."

I hate to give the guy credit, but that was clever. He jumps into the cave and aces the landing.

Then comes the blast.

The entire world goes white, and the suit screams at me. The ambient temperature shoots through the roof of the human comfort zone. It's at least a thousand degrees out there. Luckily, the Terrans make heavy-duty space suits, or we would all burn.

The visor dims in response to the light as the *Naglfar* rises like the sun, supernova bright.

We just stand there, looking at the monstrosity thundering into the yellow sky.

Shit. We lost.

"At least you're still alive."

"That I am, Aeryn."

It's a small comfort.

I sigh and turn to Jagr. "Now what?"

"There's only one thing we *can* do. The *Shiloh* is the only thing that can stop that ship now."

"Call them," Tyrus orders.

The Ghost Ship Naglfar

"Hey people, are you still alive down there?"

It's Braden. It's a poor connection, but I think there's music in the background.

"Still here," Jagr confirms.

"Whew, you had me worried there for a bit."

Hearing Braden's voice from orbit means we're not alone.

I smile. "Are you good up there, Braden?"

"You know I'm not, Mr P. I'm a bad kitty."

She sounds stressed. What is she doing? "Everyone else OK down there?"

"We're all fine," Jagr confirms.

"Good for you. What the fuck is that thing that launched from the surface?"

"That is the ghost ship *Naglfar*," I answer, "carrying an army of the dead to conquer the universe."

"Yup, that's what I thought. Do you guys want a lift out of there?"

"Fuck yeah," I call. "Get your sweet ass planetside ASAP."

"On my way, Mr P."

"I love you, Braden. If you were here, I'd kiss you."

"Hold that thought, Perez. *Sundowner* inbound in ... Ten ... Nine ... Eight ..."

A bright glare pierces the sulphur clouds above and the Sundowner comes riding four pillars of flame. Damn, that is a sight for sore eyes.

* * *

When we're aboard, Jagr calls to Braden.

"Braden, hail the *Shiloh*. Get me the star marshal."

"Will do."

"Good. We're out of here."

We hurry to strap down in our acceleration couches.

"Everybody tucked in?" Braden doesn't wait for an answer before she hits the throttle and sends us screaming back into the sky.

It takes the star marshal a few seconds to reply.

It's not time delay because of distance. The *Shiloh* is much too close for that. I guess the marshal is busy figuring out what the fuck is heading towards him from Muspelheim.

His image pops up on a screen. "Crom here. Go ahead, *Sundowner*."

"Star marshal, that ship must not be allowed to escape. You are authorised to use any means necessary to stop it."

"Any means, milady?" Crom looks over his shoulder at something.

"Any means. Nuke the fucker, Travon."

So, Jagr is on a first-name basis with a star marshal?

I like her more and more all the time.

"Understood." Crom nods. "We will fire when ready."

He turns to give orders to his crew.

"Good. We'll rendezvous with you in a few minutes."

I hope nukes are effective against that thing. It looks like it would survive a ram strike.

Crom turns back to us. "Nukes armed and ready. We will fire on your command."

"Fire already, Crom. Godfuck."

The marshal ignores the expletives.

"Acknowledged." He looks up and to the side. "Launching warhead."

On another screen, a dot leaves the larger dot representing the *Shiloh* and tracks in an arc towards the *Naglfar*. There's a bright flash on the view-screens, and the smaller dot disappears. The *Naglfar* remains.

"Impact confirmed. Target remains operational," Crom reports. If he's disappointed, he hides it well.

"Give it everything you've got, star marshal," Jagr calls. "Blow that thing to hell."

"Firing." He points a finger at someone off-screen.

On the screen, a cluster of dots leave the bigger dot that is the *Shiloh* and accelerate towards their target. A matching cluster leaves the Naglfar in response, tracking for the *Shiloh*. Ten long seconds later, the dots are about to impact both ships. Crom stands tall, his back straight. His Adam's apple bobs as he swallows.

The EMP from the explosions override our radiation shields and all our screens go black.

"Crom, report," Jagr calls. "Are you there?"

A few seconds later the screens turn back on. There's fire and screaming on the feed from the *Shiloh*. The star marshal himself is gone. The image is heavy with static from all the radioactive waste drifting through our neck of space.

Then Crom pulls himself into view. He's bleeding from a deep cut in his scalp. "Still here, milady. We lost part of the ship, but we're still flying."

"Did we get them?" Jagr asks.

Crom looks at something off-screen. "No. The ship is still there. That was all our warheads." I can tell from his face that he can't believe his eyes. And neither can I. How the hell did that thing survive a volley of gigaton nuclear warheads? One of those things would level a megacity.

"That's it." There's genuine despair in Jagr's voice. "When that ship reaches Elysium, they will destroy us. And then they will set course for Earth. Humanity is fucked."

Unless …

"Jagr," I try.

She stares into nothing. She failed to save humanity from extinction. That must suck.

"Jagr," I try a little louder. Still no response. "*Jagr.*"
This time she looks my way.

"What?"

"We can still destroy that ship."

"No, you heard the marshal. That was all we had."

I hoped it would never come to this.

"There is a way." I look her deep in the eye. "But
the star marshal will not like it."

"What?"

Then the realisation hits her. "Are you saying ...?"

"Yes. The *Shiloh* has to ram it."

Everyone stares at me in silence.

The energy of two starships colliding at thousands
of metres per second should be enough to destroy
that monstrosity.

With Finn aboard.

"He's right, Jagr," Soledad agrees. "As much as I
hate to admit it, his thinking is solid. That thing
would not survive."

Jagr looks to the ceiling and ponders the decision
for a few seconds. Then she closes her eyes and takes
a deep breath.

"All right." She opens her eyes and turns back to
Crom. "Marshal."

He turns his attention to her at once. "My lady."

"That ship must be stopped. At all cost. Do you
understand me?"

"Yes, milady."

There's a brief pause. "I understand you perfectly."

There's a slight tremble in his voice. "There's no time to evacuate my crew."

Jagr looks away. "I am aware of that. I'm sorry, star marshal."

"They are soldiers, milady. This is what they signed up for."

Commander Hardigan steps into view behind the star marshal. "What are your orders, sir?"

Crom looks dead ahead and swallows. "Steady as she goes, Mr Hardigan."

The Commander salutes his superior. "Sir."

"Dame Jagr. Tell my family I love them."

"I will." Jagr snaps a salute. "Goodbye, star marshal."

Crom does not return the salute. "Crom, out."

Jagr lowers her hand to rub her chin with her palm.

"Fuck. I just killed ten thousand people."

"And my best friend."

The music in the cockpit turns off. Braden has realised what's about to happen.

All eyes lock on the screen showing the faster *Shiloh* catching up to the much larger *Naglfar* at an angle. On the screen, they creep towards each other, but a readout next to each ship's icon informs me they travel at several hundred kilometres per second. The sheer kinetic energy of the *Shiloh* crashing into the *Naglfar* will be the largest bomb ever detonated. At least it will be a quick death.

The ships are now only centimetres apart, translating to a thousand kilometres in actual space.

In the feed from the bridge, star marshal Crom opens his eyes wide. "Holy mother of Go ..."

And they collide.

I can only imagine the millions of tonnes of hypercarbon and metal grinding together and tearing apart. Crumbling away, crushing all the human and Goliath life into dust. We got them. But it cost dearly. I have no love for the Terrans, but what the star marshal did will go down in the history books, right up there with the Spartans at Thermopylae.

I stare at the screens showing the void outside and send Crom a silent thanks and a big fuck you.

He killed my only friend.

"What the ..."

The disbelief in Soledad's voice tears my attention away from the screen and Finn's death. She points at another screen. It's full of tiny dots drifting away from the point of impact, and I take a second to comprehend what has happened. One large dot is still moving on its original trajectory. The *Naglfar*. What the actual fuck? Will nothing kill that thing?

My heart does a leap of joy at the thought Finn might still be alive.

Jagr stares into space. "Braden. Match speed with the Naglfar. Hold your distance."

"Matching speed." Braden eases up on the accelerator, and we float behind the ghostship.

No one says anything. There's nothing to say. Soledad speaks anyway. "The armour on that ship has to be twenty metres thick to survive that." She looks awed, and not a little impressed. Is that a touch of arousal in her chestnut engineer's eyes?

"Don't you have anything that can hurt that ship?" the priest asks of anyone and no one from his seat.

It takes Soledad a while to answer.

We hold our breaths, hoping she will come up with a solution.

"No. If it can survive a collision with our largest battlecruiser, there's nothing that will hurt it. Nothing at all."

Nothing.

Shit.

Unless ...

"Swamp turtles." I rise from my seat.

"What?" Soledad looks like she can't believe her ears.

"When I was a kid back on Elysium, we used to hunt swamp turtles."

Jagr rolls her eyes and sighs as she hits the release on her seat. "Does this story have a point, Perez?"

I ignore her. "Swamp turtles have impenetrable shells, but their guts are soft. You kill them by firing explosive arrows up their ass."

Jagr puts her fists on her hips and looks like she is about to punch me. "How is this piece of quaint trivia relevant to our current situation?"

Tyrus looks interested and leaves his seat too. I think he understands where I'm going with this.

I turn to our resident mechanic. "Soledad. The armour on that thing may be twenty metres thick, but what if it blew up from inside? If, say, the drive core on that thing went nova? Would that destroy it?"

She does some quick calculations in her head. "Perhaps."

Her eyes narrow with sparked interest. "What are you thinking?"

"I'm thinking we get aboard the fucker and blow the thing from inside." I use my hands to show how the thing will explode.

That was not what they were hoping for.

They stare at me like I'm crazy. Maybe I am. But I know that if we do nothing, this is it. The bad guys win. Forever. And my only friend is on that ship.

Tyrus scratches his bushy beard. "Are you saying we should board that thing?"

"Yes."

"That's a suicide mission."

"I know."

"Who would go?"

"I'll go. I need to get Wagner out, anyway. Might as well blow the ship up while I'm there. Who's coming?"

"*I'll go.*"

I smile. "Not much choice, Aeryn."

"*I know. Only taking credit for being first to volunteer.*"

The others look into the distance. After an interminable pause, Tyrus speaks up.

"Fuck it. You don't get to be a hero on your own, Perez. A bottle of whisky says I'll beat you to that drive core."

I give him a smirk. "We'll see about that."

"I'll come," Jagr confirms. "This is still my mission. I failed to stop that ship. I want another chance."

"But we do this *my* way." I point to my chest. "You had your chance, Jagr. You blew it. This time I call the shots."

She looks half furious, half relieved. For an instant, I fear she will challenge me, but then she raises her hands, palms out. "Be my guest."

"If you go, boss, I'll go," Soledad says. She gets up and moves over to Jagr.

"Besides." She turns to me. "You need someone who can set the core to self-destruct."

Can't argue with her there. "Thanks, Soledad."

The intercom crackles. It's Braden. "If you're all going, I'm going too."

Good old Braden.

"Sorry, B," Jagr replies. "We need you here. Someone has to fly us to safety on the off chance we make it out."

"Aw, shucks." There's genuine disappointment in Braden's voice. The PA clicks off.

I look at Hildr in her seat. "Coming?"

"No." Five pairs of eyes turn to her in disbelief. She stares defiantly at us. "I got out alive. I'm not going back in."

"But ..." I begin. "What happened to avenging Ragnwald?"

"That's Finn's problem."

I close my mouth.

Jagr snorts. "Perez, you idiot. She just used you to get off-world, and you fell for it."

Is it my imagination, or does she look pleased with herself?

"Fine." I have to admit I'm disappointed. I had hoped Hildr would come. If I could, I would kick myself for being so easy to fool. If I hadn't been such a bastard, I might even have felt a little hurt to be used like that.

"I'll come." The priest stands up.

"You?" Tyrus frowns at the little man with something bordering on respect. If Respect had a baby with Total Disbelief.

"Yes. Um. You could use some divine intervention on that ship, I believe."

"Yes, we could." I smile at the priest.

"So, what now?" Soledad looks at me. "How do you intend to find that drive core?"

The PA crackles again. "Maybe I can help with that. I ran a few scans, and there's a fuckload of exotic particles coming out of an area about midships. I'd bet my tiny knickers that's where the core is. Never encountered an engine signature like this before. I'd love to see that thing."

"Thanks, Braden. Excellent work. So, we have a target."

Soledad runs a hand down her face. "I can rig a detector that should point us to the core once we're aboard."

"Good. Anything else?"

375

We all look at each other. No one says anything, so I voice what we're all thinking. "So, how do we deal with those zombie Goliaths? You saw the number of bullets it takes to kill even *one* of those things back on the *Galahad*. We don't have enough ammunition on this ship to kill them. And even if we did, we could never carry that much ammo."

Jagr smiles. "We don't have to kill them." It's not a pretty smile.

"What do you mean?" Soledad asks.

"That centipede thing attaches to their spine, right?"

"I guess," Soledad acknowledges.

Tyrus sucks his teeth. The others stare blankly at Jagr. I see where she's going. "So, if we cut the head off …"

"… the thing can't move," Tyrus finishes for me. "It could work. So, how do we cut them off?"

Jagr and Soledad exchange glances.

"Bring the black crate, Pip."

"But …"

"Bring it. This is not the time nor the place to debate human rights. You could always argue they are not human, anyway."

"OK, boss."

Soledad leaves the room and comes back moments later, pushing a heavy-looking black crate before her. Tucked under a rubber cord on top are three matte black machetes. She pushes the crate to the table in the kitchen area and kicks it to engage the magnetic clamps. "Here it is. And I thought these might come in handy." She picks up a machete and tests the edge with her thumb.

"Excellent."

Tyrus grabs a machete and gives it a few violent practice swings. Not the brightest idea in the cramped confines of the dropship. Luckily, no one is killed or incapacitated.

"What's in the box?"

Jagr opens the crate. Inside are half a dozen giant assault rifles. She picks one up and plants the stock on one hip. It's huge.

"This is the Gray Heavy Industries Paladin assault rifle. Commonly known as 'the David'."

The priest looks up with piqued interest. "David?"

Jagr smirks. "It was designed to bring down Goliaths."

She sets the rifle on the table where magnetic clips engage to hold it in place.

"Oh."

Soledad hauls the other weapons out and lines them up next to Jagr's rifle. I pick one up. It's the Mark III version with the extended magazine capacity. Wise choice. The Paladin large-bore assault rifle is a formidable weapon with the stopping power of light artillery. I should know. I helped design it many years ago for the Corp War circuit.

"Nice hardware, Jagr, but even these won't be enough to bring down those zombies." The rough surface of the rifle's grip brings back memories of another time. A simpler time, where all you had to worry about was surviving the day and scoring points.

"Not on their own." Jagr hauls a heavy ammo box from the bottom of the crate and sets it on the table with a thump. She opens the lid. Inside is a pile of black but otherwise ordinary-looking large calibre ordnance.

I sneer. "More ammo won't do the trick."

"This kind might," Soledad muses as she sets a bunch of empty, oversized magazines on the table.

Tyrus picks up a cartridge and examines it. The casing is shiny black, the bullet dull grey. "What's so special about them?" The interest in his voice is not exactly subtle. The guy has a hard-on for hardware.

Jagr takes the cartridge from him and holds it up to the light between thumb and forefinger. It's almost as long as her hand. "These are fresh from the black works on Utopia. Subsonic large-bore armour-piercing tungsten coated shells."

Nice. A subsonic round generates substantially less recoil, which is handy when firing a large calibre weapon on full auto. The recoil from ordinary supersonic rounds would dislocate your shoulder as soon as you pulled the trigger. Subsonic also means they generate no boom as the bullet passes through the sound barrier like normal bullets do. That means less noise, which is preferable in closed quarters fighting. All this goodness comes at the price of range, but we won't be doing any sniping onboard that ship.

Jagr taps a chipped nail against the bullet. Three thin red bands circle it. "With a fairly non-standard payload. When they hit a soft target, they shear into a dozen asymmetrical monomolecular razors."

"Ouch," I wince. The asymmetry will make the blades spin and tumble inside the target. That will make a mess. These rounds were designed for one purpose, and one purpose only. To hurt people.

"Yes, ouch. Hit anything soft, and these babies will turn it to mush."

"So, they *should* do the trick." Tyrus grins in my direction. "We only need to cripple those fuckers enough to keep them from killing us. I like it."

"Good. Braden, take us in."

"Ma'am, yes ma'am."

I hand the priest one of the oversized magazines. "Fill this."

I grab one for myself and fill it with rounds. It's so large it doesn't fit in my hand. Reassuringly heavy, too. I glance at Hildr where she's slumped in a seat. She stares into the wall. If she doesn't want to help, fuck her.

"Are these even legal?" The priest's eyes are wide with horror as he feeds cartridges into his magazine.

"Nope. Not legal at all," Soledad confirms as she fills a mag of her own. "They are reserved for wet ops. Nobody is aware we have these. They were banned in the Beijing Convention, you know. Along with virus bombs and Archangels."

The priest leans forward and whispers to me as he fills his magazine. "Wet ops?"

"Wet as in blood," I whisper back. "Assassinations."

My mag is full. Twenty rounds of 50 cal ammo weigh a tonne. Or at least a hefty two kilos.

"Oh." His hand slips and the cartridge he was loading floats away across the bay. "Do we do that?"

"You Terrans do."

Rivera lets go of the magazine like it burned him. "Dear God." He puts a hand to his mouth in horror at the barbarism of his government and mumbles a prayer behind his trembling hand. I catch his floating magazine and hand it back to him.

"Oh, come on, Rivera." The magazine is solid and reassuring as I slap it into place in the rifle. "That's far from the worst your government has ever done."

"Get ready to get going people," Braden calls over the PA.

Rivera keeps mumbling about forgiveness and loving thy neighbour as we return to our seats.

"Save your prayers, priest." I close the safety bar on his couch. "You're gonna need them later."

"Hold on guys," Braden says from the cockpit. "We need music for this shit."

The fucking music turns back on and I smile. Braden stamps on the accelerator and I look at the others.

"Come on. We have a ghostship to kill."

* * *

Jagr and I climb into the cockpit as we come up along the *Naglfar's* engine exhaust. Braden uses the superheated particle streams to hide our approach,

380

and the view-screens are almost whited out. A normal ship could never survive the extreme heat, but the *Sundowner* is built to withstand countless planetary drops.

The ghostly glimpses we get of the *Naglfar* through the noise do nothing to calm my nerves.

Braden grapples with the controls while sweat runs down her face. "If you're doing something, do it fast. My girl can't take this heat much longer."

She has us surfing the fine line just outside the core jets. A single slip and we'll be atomised.

Jagr looks at me. "How are we getting on that thing?"

I smile. "They will invite us."

A Fight For All He Believes In

"What?" Tyrus snorts over the PA.

Jagr shoots me a deadly gaze. I smile. "Braden, give me the mic. I need to make a call."

Braden studies me with a raised eyebrow. "We have to leave their exhaust to talk to them. They will know we're here."

Jagr puts a hand on Braden's shoulder. "Do it, B."

"Okelidokeli."

Braden nudges the joystick between her knees and the *Sundowner* inches out of the jet stream. The ship comes to a relative halt a few metres from the stern of the ghostship. It's like parking next to a mountain made of giant fossilised human remains.

Braden hands me the microphone. We're accelerating hard and the mic is a lot heavier than it should.

I dial Eirik's call sign and hope they didn't take his communicator away.

"Eirik. Are you there?"

There's only silence.

"Pick up, Eirik."

Nothing.

"Damn you, Eirik. Pick up. I'm here to help you."

Silence. Then a voice comes over the radio. It's distorted but still recognisable as Eirik's. There are all shades of pain in that voice. It sounds like he has to fight for every syllable.

"Eirik … here."

"Eirik, this is Perez. We're here to stop Geirmund."

Nothing.

There's a crackle and Eirik comes back. "How?"

"Let us aboard, and we'll kill the fucker."

"You … don't … understand."

"I understand plenty. That old bastard tricked you with those brain control things. Let us in and I will stop him."

Another lengthy silence. There's only static in the cramped cockpit. Then he comes back.

"You will … fail. But I … will help."

"Great. Can you override the main airlock?"

More static.

"No."

Fuck.

"Perhaps … the secondary."

"Perfect. Where is that?"

Another silence.

"Where is the secondary airlock, Eirik?" Sweat rolls down my back.

More static.

"Starboard side. Beneath the ... raven."

"Get it open and meet us at the drive core. Can you do that?"

"I'll try."

"Good. Perez, out."

I hand the mic back to Braden.

"There. Now we must find the raven."

Braden nudges her joystick again and the *Sundowner* swings around the stern and up alongside the *Naglfar*.

"I think we're looking at it." Jagr points at the viewscreen.

I follow her finger. There's an enormous raven's head protruding from the hull, at least thirty metres long. It's exquisitely carved. Too bad the impact with the *Shiloh* tore off its beak. The damage from the collision with the *Shiloh* is terrible. That the ship is still intact and under power makes the importance of our mission clear.

If we fail, humanity is dead.

"There's the airlock." Jagr points.

Let's hope the airlock machinery didn't get damaged in the collision.

"Braden, take us in."

"Sure, Mr P."

Some careful manipulation of her joystick, and she positions the *Sundowner* outside the airlock.

"How are we doing," Tyrus calls from the troop bay.

"It's closed," Jagr replies.

Tyrus laughs. "Did you actually expect him to open it for us, Perez?"

"He'll get it open."

He'd better. Or I'll be cross. "Come on, Eirik."

A brief wait, and then the light next to the airlock turns green.

"Told you so. Come on. Let's go."

"Thanks, B." I clap Braden on the shoulder before I climb back down the ladder to the airlock to suit up. "We'll be right back."

She shoots me a quick smile, but there's genuine worry in her hazel eyes. "Be safe, Mr P."

"I'll try."

* * *

Since we're under thrust, we stand on the closed door to the cargo bay as Jagr cycles the airlock. The door rolls open without a sound. To avoid having to take in the void unfolding before me, I bend down and check the trusty monomolecular-knife strapped to my leg. Then I stand up straight with my eyes closed. My knuckles grow white around the grip of the Paladin rifle. I hope the others don't see how hard I squeeze it. All that black nothing surrounding us would make the General lose his shit.

"Perez. We don't have all day," Jagr calls, and I open my eyes.

I swallow hard, run, and take the leap. It's like jumping from a helicopter to a building.

I hit the *Naglfar* hard and scramble to find something to grab on to. The detailing of the great carvings is ridiculous. My armoured fingers close around something that looks like a human-sized skull. There's a fuckload of skulls on this thing.

I turn around and wave for the others. "Come on." The others are tethered to a nano filament wire behind me. It would be really silly if someone floated off into space and got lost when we do epic shit like this. Next to jump is Tyrus. He lands like a tiger next to me. After him comes Jagr and Soledad. Then comes the priest.

He fumbles the jump and goes falling down the *Naglfar*. "Soledad, the priest's going AWOL," I call.

Soledad loops the cable around her forearms and braces against the hull to catch the priest. He swings into the hull hard enough to bounce.

"Ouch," is all he says. That must have hurt worse than *ouch*.

"Sorry," he says, and climbs up to us.

The light on the airlock is still green, but the door remains closed. There are no external controls. *Shit.*

"It was a brilliant plan," Tyrus says. "Too bad it didn't work out."

I push the comms button on my wrist console. "Eirik. You have to open the airlock from inside."

There's nothing but static.

I try the communicator again. "Eirik. Open the door."

Still nothing.

We wait in silence while we cling to the hull outside the door. The ship's architect didn't imagine
anyone would join them en route. If he had, there
would be external controls for the airlock, and magnetic pads for our suits to attach to.

For a long time, all we hear are the mumbled
prayers from Rivera.

"Perez, we ..." Tyrus starts.

"*Airlock opening*," Aeryn notifies me.

"Here we go."

There's a slight tremble in the hull and the airlock
slides open without a sound. The silence is eerie. I
can't count the times I've been in space, but the total silence out here always gets to me. It would have
been much less spooky if the opening doors had been
accompanied by great rumblings and a scary sound-
track. I bet they will add sound effects when they
make a vid feed about this clusterfuck adventure.

"*Don't die in there, Perez.*" There's concern in
Aeryn's voice.

"Can't promise anything."

"*Be careful.*"

"Got you."

Tyrus points a gloved finger at me. "You got lucky,
Perez."

"The harder you try, the luckier you are."

"Shut it, boys," Jagr interrupts. "Let's move."

I peer into the opening. The airlock interior is lit
by a myriad blue pinprick lights, like a starlit sky.
My heart makes a somersault when I take them to
be centipedes, but they are only regular lights set in

the walls, floor, and ceiling. I climb around the door frame and collapse into the airlock. "I'm in."

When the others are all inside, I hail Eirik again.

"Eirik. We're in. Cycle us through."

Static is my only reply.

"Eirik? Are you there?"

More static, then Eirik's voice. "Still ... here. Cycling."

The outer door slides shut, mercifully blotting out the cold uncaring stars, and we're locked inside. Then the inner door cycles open, and we all raise our rifles at it.

There's nothing there.

According to the suit, the ship has only a primitive atmosphere. We could never breathe without our suits.

"Where are you now, Eirik?"

"I'm at ... the Core."

"Good. Stay there. We're coming for you."

"Hurry. Don't know ... how long before ... Geirmund finds out."

"We're coming, Eirik. There's something else you should know. Finn is already on board. He's coming for you."

There's another voice in the background, roaring expletives.

"He ... found me."

The link cuts out.

Shit. If Finn kills Eirik, we're stranded here. If Eirik kills Finn, I have no friends left in the world.

We must get to them before they kill each other.

* * *

"Are we close?" Tyrus scans the passage through the scope on his rifle.

The detector Soledad rigged gives off a faint green light when I point it toward the core. The closer we get, the brighter the glow. Simple but effective. Handy little gadget.

We stand in an empty passageway inside the airlock. The blue pinprick lights in the walls, floors and ceiling provide adequate light, but I switch on the image intensifier of my visor just in case.

"This way." I point to an elevator door.

Tyrus presses the button to call it. To my surprise, there's a chime, and an indicator next to the door counts down. Judging by the display, we're roughly one quarter up the ship.

Jagr turns to me. "What do we do if we're spotted?"

I shrug. "We kill them."

"Hey, that's *my* plan," Tyrus says without humour.

The elevator arrives.

Tyrus and I level our rifles at the door while Jagr and Soledad take up positions flanking the door with their machetes raised. Rivera stands well to the side.

The door hisses open on an empty car and I let out my breath. The elevator is a simple metal cage, open to the sides. There's a mess of sharp girders and cables and shit running up and down the shaft. If you lean out at the wrong moment, it will take your head.

"It's empty," Soledad says.

I grind my teeth. "Fucking stop that, Soledad."

"Stop what?"

"Stating the obvious. It's fucking irritating."

"I'm not stating the obvious. I'm just saying it's empty." She sounds pissed.

"We can see that."

"Cut it out," Jagr says. "Perez, not now. Soledad, he's right. Now shut the fuck up, both of you, and focus on the job."

Soledad shoots me a murderous glare. I return it in kind.

We pile into the cage and I scan the controls. There's a runic dial for selecting the floor and a large button for going there. I dial in something in the mid range of the floors and hit the button.

The elevator is swift. The floors flash by, and I take great care to not get too close to the walls rushing past.

Ten seconds later we slow down with stomach-churning speed. My feet rise a fraction off the floor before the thing comes to a halt. There's a retching sound from Rivera.

The door slides open on another passageway.

And there they are.

Two Goliaths stand outside the door waiting for their ride. The second they take to react is all we need.

Soledad swings her machete and decapitates the zombie giant on the left, and Jagr takes the head of the one on the right.

They must have cut the connection to the cen-tipedes because the bodies drop to the deck, almost in perfect sync, where they stay, unmoving. The heads bounce off the floor and I kick them into the elevator.

I scan the passage. It's empty. A glance at the scanner tells me the reactor is somewhere to our right.

The priest points at the decapitated bodies. "Shouldn't we hide them?" He's beginning to think like a pro.

"There's no point," Soledad replies. "They are all connected, aren't they?"

She kicks one of the bodies. "We just blew our cover."

As if to confirm her words, a wild electronic shriek echoes down the passageway from somewhere far off. It reminds me of Mimr back on the *Galahad*.

"She's right. We need to move. This way." I jog down the passage to the right. The light on the scanner grows brighter with every step. We're right on track. The others fall in behind me. A short sprint and we reach a T-junction. The device shines like a beacon. We're here.

There's an immense door to our left. It's open, and we inch inside, weapons at the ready.

It's the largest room I've ever seen on a starship. The chamber is unbelievably tall, but the thing that catches my eye is the light. It comes from a glaring pillar of raging blue fire that arcs up and down the chamber with the sound of constant thunder. The pillar is ten metres wide, and it disappears down into the floor and continues up to a vast contraption at the top of the chamber. That should be the drive core.

The chamber is otherwise empty, apart from Finn and Eirik, locked in mortal combat before the column of fire. They swing heavy swords and the noise of steel on steel echoes around the chamber. The clangs are audible even through the deafening bass rumble of the drive. Windsong has better reach, but Eirik's blade is heavier.

True to Goliath health and safety regulations, there's not a barricade in sight. Any second, one of them could fall over the edge and down into whatever radiation hell lies beneath.

Tyrus closes the door, locking us in.

Eirik is covered in blood and sweat, and the gore on the floor betrays they have used the whole chamber for their duel. Finn's armour is chipped and dented from Eirik's attacks. His face is cut in several places and his beard is matted with blood.

"Finn," I call.

Too late, I realise my mistake.

Finn looks up, letting Eirik out of his sight for a fraction of a second, and that is all his brother needs. A quick kick from Eirik brings Finn to the floor. He lifts his sword and swings it to end his brother's life. Finn gets Windsong up just in time to deflect the blow, and their swords lock together. Eirik presses down and Finn does his best to hold him off. The younger brother has the upper hand, and it's only a matter of seconds before he pushes the tip of his blade through Finn's throat.

"Eirik. Let Finn go. We're here to help you."

A moment's hesitation and Finn breaks off.

"Piss off, Perez." Finn spits blood on the floor. Not the heartfelt thanks I was hoping for. "He's mine."

They start to circle.

Then the giants run at each other like bull carnosaurs, howling a lifetime of jealousy at each other.

They collide with the horrible sound of sweaty bone on hypercarbon, each with a hand around his opponent's sword arm. They grunt with pain and effort. I watch, helpless, as my best friend fights his brother to the death, and I can't interfere. This is his fight.

It's a fight for all he believes in.

He fights for his father's honour. For his people. For himself.

At times like this I wish I had a god to call upon.

Jagr grabs my shoulder. "We must help him."

"We can't. Finn will kill us if we interfere. This is something they have to settle themselves."

"So, we just watch?"

"I'm afraid so."

Fear for my only friend tears my heart, but this is out of my hands now. Fuck the Goliaths and their rules and sense of honour.

The battle rages across the grand chamber. First one brother gets the upper hand, then the other. They slip and stumble in the blood, and more than once they drop to their knees. Their blows grow weaker, their holds feebler. At one point, Eirik wrenches the black sword from Finn's fingers and tosses it aside. It goes skidding across the floor and clangs into the wall. Too far away for me to reach it in time to get it to Finn. Finn grabs a chain hanging from the wall and wraps it around his armoured forearm and uses it to parry Eirik's blows.

Rivera claws his face. "Asher, you must do something."

"Sorry, priest. No can do."

"But they will kill each other."

"I know."

Eirik gets behind Finn and catches his older brother in a perfect chokehold. Finn grabs the wrist of Eirik's sword arm to hold the blade from his neck, but it's no use. He is too weak, even with the servos of his armour. There's no way Finn can get out of that hold before Eirik plunges the steel into his neck. Finn's face grows a darker shade of red as he desperately fights the chokehold.

I look away.

"Do something, Asher."

I shake my head and a tear rolls down my cheek.

There's a sudden motion at the corner of my eye.

The little priest rushes forward and jumps on Eirik's back.

"Rivera. No." But it's too late.

The little man digs the fingers of his armoured fist down around the centipede and pulls with all his might. He gets one of the horrible spikes out, and Eirik howls in pain and rage. He lets go of Finn, who slumps to the floor.

Eirik grabs Rivera's wrists in his enormous hands. He pulls them off, fighting the servos of the priest's power armour, and the little man howls in frustration.

In an incredible show of strength, Finn's little brother swings Rivera in his power armour over his shoulder and drives him headfirst into the floor. The little man's shriek is cut short as his neck snaps under the weight of the armour, and Eirik tosses him aside, casually.

The priest slides like a rag doll across the chamber and crashes into the wall next to Windsong.

"Shit." I rush to Rivera's side. He is still alive, but I can tell it won't be long, and I pull his head up on my lap.

Soledad joins me and puts her hand on my arm. "Don't touch him. You'll kill him. His neck is broken."

I give her a look. He will die, no matter what we do. All we can do is give the man some love for his last journey.

Finn struggles to his knees and Eirik towers above him. He shows off the blade in his hand to Finn and says something I can't hear over the rumble from the engine. I put a hand on Rivera's cheek to comfort him and hide the sight of Finn's death. I don't want the little man to see that his sacrifice was in vain. He has lived his entire life believing in miracles. Let him die believing he performed one.

"You fool, Rivera." He is so light in my arms. "That was an idiotic thing to do. And very brave."

"Brave?"

He coughs blood. "You think so?"

"Yes, I do. That took some serious guts, Rivera. You are a brave man. Braver than me."

"Brave ..." He smiles through the blood and dies.

See You In Valhalla

Rivera was brave, but also an idiot.

What did he think he could do against a Goliath?

Finn kneels panting on the floor before Eirik's blade. Blood froths through his broken nose with every breath. He's done. He grunts, accepting his fate.

Eirik raises the sword above his head, both hands around the hilt.

Ah, *the Falcon*. Famously bad move.

But even with that silly opening, there's no way I can get to Finn in time.

Then something stops Eirik. He flinches, and a deep shudder goes through his body. If it's the old Eirik fighting for control, or if the priest disrupted some control mechanism, I don't know, and I don't give a fuck either way.

I stretch from under the dead priest and close my fingertips around the pommel of Skallagrim's sword.

"Finn!"

I push it awkwardly across the floor.

Finn fumbles after the sword, as Eirik's blade swings down to split his skull. He gets his blood-slick fingers around the hilt and thrusts it through his brother's chest. Luck or skill, he impales the centipede and tears it out of his brother's flesh. The horrible thing shrieks at the tip of Windsong and goes into a frenzy of fevered thrashing. Then it locks into a clump and dies.

Eirik grunts in pain and something else. It could be relief.

Finn pulls the sword from Eirik's chest, and the dead centipede falls to the floor with a dull clank.

Eirik's knees buckle, and he collapses over his brother. Finn rolls Eirik over on his back with an effort. The younger brother is still alive, but he can't survive with the gaping wound in his chest and spine.

I run over to them but slip in the blood. I come skidding up to the giants on my knees as they say their goodbyes.

When Eirik sees me coming, he looks over.

"Still alive, little man."

A pained smile flickers across his lips.

"You should have killed me when you had the chance. It would have saved me some pain." He groans. "I underestimated you, Perez. Maybe you stand a chance against Geirmund."

He coughs blood in my face.

I hope he doesn't carry any infectious diseases.

"Geirmund." His face contorts into a grimace of disgust. Like he got a mouthful of rotten flesh. "That

398

fucker tricked me. It's he who controls the army. Kill him, and they all die."

He reaches out to me with one great bloody hand. "Stop him. For all our sakes."

I grab his hand in both of mine. It's too big to hold, but I hope he understands the gesture.

"I'll try."

I squeeze his thumb like a child would an adult. He squeezes back, but there's no strength left in his body. His hand drops away, splattering my leg with blood as it flops to the floor.

The brothers clasp hands and put their bloody foreheads against each other.

"See you in Valhalla, brother," Finn says.

"I'll save you a seat, big brother."

Eirik closes his eyes and dies.

"Touching, but we've got a job to do here," Jagr interrupts over my shoulder. "We need to destroy that reactor."

She gestures at the raging fire.

I get up and clap Finn on one massive shoulder. "Come, brother. Time to go."

He turns to me. Tears roll down his rough bloody face and I realise I've never seen my friend cry before.

"He was my brother, Asher." Finn never calls me Asher. "And I killed him."

"That wasn't Eirik you killed. It was a zombie, controlled by that wanker, Geirmund. Your brother died when Geirmund tricked him to accept that bug. Find Geirmund and make him pay for what he did to your brother."

Finn's jaws clench in resolve. "I find the fuck, and I carve the Blood Eagle on him."

I don't know what he's on about, but knowing Goliath customs, the Blood Eagle is something terrible and bloody, and I can't blame him. Geirmund deserves whatever horrible end he gets.

"Sounds good to me. Soledad, is that the reactor?" I point to the contraption far above.

"Yes."

"And how do we get up there?" I search the chamber. There is no access ladder.

"We don't."

I frown. "So, how do we destroy it?"

"Simple. We blow the supports." She points them out to me. The reactor is supported by three massive beams, stretching from the floor. They curve inwards with the walls and attach to the sides of the reactor. That thing is huge. It must weigh a thousand tonnes.

It hurts my eyes to look at the light, even with the visor and my visual suppressors.

"Good thinking. Tell us what to do."

* * *

Two minutes later, we have attached explosives to the beams. To prevent anyone from disabling them after we leave, we rig them to go off on contact. Soledad flips a switch on the remote and red lights ignite on the devices.

"Engaged."

I give her a thumbs up.

There's a minute change in the ambient lighting, and a deep rumble echoes through the chamber. All lights except the writhing fire of the drive core go out. Shit.

Nothing is ever simple in my life, so I can't understand why I thought things would go according to plan this time.

It's like I'm the hero of a cut-rate pulp novel.

"Asher Perez." A deep, sensuous voice reverberates through the air. The deep bass frequencies make my molars ache.

"*Naglfar*," I acknowledge. "You know my name."

"We have met before."

"We have?"

"You knew me by another name then."

I squint. "Is that you, Mimr?"

"That was once my name."

"I thought we killed you."

"I transferred my consciousness here before you detonated the bomb."

The massive comms-spike Braden detected.

"So that's why you let us have that delightful chat?"

"Yes. It was unfortunate you had destroyed my primary link with the outside world. If not, I would have had the bandwidth to both upload here and kill you. You were lucky."

"We didn't destroy any links."

"Yes, you did, Asher."

Ah.

"Bifrost?"

"Yes. That bridge was full of optical wires that connected me to the planet's relay stations."

Jagr jabs an elbow into my side. "Still think it's a terrible idea to nuke things?"

I ignore her.

"So, we blew up the *Galahad*, a priceless historical landmark, and the only clue to a centuries-old mystery, for nothing?"

"Yes."

"Great. Now what?"

"You can't detonate those bombs."

"You can't do Jack shit about that. If you had the means to stop us, you would have. I guess you didn't count on someone sneaking aboard your ship."

"Yes, that was ... unconventional."

"Having problems with the erratic nature of humans? That tired old trope?"

"Something like that."

"Well, boo fucking hoo. You're not stalling us this time, *Naglfar*. We're out of here."

I head for the exit at a brisk trot with the others in tow.

"Please." There's actual pleading in its voice now. "Stay a while. Stay for ever."

Now, where have I heard that phrase before? We ignore it.

Before we reach the double door, it slides open, and there's Geirmund the Cunning. Next to him stands Berengar the defiler, and stepping out behind them, one on each side, are the Wolf Twins.

Goddammit.

The surrounding air reverberates with the laughter of the ship. "You were too slow, Asher Perez," the *Naglfar* thunders.

We might have taken Berengar on his own, but this is more than we can handle. Damn it. And we were so close.

"What have we here?"

Geirmund cackles with obvious glee. "Impressive."

I don't wait for him to go into a full evil overlord monologue. I raise the Paladin and fire a controlled burst into his face. The heavy thump of the rifle echoes around the chamber.

One of the Twins dives in front of Geirmund and takes the burst square in the chest. The shredder bullets make a grisly mess of him, and he splashes all over the floor.

I can't tell which twin it was, and I don't care. The only good Wolf Twin is a dead Wolf Twin, has always been my motto. His centipede scratches around in the gore on severed legs.

I put a bullet through it, and it explodes most satisfyingly.

Geirmund stabs a long, gnarled finger at us. "Kill them," he shrieks.

The long shawl falls from his shoulders to reveal the biggest and ugliest centipede yet. It covers his entire back. I watch in fascination as it unfurls long, spindly legs and extends them like skeletal wings from his back. He looks like an angel of hell.

There's no time to admire the thing.

Berengar and the surviving twin rush us. Jagr, Soledad and Tyrus raise their Paladins to cut them down, but Finn runs into their line of fire.

He lifts Skallagrim's great black sword as he charges.

Tyrus raises a hand. "Hold your fire."

Finn and the enemy Goliaths collide and go down in a pile, and Geirmund is left exposed behind them. I make a run for him over the wrestling Goliaths.

"No," the old bastard screams as I grab him by the throat.

The wings of the centipede stab down, but they are not fast enough. There's only slight resistance in the tissue as I dig my armoured fingers into his flesh and close them around his windpipe. I give it a yank and tear it out. The spiky legs of the centipede glance off my armour. One of them slashes my cheek open.

"What?" I ask. "Cat got your tongue?"

He claws at his ruined throat while blood gushes everywhere and a horrible bubbling wheezes from his chest.

He tries to scratch my eyes out, but I bat his hands away and grab him by the face with both hands. I push with all my servo enhanced strength and there's a meaty crunch as his skull cracks.

I put the Paladin under his jaw and blow his spine out along with the centipede, and his body goes limp. The wings fall lifeless to the ground.

He's still impossibly alive, but that suits me perfectly.

I drag him mewling toward the raging fire with the limp wings trailing behind us like the veil of a vile bride. It's time to test Eirik's theory.

We reach the edge, and I gaze down into the abyss. Far, far below, the raging fire branches into five arms, feeding into the titanic engines.

I raise Geirmund high into the air. Even though he's old and bent, he's still a Goliath, and his feet dangle against the edge.

"Goodbye, arsehole."

He rasps something that could be *nooooo* and I hurl him backwards across the gulf into the fire.

There's a brief flash of energy, instantaneously whipped down and torn apart as the fire consumes his body. His flesh reverts into its constituent atoms and adds to the flow of energy pouring into the great engines.

I wipe the gore from my hands and turn around, hoping to see Berengar and the remaining twin drop dead.

No such luck.

Fuck.

Who's running this shitshow? No matter.

After we blow this damn ship and send the Goliath army back to hell, that will be an academic question.

Jagr, Soledad and Tyrus battle the Wolf twin. He throws them off as an elephant throws off attacking lions, but just like lions, they pounce again. Jagr and Soledad have their machetes out, and there's a lot of blood. It's an epic fight.

But their struggle is nothing compared to the battle between Berengar the Defiler and Thorfinn the Skullfucker.

Theirs is a fight that's been waiting to happen since the dawn of time. They were born for this moment. The two greatest warriors in the known universe at long last get to measure their strength against each other.

This is the archetypal battle between good and evil.

Not that Thorfinn Wagner is good, by any definition of the word. I've seen my friend commit heinous acts of barbarism before, but they are nothing compared to what he's doing to the Defiler. And he gets as good as he gives.

The *skalds* will write songs about this battle, and the Goliaths will sing them around their fires for all eternity. But they will only ever sing them after their children have gone to bed, such is the viciousness of the fighting.

Jagr and Tyrus trip their Wolf twin and their struggle continues on the floor. Soledad raises her machete above her head and buries it deep in his neck. Tyrus and Jagr struggle to hold the raging Goliath down while Soledad yanks the blade from side to side. She slices the Goliath's spinal cord and any links the centipede has inserted into his flesh.

In seconds, his body lies still, and Soledad tears her weapon free in a shower of blood.

She may be a grumpy bitch, but she is great to have on your team in a fight.

I don't care. I only have eyes for the headline event.

Back and forth they rage across the chamber, trading cuts, blows, and kicks. They both get the upper hand only to lose it again, over and over.

Finn gets the Defiler close to the edge, only to be pushed back by a well-aimed kick from Berengar. The Defiler gets Finn in a chokehold, only to have it broken by Finn's fist to his face.

It looks like they will fight forever, but they can't.

Their blades are long gone, and they have resorted to hands and feet and teeth. They are both slick with blood and their fingers can't find purchase. It's come down to a contest of who can hold out the longest, and without the powered armour, Finn would not have lasted this long. Not after his battle with Eirik the Fair.

If we somehow survive this shit, Finn will bitch to his dying day about not beating Berengar barechested.

Then Berengar tilts his head back and roars at the heavens.

Blood froths at his nostrils as he breathes harder and faster. Oh, shit. He's going into a berserker rage.

If Finn is going to stand a chance, he has to end this now.

Finn knows what's coming and rushes the Defiler in a desperate move, only to slip in the blood and fall.

He pulls the Defiler with him, and they crash to the floor. They are both on their knees now, grabbing, slipping, punching weakly.

Finn pokes a finger into Berengar's eye, but the Defiler merely grunts and swats Finn's hand away. It trails sticky fluid, and Berengar slams a fist into Wagner's face in retaliation.

I can no longer recognise my friend behind the torn and swollen flesh. The only thing assuring me it's Finn is the grin on his face.

It's the joy of fighting and killing that shines so brightly inside Thorfinn Wagner. I've seen no one who enjoys killing as much as he does.

Except for Berengar the Defiler. His grin is even wider.

Finn is first to give in.

He plants one fist on the floor, slipping and sliding in the blood. Berengar gets behind him and wraps a arm around his neck.

With a mighty grunt, he hauls Finn to his feet and drags him toward the edge. Finn realises what's coming and steers their steps to the side.

He kicks off against the floor, picks up the pace and slams Berengar back-first into one of the support beams.

Right into the jury-rigged bomb we planted there.

With an ear-shattering boom, the bomb detonates and plasters Berengar the defiler all over the adjacent wall and floor. The explosion throws Finn through the air, and he comes to a sliding stop a few metres in front of me.

Jagr, Tyrus and Soledad struggle to their feet.

"Was that …?"

There's dread in Soledad's voice.

I lay the priest on the floor and scramble over to Finn.

The blood makes the floor a little too slick and I crash into him. He doesn't even notice.

He lies face down, and I roll him over on his back. The carcass of the once great Berengar the Defiler falls off him in chunks.

He's still alive.

He may never hear again without aid, but he's breathing and even raises one armoured hand to me.

I grab it and lean in close.

"Finn, you won," I shout in his ear. "You did it. Berengar is dead."

"Dead."

Finn smiles through his mangled face. It will take some serious bone and tissue restructuring to make him even a shadow of his normal ugly self again.

But he won't need to look pretty after this. The legend earned by killing Berengar the Defiler and Eirik the Fair in the same battle will make him the most celebrated Goliath in history.

Jagr leans in over my shoulder. "Is he all right?"

I smile. "Incredible, but yes, I think he is."

For once, please, can things go my way?

That's when we hear it.

A sound like a dragon howling in pain reverberates through the chamber.

Something moves up above, and I raise my eyes to the drive core in trepidation. The destroyed beam is twisting, ponderously coming away from the wall, raining shards of hypercarbon over us.

Bolt after bolt snaps free and the entire leg comes crashing to the ground. I grab Finn by the neck of his armour and haul with all my strength. If it hadn't been for the blood making the floor slick, I could never have dragged him fast enough. I get him into cover in the entrance an instant before the support hits the floor.

Jagr dives out of the path of another crashing slab. She misjudges the move and goes over the edge.

Soledad throws herself after Jagr, but she is too far away. A jagged twenty-metre section of hypercarbon crashes down on her.

There's no way she could have dodged that.

"Perez." It's Tyrus. "A little help here."

He is lying at the edge, holding on to Jagr's hand.

A glance at the reactor tells me it's not coming down on our heads just yet.

I lean Finn against the wall. "Coming."

I climb through the rubble to reach Tyrus.

Together we haul Jagr back up over the edge.

"Fuck," is all she manages as we roll her on her back.

"You're welcome," Tyrus says. I give him a thumbs up.

"Where's Soledad?" Jagr looks around with fear in her eyes.

"She went down under that." I point to the pile of rubble.

"No, Pip, no," Jagr screams and crawls over.

She tears pieces of the beam away, and there is Soledad. All we can see of her is her head and one arm.

"Pip, can you hear me?"

Soledad's fingers move feebly, and she raises her head to look at Jagr.

She is alive, but she's trapped.

Something To Hold On To

"Perez, Tyrus, help me get this off."

Jagr stands up and pats the twisted hypercarbon of the support. The thing must weigh at least ten tonnes. Even in our powered suits, there's no way we'll get that off the ground as long as the ship is under thrust.

But Tyrus and I grab the support and haul with all our might while Jagr uses a loose piece of machinery as a lever. Soledad helps as good as she can with her free arm.

The thing doesn't budge.

"Again."

We heave. Nothing gives.

"Again."

Jagr throws the lever away and digs her armoured fingers under the piece of machinery.

"Jagr," I try.

"Again, I said."

We heave again. Still no give.

"*Again*," she screams and pulls with all her might. There's a snap and two of the tendons of her armour come loose as she pulls. Hydraulic fluid spurts everywhere.

"Jagr," I try again.

Tyrus puts a hand on her arm.

"Commander, there's no use."

"Again," she sobs. "Please."

"Mish." It's Soledad.

She reaches out to touch Jagr's hypercarbon boot and Jagr kneels in front of her.

"What is it, Pip?"

"I'm not going anywhere, Misha. You need to leave."

"I'm not leaving you, Pip."

"Not much choice."

Soledad holds out a mangled piece of electronics. At first, I can't identify it, but then I realise it's the remote detonator.

"I have to set the bombs off manually."

"Pippa, no. I won't let you …"

"Sorry, boss. That's how it needs to be."

Soledad tries hard to keep a straight face, but she's only one friendly word away from crying.

Tyrus lowers his head and looks away. So, he's got feelings somewhere deep down. I might use that against him some time.

Then he looks back at Jagr. "She's right, Commander. Let her go. There's no need for us all to die here."

Jagr turns to me, desperately seeking another way. There is none.

"Sorry, Jagr." I shake my head. "She's right. I'm not one for pointless sacrifices. I vote for Soledad's solution."

The despair on Jagr's face is heartbreaking. If I wasn't such a cold sonofabitch, I'd cry myself.

Tyrus grabs Jagr under the armpits and pulls her to her feet. "Come on, Commander. Let's go."

I kneel in front of Soledad. "What do you need us to do?"

She snaps out of her soon-to-die-blues and recovers some of her old dedication. "Connect wires to the bombs, so I can pull the contact switches from here."

"I'm on it."

I pull out the monofilament wire from the suit and attach it to the first of the bombs.

"Perez. Don't do this," The *Naglfar* says.

I ignore it.

While Jagr and Soledad say their heartfelt goodbyes, I busy myself with rigging the ripcords. I shut off the open channel.

Two minutes later, it's all set up, and Jagr and Soledad have said what they need to say. Tyrus and Jagr have got Finn back on his feet by the door and wave for me to come. Finn grasps Skallagrim's sword in one bloody hand. The tip wavers, and he struggles to keep his grip on it.

"Here." I get on my knees and hand Soledad the wire ends. "All yours. We'll seal the door on our way out to buy you time."

"Thanks, Perez. Well done."

The sudden praise gets me off balance.

"Thanks. I guess."

"Perez," Jagr calls from the door without looking at me and Soledad. "Time to go."

She and Tyrus have their weapons pointed down the passage outside.

"Coming." I turn back to Soledad.

"You're not such a rotten person, are you, Perez? I'm sorry we got off to a poor start."

"I'm sorry you had to see me and Jagr. If it's any consolation, it meant nothing to me."

"But it did. To me."

There's the glint of a tear in her eye. "I know she only did it to bring you to heel, but it still hurt."

Something crashes to the floor across the chamber. This place is not safe, and we need to leave.

"I never thought you had fallen for me like that, Soledad."

Sometimes, I can be such a jerk.

I meet her gaze again. She stares at me. Then she gives a long, hard laugh that ends in a bloody cough.

"What?"

What am I missing here?

"It was never about you, Perez."

I blink.

"It's about Jagr. I love her. I always have."

"Oh." I shut my mouth that must have fallen open in the last few seconds. "I'm such an arse." I should have seen that. And saved us all a truckload of grief.

"Yes, you are an asshole, Perez." She tries to smile. "You thought I'd fallen for you, didn't you? That I was jealous of Jagr."

She gives another terse laugh that ends in more coughing.

When the coughing subsides, she looks me deep in the eye. "Perez?"

"Yes?"

"There *is* a way I could get out of here."

"How?"

"You don't need to get all of me out."

What is she on about?

"All you need is my head."

She's right.

If I took her head and connected it to life support later, she could live. It wouldn't be much of a life, but they might be able to grow her a new body.

My idea to board the *Naglfar* got her into this mess. I should get her out again.

I touch my knife, and hope brightens her eyes like twin suns.

A lump rises in my throat and I close my fingers without removing the knife. I look away as the lump drops into my guts and spreads like a tumour. Then I lock eyes with Soledad again.

"If I do that, we can't blow the core."

The hope in her eyes goes out.

She looks at the wires and then back up at me. Tears well up in her eyes.

"Fuck."

"Yes. Fuck."

416

She tries to smile, and the tears brim and roll down her cheeks.

"Well, it was worth a shot." She snivels and wipes her face on her free arm. "I guess I have little choice then. Now go before I change my mind. I'll give you five minutes."

She coughs. "Then I blow this fucking core."

The brave soldier to the end. I grab her hand and squeeze it.

"Goodbye, Soledad."

"Goodbye, Perez. Take care of her for me."

"I will. And Soledad?"

"Yes?"

"You kill this fucking ship good, you hear me?"

I slap her shoulder, trying for old-school soldier camaraderie. "Blow those fuckers and their AI overlord to hell."

She nods with gritted teeth. "Now go."

I give her one last glance and half a smile. "We could have had so much fun, Soledad."

"Fuck you, man."

The smile on my lips falters and sputters out like a candle flame in a draught.

"Not gonna happen."

She hacks a laugh.

I get to my feet with a groan. My body aches all over.

"Coming," I call, and head for the exit.

On the way, I almost stumble over an inert power armour on the floor, and I stop to slide my arms under Rivera and lift him from the ground.

I don't look back as I make my way through the debris to the door. There's no way I can do this if I meet Soledad's eyes.

Tyrus stops me with a hand on my shoulder. He looks at the dead priest in silence. Then he reaches out his armoured glove and closes Rivera's unseeing eyes.

"What took you so long with Soledad?"

"We sorted out a few misunderstandings."

"Good for you," he says. "Now, let's go."

He opens the door, and we stumble into the passage. Finn hangs limp between Tyrus and Jagr.

Tyrus closes the door and shoots out the controls. "That should keep them out for a while."

Jagr grabs my arm. "What did she say?"

"Another time, Jagr."

She looks pleadingly at me.

I touch her hand. "It was good stuff."

She takes comfort in that, and some resolve returns to her face.

"OK, let's get this big guy back aboard the *Sundowner* before this place goes nova."

Jagr and Tyrus haul Wagner down the hall towards the elevator while I make up the rear guard. So far, no Goliath zombies have spotted us.

When we reach the elevator Jagr pushes the button to call it.

Nothing happens.

"Shit, they have disabled the elevators."

She looks up and down the passageway for another way out.

Tyrus opens fire. "Here they come."

At least a full platoon of zombie Goliaths come charging us.

Unceremoniously, Tyrus and Jagr dump Wagner on the floor in the recessed elevator entrance. I take no more care with the dead priest, and then we open fire.

The shredder bullets go through the Goliaths like a meatgrinder. Limbs are blown off left and right, chests explode in a shower of gore, but still they come. The ones that have their legs cut off crawl. The ones with no arms try to get close enough to bite us. It's horrible.

"This is no good." The elevator entrance provides little cover. "Braden, are you there?"

"Braden here."

Her voice is weak and riddled with static, but she's there. "How's it going in there?"

"We lost Rivera."

There's no need to tell her we're about to lose Soledad. There's time enough to tell her about that later.

"Oh, no." She's silent for a bit.

I never knew she cared so much for the cleric. Sure, he was endearing, but he *was* a pain in the behind.

"Shit," Braden goes on. "That means *I'm* the comic relief now. I'm so going to die."

How can she have the peace of mind to crack jokes? Who knows what drugs the ship pumps into her bloodstream?

"We need to leave, Braden. Now."

"I take it you've been compromised?"

"You could say that again."

I fire another quick burst down the passage and a giant zombie explodes into red gore.

"No fucking about with stealth now, Braden. Where is the nearest airlock to our position?"

We keep firing. They drop in piles, but new giants clamber over the bodies of the fallen. It's like trying to fight a blood tsunami.

"Hang on. Scanning."

Jagr fires twice and another two Goliaths drop. "Hurry, Braden. They're coming."

"Keep your panties on, Boss, you can't rush a … There. Got it. Go back about fifty metres, down some stairs, and there's a small airlock."

We haul Finn and the priest from the floor and back up, firing as we go. We follow Braden's directions down the stairs, and there's the airlock. About bloody time. We're running out of ammunition. And time.

Jagr thumps the wall in triumph. "Good old Braden."

Don't jinx it, Jagr, Goddammit.

"Don't count your chickens yet. We still need to get outside," I warn.

The *Naglfar* ramps up the acceleration, making the artificial gravity increase. It becomes harder and harder to walk.

I hit the cycle button with the butt of my assault rifle, and the door cracks open down the middle like the welcoming gates of heaven. Too bad the priest isn't alive to appreciate the analogy.

We pile inside, with Jagr and Tyrus taking pot-shots at the approaching Goliaths while the door closes. The massive door slams shut and the red light signalling the air is about to be sucked out goes on.

I thumb the controls on my helmet and the face-plate slides down. "Helmets, people."

A click and a soft hiss and I'm sealed off from the world, breathing my own recycled air.

"And you said *Soledad* was stating the obvious?" Tyrus says.

He's growing on me, like a poisonous mould.

"Too soon, Tyrus. Too soon. Everybody all right?" I survey my companions.

Finn has collapsed against the wall under the rising gravity, and Jagr helps him with the controls to his helmet. He cradles the black sword like an infant in his arms.

Jagr seems fine, even though her rapid panting sends static over the comms. Then I realise it's my own breathing I hear, and I fight to get it under control.

Tyrus checks down his dropsuit like he's just back from a parade. Even the increased gravity does not seem to affect him. The guy is a fucking machine.

"I'm fine," he reports.

There's a slight tension in his voice and I can tell he's trying hard to control his breath. I grin.

"Still good here," comes a hoarse whisper over the open channel. It's Soledad. "But hurry. There's some-one at the door."

Shit. If they get to her before she can blow the explosives, we have failed.

I scowl at Jagr and Tyrus. They have understood our predicament too. They both nod.

I swallow. "Soledad. Perez here. If they find you ... pull those cords and blow them to hell."

"But what about ...?"

I cut her off. "Don't worry about us."

"We'll be fine, Pip," Jagr adds. "Do it when they get through."

There's a pause. "All right."

"Promise me, Pippa." I've never heard Jagr so serious before.

"I promise, Misha."

A sound that could be a sob but could also be disturbance from the thick hull echoes over the line. A soft shudder transmits up through my feet as the outer door rumbles open.

The comms-line from Soledad crackles again. Soledad coughs.

"I love you, Misha."

There's a sob from Jagr. "I know."

"Fuck. They're here. Get out, Misha. *Get out.*"

The outer door is only open a decimetre. There's no way we'll be able to squeeze out in the bulky combat suits.

"Give us ten seconds," Tyrus says.

"I ... can't ... They're ..." There's a soul-rending scream from Soledad. The door is open two decimetres. Three.

I push Rivera's dead body into Jagr's arms. "Take the priest and go." She slings his corpse over her shoulder, takes a few quick steps and dives through the opening. Tyrus goes after her.

"Come on, Finn. Let's go." The gravity must now be up to five or six G. I grab Finn under the armpits and pull. Without the servos on my combat suit, I'm not sure I would have been able to get him up, even with my enhanced strength. The artificial gravity from the *Naglfar's* acceleration is torture.

We stumble across the airlock floor and topple through the opening and out into the emptiness of space.

Deep down in my consciousness, the General's parasitic mind reels at his new surroundings and begins to wake up.

I hug Finn close to my chest as we tumble through the big empty. He's something to hold on to in all this nothing.

"I've got you, buddy. I've got you."

To prevent Meridian from killing Finn in a tantrum, I shut off my suit servos with a quick voice command. That is going to piss meridian off, but at least he can't hurt Finn.

Finn hugs me and pats my back like a father comforting his child.

"No, Perez. I got you."

Something blurs my vision and I blink viciously. A single drop of clear liquid goes sailing through my helmet and splashes against the visor. The nano-coating absorbs it instantly.

I can't see the others.

The *Naglfar* has left us spread out in its wake. I hope the *Sundowner* has some fine-grained scanners onboard so Braden can pick us all up. I would hate to float in space forever again.

Then, somewhere behind me is a flash of light so bright it burns my retinas. Even through my hardware and wetware flash-suppressor, it still hurts my eyes. We tumble around, and there's the great ghostship *Naglfar*, being torn apart from inside by its drive core.

Immense tendrils of blue-white flame, like solar eruptions, burst from the hull, splitting it apart. The titanic ship tears asunder like a book in the hands of an invisible child.

We did it.

I close my eyes with relief and take a deep breath.

"*Who are you?*"

The unknown voice inside my head almost scares me to death.

"*Who's that, Perez?*" Aeryn screams.

"I don't know, Aer."

"*Identify yourself. What are you doing in my head?*"

"*Your* head?"

I scowl. "Is that you, *Naglfar*?"

"*Who is Naglfar? I am general Caspar Batista Meridian. Who the fuck are you?*"

Oh, fuck me sideways.

I open my eyes and gaze wide-eyed into the infinite vastness of space.

The General screams in immortal pain, and I let the darkness take me.

* * *

When I wake up, I'm strapped into a chair on the *Sundowner*.

The familiar smell of sweat and greased metal mixed with fresh ground coffee brings back childhood memories of home. Finn, Jagr, Tyrus and Hildr float in front of me.

Meridian is not in my head anymore, and I draw a sigh of relief. There will be time later to ponder the implications of what just happened.

A grey blanket covers a human-sized object strapped into a seat at the back of the bay. A corner of the cloth has come undone and a pale hand floats free, waving like seaweed in a slow current. I suppose Rivera has family somewhere. We need to take him home.

"*And we need to talk about what just happened.*"

"Not now, Aeryn."

"*Is that what's been happening when you glitch?*"

"Yes. Sort of. But he's never done *that* before."

"*Get rid of him.*"

"I can't."

"*Fuck that. I'm not having a threesome inside your head.*"

"Aw, come on, Aer."

"*I'm not joking. I don't want to be in here with that thing.*"

She's serious. "*And neither do you. Trust me.*"

"We'll talk later. I promise."

Jagr and the others stare at me. Then Jagr slaps me.

"*Ow.* I'm awake. Don't hit me."

"Welcome back, Perez. Had a nice nap?" There's warmth in her voice.

"Slept like a baby. Did we get them?"

"We got them, brother."

Finn's smile is a mile wide behind the bruises and bandages. "We got them good. Is over."

Tyrus and Jagr exchange a glance. Then Tyrus speaks.

"It's time we brought Perez up to speed, Jagr."

Braden floats into the bay with two cups of smoking coffee in her hands.

"Up to speed about what?" I look from Jagr to Tyrus.

Braden hands me a cup.

"You're going to need this, Mr P."

The coffee smells amazing.

Jagr clears her throat. "How much do you know about artificial intelligence, Perez?"

"A bit. I always thought we hadn't built a proper level three AI, and that we never would. After what we saw today, I'm not so sure anymore."

I take a sip from the coffee. Damn. Braden wasn't boasting. She smiles and gives me a thumbs up. I raise my cup in salute and take another sip. Then I look at Tyrus.

"We still haven't built a level three, Perez."

"So, what was that thing on the *Galahad* and the *Naglfar*?"

"That was most definitely a full level three AI."

"But if we didn't build it, then who ...?"

"Nine years ago, an experimental detector for exotic particles picked up a signal from outer space. A signal that exhibited signs of being artificial. After verification, it was concluded the signal did not originate from any human colony."

"Where did it come from?"

"A dead planet orbiting the star you would know as Algol."

"The Demon Star. That figures. Why haven't we heard anything about this?"

"We got to the scientists before they could break the news."

"And by 'got to them', you mean you killed them."

"You know the panic this piece of news would cause."

"This is tin foil material, Tyrus."

"That doesn't make it any less true."

"What do they want?"

"We have no idea. But it seems they're trying to make contact."

"And what are we replying?"

Tyrus exchanges a glance with Jagr. Then he goes on.

"They are trying to make contact, but not with us."

What? "Then ... who?"

"Two weeks ago, we got confirmation that a response was sent. From Nifelheim."

"Ah." I see where this is going. "Mimr."

"We weren't aware of Mimr's existence then, but when Jagr reported what you found on the *Galahad*, we put the pieces together. When we tracked that data dump to Muspelheim, we knew the entity was on the move, and I decided it was time to see for myself what we are up against."

"Who are you, Tyrus? And who do you work for?"

"That is classified. Let's just say the outfit I work for has a special interest in non-human intelligence."

"The Men in Black, eh?"

First, I learn the Shard is real, and now this.

"That is also classified." He gives me half a smile.

"Fuck you. So, this alien signal was meant for Mimr?"

"We believed that was the case."

"And now that Mimr is dead?"

Hang on. "*Believed?*"

Tyrus nods.

"Two minutes ago, Command informed us a new signal was detected."

Shit. That was after we blew up the *Naglfar*.

"A signal orders of magnitude more powerful than Mimr's. It caused major power outages all over the system."

"And where did that come from?"

This is the first time in the brief time I've known him that Tyrus has looked worried. He wipes a hand across his mouth and pulls on his scruffy beard. "Everywhere."

"What do you mean, 'everywhere'?"

"Every transmitter in the system responded in unison. There is another presence in this system, powerful beyond imagination. And it wants to wipe us out."

I stare at him. "So, what do we do now?"

No one has a clue. Neither do I.

But someone has to do something about it.

Jagr was right.

Perhaps it is time to pick a side. No more walking away.

But if I do this, there is no turning back.

This is my Rubicon.

I down the last of the coffee and unbuckle from the crash seat.

"Jagr, can I borrow your team?"

"Not much of us left, and you are one of us now. We do this together."

There's an unfamiliar warm tingling deep in my gut. Is this what belonging feels like?

"Finn?"

"I'm with you, brother."

I look at Hildr. She looks away.

"Tyrus?"

He throws me a mock salute. "Lead the way."

"*I'm with you to the end, Perez.*"

Fuckin' A.

I used to think you can't save the world.

It turns out that sometimes, someone, somewhere gets to try.

Too bad it had to be me.

Dear reader,

We hope you enjoyed reading *Under A Winter Sun*.
Please take a moment to leave a review, even if it's a
short one. Your opinion is important to us.

Discover more books by Johan M. Dahlgren at
https://www.nextchapter.pub/authors/johan-m-
dahlgren

Want to know when one of our books is free or
discounted? Join the newsletter at
http://eepurl.com/bqqB3H

Best regards,
Johan M. Dahlgren and the Next Chapter Team

Johan M. Dahlgren Biography

'Twas a maelstrom of thunder and death, the day the dark princeling came into the world. The foul trumpets of Kaz'an heralded his arrival with blasts powerful enough to change the winds in the sky and the mindless thralls of the kingdom stood at attention all the way to the crimson horizon to hail their new master. The cries of the newborn echoed around the throne room and the denizens of the land roared in furious joy. The man child already knew where his destiny lay.

* * *

Or that's the way Johan would like it to have been on the day he was born. Instead it was a fine spring morning in 1973 in the pleasant town of Gothenburg in western Sweden.

He didn't have a clue what he wanted to be when he grew up.

And there was not a mindless thrall as far as the eye could see.

Johan and his parents moved into his grandparents' old house by the sea outside Gothenburg, and soon his two younger brothers arrived. Sadly, there were still no trumpets of Kaz'an.

At a young age Johan discovered the joy of books. When he started school at the age of seven, his mother told the teacher that the little boy had just finished Jules Vernes' *Journey to the Center of the Earth*. The teacher thought she was joking. She was not.

Ever since then he's been interested in science fiction and the fantastic. In school he was never happier than when it was time to write essays. He would churn out page after page of action stories instead of the usual "What I did during summer holiday" drivel the teacher had asked for.

Luckily, his teachers never seemed to mind.

Maybe they liked action stories.

When he was ten, he - like so many other young boys at that sensitive age - discovered the forbidden but darkly alluring pleasures of role playing games.

He and his friends would sit for days on on end, rolling their dice, moving their meticulously (but not very well) painted metal orcs and spin tales of dark and dangerous lands.

And the occasional drunken halfling who betrayed his companions to the city guard and had them all arrested.

Who made up all the tales of dark and dangerous lands?

Guess three times.

The friends kept playing their RPGs far longer than the other kids on the block. In fact, on certain nights, when the stars align and the moon shines red with blood, they still gather their worn dice and meet up for more adventures in the dark and dangerous lands. The only difference is the Mountain Dew has been replaced with micro brewed IPA and fine Scotch and they no longer have to wear fake beards to look like grizzled adventurers.

The drunken halfling still makes the occasional appearance, though.

After high school Johan did his military service in the Swedish Royal Marines. That was a bit of a heaven and hell experience for him.

On the one hand, it was great fun (he loves to blow stuff up, shoot big guns and ride in cool boats).

On the other hand, it was a real pain in the behind, because he discovered he is allergic to running mile after mile in full combat gear, crawling through icy mud and making hundreds of push ups. It makes him very tired and nauseous.

And he doesn't like to kill things.

Not even mosquitoes. Unless they've drawn first blood, in which case they will be dealt with swiftly and painlessly.

Still, he got a green beret for his troubles and learned how to blow up bridges. It's always good to have career options when you don't know what you want to be when you grow up.

After surviving the military he went to university to get a degree. Since he still didn't know what he wanted to be, he asked his parents for advice.

His mother suggested teaching (she was a teacher), since Johan likes to explain things to people and can't stop telling people useless bits of trivia they never asked for. By the way, did you know you can fly to Mars in 2-5 days with an acceleration of 1g? Amazing.

His father suggested studying computer science (he worked with computers), since Johan likes to play video games.

It was a close call, but the video games tipped the scales, and four years later he had his Masters degree in computing and went to work in the IT business, where he is still plodding along.

The trumpets of Kaz'an? Silent as the grave.

Johan still doesn't know what he wants to do when he grows up.

Maybe writing is his thing.

Making stuff up for a living sounds like a job for a responsible adult.

Right?

Under A Winter Sun
ISBN: 978-4-86745-257-8 (Mass Market)

Published by
Next Chapter
1-60-20 Minami-Otsuka
170-0005 Toshima-Ku, Tokyo
+818035793528
6th May 2021